Loretta Hill was born in Perth, the eldest of four girls. She enjoyed writing from a very early age and was just eleven years old when she had her first short story published in *The West Australian* newspaper.

Having graduated with a degree in Civil Engineering and another in Commerce, she was hired by a major Western Australian engineering company and worked for a number of years on many outback projects.

But through all this she continued to write, and her first novel, a short romantic comedy called *Kiss and Tell*, was published in America in 2009 under the name Loretta Brabant.

The Girl in Steel-Capped Boots, her debut in mainstream women's fiction, was an acclaimed bestseller in 2012.

She lives in Perth with her husband and four children.

Also by Loretta Hill

The Girl in Steel-Capped Boots

The Girl in
the Hard Hat

LORETTA HILL

BANTAM
SYDNEY AUCKLAND TORONTO NEW YORK LONDON

A Bantam book
Published by Random House Australia Pty Ltd
Level 3, 100 Pacific Highway, North Sydney NSW 2060
www.randomhouse.com.au

First published by Bantam in 2013

Copyright © Loretta Hill 2013

The moral right of the author has been asserted.

All rights reserved. No part of this book may be reproduced or
transmitted by any person or entity, including internet search engines
or retailers, in any form or by any means, electronic or mechanical,
including photocopying (except under the statutory exceptions
provisions of the Australian *Copyright Act 1968*), recording, scanning
or by any information storage and retrieval system without the prior
written permission of Random House Australia.

Addresses for companies within the Random House Group can be
found at www.randomhouse.com.au/offices

National Library of Australia
Cataloguing-in-Publication entry

Hill, Loretta.
The girl in the hard hat /Loretta Hill.

ISBN 978 1 74275 680 6 (pbk.)

A823.4

Cover design by Christabella Designs
Cover images: (landscape) Peter Walton Photography/Getty Images;
(woman) Fabrice Lerouge/Getty Images
Internal typesetting and design by Midland Typesetters, Australia
Printed in Australia by Griffin Press, an accredited ISO AS/NZS
14001:2004 Environmental Management System printer

Random House Australia uses papers that are natural, renewable and
recyclable products and made from wood grown in sustainable forests.
The logging and manufacturing processes are expected to conform to
the environmental regulations of the country of origin.

For my darling husband, Todd.
Ever since we got married we've done everything as a team.
I couldn't have got through the last few months without
your faith, enthusiasm and support.
Love you for always,
Loretta

Author's Note

The majority of this story is set at Cape Lambert Port Facilities, the home of one of the tallest, longest and deepest jetties or open-sea wharves in the world. It is owned by Rio Tinto and is operated by Pilbara Iron. The nearby town of Wickham was built specifically for the purpose of supporting the wharf and other functions of the port, such as train-dumping, primary and secondary crushing and screening, stockpiling and blending of iron ore.

This ore wharf, which is approximately three kilometres long and thirty metres tall, has two cranes or ship-loaders that are able to load three ships at the same time. The wharf currently exports fifty-five to fifty-seven million tonnes of iron ore every year to steel mills in Japan, China, Korea, Taiwan and Europe.

My heroine takes on a role as safety manager for a construction team who are there to lengthen and widen this wharf, which was originally completed in 1972. Over the course of its existence the Cape Lambert wharf has undergone many upgrades of this nature to increase its life and capacity. I was lucky in my career as an engineer to witness and participate in one of these upgrades in 2001, which forms the basis of the background of this story.

It is important I highlight the time frame of the project in this story because in terms of safety standards in this industry, a decade is rather significant. Although the dangers still exist, regulations have become much tighter and company cultures much more accepting of them. Policies and procedures have improved not only for safety in the workplace but also for the standard of living in the camps. The attitudes of the workers in the fictional company Barnes Inc, depicted in my story, would be rare these days.

Also, to reduce the number of characters and engineering jargon in this story, I have condensed certain roles of some of the characters: for example, Carl is the project manager, but in my novel he also performs the duties of a construction manager. In real life, his job would have been done by two people. I have also ignored a lot of the other functions of the port and the shipping schedule, which would definitely have interfered with the project. It has been my aim to show the culture and flavour of the people in this environment, rather than absolute technical accuracy. Nonetheless, it is important to note that all characters and companies shown here are entirely fictional. Any resemblances to any real persons or entities are purely coincidental.

I adore the Pilbara and the people who work and live upon its majestic beauty. But the Pilbara can take as much as she can give. Cyclone James, the storm depicted in this novel, is fictional and was researched by looking at other cyclones which occurred on the Pilbara, in particular Cyclone Vance in 1999. Incidentally, I named my fictional cyclone after my second son, James. This is actually how real cyclones are named. If you would like a cyclone named after your child, you can actually add their name (free of charge) to a list managed by the Bureau of Meteorology.

This book is all about the hazards associated with working the land – not only those of humanity's own making, but also the results of Mother Nature's wrath. I wanted to show the challenges and dangers men and women face on jobs like this. The lifeblood of Australia has always been humour in the face of hardship. I hope this is one theme readers take away from my work.

Chapter 1

Wendy knew something was wrong the moment she stepped into TCN's open-plan office. Perhaps it was the frosty looks she got from the staff as they peered at her over their short cubicle walls. Or the fact that the receptionist wouldn't let her step beyond the hat hooks by the front door, but directed her instead to a room set apart from the main office space.

'You'll have to sit in the meeting room until Mr Hullog is ready to deal with you.'

Deal with me?

The woman made it sound like she was a toddler with a dirty nappy. This was supposed to be her first day of work. She had dressed carefully in the TCN uniform that Dan Hullog had given her just the day before. Her shirt was ironed, her khaki pants neat. Her blonde hair was tied modestly at the nape of her neck with black elastic.

So if it wasn't her appearance that offended them then what had happened between yesterday and today that she didn't know about?

She walked into the meeting room. It was furnished in the usual sparse style of a construction site donga office. A white

1

trestle table and eight plastic chairs filled the space. The vinyl floor was marked red with boot prints and the white board on one wall held a list of milestone dates. The chairs were uncomfortable to say the least and after twenty minutes of sitting in one she had to get up and walk around to stave off a numb bum.

Where is he?

She looked out the window, anticipation momentarily over-coming her concern.

The Cape Lambert iron-ore wharf stretched out before her – a majestic masterpiece almost like a painting framed by the dingy donga office window. Standing nearly five storeys above the water, the jetty stretched out more than three kilometres across the sea. The end of it was imperceptible as it faded into the horizon. Every day, ships from around the world docked there, picking up tonnes and tonnes of the precious red dirt that fuelled Australia's economy.

A shiver of both excitement and trepidation flitted through her body.

I can't believe I'm going to be a part of something like this . . . again.

She heard the snap of a door closing and spun around.

A tall, dark-haired man with the most intense blue eyes she'd ever seen advanced into the room.

'I'm sorry to have kept you waiting, Wendy.'

'Er, that's okay, Mr Hullog.'

'Call me Dan.' He indicated the chair she had been sitting in before and took the one opposite it. He laced his hands together on the white chipboard, transforming their encounter from backyard picnic to boardroom meeting. 'I have to ask. Do you know how you got this job?'

Her eyes narrowed. 'My uncle said you owed him a favour.'

Dan grimaced. 'That's putting blackmail politely.'

Red-hot heat worked its way up from the base of her neck. She knew she shouldn't have trusted Uncle Mike. She barely knew him and he seemed as inclined to want to get rid of her as to help her. But she had been at her wits' end. Out of money and out of luck. When she'd stumbled across him in Karratha, she had thought it was the hand of providence not the bite of corruption.

What had her mother told her? *Oh yeah: 'Nobody does anything for nothing.'*

She swallowed hard before casting an apology at the man before her. 'I had no idea. Honestly. I hadn't seen Uncle Mike in years. I should have checked his motives more closely.'

You should have listened to your conscience.

She had known Mike was the black sheep of the family. No one talked about him unless they absolutely had to and even then their comments were never complimentary. Still she wasn't exactly number one with the family at the moment either. When she'd run into Uncle Mike unexpectedly, it had almost been like meeting a kindred spirit.

How wrong you were.

She waited on Dan's response with breath held.

'I had a feeling from our conversation yesterday that you had no idea what the full story was. The truth is,' he sighed, 'there is no real position for you here. I have a safety officer already and he does a very good job.'

Her heart sank. He wasn't going to take her on. He had been her last hope at a job in the area.

'Also,' he lifted an unsmiling face, 'I no longer care what your uncle says or doesn't say. The person I was protecting . . .' He changed tack. 'Let's just say, his so-called silence is no longer of any value to me.'

Pride stiffened her back, causing her to stand. 'Well, I'll just get out of your hair then, shall I? There's no need to drag this conversation out.'

'Wendy, whatever beef I have with your uncle is nothing to do with you or your ability. And I'm mortified that you have been used as a pawn in a very tasteless game.'

Used. Yep, that's me.

But Dan was still talking. 'I want to honour the agreement, not for his sake but for yours.'

She paused in the act of turning away. 'But you said there was no job.'

'Not here. But somewhere else.' His tone softened. 'Please sit down and let me tell you what I have arranged. TCN is the Engineering, Procurement and Construction Manager or EPCM for this project. Do you know what that means?'

'You run the show, don't you?'

'Sort of.' Dan smiled. 'The wharf owners make the rules, so we don't have a choice about that. But essentially we govern the place for them. As in, we make sure everyone else, such as our principal contractor Barnes Inc, follows the guidelines set by the wharf owners.'

She didn't say anything but sank slowly back into her chair.

'Unfortunately Barnes Inc have not been meeting the safety standard set by the wharf owners for some time now. They have a safety officer over there but he doesn't seem to be able to keep up with the workload. On behalf of the wharf owners I have rung Barnes Inc and told them that they need to take on another safety person in addition to the one they already have. I've suggested you as a likely candidate.' He paused. 'The project manager at Barnes Inc, Carl Curtis, said he is willing to interview you this morning.'

A job was a job. This office. That office down the road.

What did it matter as long as she got paid?

She licked her lips. 'When?'

'Now.'

Relief swept through her. All was not lost. 'Well, that's not a problem.'

'I assume you brought your vehicle with you?'

She nodded. She'd passed the Barnes Inc office dongas on the way to TCN so she knew how to get there too.

Okay, let's do this. She stood up more firmly this time, holding out her hand. 'Thank you for this opportunity, er, Dan.'

'I'm very sorry that I didn't have a job for you.' His tone at least was genuine. 'I really think we could have worked well together.'

'Thank you.' She had an inkling that Dan Hullog was an honourable man, unlike her slimy excuse for an uncle. What the hell was Mike's game anyway?

She gritted her teeth as she made her way out. Was there no end to the lies she had been fed by her family her whole life? The betrayal just seemed to go on and on. All those years in a boarding school had allowed her to wonder what was wrong with her. Out here in the outback, far away from Perth, she had thought she was beyond all that. But no, the one uncle she thought might understand her was keen to use her as a bargaining chip as well.

Enough is enough.

She couldn't wait to give him a piece of her mind later, but right now she had a job to score *on her own merit.*

TCN had three office dongas lined up in a row, framed by red rock on one side and a car park on the other. Her car stood out easily amongst the dirty white utes in the car park – a blue Nissan with floral seat covers and a collection of stuffed animals peering out the rear window. It looked completely out of place against the backdrop of iron ore stock piles, cranes and conveyor belts.

She made her way down a well-trodden path towards it, the only asset she still had after her trek across the state over the last six months. For a while, it had been her sole companion in this search that never seemed to end. And those toys had brought her luck. Even in their sun-damaged state, she'd never throw them out.

She got in her car and started the engine. It was only a five-minute drive down a long gravel track that ran alongside the red beach and through the port facilities. As at TCN, there were three Barnes Inc office dongas. An odd-looking flag with an extra thick circular pole had been pushed into the ground in front of one of them. The flying emblem of the company was bolted rather than strung on the pole and a group of guys were having smoko underneath it on a couple of park benches. Two more were sitting in the back of a ute, chowing down on Mrs Mac pies still half in their plastic microwaveable wrappers. When they saw her car, they immediately all stood up and waved. She parked and they cheered as though she had stopped for them.

Oh brother!

Clearly, they hadn't seen a new female face on site in a while.

She alighted cautiously from her car, noting that maybe at some stage, sooner rather than later, she should move those stuffed animals into her boot.

'Hey, love, where are you going? Wanna stop for a bite?' One of the guys grabbed his friend's pastry as it was on its way into said friend's mouth and held it up in the air like a trophy. 'We've got a spare one!'

She chuckled at the original pie owner's expression of outrage and watched him snatch it back before shoving the thief in the chest. Maybe it was the thief's lack of attention or the roughness of the shove but the man fell out of the side of the ute and landed starry-eyed in the dirt.

The others lost interest in her and roared with laughter. She took the opportunity to slip by the group and enter the Barnes Inc main office donga.

Compared to the TCN equivalent, it was an absolute mess. All the desks seemed to be covered in a film of dust and papers, with the occasional computer poking through the chaos. There was no official reception desk.

The two guys seated closest to the door both eyed her up and down before one said, 'And who might you be, blondie?' The guy who addressed her had his eye fixed on her shirt pocket. The TCN logo seemed to repulse him. She wished she'd had a change of clothes in the car. The last thing she wanted to do was give anyone any false impressions.

'I'm Wendy Hopkins. I'm here to see Carl.'

The man raised his eyebrows. 'I'm John Lewis. Pleased to meet you. Do you have an appointment?'

'No . . . I –'

'Just pulling your leg.' He grinned. 'I don't think Carl makes appointments. He's never around for them. He must be expecting you though because he's in his office.'

Not quite knowing what to say to this, she merely nodded. 'And which way is that?'

'Only office in this donga, darlin'.' He jerked his thumb over his shoulder. 'Down the end next to the kitchen.'

'Thanks.'

She knew John's eyes were on her rear as she walked off in the direction he had indicated. Her skin prickled in annoyance but she decided it was a fight best saved for another time. The door to Carl's office was wide open so she heard the man before she saw him.

'What the fuck do you mean there's no fuckin' bolts with it? . . . How the fuck should I know? . . . Didn't a pallet arrive last week? . . . Why the fuck would I cancel it? If it's not there then it must be somewhere else . . . Have you looked up your own fuckin' arse before you've shoved your head in mine? *Fuck*!'

SLAM!!!

Carl looked up at her standing there with her hand frozen in the 'about to knock' position.

'Who the fuck are you?'

Wendy closed her gaping mouth and licked her lips. 'I'm Wendy Hopkins. Dan Hullog said –'

'Oh shit! You were fuckin' quick! Come in, come in.' He waved his hand at her in resignation. 'And shut the door behind you.'

She complied and then took the seat in front of his desk. He was a heavy-set man in his late forties with dark brown hair and skin that tanned easily. In fact, he'd probably be quite good looking, if he didn't radiate stress like a wild bird in a cage.

'So you're in OH and S, are you?'

'Yes.'

'What's your experience like?'

'I've done seven years in the field. My last job was at the Parker Point Wharf in Dampier two years ago. So I actually do have some jetty experience in my –'

'You've been out of work two years. Why?'

It was a perfectly reasonable question – one that a prospective employer was definitely entitled to ask. Her reasons, however, were many, personal and complicated. So she decided to tell half the truth. 'I wanted a holiday.'

'Pretty long fuckin' holiday.'

As she began to bristle defensively, he put his hand up to stop her responding. 'The reason I ask is if I hire you, I want you to stay for the duration of this project. So if you feel like you might need to take off again, "on holiday", you need to tell me now.'

He said the words 'on holiday' like he didn't entirely believe them. Not that she blamed him, but at least she could reassure him on one point.

'I will definitely be staying to the end. If you're worried I won't take this job seriously, don't be. I'm not going to let anything happen to Barnes Inc's people. I have a debt to pay to myself and there's no better motivation than that.'

'A debt, eh?'

She buttoned her lip, not really wanting to elaborate any further. She'd already said too much. If he was a gentleman, he wouldn't press her.

'You don't want to fuckin' tell me, do you?' His smile was unsympathetic. 'That's going to cause problems for you, missy.'

He wasn't a gentleman.

She winced.

Maybe this was a bad idea.

I shouldn't have come back to this industry.

I could have got a job in a bar or a kitchen.

Carl eyed her cynically. 'No point in pretending you're not aware of what the fuck I'm talking about because we both know that ain't true. It's not that I don't respect your privacy but, believe me, in this fuckin' place no one else will.' She swallowed. He sat back in his chair and it creaked loudly in protest. 'There aren't any secrets here. There's only one commodity traded more often on this wharf than fuckin' ore. It's called gossip.'

When she said nothing, he shrugged. 'I'm just trying to fuckin' warn you. You'll be gossiped about from one end of the fuckin' wharf to the other so just be prepared to deal with it. If you have any major problems, like harassment, please don't fuckin' wait on it. Come see me.'

She looked up hopefully. 'Does that mean I've got the job?'

'When Bulldog barks Bulldog gets.' He seemed mildly put out by his own analogy.

'Bulldog?'

'That's Dan Hullog's name on this side of the fence.' He sighed. 'The thing is, our current safety guy, Neil Cooper, can't keep up with his workload. With fuckin' cyclone season coming things are only going to get worse. I gotta make some fuckin' improvements around here or we'll all be up shit creek faster than this morning's turd. I think Neil will be fuckin' glad of an assistant.'

An assistant.

Her body stilled.

Great! Maybe you were better off in a bar.

She cleared her throat. 'Well, I've got a lot of experience working on sites like this one. I'm really looking forward to the challenge.' She hoped these words indicated that she wanted to be more than just an assistant.

He didn't rise to the bait. 'It'll be a fuckin' challenge, all right. Pushing safety around here is like serving Brussels sprouts to children. Nobody wants a fuckin' bar of it.'

Well, she was used to that. When people had work to do, they just wanted to get on with the job, take precautions later. They didn't want to listen to what she had to say. But construction on water took danger to the next level, especially if the weather got bad. She would have to stay on top of things.

'There's just one other thing.' She took a breath. 'I'd like to live in the camp.'

His eyebrows jumped. 'Fuck! If you've already got accommodation, I'd keep it.'

She tried to explain. 'I think the camp will be a bit more convenient. Travelling from Karratha every day will be really painful.'

Besides, I'm done with Karratha.

She had already dropped in at every steel mill there. No one could answer her questions or give her a new lead. Time to venture a little further out of town.

'Well, fuck me if you don't get a big welcome.' He paused. 'But it's no hotel. And there are only five other women in the camp.'

'How many men?'

'Three-fifty.'

She swallowed. 'Right.'

He seemed unperturbed by her alarm, rising from his chair and opening his door. 'Well, I suppose you'll want to be meeting fuckin' Neil. Come with me.'

They walked back through the open-plan office and she felt all eyes drilling holes in her back. They passed John Lewis, who did not look up, and stepped outside.

Carl led her across a short courtyard to another donga. They went up the steps and were soon inside. This donga was just as untidy as the first but much smaller and much more claustrophobic. It was also colder. The air conditioner was running so high, it was rattling in its socket on the wall. Wendy rubbed her arms as a chill went through her both literally and metaphorically.

A sweaty-looking man was standing by a sink and a bar fridge that passed for a kitchen, dipping a tea bag into some hot water. He was dark and swarthy and obviously didn't deal well with the tropical weather. His glasses, which were slightly foggy, sat right on the tip of his wet nose. A large packet of Marlboros bulged from the top pocket of his shirt.

He jumped when he saw them. 'Carl!'

'I got a fuckin' present for ya, Neil.'

'You . . . er . . . do?'

'I've got you some help. This is Wendy Hopkins. She's got seven years' experience in the field and I've employed her.'

'She's from TCN,' Neil protested, his eyes on her uniform.

'Huh?' Carl glanced at Wendy, belatedly noticing her attire. 'Fuck! Forgot about that. Not an issue, Neil. It's all bullshit. She's not working there any more. Are you?' he prompted her.

'No.' Wendy shook her head.

'There you go.' Carl nodded. 'All right and tight. Put her to work. I want to see some fuckin' improvements around here.'

On this note he left, leaving her standing there awkwardly with his subordinate, who was yet to give her a friendly welcome.

'You got a lot of nerve, coming here in a bloody TCN uniform.'

'It wasn't intentional.' She tried to reassure him but it was like she hadn't spoken.

'And who said I needed help? I don't need any help.' His tone was contemptuous. 'I just hope to God you don't make things worse by getting in the way.'

Although profanities had slipped off Carl's tongue like butter on a hot pan she'd found him less offensive in the half an hour she'd spent with him than she did this guy after only five seconds.

'Well, Carl seemed to think that you were under the pump –'

'What would Carl know?' he snapped. 'He's never around. Never comes into this donga. Keeping safety up to scratch is something I do *on my own*. He should have asked me first.'

Frankly, Wendy thought Neil was a little full of himself. Carl was the project manager. It was his right to hire and fire as he saw fit. She said nothing, however, not wanting to rock the boat further. After all, she was going to have to work with this guy. Better to shut up and make peace as quickly as possible.

'Well, I want you to know,' she said slowly, 'that I'm only here to make your life easier. Whatever I can do, just say the word.'

His greasy mouth tilted into something she couldn't quite call a smile. 'I need some milk for my tea and our fridge is all out.' He pointed at the door. 'The smoko donga is down that way.'

Her mouth dropped open in disbelief as he turned and walked away from her. She opened her mouth to yell back at him when a man stepped conspicuously in front of her.

'I wouldn't. Wait till you've calmed down a bit.'

'Conspicuously' was actually an understatement. Her advisor was, in a word, massive. Both tall and wide, with an arse and stomach so generous that Wendy would be surprised if he didn't have to turn sideways to get through the door. Brown haired and in his early forties, he gave her a sympathetic smile.

'I'm Bill Walden, by the way. But everyone around here calls me Chub.' He leaned in, patting his belly affectionately. 'Yes, that's short for chubby. But just between you and me, most of it's muscle.'

'Right.' She blinked.

'I'm the HR manager. So I think you better come with me for the moment. I can get you a new shirt. That one is currently causing a few problems around here, if you know what I mean.'

'Why is everyone so against TCN?'

He tut-tutted. 'That's like asking why everyone smoked in the sixties. It just is, love, and if you want to fit in you better learn the rules of the fraternity. Rule number one, all TCN are scum.'

'What's rule number two?'

'Under no circumstance should you forget rule number one. Okay.' He rubbed his pudgy hands together. 'Let's get you a Barnes Inc wardrobe. Now when I turn around to lead you off to our storage container, don't look at my arse. It makes me uncomfortable.'

Wendy choked.

'I've been told it's a real chick magnet. But I wouldn't know. Never seen it myself.' He indicated his thick neck with his pointer finger. 'Can't get my head around that far.'

He was absolutely shocking, yet seemed to be the first person in this town she actually found herself liking without hesitation.

She returned his grin with one of her own. 'No problem.'

'Cheers.' He gave her the thumbs up before turning around. 'Okay, let's go.'

He led her to an old shipping container outside the donga which appeared to act as a storeroom. There was a lot of PPE, Personal Protective Equipment, in there – which was good to know.

'Try not to let Neil get to you,' Chub offered as they trotted out. 'He doesn't eat much and I think he must suffer a lot from hunger pains.'

She giggled.

'He may warm up to you yet,' he added optimistically.

If Neil generated any warmth at all over the next six hours he certainly didn't share it with her. After dumping a five-hundred-page safety manual about permits and tagging on her desk and telling her to study it, he pretty much left her to her own devices.

The room itself seemed to get colder and colder as the day progressed. Neil kept the air conditioner up so high, going outside was actually a relief from the icebox that was now her office. She wondered why the other occupants of the donga didn't complain until she realised that most of them didn't spend the majority of their time there the way she, Neil and Chub did. They'd grab their hard hats off the wall and be out most of the day.

As she shivered through the afternoon, it became clear that Neil was under pressure. He was on the phone practically the whole time and most of the calls sounded like complaints. He had a pile of memos on his desk almost half a metre tall. And there were small piles of foolscap files sitting on the floor behind his desk rather than on the empty bookshelves against the wall. She couldn't work out what his system was but was anxious to get in and lighten his load.

The other thing was, he didn't look well – what with the sweating and the occasional hand tremors. The guy clearly had a problem but refused to ask her for help. When she tentatively suggested she might take a couple of files off him he practically bit her head off. In resignation, she retreated back to her desk.

By six pm, she didn't know whether her brain was numb from the cold or the dryness of the material she was reading. In any event, she was very thankful to be getting out of there. The next day she was coming in late so that she could sort out her accommodation and have her safety induction in Wickham at ten o'clock. Once that formality was out of the way, perhaps she'd start getting out of the office too and into the real action.

She said goodbye to her colleagues. Neil ignored her, Chub gave her a jovial wave and she stepped out into the warm, balmy air.

The red sun, halved by the horizon, made the blue sky pink and the ocean violet. Clouds struggled to keep their own colour too, streaking across the sky, lit from behind.

She decided to take this beautiful sight as an omen. Everything was going to be okay. Her search for her father was coming to an end.

Here.

She got in her car and started her engine. It was a forty-five-minute drive back to her hotel in Karratha. This evening, she didn't mind the long commute. She was feeling a little philosophical and whiled away the time reminiscing about past fly-in/fly-out roles she'd taken. If, fingers crossed, things with Neil improved, it would be good to be back doing the work she loved.

After the incident at Parker Point she hadn't been able to face working there any more. Sure, nobody knew what she had done. But she did.

So she'd fired herself. Being out of work for a couple of weeks hadn't really helped, so that's when she'd decided to extend her sabbatical to a year. Backpacking around Europe had seemed like a good way to get her mojo back. And the time had given her perspective. She'd realised she couldn't give up a job she loved because of one stupid mistake. After spending more than a year overseas, she'd been ready to start again and prove to the world exactly what she was made of.

She went job-hunting and even had a post lined up in Port Hedland. She'd been all set and ready to make a comeback . . .

Then along came that awful moment that she'd remember for the rest of her life. The revelation that had tipped her world on its side.

Chapter 2

Eight months earlier

'Department of Births, Deaths and Marriages.' Wendy smiled at the boredom in the clerk's monotone voice down the phone.

'Er, hi. My name's Wendy Hopkins.'

'Uh-huh.'

'I'm starting a new job in Port Hedland and I need to provide my employer with a copy of my birth certificate.'

'Uh-huh.'

'I've moved a few times and seem to have lost my original. Could you send me a new one?'

'There is a fee for birth certificate replacement.'

'That's all right.'

'Very well.' Wendy heard the sound of paper rustling, a chair creaking and a tongue clucking. 'Let's see. What did you say your name was again?'

'Wendy Jane Hopkins.'

'Place of birth.'

'Perth, Western Australia.'

She heard the *click-click* of fingers fluttering across a keyboard, pushing keys, pulling files.

'All right.' The clerk seemed to have found it. 'Would you like the original certificate or the one after adoption?'

Wendy's brow furrowed. 'I think you have the wrong Wendy. I'm not adopted.'

'When were you born?'

'March 15.'

'And hospital of birth?'

'St Bernard's. My mother's name is Helen and my father's name is Parry Hopkins.'

'Yes.' The clerk clicked her tongue. 'Parry is not on the original certificate.'

Wendy's heart stopped. '*I don't understand.*'

She heard the ruffling of papers. 'It seems after your adoption you were issued with a new certificate. Shall I issue both the original and the adoptive one to you?'

Wendy grabbed her chest as she struggled to breathe.

'Hello?'

She put the phone down and stepped back from it like it was diseased. Sweat broke out on her brow. Her eyes blurred.

I'm adopted.

No.

I can't be.

She was shaking from head to foot.

Can't you?

Milestones in her childhood that had before seemed strange now stood out like big flashing neon signs, all pointing towards this conclusion. She paced the room, rubbing her arms as a chill spread through her chest. It was a thirty-five-degree day and yet she had goosebumps.

Didn't people adopt because they wanted a child?

When she thought of her parents, she couldn't help but see them as the least likely people in the world to adopt a baby. After all, didn't she spend half her childhood in boarding school? After the age of six, she was away from home more than she was there. Why would her parents adopt a kid when they didn't really want to raise it?

An awful thought that had plagued her from very early in her life seemed to be confirmed. *Maybe I was a disappointment. Not the type of child they wanted.*

She stopped pacing and sat down, wondering what to do.

In the end she got in her car and went in person to the Births, Deaths and Marriages department in the city. She purchased both her certificates. They were printed there and then and handed to her across a beige counter by another uninterested clerk.

After a quick scan she could see they were identical in nature except for one crucial detail.

The first certificate read, *Father: UNKNOWN.*

The second read, *Father: Parry Hopkins.*

So it seemed her mother was still her mother – it was her father who was in doubt. This new information should have given her some reassurance but it only seemed to disturb her even more. How could there be a secret in her own past that she didn't know about? Had her mother really lied to her her entire life? Or was there just some sort of misunderstanding?

She went to her parents' place situated north of the Swan in their own private patch of suburbia. Her father was at work. He owned a pub in Leederville and always seemed to be busy. Her mother had had many jobs in Wendy's lifetime but currently, at the age of fifty-eight, she was a homemaker. She had been in Perth since she was twenty, having originally come to Australia on a working holiday when migration through marriage had occurred.

Very English and very proper, Wendy's mother had never been an overly affectionate parent, but Wendy had put that down to her background. Now, as she knocked on her parents' door, she had to wonder.

Helen Hopkins took her time in answering. 'Wendy,' she said from behind the flyscreen door. 'I wasn't expecting you today.'

Wendy realised with a wince that she usually made 'an appointment' before turning up. Pop-ins, drop-ins, just weren't done in her family.

She licked dry lips. 'Can I come in?'

'All right, I've just made a pot of tea. Do you want some?' Her mother opened the door and turned to walk back into the house. Wendy followed.

'No thanks.' She closed and locked the door before joining her mother in the living room.

'I wanted to talk to you about something I found out today from the Births, Deaths and Marriages department.' She took both certificates out of her handbag and gave them to her mother, who had already sat down calmly on the couch.

'Oh.' Her mother took the papers and scanned them.

'What does this mean?' Wendy felt panic bubbling up her throat again. 'Is my father not my real father?'

That white-blonde hair, pale English skin and blank blue eyes, all of which she'd inherited, just stared back at her crossly as though it was she who had put her mother to gross incon-venience. 'I really wish they would be more careful before handing out private information like that.'

'Private information,' Wendy repeated, scarcely able to believe what she was hearing. 'We're talking about *my* birth certificate here. Don't you think I have a right to know who my father is?'

Her mother raised her eyes, seeming to realise, perhaps for the first time, how distraught Wendy was over the situation. 'Darling, I'm sorry if you are upset. I just thought all this was behind me. I never meant to get you involved.'

Red sparks flew behind Wendy's eyes. 'I think I'm pretty much front and centre of this story, Mum, and I want to know everything. *Now.*'

Her mother frowned and was silent for a moment. 'All right. But for goodness' sake, sit down. You're giving me a crick in the neck having to look up at you like that.'

Wendy sat on the couch opposite her mother. It was a very English-looking couch, cream coloured with a pink rose print across the fabric. It made Wendy think of how reserved and withdrawn her mother had been all her life. Even her father had been more loving – until she got older, of course, and was sent away. She braced herself for the truth, gripping her hands in her lap.

'Well?'

'I was young and stupid.' Her mother couldn't meet her eyes. Gazing out the window across the room from them she continued with a careless flick of her hand. 'I was engaged to one man and had an affair with another. You know, I guess I wanted to get married but at the same time I had cold feet. And so I did something very, very silly.' She finally turned to meet Wendy's eyes. 'The long and the short of it is, I got pregnant and both men dumped me, having by then found out about each other. So I had you, alone.' Her face shrivelled up at that point and for a moment Wendy felt sorry for her. It probably would have been scary, to be a first-time mum cast adrift. But it wasn't like it hadn't happened to women before. Her mother seemed inclined to stop talking, so she quickly tried to bring her back on point.

'My original birth certificate says the father is unknown.'

Her mother hunched a shoulder. 'Well, I didn't know which of my two lovers was the father, did I? And frankly, at that stage, I didn't care to find out. Of course when you were a year old, Parry forgave me for cheating on him while we had been briefly engaged. He adopted you and we got married as we had always intended. That is exactly what happened.'

Wendy could feel her anger rising again. 'That may be exactly what happened. But it explains nothing to me! Who was the other man? The man who could be my father?'

Her mother's face seemed to close. 'He is gone.'

'*Gone where?*'

'When he found out I was pregnant, he left.' Mrs Hopkins snapped her fingers as though she were illustrating how fast he'd retreated. 'I wouldn't worry about him if I were you. Parry is your father. He loves you. He's accepted you. He adopted you, for God's sake. What extra proof do you need of his commitment?'

'It's not his commitment I question.' Wendy stood up, unable to sit idle any longer. 'It's your honesty. Why didn't you tell me he might not be my real father?'

'You didn't need to know.'

'*Why not?*'

Her mother threw up her hands, glaring at her as though she were a spoiled brat. 'How would you have benefited from knowing that you could have a father who existed but didn't want anything to do with you? Parry is your father. We were married. Better to keep it simple.'

'Better for who?' Wendy shouted.

'Don't you take that tone with me. I could have given you up for adoption! In fact, I almost did. Be grateful that you got the upbringing you did.'

Wendy reeled, almost tipping backwards at her mother's words. 'So if you were that keen to get rid of me,' she returned icily, 'what made you change your mind?'

Her mother said nothing. Lifting her chin, the woman retreated behind that mask of English propriety.

Why did they send me away to boarding school?

Why did Daddy change after I turned six?

Why does he look at me with such sad eyes when he doesn't think I notice?

The reason hit her like a blow to the chest. Winded, she sank onto the couch again. 'Oh hell, you used me to get Parry back. You told him you knew for certain I was his, didn't you? And he found out that I wasn't later.'

It was logical really – young girl with a baby and no support from a family back in England. Reasonably wealthy young man with strong family values who owned his own business. If she could land him, it would be a nice move out of poverty and into the easy life.

'Don't judge me for what I did,' her mother shot at her. 'I did the only thing I could do at the time, for you and for me.'

'You didn't do it for me,' Wendy choked out. 'You used me to play your games. When did he find out I wasn't his?'

Her mother looked away. 'We tried to have more children but couldn't. When you were around six years old, Parry had himself checked out. He discovered he couldn't be a father.'

Wendy's ears tingled. The timing made complete sense. 'So that's when he had me exiled to boarding school. Couldn't stand the sight of me, could he?'

'Oh, for goodness' sake.' Her mother dismissed her with a wave of her hand. 'You make it all sound so sordid, when it was really nothing like that. It's just the way of the world, darling. People sometimes do things to survive. You can't live on love and fresh air, you know. Nobody does anything for nothing. Remember that.'

How could she forget it?

It was the first of the many fruitless arguments that had followed. Some with her mother, some with her adoptive father. Her parents seemed to raise more questions than they answered. When she tried to enquire after her biological father's whereabouts, they said they didn't know. When she asked about his origins, his personality, his relationship with her mother, they said they had forgotten all that information long ago. After he had disappeared, they'd both allowed him to fade from their memories.

Yeah right!

She didn't trust them. Why should she, when they had lied to her most of her life?

She didn't take the job in Port Hedland but instead stayed in Perth to resolve things with her family. It was becoming apparent that all of Parry's relatives had known of her adoption.

Her grandmother, her aunties, even some of her cousins. After all, Parry hadn't married her mother Helen until after she was born. No one had seen fit to tell her, though – much easier to just keep her in the dark. She was furious.

Furious and betrayed.

She had expected her mother to act differently too. After all, she was supposed to love her, right? Surely she would understand how much pain this revelation had caused her daughter and at least try to ease some of it. It seemed inconceivable to her that her mother could just forget someone who had played such a significant role in her life.

'You must be able to tell me *something* about him. You were his lover. You can't ask me to believe that you remember nothing.'

Her mother had blushed deep red but words that seemed torn from her by force finally came out. 'Your biological father was a free spirit. A drifter, who couldn't stay in one place. He loved the outback and lived from one mine to the next. He worked in many towns as a welder. Even when he had that terrible accident on the Pilbara, he still wouldn't give up his career.'

'An accident?'

Her mother looked uncomfortable, like she'd said too much. But after a moment's hesitation, she told Wendy the rest of the story anyway. 'He lost a couple of toes on his right foot while working at a steel mill near Karratha. He dropped an angle grinder on it.'

Wendy's eyes widened. 'Ouch.'

'You don't see my point,' her mother chastised her. 'He was still willing to go back to work. But when it came to love, family and commitment . . .' She snorted. 'He didn't want to be tied to me or, I'm afraid, to a possible son or daughter. You need to let it go. It was better that he left and I married someone else.'

'But who was he? What was his name?'

23

Finally her mother gave her a first name and a vague physical description. It wasn't much, but it was a start.

The start of a search.

Her parents were against the endeavour but Wendy couldn't be satisfied with so vague a history. How many more shocks were there around the corner? She couldn't relax. All she wanted now was the truth, so that her world could never again be ripped out from under her like it had that day on the phone.

So she put her whole life on hold.

For six months she'd searched for the drifter who was her father – driving from town to town in northern Australia. She was now more at home on the road than she was anywhere else.

But dark-haired Hector, the welder, with two toes missing on his right foot, a taste for red dust on his boots, and a bag on his back, seemed more like an Aussie myth than a miner with a daughter he'd never met.

Chapter 3

The air conditioning in her car had long since died. So Wendy wound the windows down and cranked up a CD player, revelling in the freedom of the open road. The stark red space sported more shrubs than trees. Families of kangaroos bounced between them looking for food. It was nearly dusk and they were just starting to become more active. Some of the tension that had wound around her heart loosened as the Pilbara took over.

A couple of CDs later, she turned her car into her hotel car park and was surprised to see her uncle waiting for her there, leaning against the side of a Barnes Inc ute that needed a good wash. He was still in his uniform. Pale blue shirt. Navy pants.

She jumped out of her car. 'Uncle Mike, what are you doing here?'

He looked decidedly cranky. But then Uncle Mike always looked cranky. He was shorter than her, bald and heading towards a pot belly. She reckoned that he must frown often with those lines etched so deeply into his forehead.

'What *the hell* happened?'

'W-what?' she faltered.

He pushed off the side of his car and put his hands on his hips. 'Dan Hullog was supposed to give you a job, so why on earth am I hearing rumours that a TCN spy is now working with us?'

She lifted her chin. 'They're not rumours. Dan didn't have a job for me so he helped me get one at Barnes Inc.'

'That wasn't the deal,' he ground out.

'Well, then you shouldn't play dirty.' She glared at him and he had the grace to redden.

'Told you about that, did he?'

'I don't appreciate being part of some scam you're running.'

'It's not a scam,' he retorted. 'I want to help you.'

'Then why didn't you get me the job at Barnes Inc instead of some dodgy deal over at TCN?'

'Well, for one thing, I didn't know about it and for another, do you think I want to be accused of nepotism? You better not have told anyone that you're my niece.'

The jab hurt, particularly because she'd told him a couple of weeks ago that she'd found out she wasn't *really* his niece. She'd been hoping for a kind word, maybe a bit of information that she hadn't already discovered. But he'd been as cold as the rest of the family, if not colder.

'Don't worry,' she muttered sarcastically. 'I'm not in the habit of lying.'

His eyes narrowed. 'Just because my brother isn't your real father doesn't mean he doesn't love you.'

She tossed her head. 'I'll be the judge of that.'

'You're right.' He glared at her. 'It's none of my business. In fact, I wish you hadn't told me. The last thing I need is a female with issues on my back.'

She gasped.

He spread his hands with callous indifference. 'Being adopted is not a big deal. You should be grateful that you had a roof over your head and food on your plate.'

His complete and utter lack of sensitivity was like a slap in the face.

'I can't believe you just said that.'

'Well, believe it.' He nodded and turned as though he were about to get back into his vehicle. 'I'll see you when I see you.'

She decided to throw her own dart out there. 'It'll probably be at dinner tomorrow.'

He started. 'W-what?'

'I'll be living in the camp.'

'What for?' he barked, spinning back with surprising speed.

She folded her arms crossly. 'Well, I can't live in this motel: it's too expensive and also inconvenient. I don't want to drive forty minutes every day to get to work by six am. I'd have to get up at four!'

'So get a house in Wickham!' he cried. 'That town is five minutes from site.'

'What's wrong with the camp?'

'It's not safe.'

'Why wouldn't it be safe?'

'There's no women there.'

'I was told there were five women there.'

'Idiots, all of them,' he retorted. 'Don't be a young fool.'

She gasped. 'I'm nearly thirty. I think I can take care of myself.'

'You look too much like your mother.'

She rolled her eyes. 'Well, since I last checked being blonde isn't a health hazard. Is it really that much of a problem for you to be seen with me? I mean, I'm sure we won't come into contact that often.'

He grunted.

She stared at him.

He was the distant relative who had never been around. Not even at Christmas. She hadn't thought that was his fault. His wife was a dragon and she'd had a theory it was Patricia who had prevented him from attending anything but weddings or funerals. But maybe not. Maybe Uncle Mike *was* the cold-hearted bastard everyone reported him to be.

So then why had he helped her? Why had he told her to go to Dan Hullog for a job?

He seemed to read her thoughts and sighed. 'Look, it's not that I have a problem with you or anything. I know Parry would have wanted me to help you. But you walked into the job wearing a TCN uniform. There's enough gossip surrounding you already without dragging me into it.'

'Relax,' she responded cynically. 'This sinking ship isn't taking you down with it.'

His face hardened. 'I think that remains to be seen.' He opened the door of his vehicle. Just before he stepped in, however, he looked up at her.

'There's a female engineer called Lena Todd who lives in the camp and works for Barnes Inc. She'll help you.'

'What? Help the TCN spy?' she snapped sarcastically.

'Lena won't care about that. Like I said, she's an idiot. You'll probably get on.'

She didn't know whether to be grateful or affronted as he finally slid into his ute and sped away in a cloud of dust. She shook her head and turned around to enter her hotel room. The familiar smell of musty carpets and empty ashtrays assailed her nostrils.

No matter how bad the camp was, it would be fantastic to get out of here.

Wendy got her first taste of her new accommodation the following morning. The Cape Lambert Work Camp was located on the outskirts of the small town of Wickham – a maze of dongas sitting on unkempt weed-ridden dirt. The central brick building, which housed the reception, a gym and the mess hall, had seen better days. It was past eight am when Wendy arrived, so the place was like an eerie ghost town of aluminium bedrooms-for-one. The only sounds were the clicking of insects and the scrape of her boots on red pebbles.

A bell attached to the door rang as she walked into reception and a woman in her late forties, with her feet on the desk, looked up from her nail file. She had knotty hair and a rather unfortunate face that settled into a resigned expression around her dry cracking lips.

'Oh great! Another one.'

'I beg your pardon?'

'There's no sense in apologising. You can't help what you are.'

'My *name* is Wendy Hopkins. And I'm here to organise a donga for myself. I just started with Barnes Inc.'

'So you're the TCN spy everybody's been talking about. Don't look like you've got much gut in you, do ya?'

By now Wendy was finding it impossible to ignore the fact that this woman was being a bitch simply for being a bitch's sake. 'I'm not a spy.'

The woman grinned, exposing her bad teeth. 'He said, she said. It's all about credibility, isn't it?' She went back to filing her nails, the scratchy sound grating on Wendy's last nerve. 'The name's Ethel, by the way, girlie.'

Girlie?

It was clear this woman was the resident bully. Wendy put her hands on her hips. She'd had enough stress, rude remarks and wisecracks the last couple of days to last her a lifetime. She was over it. 'Just so you know, *Ethel*, I've been around the block a few times and I don't take shit from anyone. So get your feet off the desk, put that nail file away and get me a bloody donga now!'

Ethel narrowed her eyes. Her mouth curled in a manner that let Wendy know she'd gone too far.

She waited.

With painstaking slowness, Ethel put the nail file down, took her feet off the desk and turned to the pigeon holes behind her. She pulled some forms from the boxes and a set of beaten-up looking keys that for some reason were set apart from a pile of others.

She turned around and slapped all this on the counter. 'I got the penthouse just for you, honey.'

Her grin was positively evil. But Wendy shrugged, refusing to buy into such tactics. She grabbed a pen and quickly began filling in her emergency forms. She skipped the television form and took the maps.

'Enjoy.' Ethel's smoker's cackle sounded in her ears as she swiped the keys off the countertop and left.

She went back to her car first and grabbed the large duffle bag that contained her life. The key was marked B39 and the donga was easy enough to find with the aid of her map. Unfortunately it also kind of stood out from the ones around it.

There was a sign hanging from the door knob. *Out of service*.

Next to the door, the flyscreen from the window had obviously popped out, because it was under it, leaning against the wall. It had a couple of giant holes in it too. So a fat lot of good it would do if it was in anyway.

For a split second Wendy thought that Ethel must have made a mistake and then realisation dawned on her. Okay, so the woman was more than a bitch. She was the devil incarnate.

But there was no way in hell she was going back to reception with her tail between her legs to beg for a different room. It couldn't be that bad, could it?

It could.

The door creaked open and she saw an unmade bed with ripped sheets. The donga clearly hadn't been cleaned since the last occupant had left it. It smelled like feet and stale beer – a dreadful combination. The fridge was open but luckily switched off. There were empty cans spilling out of it and a rather suspicious looking puddle on the floor. She noticed, after further inspection, that there were some glass pieces in the puddle and looked up. The light bulb was not only blown, it was smashed. The leg of her desk was broken and the door of her wardrobe was hanging by one hinge. If she didn't know any better she'd say a brawl had taken place in there. She left her bags outside and went in to switch on the air conditioner.

Yep. Broken.

Great.

She was on the verge of swallowing her pride and returning to Ethel when she heard someone humming outside. Marching out of the donga she spied a trolley laden with fresh linen and some other cleaning products on the gravel across the way. A donga door a little way down from hers was open. It seemed housekeeping was currently moving through these parts.

She crossed the gravel path and poked her head into the aluminium box. A small woman in her thirties with a net over her blonde hair was busy making up a bed.

'Hey,' Wendy said. 'I've just moved into the donga that's out of service. I was wondering if I could borrow your Spray n' Wipe.'

The woman straightened. 'What? It hasn't been refurbished yet.'

Wendy's mouth twisted. 'I think Ethel's refurbishing it with me.'

The woman grinned. 'Pissed her off, did you?'

Wendy chuckled. 'Must have.'

'Come on then.' The housekeeper came out of the donga. 'I'll help you. I'm sure we can do more than Spray n' Wipe.'

She pushed her trolley over to Wendy's donga and together they cleaned out the bar fridge, closed the door and switched it on, wiped up the spill and a few other stains on the floor and replaced the bedding with good clean linen.

As they completed the job together, Wendy found out the woman's name was Alison. She was a recent Wickham local who had taken this part-time job as a means to earn extra money.

'So what about the light bulb, the wardrobe and the desk?' Alison asked when they were done.

31

'I won't use the desk. I'll just keep my clothes in my bag – I don't have much with me – and if I close the wardrobe door it'll be out of the way. And I can pick up a light bulb in town on my way home.'

Alison nodded. 'Sounds like a plan. You won't get far without air conditioning though.'

'We'll see.' Wendy was prepared to do without it as long as she could, just to prevent giving Ethel the satisfaction.

With her accommodation finally sorted, it was time to attend her safety induction in town. Actually, past time. She was twenty minutes late due to the donga debacle but the presenter let her sneak in without a word.

The safety induction was organised and run by the owners of the wharf. Anyone who wanted to work on their site had to attend this five-hour session explaining policy, protocol and what to do in an emergency. Wendy listened very carefully and even jotted down notes. She noticed that nobody else did and had that feeling she hadn't experienced since high school. Amongst the popular kids, the sports stars and the musicians, she was definitely *the nerd*.

During morning tea one of the guys, a scaffolder for Barnes Inc, said to her, 'Don't worry so much, honey, there's no test at the end.'

She raised her eyebrows at him but said nothing. Maybe the truth was that the problems with safety on this site started on day one.

The group was made up of new starters for TCN, Barnes Inc and some other minor subcontractors. But she was definitely the only female in the room.

By three o'clock she was gutted. Her colleagues weren't much better. She knew they had no intention of going to Cape Lambert to finish off the rest of their working day. *Especially* when they invited her to join them for a round of drinks outside one of the boilermaker's dongas.

'Er . . . no thanks. I think I might go in to work.'

They all exchanged a look.

Geez. No points for work ethic around here either.

In the end her trip into Cape Lambert was a mistake. Neil was very disappointed to see her. 'I thought you had the induction today.'

'Yes, but it finished at three.'

'Well, I didn't expect you to come in. I don't have anything for you to do.'

She was beginning to get rather cross with him, considering she could see for herself that the man was more overloaded than a freight train en route to Queensland. 'I find that very difficult to believe.' She looked pointedly at the piles of memos on his desk.

'I can't just hand you that stuff raw,' he protested. 'You need to have some background knowledge of this job before you wade in. You'll just get lost in it without my guidance . . . and frankly, I don't have the time.'

She pounced on this. 'Well, if I need some background knowledge why don't I catch the bus out onto the wharf? Have a look around myself, so to speak.'

'You're not going on that wharf on your own,' he snapped at her a little too quickly.

'Why? I've had the safety induction. I'll be perfectly fine.'

'There's too much for you to do here.'

'You just said there was nothing for me to do here!'

'Nothing on this desk.' He pointed at his own. 'But you've still got a heap to get through on yours.'

She looked over at her desk. That giant safety manual he'd given her yesterday was sitting there but next to it was now another file of similar shape and proportions. On its spine, in dark black ink, was written *Volume 2*.

You've got to be kidding me.

'When you've read all that,' he waved his pointer finger at her, 'then we'll talk.'

As he walked away, she suddenly wished she'd killed the last few hours of her day in Wickham searching for her father instead. There was a steel mill on the outskirts of town.

Wickham had a health centre too. She could have checked that out. Ask if anyone had come in with an injury to his right foot more than thirty years ago. Not that she knew if their records went back that far, or if they'd pass out personal details to a stranger. It was definitely a long shot at best. But it was why she had come back to Karratha and this part of the Pilbara in particular: to discover any clues she may have missed before.

Her father's injury was the one unique and solid fact she had. And if it meant researching the rise and fall of every steel mill in the area, she'd do it.

Though obviously not today.

She dragged her feet back to her desk and slumped in her chair, looking at the files with such resentment that a low laugh next to her made her jump.

It was Chub.

'Do they offend you in some way?' he enquired and then held out an open jar of jelly beans to her. 'Here, have one. It'll take the edge off. Always does for me.'

She grinned and stuck her hand in the jar.

'Okay, when I said one, I didn't literally mean one. You can have five or six or fifteen,' he amended generously. 'Whatever it takes to lift your mood.'

'Thanks, but one's fine.' She popped the purple bean in her mouth and chewed. The intensely sweet blueberry flavour gave her an instant sugar jolt. 'I just don't get him. Why does he have such a huge problem with me?'

'It's not you. It's him.'

'How do you mean?'

'He doesn't have a problem with you, he just has a problem period.' He was about to put the lid back on his jar when he shook his head. 'Aw, screw it.' He tipped out a handful, tossed them back and then set the jar down. 'You should do what I do,' he said with a mouth full of sugar.

'What's that?'

'Don't talk to him.'

She laughed. 'I can't do that, he's my boss.'

'Well, I didn't say it was going to be easy.' He sighed. 'Nothing here is easy.'

She smiled sadly. 'Nothing worth it ever is.'

'Well, aren't you a philosophical little mate? I just hope they don't crush your spirit.'

She lifted her chin. 'They'll find that very difficult, cobber.'

He grinned at her and she grinned back. She could tell he got a real kick out of the word 'cobber' springing off her lips. Not just because it was a word usually employed by older men amongst their cronies but because she hadn't called him Chub.

Nor would she ever.

From that day forwards, it was always 'little mate' and 'Cobber' between them. And in the hard times ahead, it was one of the few comforts she had.

When work ended at six that evening, it was still light. She had picked up and installed the new light bulb but there was still time to kill. So she decided to go for a jog up Water Tank Hill. It was the lookout point for Wickham. The gym was her other option to burn off frustration but she desperately wanted to be alone. In her experience, gyms on jobs like this also functioned as pick-up joints. Given there were only five women in this camp, her odds of being approached were pretty loaded. Besides, the lookout wasn't that far from the camp and it would provide an excellent view of the town at sunset.

Back at her donga, she changed into a pair of black bike pants and a loose pink T-shirt, tied her hair in a ponytail and stuck some earphones in her ears. All she wanted to do was zone out.

As she jogged through the main car park to get to the road, a man who had been leaning against his ute straightened and she noticed with a flush that he was *very* good looking. Sandy brown hair, soulful brown eyes and a healthy tan. He brought the same sort of visual pop to her eyeballs that Brad Pitt brought to the big screen. She ignored that familiar *zing* that had got her into trouble so many times before and kept running. Apart from the fact that she had serious desertion issues and a truckload of emotional baggage she was trying to figure out what to do with, she just didn't have time for romance.

Her last boyfriend had certainly made that clear when he'd dumped her for ignoring him. 'I don't know, Wendy. For the last two months you've been pretty preoccupied with your family. I'm starting to feel like a third wheel.'

If she were honest, Nathan had only ever been a holiday fling. All the same, his rejection had hurt. There was no sense in going through that again. She had already made the decision that any time off she had here was going to be spent looking for her father.

Maybe it was because of the music in her ears or her pre-occupation with her own thoughts but she didn't notice that the man from the car park had started following her until she was about halfway to the lookout.

On a bend in the road, she caught him out of the corner of her eye jogging only a couple of metres behind her. Was he tailing her?

An awful thought occurred to her.

Lone female.

On the top of an isolated hill.

No witnesses present to see her dragged behind a bush.

Her blood boiled. Not in this lifetime!

She took a wrong turn to see what he would do. He turned off in a different direction. She breathed an inwards sigh of relief that was closely followed by guilt. Was she always this

distrustful and paranoid of people? Or just since she'd found
out she was adopted?

Get a grip, Wendy!

After jogging down another street, she looped back and
headed up to the lookout again, increasing her speed. She
really needed to stop jumping to conclusions so fast. It was
doing her head in. The world had not changed. She just knew
more about it.

She jogged up to the top of the grassy mound and surveyed
the town laid out before her in the dim twilight.

'Hey, gorgeous!'

The suggestive tone had her spinning around faster than an
eighties yoyo.

'You again.'

The good-looking stranger was standing a mere metre
and a half behind her. Tall, well built and a little too close in
her opinion. She glared at him. He put his hands on his hips,
sweat from his jog glistening on the parts of his chest that were
exposed by his loose-fitting tank top.

His lips curled. 'I thought you might be coming up here.'
He took another step towards her.

In her startled state, it seemed like all the proof she needed.
Her hand pulled back and . . . *THWACK!* She struck him full
against his jawline. He staggered back, his palm to his cheek.

'What the hell did you do that for?'

She widened her stance and raised both hands. 'I'm warning
you, I've taken self-defence classes.'

He seemed amused. 'Karate?'

'Among other things.'

'I see.' He rubbed his jaw but didn't step back.

Her alarm heightened. 'Who are you? Where are you from?'

'I'm from the camp, same as you.' He took another step closer,
hands spread wide. 'Just calm down, I'm not here to hurt you.'

'Don't tell me to calm down.' She tossed her head and main-
tained her stance. 'Why were you following me?'

He ignored her question, however, as he eyed her thought-fully. 'You know, I don't know what they were teaching you in those classes but if you want to exert more damage on your opponent, you shouldn't use an open palm. Try a fist or kick next time. In fact,' he nodded as though he were doing her a favour, 'if you want to practise on me now, go ahead. I promise I won't fight back.'

Her bravado faltered and her hands dropped slightly. A would-be attacker didn't usually offer free punches to his victim. Annoyance replaced her fear as she studied him. She didn't need a psychic to tell her that those love-you-today leave-you-tomorrow eyes were Trouble with a capital T.

'I don't want to hit you again,' she snapped.

He sighed. 'Would you prefer it if I provoked you in some way?'

'*Huh?*'

Without explaining further, her leaned in and kissed her.

It was the most unexpected, outrageous, incorrigible thing that anyone had done to her.

Ever!

What was even worse was the fact that while he took her mouth, he didn't touch her. She could have jumped away from him. Run off down the hill. Instead, like a cobra entranced by a snake charmer's flute, she closed her eyes for just a few seconds to enjoy his gentle caress.

And then reality hit. *What are you doing? Why are you still here?*

She pulled away and this time did curl her fingers into a hefty fist and punch him in the face. 'You arse!'

The red mark on his cheek almost made her feel guilty until she saw that smile of his again.

'Okay, I deserved that one.' He nodded. 'I really shouldn't have done that. It's one of my worst faults actually. Kissing girls who don't want to be kissed. You'll have to accept my apologies.'

She had absolutely nothing to say to this brazen remark so turned to go.

'Don't suppose you'll have dinner with me some time, will you?' His voice struck her from behind, right between the shoulder blades.

She spun back incredulously. '*What?*'

'Well, that *is* why I followed you.' His tone was finally apologetic. 'To ask you out. Guess I kind of botched it, didn't I?'

With hands on hips, she eyed him with utter contempt. 'Yeah you did.'

'No worries.' He nodded and then, without saying goodbye, jogged off down the hill again, which couldn't help but infuriate her even more.

She was the one who was supposed to make the dramatic exit.

She had wanted to leave him standing there staring like a stunned mullet, not the other way around.

Dragging a hand across her lips, she symbolically tried to wipe away his touch. But the smell of him still clung to the air around her, or more like the sweat from the jog they'd taken. She shook her head with disgust. *I need a shower.*

Whoever he was, she hoped he worked for TCN or in a hole in the ground somewhere where she wouldn't run into him again anytime soon. Embarrassment didn't even begin to cover how she was feeling right now.

After she'd allowed five minutes to crawl by, she jogged down the hill to the showers. There was only an hour left till the mess closed and she needed to get some dinner before bed.

It was her first time in the mess since she'd arrived. Given the gossip about her that was already circulating, she was expecting to make a bit of a stir. However, the reality was still a bit galling. All she wanted was a low profile, especially after her experience on the hill, but she felt like a thousand pairs of eyes followed her into that mess hall. From the rows and rows of trestle tables they watched her walk across the room to the buffet. They nudged each other when she took a spoon of mashed potato, followed by a side of beef and gravy.

Why was that controversial?

She wished she'd tied her hair up after the shower, but it was wet, so she'd left it out to dry. It felt too feminine now, having it all loose like that.

With shrug of rebellion she put another scoop of mash on her plate and turned around. After the evening she'd had, she was done dancing to the tunes of men.

To her surprise, two women sitting at a trestle table by themselves were waving at her. A redhead with laughing blue eyes and the prettiest honey blonde she'd seen in a very long time.

They beckoned her eagerly.

With the impossibility of her day getting any worse, she decided to join them.

'Hi, Wendy,' the redhead greeted her. 'I'm Sharon.'

Her mouth fell open in surprise. 'You know my name?'

'Honey, word travels faster around here than nits in a class-room.'

She didn't know whether to be flattered or worried. Instead she lowered her voice. 'I just wish they'd stop staring at me.' She sat down slowly, self-consciously tucking her hair behind her ear.

'They will in a minute. First they had to see what you'd get for dinner. There's been a bet going round you were going to just eat a salad over the roast.'

She was startled. 'Really?'

'Skinny thing like you.' Sharon chuckled. 'You've had them all confounded. I think that lucky guy over there's made $175 on your mash potato grab.'

'Seriously?'

The honey blonde laughed. 'Oh yes, and it's quite made up my mind about you.' Her green eyes danced. 'You're going to be heaps of fun. I'm Lena. Lena Todd. Very, *very* pleased to meet you!'

Wendy held out her hand and found it shaken warmly.

'So you're Mike's niece, are you?' Lena asked.

'You know Mike?'

'Yes, you could say I know Mike *extremely* well.' Lena exchanged a glance with Sharon.

'Sounds ominous.'

'Oh it's nothing.' Lena rolled her eyes. 'Past tense really.'

But Wendy's curiosity was caught. 'No, tell me.'

Lena's eyes narrowed on her. 'You honestly don't know, do you?'

'Don't know what?' Wendy spooned a little mash into her mouth.

'Your uncle didn't share his *intel* with you?'

That caught Wendy's attention. 'No.'

'The truth is, I'm dating the client. Which is a little controversial in these parts. Mike found out about it when Dan and I were trying to keep it all a secret.'

A couple of cog wheels in Wendy's head slipped into gear. So this was the leverage her uncle had thought he had over Dan Hullog. Made sense, considering everyone at Barnes Inc seemed to hate everyone at TCN – it would have caused one hell of a Romeo and Juliet scandal.

She winced. 'He didn't threaten to expose you, did he?'

'Well,' Lena cleared her throat. 'I wasn't going to mention it. But turns out your uncle does have a taste for blackmail. Luckily, Dan doesn't give a damn what people think and neither do I. I've proven that I can do my job well without any special favours from the client.'

Wendy nodded. 'Good for you.'

'So how are you and Dan going anyway?' Sharon asked, and for a moment the two friends forgot about Wendy and her uncle.

Lena's face seemed to light like a bulb although she swatted the air with studied casualness. 'We're fine. But I mean, we only just went went public.'

41

'And the guys aren't still hassling you?' Sharon wanted to know.

'Are you kidding me? This morning Dan exited his donga accompanied by "Unchained Melody" played from his neighbour's two loudspeakers.'

Sharon grinned. 'Nice.'

Wendy licked her lips. 'I'm sorry if my uncle is one of those people who've been heckling you.'

Lena looked at her in surprise. 'No, Mike's a lot of things, but he's not juvenile.'

Wendy looked the engineer dead in the eye. 'You don't like him, do you?'

Lena's lids fluttered open. 'Oh, it's not that he's . . .' Her shoulders slumped. 'Okay, we don't get on but I'm sure he's a fabulous uncle.'

Wendy grinned. 'He's not.'

'You mean he's moody with you too?'

Wendy nodded. 'Pretty much.'

'So I take it you're not close.'

More like dysfunctional. Wendy's mouth twisted. 'Not really. Never saw much of him when I was growing up. He put a lot of people's noses out of joint back in the day and has kind of stayed out of reach of the family. Even my grandmother thinks he's strange and he's her son.'

'That's a shame.' Lena sighed. 'Here I was thinking there might be a different side to him. You know, the nice side he reserves for his loved ones.'

'Well if he's got loved ones, I'm not one of them.' Wendy nodded a little sadly. 'When I ran into him in Karratha by accident, I thought I might be able to mend a few fences but it just didn't work out. So,' she changed the focus to Sharon, 'do you have a boyfriend too?'

Sharon coloured up. 'Yes, it's Carl.'

'As in Carl Curtis?'

'That's the one.'

'Wow!' Wendy laughed but her brain was doing flips. She'd just run into the two Alpha Women of the site, each one bonded to a powerhouse. She was going to have to be careful around these two. However, they had already lost interest in her again and returned to their previous conversation.

'I can't believe Dan is your boyfriend. It's so weird.' Sharon was shaking her head.

'It's not weird,' Lena protested. 'But I can see what you mean about the word "boyfriend". It doesn't really suit him. Do you think I should call him my partner?'

'That's a bit serious.'

'Well, I think we're serious. Do you think we're serious?'

'Lena, if you're asking me then you're not serious enough.'

'Right, okay.' Lena chewed happily on her lower lip. 'Well, I'm just happy to see where it goes from here for the moment. I've got a date tonight.'

'*Really?*' Sharon's eyes widened. 'Imagine that? A social life in Cape Lambert. Miracles do happen.'

'Well,' Lena threw a teasing smile in Wendy's direction, 'if there's anything I've learned in the last few months it's that if you put your mind to it, you can accomplish anything.'

Wendy nodded and Sharon raised her cup of water. 'Damn straight!' she toasted them.

Chapter 4

After a night of mashed-potato bets, a stolen kiss and an invitation to join the popular girls' group, Wendy was more than ready to find some semblance of normality in her life again. The place she hoped to find it was at work. With the luxury of having her own car, she turned up ten minutes early. Neither Chub nor Neil had arrived yet and she snuck over to the air conditioner, fiddled around with the temperature setting and managed to increase the thermostat by a couple of degrees. She hoped her two colleagues wouldn't notice but the slight adjustment made a world of difference to her.

She sat down and read her files. Chub arrived on time, but Neil showed up ten minutes late.

'Why the hell is it so hot in here?' he snapped, the sweat beading on his forehead like water droplets on a boiled egg. He immediately walked over to the air conditioner and turned the temperature setting down.

Four degrees.

Wendy groaned inwardly. Pretty soon she was going to grow icicles on her nose hairs. Should she go to her car and fetch that blanket she kept in her boot? How stupid would she look?

A plastic packet flew from her left and landed in front of her. It was a fluoro yellow safety vest. She looked over in the direction it had come.

'It might help.' Chub winked at her. 'Marginally.'

'Thanks.' She smiled but didn't immediately open it. Instead she got up and walked over to Neil's side of the office.

'Er . . . Neil,' she began.

'Not now,' he snapped. 'Can't you see I'm busy?'

The truth was he didn't look busy at all. He was just sitting there – pale and sweaty with bloodshot eyes.

What he did look was *sick*. 'Are you okay?'

'Just go away,' he croaked.

It was the sound of his voice, rather than the command itself that made her turn helplessly away. After she sat down, she looked across the room at him. He was sitting slumped in his chair, head down, eyes fixed on the floor like he was suffering.

Her brow wrinkled. 'Hey, Cobber,' she whispered to Chub. 'Should we call someone, like the medic?'

'Nothing to worry about, little mate, he's just hungover.' He continued to type away on his computer as though the announcement were commonplace.

'How do you know?' she asked.

'A lot of guys here like to drink after work. Neil *especially*. He's committed.'

'He's committed?'

'Yeah, he's like this every morning.'

Warning bells like the chimes of Big Ben sounded in her ears. '*Every* morning?'

Chub looked up. 'Are we playing like a game, where you repeat everything I say?'

'But that's disgraceful!' Wendy ignored his question, her voice losing its whisper quality.

'Not too loud.' Chub put a sausage-like finger to his lips. 'You'll wake him up.'

Just then what sounded like a snore erupted from Neil's slumped body.

'Please tell me he's not sleeping.'

'All right.' Chub complied agreeably and said no more.

An awful realisation dawned on Wendy. 'And I suppose he does that every morning too?'

'Pretty much.'

'But that's outrageous. Why haven't you reported him?'

'And be a snitch?' Chub snorted. 'Little mate, you don't know the rules of the game around here.'

'What game?'

'You don't dob on your peers. It's very bad form. I'd be ostracised. So would anyone else who blew the whistle. You protect your own.'

She gaped at him. 'But don't you get it? He's supposed to be protecting you, not the other way around. Who else knows about this?'

'Everyone.' Chub raised his eyebrows. 'Well, maybe not everyone everyone. Carl obviously doesn't know.'

'He's an alcoholic,' she whispered, glancing over at Neil's snoring form. The horror that Parker Point was repeating itself was like a slap across her face. 'I mean, he's gotta be.' Was she going to be asked to protect this guy from himself too?

Just like Adam Booth. The man she had unwisely decided to give a second chance to.

She turned angrily on Chub. Her reaction, she knew, was slightly overboard but she couldn't help it.

'I can't deal with this.'

'Which part?'

'All of it! You can't have a safety officer who's an alcoholic! Even saying it sounds ludicrous.'

'Well don't say it then,' Chub offered. 'It'll make you feel much better. Hell, it'll make me feel better.'

'No it won't. No wonder Barnes Inc has dropped the ball on safety. It's all because of him.'

'Well, there's no need to get your knickers in a knot.' Chub reached for his jar of jelly beans.

'I don't want a jelly bean!' She bolted to her feet. 'I'm going to see Carl.' The anger boiling in her blood was like a shot of adrenaline.

'But, Wendy,' Chub began, 'wait –'

It was too late. She was already striding from the room. It was only about fifteen minutes into Wednesday morning, so Carl was still in his office, just downloading his morning emails.

'Fuck! Fuck! Fuck!'

Obviously, none of them were good news.

'Good morning, Carl.'

He didn't look up from his computer screen as she positioned herself in his doorframe.

'Morning, Wendy.'

'How are you?' she asked politely, wondering whether to ease into her complaint or cut to the chase.

'Fucked.' He still didn't look up.

Cut to the chase.

'Speaking of which, did you know that Neil Cooper has a drinking problem?'

He finally pulled his eyes from his screen. 'What the fuck?'

'The reason why we have such a poor relationship with the wharf owners is because Neil can't get through the work. Every morning he's hungover.'

'You've been here . . . what? Three days? And that's your assessment. A bloke is allowed to be fuckin' hungover occasionally. Especially in these parts.'

'Well, according to Bill Walden, and probably anyone else you care to question, Neil is like that every morning without fail.'

'Who the fuck is Bill Walden?'

She sighed. 'Chub.'

'Right.' His eyes cleared in recognition. 'Well, why didn't Chub tell me himself?'

'Because,' she rolled her eyes, 'nobody wants to be a whistle-blower.'

His eyes narrowed upon her. 'You, on the other hand, are fuckin' happy to do it.'

She reddened. 'It's not that. I don't enjoy anyone's misfortune or deliberately want anyone to suffer whether they've made a mistake or not. I firmly believe that everyone should get a fair go and definitely some room to stuff up and get back up. But, Carl, I've seen how much work he has on his desk. And I've heard the number of complaint calls he gets. This is a situation of long standing. I've had my safety induction but he won't let me on the wharf or give me any real work. He's too scared I might find out exactly how much he's missed. It's too dangerous to give him time to realise the error of his own ways and change. He's in charge of people's lives, for goodness' sake – making sure that every person on this job is not at unnecessary risk of injury, or worse, death. You can't just let something like that slide. Particularly for an *alcoholic*. His condition is a disease. He's not going to right the wrongs he's committed overnight, even if he admits today that he's got a problem. He needs help. Professional help!'

Her voice faltered as bad decisions she couldn't make again threatened to choke her. But she pushed through the feeling.

'Even if the lives and well-being of your men aren't that important to you, what about Barnes Inc's risk of liability? If anyone so much as breathes the word negligence, we won't have a leg to stand on. Maybe I'm the new girl in town and maybe I've only been here a few days but, Carl, I can promise you, if you come with me now, just for five minutes, you'll be able to see firsthand *exactly* what I'm talking about.'

She found herself panting slightly as she came to the end of this impassioned speech. And Carl, who had watched her whole diatribe in wide-eyed shock, continued to sit there in silence for a few more seconds before exclaiming, 'What is it with the fuckin' women on this job?'

While she was still trying to decipher the significance of this question, Carl put his pointer finger to the desk. 'This,' he growled, 'is a construction project. It's not a cause. I have no place for soapboxes on this job.'

Wendy wrung her hands. 'I know but –'

'But,' he held up his finger, 'if you think you've got something to show me then, fuck, show me, and make it quick.'

She nodded curtly. 'All right then.'

She led him out of the main office donga, across the patch of dirt separating it from the icebox and back to Neil's desk. It took Carl only five seconds to notice that Neil Cooper was asleep and another two seconds to smell him.

'Fuck!' Carl turned on Chub. 'And you say he's like this *every morning?*'

Chub looked heavenwards. 'Why do I feel like there's an echo in here?'

'Just tell me the fuckin' truth.'

Chub quickly sobered. 'Yes. It's pretty much his routine.'

Carl bent over and shook Neil's shoulders. The man started as he opened his eyes.

'Neil, you're fired. Pack up your things and leave. Wendy,' Carl turned to her, 'you've got his job. I want you out on that wharf. You find out everything this motherfucker has missed and I do mean *everything.*'

Chapter 5

Gavin Jones was not a man who normally gave much time to gossip. Unless, of course, it was about himself, which generally didn't happen that often. After the awkward incident with Lena Todd a couple of months earlier he'd made it his personal mission to stay out of the limelight.

It wasn't to say he didn't enjoy a good laugh with his men over their drunken antics and hook-ups with women gone wrong. He just didn't want to be the subject of one of those stories again, which, once circulated, were followed by all and sundry like a TV soap.

Today, however, as he sat in the TCN office with Lena waiting for Bulldog to deem them worthy of his presence he couldn't help but listen with half an ear to her musings.

'Did you know she had Neil fired this morning? She's taken his job. Just swiped it right out from under him.'

'Really?' His tone implied vague interest. 'And who is Neil again?'

Lena rolled her eyes. 'He's our safety guy.'

'We have a safety guy?' Gavin rubbed his chin. 'Never heard of him.'

'I think that's half the problem.' Lena put her foolscap file in a standing position and leaned heavily on the top of it. 'Things are going to change around here big time. I just know it. Radar was saying that after firing Neil she got on the wharf and started going around taking a heap of notes. Apparently, there's all these improvements we need to make.'

Did that mean he was going to be seeing more of that stunning blonde striding around the deck? He couldn't wait.

'She reckons we're not ready for cyclone season. I suppose that's true, considering I don't even know when cyclone season starts.'

'November.' Gavin's excitement increased. 'She'll probably want to do a pre-season clean up.'

'That's what Radar said,' Lena groaned. 'That's going to slow us down, isn't it?'

Gavin sighed as he thought about Wendy's pouty mouth, and long-lashed lids. 'Oh, give the girl a chance. Safety is, after all, very important.'

'I know.' Lena bit her lip. 'And I shouldn't be complaining after everything Dan's been through. I just have a bad feeling, you know.'

'About Bulldog?' Gavin grinned. 'That's perfectly natural.'

'About *Wendy*.' Lena tutted. 'She's a nice girl who's in for a very hard time of it. The boys around here are pretty much set in their ways with their "Why fix it if it ain't broke?" attitudes. I doubt they'll be very accommodating of her new ideas. Maybe I should warn her to be careful.'

She *should* be careful all right. That gorgeous tight little arse encased in black Lycra running through the streets of Wickham at twilight, taunting a man with delights he dared not imagine. *Is that get-up even legal in these parts?*

'What are you smiling about?' Lena demanded. 'I swear you're like a stoned puppy to talk to this morning.'

'Nothing.'

'You're thinking about going after her, aren't you?'

Been there. Done that.

'For goodness' sake, Gavin, have you even met her yet?'
Kissing her was the highlight of my week.

'Sort of.' He lifted an arm to self-consciously rub the back of his neck. 'We kind of didn't get off to a good start. I think I'm going to have to work on my manners.'

Lena sniffed. 'Got that right.'

He threw her his most whimsical smile. It usually melted away the annoyance on the crankiest woman's face. 'You're not still dirty about what went down between us, are you?'

But Lena wasn't most women. She'd proved her immunity to him with gleeful dexterity. 'I'm too in love with Dan to be worried about the likes of you.'

'Of course.' He glanced dryly at his watch. 'I just wish that boyfriend of yours cared a little more about this meeting. We've been waiting for his majesty for nearly half an hour now. I've got things on the wharf I need to do.'

Lena stiffened defensively. 'He's a busy man. He's got lots of people demanding his attention.'

As if to echo this sentiment, the door to the client's office swung open. Preceded by a swirl of red dust, a woman entered the reception area.

A gorgeous brunette.

Gavin immediately sat up straighter. He definitely had a preference for blondes but this bird was something special. She looked completely out of place standing in front of that dirt-smudged white reception counter. She was wearing a cream summer dress with a faint pink floral print. It had a lace-trimmed sweetheart neckline leaving her shoulders, arms and the round tops of two perfect breasts exposed. On her feet were a pair of flimsy pale pink sandals, a rare sight at Cape Lambert, where every foot was encased in steel-capped boots to avoid censure from the client, or crushed toes – whichever seemed like the priority at the time.

Her skin was the fair kind that obviously only saw sun on those rare occasions she thought a well-catered picnic on the beach sounded like a good idea. Her hair, a generous cascade of glossy chestnut-coloured curls, trailed down her back with inviting warmth.

'Hi-iiii.' She drew out the word in a sing-songy gush to the receptionist, who lifted her eyes from her computer screen only to have her jaw drop in astonishment at the sight before her.

'Er . . . Hi.'

'I'm Annabel George. I'm sorry I don't have an appointment. It was kind of a spontaneous decision to come down when I found out from my friend Alison, who just took a job at the camp, that *Daniel Hullog* was project manager here.'

To Gavin's amusement, Lena, who was still resting lazily on her file, jerked in her seat.

'Is he available?' Annabel asked. 'I'd love to see how he's been doing.'

'Er . . .' The receptionist was still too stunned to reply.

Conveniently, Bulldog walked into the lobby at that moment, looking brisk and ready for business. He was immediately bombarded by the floral-scented bouquet that was Ms George.

'Daniel!' She gasped at the sight of him, throwing her arms around his neck and pecking him on the cheek. 'You haven't changed at all!'

'Annie?' Bulldog pulled back from the hug to register her face.

'The one and only.' She touched his cheek with French-tipped fingernails. 'Miss me?'

'Who is that woman?' Lena hissed at Gavin.

'Damned if I know.' He grinned and then added in a low voice, 'But I'd like to find out if the whole Wendy thing goes cactus.'

'Forget Wendy,' Lena whispered forcefully. 'You have my full permission to try your hand at Annabel George.'

They both returned their attention to the scene before them.

'It's been such a long time.' Bulldog held Annabel at arm's length, studying her face carefully. 'How are you doing?'

'How am I doing? Believe me, Daniel, a lot has changed since we were an item.'

'An item?' Lena squeaked. 'Okay, that's it.' She stood up. 'Hey, Dan.' She walked over to the little reunion. 'Who's your friend?'

Annabel blinked twice at the sudden intrusion, turning to give Lena a particularly unwelcoming look.

It was the first time Gavin had ever seen Bulldog even vaguely embarrassed. The faintest of pink tinges crept up his neck as he raised one long finger to insert it into a collar that really didn't look that tight.

Gavin smiled.

Poor bastard.

This was exactly the reason you didn't let a woman under your skin. In your bed maybe, but that's as far as it went. He, for one, had absolutely no intention of ever being in a scenario such as this one. It was imperative that he kept his hands clean.

'Oh, Gav, you're such a cynic,' his sister had told him once. 'You'll only fall harder than all the rest when the time finally comes.' The memory sobered him.

It had been years since he'd had a coffee with Kate, just to chew the fat and catch up. He had no idea when the next time would be. And, as things stood, he didn't expect it to be any time soon. He refused to let the thought damage his mood. Things could be worse.

A lot worse.

'Hi.' Lena was holding out her hand to Annabel George. 'I'm Lena, Dan's girlfriend.'

'Oh, Daniel,' Annabel gushed, tapping the knuckles of her right hand against Bulldog's chest, 'she's simply *gorgeous*. Those eyes, that hair, those ...' She paused, frowned and then tipped her head to one side for the moment before saying to Lena with exaggerated concern, 'You do realise though, darling, that that shirt is too big for you. Tucked in like that, it does absolutely nothing for your hips. And ponytails, love, the higher the better. Middle range screams dumpy. You know, I could give you a few make-up tips if you like. Don't be afraid of a little mascara. It'll just bring out those eyes of yours.' She patted Lena on the shoulder as one might tap a child affectionately. 'Any time, darling. Any time.'

'*Really?*' Lena threw a look at Dan, whose expression pleaded mercy.

Gavin covered his mouth as he choked back a laugh. Bulldog with two women busting his chops. This was going to be more fun than the time Tobias's topee had fallen onto the conveyor while he was in the man cage.

He stood up. 'Er, Dan . . . would you like to do this meeting now or should we come back later?'

'Yeah, Dan?' Lena demanded. 'Would you like us to come back later?'

'No, no.' Bulldog cleared his throat and turned to his visitor. 'Annabel, can I call you this afternoon?'

'Sure, honey.' She smiled. 'I'll leave my number with your receptionist and go home to wait by the phone.'

Chapter 6

If Wendy thought that having Neil fired would solve all her problems, she was dead wrong.

There was nothing like the rumour 'The TCN spy has stuck it to one of our own' to rile up the boys. There were only a handful of men who knew for certain that Neil was an alcoholic – those who had worked most closely with him and those who drank with him. These people, who no doubt were also the ones who had been protecting him in the first place, did nothing to squash the stories that he had been unfairly dismissed by an over-anxious female with a bee in her bonnet.

Short of putting out a memo that argued both her soundness of mind and her legitimate employment by Barnes Inc, she couldn't see how she was supposed to change their opinions of her. Safety managers were never liked at the best of times but a new one who had just made a drastic change to the status quo was going to have a very tough time bringing people round.

The truth be told, she had put a couple of memos out there already just to test the waters. She had pinned them on the smoko donga notice boards. Nothing too demanding, just tentatively asking men to be tidier and more thoughtful with their equipment. The next day she had found them under the trestle tables turned into paper planes.

'What am I going to do, Cobber?' Wendy asked, unable to hide the bewilderment she felt. 'Everybody hates me.'

'Well, I have always believed in the old adage, the way to a man's heart is through his stomach.' He rubbed his own with a dreamy expression on his face. 'Just a quick tip, get something with meat in it.'

'Cobber, I'm serious.'

'And I wasn't?' He raised his eyebrows as he turned towards her.

She sighed. He wasn't going to be any help at all. But he surprised her.

'Look, maybe you just need to give it a little time. You've just had Neil fired and taken his job. There's bound to be a few noses out of joint for a couple weeks. Just do your job and do it well. They'll come around.'

She decided that this was possibly the best plan she'd heard since she'd got there and did her best to dive right into it.

On Thursday morning, with Carl's permission, she called a meeting of all the engineers. After cruising around the site on Wednesday, she had definitely noticed a number of areas that needed work in terms of safety. She wanted to discuss some new procedures with them. As leaders of each team, they needed to be on board with her ideas.

She set the meeting for seven am, hoping to catch them all before they got too engrossed in whatever task they had set for that day. There were about six engineers in all required to attend the meeting. It was apparent when the clock indicated they start that three of them were either late or had no intention of showing up. Lena, who was seated closest to Wendy at the long trestle table in the Barnes Inc meeting room, grimaced sympathetically.

'I'm pretty sure they got the email.'

Wendy glanced at her watch, which now read ten past. 'Do you think I should start?'

Lena shrugged. 'I guess so. They've probably just got caught up with something.'

Or maybe I'm not worth their time.

This attitude seemed to be an issue of debate amongst the people who had shown up as well. She could tell that some of them were beginning to regret having left their posts. When she began explaining that she wanted every man on the job, not just the managers or the supervisors, but *every man* to stop what they were doing and take a JSA – short for Job Safety Analysis – there was almost an explosion of outrage.

'Now hang on a minute there, missy,' a burly man with a dirty safety vest on protested. 'You can't just dole out extra paperwork like lumps of cream on scones. We've got a job to do, which won't get done if we've got all this crap on our plates as well.'

She was trying to explain that they could delegate some of this paperwork when the door burst open and three men, in full PPE, strode into the room talking loudly as though they were not half an hour late.

The first was a rather skinny, lanky-looking individual who obviously gave very little thought to his physical appearance. The second, a freckle-faced, ginger-haired man who seemed to be the youngest of the three. And the last . . .

The tips of Wendy's ears grew hot and her throat went dry.

The last was the man who had followed her up Water Tank Hill and kissed her.

You've got to be kidding me!

She was glad she was sitting down because she was sure her knees would have visibly trembled at the sight of him. Thankfully, instead, she was able to clutch them firmly under the table to stop any embarrassing wobbling as she stared at the newcomers, momentarily bereft of speech.

They were not so incapacitated, rudely continuing their conversation as though the people seated at the table weren't even there.

'So I'm not sure which class I should go for,' the ginger-haired young gun was saying. 'Karate or judo. They're holding night classes in the community hall in Wickham.'

'I'd go karate,' the skinny man announced. 'Isn't there more belts or something?'

'I don't know.' The man who had kissed her looked across the room and met her eyes. A lazy smile tickled his lips as he addressed the room at large, 'Anybody know anything about karate?' He broke their gaze to remove his hard hat.

Wendy could feel her face filling with colour and hastily looked down.

Lena, obviously angry on her behalf, stood up. 'Gavin, stop being a pig! Can't you see we're having a meeting here?'

He put his hat under his arm. 'Sorry we're late.'

The skinny guy with longish brown hair, currently tied in the knottiest ponytail Wendy had ever seen, finally turned around and scanned the group.

'Where the hell is Neil?'

This one tactless statement was all it took for Wendy to get her game face back on. She stiffened. 'I'm sorry to be the one to inform you but he was let go.'

'Let go? When?'

'Yesterday morning,' she responded tightly.

'Didn't you know, Fish?' Craig, the engineer for construction of the new berthing dolphins, addressed him from across the table. The berthing dolphins were located on the sides of the jetty and assisted in the ships docking. 'Where've you been the last coupla days?'

'Crabbing,' said Fish and then he turned to the group at large. 'I've got a new trick. What you do, right, is you cast a net first thing in the morning before work, put pierced cans of cat food in it and after work you'll pick up a full net. I've done it the last three mornings with a few checks here and there at smoko and lunch. It works a real treat.'

'Seriously.' Gavin eyed him with some interest. 'Maybe I'll have to try that sometime.'

'I'm telling you, mate, it's –'

Fury swept through Wendy's body. 'If you don't mind, I didn't call a meeting here today to talk fishing.'

Fish closed his mouth for a moment and then asked sullenly, 'So who are you?'

'I'm Wendy Hopkins, the new safety manager. And you are?'

'Lance.' He shrugged. 'The deck engineer. But everyone calls me Fish because –'

'No need to explain, it's perfectly obvious,' she snapped. 'And you?' She turned to the ginger-haired gentleman, who was now starting to look rather self-conscious.

'I'm Anton.' He shuffled from foot to foot. 'I do a lot of odd jobs where it's needed.'

Before she could address the last man, he thrust his long tanned fingers into her field of vision.

'I'm Gavin, the piling engineer.'

She took his hand and nodded curtly. Perhaps it was because he knew it would embarrass her or maybe he was just fundamentally a pig as Lena had described him. But he deliberately held onto her hand a few seconds longer than necessary, forcing her to twitch her fingers out of his grasp. She could feel herself colouring up like a beetroot and wished to God she had more self-restraint.

'All right.' She turned away without meeting his eyes. 'Let's get on with this. We have a lot to get through.'

She wasn't lying about that.

At the same time she knew she'd lost them all after the words 'Hazard Cards' and 'Incident Reporting' came out of her mouth. It wasn't that they didn't know that they should be reporting possible areas of risk on the job or where the paperwork for that reporting was to be found. It was just that they seemed to only want to do it 'when there was time'.

Wendy had to face it. On a job like this, there was never any of this 'time'. Engineers didn't just go back to work after a lunch hour and think, 'Hey, I've got a spare few hours, I might analyse the safety of our methods.' It was something they had to *make* time for. By the end of the meeting she knew she was banging her head against a brick wall. She hadn't really persuaded them to change their habits at all. Perhaps she'd taken the wrong approach getting them all together like this, so that they could gang up on her. She resolved to raise the issue with them again individually in the coming weeks. Maybe she would have more progress that way.

'Just one more thing before everyone goes.'

Everyone with the exception of Lena sighed. She stubbornly ignored it. 'It has come to my attention that we do not have a CMT.' Their faces were blank. 'Cyclone Management Team,' she clarified. 'In the event of a cyclone, it's these people who will give this site direction. Carl has suggested that the following personnel form this group in addition to himself. They are Gavin, Lance, Bill, Lena and myself.'

'Who's Bill?' Fish demanded.

Wendy sighed. 'It's Chub.'

'Oh.' Everyone around the table murmured, understanding.

'*Anyway*,' Wendy pulled them back on point, 'just giving you a heads up because I'll be calling a meeting of these people next month.'

No one deigned to reply to this remark, which she figured showed perfectly their levels of enthusiasm. She let out a breath. 'All right, that's all. You can go.'

It was like the school bell just went. Their faces lit up as they pushed out their chairs and shoved on their hard hats, practically jumping over each other to get out the door.

One of the engineers, however, wasn't so lucky making her quick escape.

Wendy waylaid Lena at the door, hoping to make a start on studying and coaching individuals immediately. Also, perhaps a fellow female might be able to give her some support. But Lena looked wary when she heard her request.

'Do you mind if I tag along with you out to the wharf? I feel like I need to see a team in action before I can make any more judgements.'

'Er, sure . . . when?' She couldn't miss the uncomfortable hesitation in Lena's voice.

'Right now.'

Again Lena seemed reluctant, looking away as though searching for an excuse. Wendy sighed inwardly. So the one person she thought might give her a chance was also going to let her down. It was going to be an uphill battle all the way. She opened her mouth to say, 'Don't worry about it,' when Lena suddenly straightened her shoulders.

'Of course.'

'Really?'

'Definitely.' The honey blonde gave her a lovely smile. 'Come with me.'

They grabbed their hard hats and boarded Sharon's bus together. Sharon was happy to see them. 'You ladies look like you're up to no good.'

'Don't look at me,' Lena joked back. 'Wendy's the one springing the surprise inspection.'

Sharon raised her eyebrows and Wendy wrinkled her nose. 'Oh, it's not like that – just a friendly visit.'

'Speaking of friendly visits,' Sharon grinned at her in the rear-vision mirror. 'Why haven't we been seeing you at dinner?'

Wendy blushed. 'Oh, I . . .' she began and then was unable to finish. The can of worms labelled *I'm looking for my father* was one she didn't want to open in public.

'The boys say you've been taking off into Wickham every evening in that cute blue Nissan of yours,' said Lena.

'Have you got a fella who lives there?' Sharon enquired.

'If she did, I'm sure Radar would know about it,' Lena scoffed. 'He swears she's single.'

Sharon rolled her eyes. 'Yeah, because Radar is the most reliable source on the wharf. He also thought that poor guy in

Fish's team had plastic surgery and Biro was cheating on his wife when his daughter picked him up from the airport.'

'I am sitting right here, you know.' Wendy laughed. 'I can answer for myself.'

'Oooh, please do.' Lena rubbed her hands together. 'I'd love to have one up on Radar.'

'I'm afraid there's no fella to speak of. I'm single and staying that way.' For some reason, the image of a cheeky smile and a confident swagger intruded upon her vision. She gritted her teeth and pushed it away.

'Damn.' Lena pouted. 'I was hoping for a juicy story.'

'Speaking of juicy stories.' Sharon threw Lena a look over her shoulder. 'Who the hell is Annabel George?'

Lena looked cross. 'A bloody pain in the arse, that's what.'

Wendy glanced at her in surprise and also saw Sharon's eyebrows rise in the rear-vision mirror again.

'So the rumours are true,' the bus driver murmured. 'I honestly didn't credit it when I heard a woman in four-inch red heels turned up on Saturday with a couple of lunchboxes full of muffins and biscuits for Bulldog.'

'She made them herself,' Lena revealed sourly.

'Were they any good?' Wendy enquired.

'Absolutely bloody delicious.'

Sharon snorted. 'Why is she baking for him?'

'Dan says she's just being nice. But I know what it means.' Lena rolled her eyes. 'She wants him back.'

'Back?' Sharon started. 'Bulldog has an ex?'

Lena threw her hands in the air. 'I thought I knew everything there was to know about Dan. But I completely forgot about his love-life. I mean, obviously he must have had one before me but I didn't expect it to come boobs blazing back into his life out here. I mean this is Cape Lambert, for goodness' sake.'

'What does Dan say?' Sharon asked.

'That I have nothing to worry about and not much else. You know how forthcoming he is about his feelings.'

Wendy could definitely picture Dan as the strong, silent type. 'Well, maybe you should just wait a bit. Maybe this woman will get sick of baking him treats and leave him alone.'

'Amen to that,' Lena nodded.

On this positive note, the bus came to a halt in front of the wharf boom gates so there was no opportunity for them to question her further. An inspector came on board to make sure everyone was wearing their PPE – the main items being hard hats, vests and boots. She and Lena passed the test and so did the two guys slumped in the back row. The inspector got off and the boom gates were raised.

The hum of the wharf conveyor penetrated Wendy's ears, and then she saw it. Lumps of iron ore rolled beside the bus on a belt stained red with years of service. She could see two ships docked at the end waiting for this precious cargo. It was amazing that Australia made so much money from selling dirt.

The bus picked up speed again, though not much. The red-dusted road was narrow and had no guard rail. One false swerve and they'd be over the edge and into the ocean or – worse – in the conveyor. Wendy remembered that on her first bus ride out on Wednesday morning she'd clutched her seat in trepidation. Now at least she was able to sit there with some semblance of calm.

After five minutes of silence, Sharon braked near the centre of the jetty beside what was called the skid frames. The frames were two table-like steel structures that straddled the conveyor and basically provided a platform for the men to work on while ore could still move beneath.

'I believe this is your stop,' Sharon announced cheerfully.

'Thanks.' Lena stood up. 'I'll see you on your way back.'

The bus driver nodded as Lena and Wendy jumped down the steps and onto the road. Wendy shaded her eyes and looked up. She could see all the members of Lena's team scurrying around on the top of the skids, taking orders from the skid supervisor, who turned out to be her Uncle Mike.

Her eyes widened when she saw him. 'My uncle is your site supervisor?'

'Yeah.' Lena mirrored her surprise. 'Didn't he tell you?'

The truth was they hadn't spoken since that day in Karratha at her hotel. She hadn't seen him at dinner either, even once. But she didn't want to delve into her family issues again so she merely said, 'No,' and then looked at the other team members. 'You'll have to introduce me to everyone.'

'Sure.' They climbed the vertical ladder on the side of one of the skid frames. Their arrival drew immediate interest.

'Well, well, well.' A brown-haired, brown-eyed and brown-skinned man sauntered up to them. A flash of white teeth broke up the monotony of his features. 'Aren't we flushed with female company this morning?'

'This is Radar.' Lena rolled her eyes. 'He's been dying to meet you.'

'Really?' Wendy responded cautiously.

'So how you finding it all?' He grinned good-naturedly at her and spread his arms wide as though he were in fact the owner of the wharf and was presenting it to her for the very first time.

'Really good actually,' Wendy returned and decided that maybe that sounded too much like the fib it was and so retracted a little. 'Of course, Ethel did give me that donga that's supposed to be out of service. The lack of air condition-ing is killing me but otherwise all fine.'

Radar gave a low whistle. 'What did you do to piss her off?'

Wendy flicked him a secret smile. 'When I find out, I'll let you know.'

'Oooh,' he tipped his hat at her, 'the crab is in the pot now, isn't it? Got any other interesting titbits you want to tell me?' He folded his arms and tapped a thoughtful finger to his chin. 'I was shocked to hear that you and Mike are family. If you've got any dirt on him I'd love to hear it.'

Wendy glanced over at her uncle, who seemed to have noticed her presence for the first time. She tried to smile at him.

But he threw her a 'How dare you invade my territory' glare before striding over to the far side of the platform, as though trying to put as much distance between them as possible.

'Whoa, no love lost there,' Radar observed keenly. 'Anything going on?'

'Tell him nothing,' Lena warned as Wendy tore her gaze from Mike's back. 'He's just trying to build your case file.'

'My case file?'

Lena grinned. 'Radar's got a reputation to maintain as the pulse of Cape Lambert. Anything he can pick up on his radar, so to speak, is going to get circulated. That story about you and Ethel will be all over site in a couple of days.'

Wendy raised her eyebrows. 'Thank you for telling me.'

'Come on, Madame E,' Radar rolled his shoulders forward petulantly, 'don't spook her. She was just about to tell me *everything*.'

'Really?' Wendy chuckled. 'That good, are you?'

'You know it.' He flicked his chin at her before answering a call from one of the other men. 'Yeah, yeah. I'll be right over.'

'Any problems today, Radar?' Lena asked him.

'Mike's swallowed a spider. But apart from that, we're looking good.' He strolled off, trailing his harness behind him.

'Is he always like that?' Wendy asked.

'Oh yes. Always. Radar is definitely a character but he's a good rigger.'

'Madame E?' Wendy repeated the phrase that had intrigued her. 'What's that?'

'My nickname,' Lena grimaced. 'The long version is Madame Engineer. If you're lucky enough you'll get a nickname too.'

'I'm not sure I like the definition of lucky around here,' Wendy observed dryly and Lena laughed before throwing her a sideways glance.

'So what do you think of my skids?'

Wendy stepped back and looked around with interest. Bolted to the checker-plate deck of each skid was a five-tonne crane. At the moment, the cranes were working together to hold a pre-fabricated truss over the side of the wharf so that the men could weld it in place. The truss was one of the many building blocks being used to widen the wharf. She couldn't see any immediate hazards in what they were doing. But she'd need to look over the method statement for this installation before jumping to any quick conclusions.

'It looks like you've got a pretty tight operation going on here,' she said instead.

'Tight and fast,' Lena nodded enthusiastically. 'The client wants everything done yesterday.'

Working fast and working wise were two attitudes that often didn't run parallel. Wendy stayed for a little while longer, confirming her suspicions that they were sometimes a little lax with safety protocols in order to keep things moving. They were only minor things though, so she decided not to say anything to Lena yet and maybe check out the other teams at the end of the wharf. Perhaps then she could issue a statement across the board so that Lena wouldn't feel like she was being picked on.

She walked up to the engineer to take her leave. 'I think I'm going to head up to the end of the wharf to check on Gavin, Fish and Craig.'

'Yeah, sure, no worries,' Lena replied easily enough and then asked unexpectedly, 'Hey, has Gavin been hassling you?'

Wendy immediately felt her hairline stiffen. 'W-why do you ask? Have you heard rumours?'

'No,' Lena denied. 'It just seemed pretty tense between the two of you this morning, that's all. I wondered if it was my imagination.'

'Oh.' Wendy licked her lips, searching for a half truth she could give by way of explanation. 'Well, I was annoyed that he and the others were late. I thought it was pretty rude of them.'

'Yes, it was.' Lena nodded her agreement and allowed the subject to drop.

The walk up the remainder of the wharf was a pleasant one. The sound of waves and gulls provided relaxing mood music for a stroll in the sunshine. She smelled sea salt and wet earth – an interesting combination. The ocean views were gorgeous. White-tipped waves saluted her. She had a feeling it was the only mark of respect she was going to get around here for a long time.

As she got closer to the pile hammer, which unfortunately she could not see yet, it started driving another pile. She knew this because the deep, melodic and extremely loud thump of its operation exploded into her ear canals.

BANG! BANG! BANG!

Like the rhythmic counting of an oversized tribal drum, it pounded her skull. Reaching into her pocket she quickly removed a couple of foam ear plugs and pushed them into her ears. They didn't completely squeeze out the noise but certainly took the edge off.

Then the barge or SEP, Self Elevating Platform, came into view. It was a giant freestanding structure, separate from the wharf, and standing above the waves on three cylindrical legs. Wendy knew these legs could be jacked up at any time to turn the platform back into a barge. Then it could float away to set up and drive a pile somewhere else.

Wow!

Although she had seen the structure a couple of days earlier, she hadn't seen it in action yet. The giant claw on board the barge was holding a pile in place, while the hammer, a humongous sleeve that fitted over the pile, dropped a weight on its head every five seconds.

She strode to the railing where Fish, Craig and Gavin were all leaning over the side looking at something below. She also glanced down to see what they were gazing at and had to smile.

They were looking at fish.

There had to be twenty or more, floating on the surface of the waves. Not dead but stunned by the vibration in the water, bobbing there helplessly around the pile that was being driven.

Big fish too.

Big fish that Fish would be dying to have on the end of his hook. *It must be driving him crazy*, she thought. The hammer ceased and Wendy removed her plugs just in time to have her suspicions confirmed.

'What I wouldn't do to be in a little fishing boat down there, scooping the barramundi off the surface of the waves.' Fish smacked his lips together. 'As easy as taking candy from a baby.'

'Well, you know they hire those boats out in Wickham,' Gavin began. 'I've seen –'

'Don't even think about it.'

All the men spun around at the sound of her voice.

'Oh shit,' Fish started and began wringing his hands, 'it's the cops.'

'Not quite.' She couldn't help but grin a little at his comically gawking face and the red guilt staining the cheeks of the other two men. 'But I will say this. As long as I'm around no one is fishing on the job.'

'Really?' Fish cocked his head to one side in deep disappointment. 'It's not dangerous if a man knows what he's doing.'

'And I suppose,' her lips twitched, 'that man would be you.'

'Well,' Fish replied enthusiastically, 'I was going to get Gav to drive the boat because he's better at that. But I'll have the net and nobody can drag in a catch better than me.'

She looked at them all sternly. 'Nobody is getting any nets or boats and that's final.'

Gavin, in typical cavalier style, was the first to recover. 'Guess you better haul me away to the station then, Sergeant.' He presented his wrists as though expecting to be cuffed. She shook her head at his suspiciously meek expression.

'Sergeant,' Craig repeated the name Gavin had given her. 'I like that.'

Fish groaned. 'You don't just hand yourself in,' he scoffed. 'Where's your bloody spine?'

Craig chortled and cast Wendy a knowing glance. 'He ain't handing himself in, Fish. He's chasing tail.' He glanced at Wendy. 'You be careful, honey.'

Wendy squared her shoulders. 'I can take care of myself.'

'Yes you can,' Gavin murmured and dropped his wrists.

She tried to give Gavin her best 'I don't play games' look but under the lazy predatory twinkle in his eyes, her gaze faltered. And it wasn't long before she desperately turned her face to the ocean to get away from the feeling that he had her completely surrounded.

By this time, however, Fish was thoroughly over the turn the conversation had taken.

'I can't believe we're back to this again,' he reproved Gavin. 'When are you and Carl going to learn? Women are like trees – eventually they all leave. And then you end up cleaning your own house.'

He didn't stay for Wendy's gasp of outrage and Gavin chuckled softly. 'I'd say that poor fella's cruisin' for a bruisin', fishing boat *or not*.'

That evening, as though to lend proof to Radar's reputation, she arrived back at her donga to find that someone had replaced her flyscreen. No note had been left: it was simply done. Good as new. It lifted her spirits. Not only would she be able to sleep with her window open now – a great relief given she had no air conditioning – but it also indicated that maybe not *everybody* on this site had it in for her.

In the days that followed, Wendy doubled her efforts to make the Barnes Inc operation a safer and more procedure-oriented workplace. As a result she also raised her profile as the most annoying and avoided person on site.

She was not sure how or when but somehow it had got around that Fish had labelled her the cops and that Gavin had christened her Sergeant. It was now her nickname, bellowed from scaffolding and utes alike whenever she was passing through.

'I don't know,' Chub commented on Saturday afternoon. 'I kind of like it. Sort of comments on the authority you have, wouldn't you say?'

'Or mocks it,' Wendy returned dryly.

After that the pranks started. Thankfully they weren't nasty or dangerous, just excessively annoying.

One day, she was out inspecting the end of the wharf and left her camera in the small office donga. When she took it back to the main office, she found all her previous photos deleted and a set of new ones in their place showing a bunch of faceless men pretending to do some ridiculously unsafe things with a flame cutter – like using it as a cigarette lighter.

On Sunday, someone nicked a packet of her *Hazard* and *Out of service* tags. These were basically colour-coded plastic rectangles that were tied onto equipment that was faulty or too dangerous to use. When she left the office at the end of the day, she found that someone had tagged her blue Nissan all over. From the wheels to the side mirrors, to the door handles and the windscreen wipers. Her car looked like it was about to perform in a Pride parade. She had been experiencing trouble starting her car from time to time, mainly because it needed a battery change. But this was ridiculous. And how would they know anyway, unless they'd been spying on her?

It took her half an hour to get all the tags off.

But Monday morning really took the cake.

She should have seen it coming. The day before she had stepped in some particularly muddy ground on site but couldn't be bothered cleaning her boots after work. Thinking that by morning the mud would have dried and she could just bang them together and the dirt would slide off, she left her boots outside.

But when she stepped out of her donga Monday morning, in sock-covered feet, her boots were gone.

As she stared in confusion at the place she'd left them, realisation dawned. She closed her eyes and let her head flop back. *You stupid fool.*

Obviously they'd been taken. It was another prank. She spun around, hands on hips, going through her options – though there was really only one. She'd have to put on her sandals and go to Karratha to buy new boots. Better that than the humiliation of asking around if anyone had seen her old ones.

She'd never find them anyway. They could be anywhere, probably set in concrete by now if she knew the mentality of the boys. Just as she finished the thought, she happened to look up and see her boots, mud still intact, on the roof of the donga opposite hers.

Okay, so maybe I was wrong about not being able to find them.

The problem, of course, was how would she get them down?

She stepped off the front step of her own donga and walked across the dividing gravel path. Jumping up and down didn't put her any closer to reaching distance.

I wonder if . . .

She raced back into her donga and brought out the plastic desk chair they were all furnished with. Putting this up against the wall of the demountable, she stood on the seat and tried to swat her boots down with a rolled up towel.

No, she still couldn't reach them.

'Hey, Sarge.' An all-too-familiar drawl permeated her senses. 'That's a weird place to put your boots.'

She snatched her hand back and spun around, realising that she must look absolutely ridiculous standing on a chair in her socks. He, on the other hand, appeared as handsome and cocky as always, a backpack flung over his shoulder, a rascal of a grin curving his mouth. 'Need some help getting them down?'

Clearly, he'd been on his way to the car park until luck put him in the wrong place at the right time.

'No, I'm fine, thanks,' she returned tightly, looking away.

'You don't seem fine to me.'

'Just a little hiccup.' She jumped off the chair. 'I'll figure it out.'

He put down his backpack. 'I reckon I could give you a boost and you'd reach them.'

She blushed. 'No, that's all right.'

'Geez, Wendy,' he said crossly. 'What are you going to do if I walk on? Pull out the desk and put the chair on top. I have to say, I think that's *grossly unsafe*.'

She stuck her tongue out at him. 'I can't use my desk, it's broken. I got the dud donga, so rest easy.'

'Oh yeah, that's right,' he grinned, 'so I heard. So what's plan B?'

They stared at each other for a few seconds until she could stand it no longer. '*All right*. I'll let you give me a boost. But no funny business.'

His triumphant expression was positively shameless. 'If that's a warning not to kiss you again, I promise I'll control myself.'

Embarrassment whipped through her like a hot flush. 'Let's just hurry up and get this over with.' She averted her eyes, not even wanting to acknowledge their first meeting. Better not go there at all!

He came over and stood between the wall of the donga and her, offering his hands laced together as a stepping platform. She gave him one last warning look, before putting her foot between his palms. Feeling decidedly self-conscious, she put her hands on his shoulders to steady herself as he slowly lifted his palms. As she got higher she put her hands on the donga to keep her balance. By this stage she could feel his cheek under her knees as she leaned against him to keep from falling.

This is so not how I wanted to be doing this.

And then her boots were within reach. She took a swipe at them and they fell off the roof and bounced on the gravel a few feet away.

'I got them,' she called. 'You can put me down now.'

Instead of lowering her, however, she felt his hands jerk upwards before releasing her foot. She half gasped, half screamed as she fell, arms flailing, only to feel her body caught seconds later, bride-over-the-threshold style.

I might have bloody known it.

Her face burned as he beamed at her with all the boyish satisfaction of one who had got his way. His face was the very picture of mischief.

'Put me down,' she said through her teeth.

His eyes danced and his arms tightened. 'Do you want me to carry you over to your boots, so you don't have to walk on the gravel?'

'No.'

'Because it's no trouble.'

'No.'

'Or I could put you in the chair, bring your boots to you.'

'Gavin, put me down!'

'Oh, all right.' His voice had a distinct 'spoil sport' attitude in it before he set her on her feet with a lot of unnecessary assistance.

'Thank you,' she said huffily, swatting his hands away as he attempted to dust off her jeans.

'Will you stop that?!'

'Sorry.' He grinned. 'Guess you'll be fine then.'

'Yes, I'll be fine.'

'Okay. My work here is done.' He nodded, picked up his backpack and walked off.

She watched him, unable to stop a silly smile from playing on her lips as she shook her head.

Chapter 7

On Monday while she was at work, someone – presumably Ethel – had replaced Wendy's air conditioner. When she arrived back at her donga that night, she found that the old one had been pulled out of the back hole in the wall and a brand spanking new one pushed into place. She plugged it in and turned it on.

It worked like a dream.

Relieved that Ethel had finally decided to make nice, she resolved to go some time soon, thank her and offer the hand of friendship. After all, there were so few women in this camp: shouldn't they all stick together?

As Tuesday drew to a close, she decided that she was making good progress. Lobbying individuals was definitely working better. As a result, she thought Carl might let her get away early. After speaking to Ethel, she could go into Wickham and make a few more enquiries about her father while it was still daylight. Perhaps there were a few rocks she hadn't turned over yet.

Who are you kidding?

She had to face facts.

Wickham was another dead end.

She'd already been to the health centre twice. No one by the name of Hector had been treated there for the loss of two toes on his right foot. The steel mill on the outskirts of town was apparently only ten years old and none of the locals seemed to know of any older mills that had perhaps closed down years earlier. So she decided to widen her search.

Roebourne Golf Club had no memberships under the name Hector. Not that she knew if he was into golf. She just went anywhere that might have a list of names and details to look at. God help her, she'd even driven to Roebourne Prison one scary night to check out their inmate list. No Hectors there. At least she'd been thankful about that one.

The only place she hadn't looked yet was at work. And as unlikely as it was that her father could be working on the same project as she was, she was reluctant to start asking people if they'd heard of or seen a dark-haired welder called Hector.

What a great way to make a public spectacle of herself.

If she wasn't one already.

She knew how much the men loved to make fun of her. The 'TCN spy' theory was still alive and well. If there was one thing this project loved, it was a good story. Woman searching for a father who deserted her before birth seemed like just the sort of gossip the guys would latch onto and never let go of. If she ever did find her father, it'd be like having a reunion show on *Oprah*!

Her chin sank heavily into her palm. No, she definitely did not want to start more scandals about herself.

Wouldn't it be great if she could just quietly get her hands on the Barnes employee manifest? A quick glance at that would give her the truth without any need of a fuss. Barnes Inc and their subcontractors had to amount to the majority of personnel on this site. TCN would make up the rest, plus the usual guys who worked for the port.

She glanced at Chub. He was possibly the kindest person she'd met since she'd started working at Barnes Inc. If she asked nicely, he'd probably let her have an unauthorised look. Still, there was no incentive for him to do so. He may even get into trouble for it. Even nice people had their limits, or as her mother had warned, *their price*. She drummed her fingers on the desktop.

Should she ask him and risk him wanting something in return? She hated being obligated to anyone.

'It's my biceps, isn't it?' Chub said without looking at her. 'That's why you're staring at me.'

'Er . . .'

He held up an arm so that she could have a better view. 'They're pretty big, aren't they? If only they didn't *hang* like that . . .'

Her mouth slowly turned up. 'Cobber,' she began slowly.

'Yes.' He tucked his two chins in his chest as he looked over the rims of his small round spectacles at her.

She wheeled her chair closer to his desk, clasping her hands in her lap so tightly the knuckles turned white. 'I was wondering if you might help me with something. You see I've been trying to locate someone in town. And it would make my search process so much shorter if you'd allow me to look at the Barnes Inc employee manifest.'

She grabbed her lower lip between her teeth and held it.

Chub was silent for a moment, as he continued to study her over his glasses, then without blinking he said, 'What's their name? Maybe I could look for you.'

Her breath eased out. 'His name is Hector. Not sure of his last name but I know he is or was a welder.'

Chub turned back to his computer and started moving his mouse and pressing keys. She clenched her teeth in excitement, unable to relax.

He only kept her waiting a few minutes and she couldn't help but wish she had asked this before.

'I've found one Hector on the list. Hector Warner is his full name. He's not a welder though, he's a site supervisor on Gavin's team.'

The beat of her heart roared in her ears. It was entirely possible that her father, having been a welder when he was

77

with her mother, had now risen through the ranks to become site supervisor. Was it all finally coming together today? Had she found her father after all this time, and so easily too?

She put a hand to her chest. 'What colour is his hair?'

Chub looked up at her in some amusement. 'I don't know. Are you okay? You look like I do after I discover I've eaten my lunch for morning tea.'

Her colour returned and she managed a wry smile. 'Yep, it's just been a long time coming.'

'Been looking for this guy a while now, have you?'

'Sort of.' She didn't meet his eyes.

'It's an ex-boyfriend, isn't it?' he enquired. 'The bastard owes you money, doesn't he?'

'No, no.' She laughed evasively. 'Nothing like that. I can't wait to meet him though. Would he be on the wharf if I took the bus out?'

'He would be,' Chub began tentatively, as though he were about to deliver some bad news, 'if he hadn't resigned a few weeks ago.'

'*What?!*'

'I know,' he shrugged. 'Awful luck but that's what it says on the list.'

'May I look?'

'Sure.' He slid back.

She moved her chair closer so she could view his screen. Chub was right, the list provided no more information than he'd already told her. Name, occupation, site team, start date, end date.

'How do I find out how old he is and where he's from?' she asked. 'Do we have a copy of his resume or licence to practise?'

Maybe it had his birth date and/or contact details on it. After all, if he was in his thirties or something she could end the search there. But if his age seemed reasonable, at least she'd have a possible address or phone number.

'Yes, actually we do. But it's not in this file.' He closed it and as he did so his computer froze. 'Oh shoot, looks like the server's down again.'

If it were socially acceptable to scream in frustration she would have done so. Instead she was forced to sit there, on the edge of her seat, in silence, as Chub tried a number of manoeuvres to unfreeze his computer, all without success.

'I'm sorry, little mate, I'm going to have to get back to you later.'

Unfortunately, the server did not come back on before knock-off. It was the most frustrating hour of Wendy's life. On the return drive to camp, she hit upon the idea to ask Ethel about it when she went to see her about the air conditioner. If Hector had lived in the camp he may have left a forwarding address with the camp administrator. Hadn't she herself filled out her Perth address on those forms Ethel had given her to complete?

As luck would have it, when she reached the camp reception Ethel was away from her desk – a *Back in fifteen minutes* sign was taped to the counter. She stood outside reception, leaning on the wall by the door. She would see Ethel literally the second she returned.

It was a typical Pilbara evening for early October: warm and balmy. The camp smelled faintly of red earth and old leather. Insects clicked, keeping time as she waited. Just then she spied a blue-tongued lizard sitting right in the middle of the main road across from reception. The beast was fully grown, at least half a metre in length, and it looked like a mini dragon, its scaly pewter coat decorated with glossy black stripes.

Majestic little fellow, she thought, hoping he would move soon. It was knock-off time and ute traffic was pretty busy. She looked down to find a stick. Maybe she could poke him on his way.

Just then she heard the roar of an engine – probably someone eager to get back to camp after a hard day's work. She stepped away from the reception building, fear for the blue-tongue propelling her forwards.

Sure enough, a Barnes Inc ute was tearing up the road. She put a hand over her mouth but just at the last second the vehicle screeched to a halt about a metre in front of the lizard.

She watched in amazement as the ute door opened and Gavin jumped out. The sight of his windswept hair made her falter and step back a little. Goosebumps broke out on her flesh even though it wasn't the least bit cold.

He hadn't noticed her though; his eyes were trained on the blue-tongue. With swift, purposeful movements, he walked over to the languid lizard and expertly picked it up.

Her eyes widened as she watched him speaking to it. She couldn't hear what was being said because she was too far away, but from the lopsided grin on his face she guessed it was a friendly telling off. He walked over to the side of the road and placed the lizard under an acacia tree. It turned its back on him and trotted off over the red pebbled earth. With a smile and shake of his head, Gavin returned to his vehicle and drove into the camp car park.

'What the hell are you looking at so bloody intently?' an abrasive voice asked.

Wendy jumped almost guiltily as Ethel joined her at the door of reception. 'Oh, er . . .' She rubbed her temple. 'Nothing.'

'Whatever you say,' Ethel replied, utterly uninterested. 'Are you just darkening my door to be a pain in the arse or do you actually want something?'

Wendy cleared her throat. *Am I missing something here? Or are you still a bitch?*

She tried her luck anyway. 'I just came to thank you for the new air conditioner.'

Ethel's bushy eyebrows met over her nose. 'What air conditioner?'

Uh-oh. Wasn't her.

Anxious to change the subject in case Ethel decided to take the new air conditioner off her, she shrugged. 'You know what, doesn't matter. I actually have something else to ask you – something more important.'

Not that she believed for a second Ethel would help her find Hector given her lack of knowledge about the air conditioner. But what did she have to lose in asking? She followed Ethel into the reception building. 'I'm looking for someone who I think might have lived in this camp. I was wondering if he left a forwarding address.'

To her surprise, after a moment, Ethel grunted, went behind her desk and sat down. 'I'll look it up for you this once. But I'm not running a free friend-finding service here. Next time, just get his mobile number and track him down in your own time.'

'Absolutely,' Wendy readily agreed.

Ethel adjusted her computer screen and then put her hands to the keyboard. 'What's the name?'

'Hector. Hector Warner.'

Her bony hands flew across the keys and then pressed enter with a flick.

'Hmmm.' Ethel leaned in, putting her chin on her palm. It took all Wendy's willpower not to reach across the desk and swivel the screen around to face her.

'Nope.'

'Nope what?' Wendy faltered.

'He never lived in the camp.' Ethel clicked the menu off and sat back in her chair. 'So how are you liking your donga?'

'Huh?' Wendy was still busy trying to process the first part of Ethel's response about Hector.

'Your donga,' Ethel snapped impatiently. 'The one I specially picked out for you, girlie.'

It was then that Wendy realised why Ethel had helped her with Hector. It was because she wanted her to stay longer so she could gloat about the donga.

Nobody does anything for nothing, remember?

Her mouth stretched into a wide grin as she realised her silence on the subject must have been killing Ethel.

Clasping her hands together in front of her chest, Wendy said, 'It's perfect! Thank you! Wouldn't change a thing.'

At Ethel's chagrined expression, she left the building, dusting her hands with satisfaction as she shut the door. It was her first gratifying win since she'd got there.

The only thing was, if Ethel hadn't given her a new air conditioner then who had? Was it the same person who had fixed her flyscreen? A Good Samaritan?

Or a secret admirer.

Was it something she needed to worry about? She didn't know. So far this person's actions hadn't been creepy so much as nice.

Nobody does anything for nothing.

She frowned. She had no choice and no leads. She'd just have to wait and see.

Her mind returned instead to the news about Hector. Technically, there were no hard and fast rules that if you worked on the job you had to live in the camp. Maybe he lived in Wickham or Point Samson or even a bit further out. The point was, even though he'd quit Barnes Inc, he might still be living very close by.

Her excitement kicked back up.

So close.

After a quick, cleansing shower she went straight to the mess for dinner. It was the first time in a week since she had done so, so unwittingly she created a bit of a buzz when she walked in. If she hadn't wanted to be alone with her thoughts, her spirits would have lifted slightly. It was the first sign of friendliness the guys had shown her in days. Ever since she'd started handing out memos and carrying out inspections, they'd been doing their absolute best to avoid her.

On the one hand, it was great not to have to deal with the flirtatious teasing. On the other, it was just as unpleasant to be treated like someone with an infectious disease. It wasn't as though she was deliberately picking on people. Any criticism she made, she gave serious thought to and only delivered if absolutely necessary. Tonight, however, she was off duty and the men in the mess seemed to sense that. They waved to her, shouted greetings across the room and offered the news that apart from lasagne there was a lamb roast which she might like if she thought Charlie's efforts were 'safe' enough to taste.

Charlie was the new chef who had started last week. He was very young and very shy. She had a feeling the guys enjoyed embarrassing him as much as they did her. She smiled reassuringly at him as he stood behind the steaming counter and requested a little of his lamb roast. Relief swept through her as she spied Lena and Sharon sitting nearby. She made a beeline for them.

'Hi, guys!'

Surprisingly, they were equally pleased to see her. She knew Lena had been struggling a little with Wendy's role as safety manager. All the engineers were. But to give the girl some credit she hadn't uttered a single rude word to her, which couldn't be said about Fish or Craig or any of the other engineers.

Except Gavin.

Gavin had said nothing at all. Stone cold silent on the subject.

Do you honestly want him to say something? Isn't it better that he stays away from you?

She blushed as her mind automatically revisited each encounter they'd had. He was flirtatious, shameless and persistent. But she still had no intention of taking him up on the offer he was obviously making.

Lena interrupted her thoughts.

'We were just talking about you.' Her smile was bright. 'What are you doing on the weekend?'

'Oh, we have this Sunday off, don't we?' The realisation was like picking up fifty bucks on the side of the road. 'I completely forgot!'

'How on earth did you do that?' Sharon laughed. 'I've been counting the days.'

They only got one Sunday off a fortnight. They had to wait five weeks before they earned R and R, which was a week off.

Most of the boys flew home for it, but some stayed to bum around in town. It was definitely a long time to wait for a break but Wendy had been so preoccupied with her search for her father and getting a head start on her new job that every day had seemed to blend into the other.

Radar and a man called Leg were also seated at the same table. They immediately put their cutlery down. 'What's it to be this time, Madame E? Another fishing trip?'

Lena stuck out her tongue. 'Who said I was inviting you? This is going to be a Girls' Day Out.' She turned to Wendy. 'What do you reckon? A day on the beach, bit of a swim and a sunbake with your gal pals? We can have lunch in Point Samson or something.'

'It sounds wonderful. But . . .' *I might be tracking down Hector Warner that day.*

'But what?' Lena seemed disappointed. 'You can't mean to stay in the camp. You'll be bored batty. Tell her, Sharon.'

'Lena has a point.' Sharon nodded. 'You'll be stuck with these guys and all they're going to do is drink and read dirty magazines.'

Leg sniffed haughtily. 'You don't know that.'

Radar snorted.

Wendy shifted uncomfortably in her seat. She didn't want them to think she was a snob. She had too many other labels already, like: nit-picker, spy, tattle-tale, Bossy Boots Barbie.

She could do without adding Snooty Snob to the list as well.

It wasn't that they didn't seem like nice enough people. Under any other circumstances she'd be all for socialising. But at this point she thought keeping to herself was a more preferable option, especially with her search for her father still on the go.

'Come on, Wendy.' Lena grabbed her hand. 'It'll be fun.'

Wendy was touched by the other woman's affection. 'Okay,' she smiled. 'I suppose there's no harm in kicking back a bit.'

Lena whooped. 'That's the spirit. And now on to my next question.' She reddened slightly. 'Can you drive? We kinda don't have a car.'

Sharon swatted her. 'You are shocking, girl!'

'Oh well, you know . . .' Lena rushed out quickly, 'we could ask Carl for a ute if we need to.'

Wendy laughed. 'No that's fine. I'll drive if my battery holds. It needs changing.' She paused, pushing her fork through her coleslaw with studied casualness. 'Hey, have you guys ever met a man called Hector Warner on this job?'

They all shook their heads and then Leg added, 'It's hard to say though, Sergeant. Almost all the guys around here have nicknames, so your Hector might not be called Hector, if you know what I mean. Look at Radar here. I can't even remember what his real name is.'

'It's –' Radar began but Leg held up his hand.

'No, no, don't tell me, it spoils the romance.'

Radar chuckled and then turned back to Wendy. 'Why do you ask? Who's he to you?'

'Just someone I used to know back in Perth.' She put a forkful of dinner into her mouth so that she literally could not talk any more.

'Oh.'

She could tell by the glaze in Radar's eyes that he'd lost interest. He proved it by turning back to the group at large. 'Well, you ladies are going to be kicking yourselves that you didn't stick with us. As it happens we've got some super fantastic plans for this Sunday too.'

'Yeah right.' Lena pulled a face at him.

He looked down his nose at her and said mysteriously, 'You just wait and see.'

The next morning, Wendy could have been at work an hour early. She certainly got up in time to make that. The knowledge that Hector Warner's resume and possible location was sitting on Chub's computer just waiting for her had her feeling like a kid at Christmas. She could not sit still or, in this case, lie still in bed. In the end, she went for a jog up Water Tank Hill before work. This time nobody followed her, though she could have done with some distraction.

She managed to restrain herself from getting into her car before five-thirty am and arrived at work a mere ten minutes ahead of schedule. Chub was not there so she whiled away the time checking to see if the server was back up.

It was.

Her body tensed with excitement.

Not long now.

'Hey, little mate.' Chub arrived, throwing a large backpack down on his desk and then removing from it four lunchboxes that he intended to put in the bar fridge.

'The server is working,' she announced as she followed him to their poor excuse for a kitchen. He put his food in the bar fridge and turned around.

'Is it now? Do you think I have time for a coffee first?'

'You can't possibly mean to do that to me.'

'All right, maybe not.' He sighed and hunkered back to his desk to sit down. She peered over his thick shoulders as he tried to call up the screen he'd been looking for yesterday. In less than a minute, he had found Hector's resume and was sending it to the printer.

Her chest swelled as the small bubble-jet creaked noisily to life. 'Now obviously I can't let you keep it because it's a breach of his privacy. But,' Chub winked at her, 'I'll let you look at it for as long as you like.'

'That's perfect.' She nodded breathlessly.

Her hands trembled slightly as he handed her the papers. 'Now I think I'll get that coffee.' He rose with effort. 'I don't know why they don't have donuts in the mess. Such a lack of foresight.'

The comment flew over Wendy's head as her eyes were already on the page, devouring every word – calculating Hector's age from his birth date.

Oh wow! He's sixty-five.

That made him a very plausible candidate indeed.

He was married. His address was in ... *Wickham*! She scanned down the list of his credentials and began to feel rather light-headed.

There it was. He'd started as a welder. He was a site supervisor now but he definitely fit the bill. A shame there was no photo. If Chub hadn't been in the room, she probably would have jumped up and down, laughing and screaming. Instead, she put the resume down on his desk, giving it a swift pat. 'I don't know how I'm going to get through today, but I'm just going to have to.'

'Why, what's on tonight?' Chub asked as he returned to his desk.

'Something big, I hope.' She pulled open her drawer and drew forth a brown paper bag. With great delight she tipped the contents of it onto Chub's desk. A large selection of chocolate bars she had purchased from a machine outside the camp reception spilled forth in all their glossy glory.

'I know it's not much,' she smiled, 'but I wanted to give you a little gift for helping me out.'

Nobody does anything for nothing.

So now her debt was paid.

'Geez, Wendy,' Chub's eyes widened, 'you didn't have to buy me chocolate. You'll ruin my figure.'

'Do you want me to take it back?'

Chub's expression was pained. 'Well, I wouldn't want to be rude.'

She laughed. 'Then don't be.'

She sat down to focus on getting through the day again. This included enduring an absolutely dreadful meeting with TCN. The attendees were herself, Carl, Dan and Frank, the safety manager for TCN.

As usual it was a short trip to the client's office and a long sojourn in the waiting room. To Carl's entertainment, the woman Wendy could only assume was Annabel George arrived shortly after them. She was dressed in a figure-hugging short green dress accessorised by a giant gemstone-studded handbag hanging from one shoulder.

The receptionist seemed to regard her with almost as much disdain as she regarded Barnes Inc staff, because she waved the brunette to a chair without so much as a greeting.

'No problem. I'm happy to wait.' Annabel George sat down next to Wendy, beaming. 'Are you here to see Daniel too?'

'We have a meeting.' Wendy inclined her head.

'Do you know him well?' Annabel put a hand over her heart. 'He's such a sweet man, isn't he? Did you know when he was in high school he used to play guitar? He wrote me a song once. I still have it on cassette tape.'

Carl's eyebrows practically hit his hairline. 'Ffffuuuuck.'

'Yes, well,' Annabel smiled modestly, 'I was thinking about that keepsake the other day and I thought, you know, he should really have one from me too. So . . .' She paused for effect. 'I made him a photo book.'

'A photo book?' Wendy repeated faintly.

'Fried fuck and onions,' said Carl.

'Oh yes, I'd love your opinion.' Annabel withdrew a professionally bound hardcover book from some digital photo studio and reverently opened it.

The first page featured a large picture of Annabel blowing a kiss at the camera dressed in a purple bikini that left little to the imagination. The picture itself was surrounded by sprigs of lavender. Annabel leaned over the book and whispered excitedly, 'Did you know lavender is for Yearning?'

'Get fucked.' Carl baulked.

'I didn't know,' Wendy responded, searching the woman's eyes for dilated pupils.

A shadow crossed their chairs and all three occupants looked up to find Dan standing over them, frowning.

'Sorry I'm late.'

Carl stood up but not in greeting. He simply placed a firm and sympathetic hand briefly on one of the client's broad shoulders before turning away and entering the meeting room behind him.

Dan turned to his admirer first. 'Annie, why are you here again?'

'Sorry, Daniel.' Annabel also rose from her chair. 'I know you said not to come but I just wanted to drop this off. I'll be out of your hair in two blinks of an eye.'

She presented him with the album before patting his other shoulder. 'See you soon, sweetheart.' She blew him a kiss.

As the front door shut behind her, Dan's eyes flicked back to Wendy, who refused to mask her amusement.

Dan Hullog was normally the embodiment of extreme professionalism, mixed with a hawklike intelligence that favoured perfection and the achievement of tough deadlines. He was a man's man whose rough edges hadn't quite been polished smooth. It was clear that he had absolutely no idea how to deal with Annabel George. He couldn't fire her because she didn't work for him. But he wasn't mean enough to tell her to get lost either.

A muscle spasmed below his chiselled cheekbones as a dark cloud descended upon his brow.

'I'm big in trouble, aren't I?' he demanded.

'You bet.'

She would have taken pity on him then. Perhaps offered him some advice. But the moment was lost when his safety manager, Frank, came stumbling out of the main office area burdened with a stack of foolscap files.

'All set, Dan,' he was saying. 'Shall I put these in the meeting room?'

'Yes,' Dan nodded and then swept a hand before himself, indicating for Wendy to proceed.

Wendy found herself once more confronted by the white trestle table and eight uncomfortable chairs, one of which was already occupied by Carl. She had never liked this room, both for its ambience and the conversations that had taken place in it. The room, in turn, didn't redeem itself when, after initial pleasantries and updates, the discussion proceeded to deteriorate.

'I'm sorry to have to inform you,' Dan began, 'that we are still receiving complaints from the wharf owners.' He laced his fingers on the tabletop. 'I know you have terminated Neil Cooper and stepped up preparation for cyclone season but TCN and, indeed, the wharf owners are still concerned about your day-to-day operations.'

Carl and Wendy squirmed in their uncomfortable seats. It wasn't that she didn't know they had a long way to go. It was just getting those improvements implemented at an acceptable rate was really, really hard. The men were getting better but they were still pretty unreceptive. Only one in four orders she issued got listened to. What else could she do?

Perhaps she didn't have all the information she needed.

'What are their complaints?'

It was a mistake to have asked for specifics because it was not Dan who responded to her question but Frank. He happened to be one of those annoying people who given a very small amount of power had allowed it to go to his head. He opened the large file in front of him and began reading from a list with smug superiority.

'They smoke anywhere they like. The toilet dongas are a breeding ground for disease. They litter. They forget to wear their PPE, or the PPE they do have is damaged or inadequate. They drive their utes too fast. There is a speed limit, you know. They break things. Last week someone backed his ute into the conveyor and bent one of the struts! Luckily, no serious damage. They don't wait thirty minutes after hot work before clearing the site. They don't tag damaged equipment, they just chuck it in a container so some other person can re-discover it and not tag it all over again. They don't read safety memos! They are constantly –'

'Okay, you can stop now, Frank.' Dan held up his hand. 'I think they get the message.'

'We're doing our fuckin' best,' Carl protested. 'But you can't expect this sort of shit to improve overnight. Wendy needs a chance to fuckin' find her feet.'

'Then I hope she finds it by next month because the wharf owners have instructed us to do a safety audit of your team then.'

'What?' It was Carl who gasped the word out loud but Wendy felt the blow equally. She was finding it difficult to breathe, as if a sack of potatoes had been dropped on her chest.

Dan sighed, rubbing his temples in an obvious attempt at restraint. 'Carl, it may come as a shock to you but I am as reluctant to shut Barnes Inc down as you are. That is why, even though I'm not supposed to, I am giving you fair warning. TCN *will* be auditing you next month. Clean your men up.'

Static buzzed in Wendy's ears. How on earth was she supposed to fix everything in less than a month? There was just too much to do. She hadn't counted on this job being so stressful, in addition to the other emotional baggage she was carrying around. The plan was to be functional at work so that she could be a basket case in her free time. Bad enough she was already very nervous about tonight. She didn't need this on her shoulders as well.

Thinking about her father and what she would say to him when she met him always put her on edge.

Not that she had any expectations. If he hadn't concerned himself about her in all these years, chances are he probably wouldn't be moved to become part of her life now.

No. All she wanted was a little information. *Do I have any brothers or sisters? Who are they? And where do they live?*

She relived that day on the phone with that awful government clerk over and over in her nightmares.

The hurt.

The betrayal.

The uncertainty.

If she were honest, she didn't want to know why her father had abandoned her. That might be too painful. It was more about needing to know what he had left her with. Knowing that she had this whole other identity out there – that could be sprung on her at any time – was enough to give her a panic attack. And, back when she first found out about her father, often did.

She didn't want any more shocks.

Wendy was a planner. Ever since her parents had shipped her off to boarding school, getting control of her life back had been a goal. As an adult she'd prided herself on her independence and being in charge of her own destiny.

Now she felt that hard-won power was out of her hands, somewhere out of reach. *But* she was so close to getting the answers she wanted and her identity once again something of her own making. Hector Warner was finally within driving distance. So she decided to put the audit out of her mind, at least till the following morning. This evening she might just be able to put her fears to bed once and for all.

But luck still wasn't on her side.

When she turned up that evening at the address she'd received from Hector's resume, the house was locked up, dark and quite obviously vacated. On the front lawn was a huge real-estate sign advertising the property, and a large sticker had been placed over the front of it.

SOLD, it read.

Her palms went sweaty on her steering wheel and her heart rate jumped. Hector and his wife were gone.

Foiled again.

Could she not get a break here? If she didn't know any better, she'd say he was actively running from her. Maybe he was. What did she know? She knew nothing.

She closed her eyes, willing her shallow breathing to deepen, and it did after a moment or two. It wasn't the end of the world.

She took down the real-estate number from the sign board. Perhaps Hector had left a forwarding address with them.

When she got to work the next morning, she called the real estate first thing. The receptionist who answered the phone was as bored with her as the clerk at Births, Deaths and Marriages. Apparently, the Warners had not left a forwarding address or phone number. The agency could not help her.

'Why so glum, little mate?' Chub asked her as she hung up the phone.

'The address in that resume was a dead end.'

'Well, why don't you go speak to Gavin? He might know where his man moved.'

It was the very last thing she wanted to do. But unless she wished to concede defeat, it was the only option left.

A gentle, tropical breeze whispered against her sun-kissed cheek. She'd never get sick of this balmy spring weather. The Pilbara always delivered on atmosphere. Pity there wasn't a deckchair to hand. She smiled at the ridiculous image it created in her mind. A deckchair on this wharf would look as out of place as Annabel George in the TCN site office. Her smile faded as soon as she spotted him.

He hadn't seen her yet. His back was to her and he was leaning on the railing talking to one of his subordinates. A perfectly proportioned rear encased in navy Hard Yakka couldn't help but draw her notice. She marched up to the pair of men with determination that was more for herself than for them. As soon as she was within a metre, however, she realised she was intruding upon a private conversation and awkwardly hung back.

They still hadn't noticed her, so engrossed were they in the subject matter.

'I don't know what to tell you, Gav. I'm fuckin' freakin' out here. I just can't concentrate.'

'Then you should go to her, Craig.'

'Carl will have ten fits. The berthing dolphins are the most behind schedule.'

'I'll cover for you.'

'I couldn't ask you to do that,' Craig protested. 'Your R and R is coming up next week.'

'You can pay me back when you return.'

'You can't just work through.'

'Why?' Gavin grimaced. 'Bulldog does it.'

'That's different. He's a fuckin' robot.'

'I'll survive.'

Feeling like a guilty eavesdropper, Wendy tried to take a couple of steps back, and that's when they noticed her.

Craig turned around first and coughed. 'Oh, it's the Sergeant. Didn't see you there, Wendy. What can we do for you?'

She waved her hand in a gesture of denial. 'I didn't mean to interrupt. Shall I come back later?'

'No, no.' Craig shook his head. 'I was just about to head back to my men. Did you need to see me?'

'Er, no, I actually wanted to speak to Gavin.'

'No worries.' Craig tipped his hat and walked off.

'Miss me, Sarge?' Gavin threw her a whimsical smile.

'Like a fly in my tea.'

His smile only broadened unashamedly. 'So I guess you're not here to offer to take me to dinner for getting your boots back?'

'Nope.'

He sighed. 'A man can always hope.' He turned around to lean on the rail and she followed his gaze.

They were standing right on the end of the wharf. Before them was the ocean, sunshine sparkling on its surface. She could hear the sounds of waves crashing against the piles beneath the deck. A couple of lone piles that had been driven but not built on yet stuck up out of the water in front of the wharf. She couldn't help feeling like she was one of them. Alone, in an ocean of waves crashing all around.

Beyond these, setting up to drive another pile, was Gavin's barge. With a sigh, she also leaned against the rail. 'So you're not taking R and R this time?'

His lips twitched. 'Eavesdropping on a private conversation, were you?'

'I didn't mean to. I just showed up when –' She broke off, knowing it was probably useless to try to explain herself. 'Are you sure you should skip your break?'

'Yep, pretty sure.'

'It's not good for your health.'

'Are you going to give me a safety lecture, Sarge?' He glanced at her ruefully. 'I wouldn't bother.'

'Everybody needs to re-charge. Working the hours we do –'

He cut her dead. 'Craig and his wife just found out she has cancer. He needs to go home and see her.'

Wendy's heart lurched.

'Craig needs to put his family first right now and if I can't help with that, what kind of friend am I?'

'I . . .' Wendy swallowed, feeling both out of line and concerned. 'I didn't know . . .'

'Then save it.' He shook his head. 'It's between me, Carl and Craig anyway.'

She grimaced, knowing that much was true. Not that she wanted to stop him if Craig's need was so dire. But she was worried about him; that was all.

As an employee of Barnes Inc, of course.

An employee who wasn't getting ample rest and recuperation.

His gaze returned to the barge or SEP as his expression morphed into annoyance – with her or with himself? She couldn't tell.

For the first time, she wondered, could Gavin be her mystery handyman? Her Fairy Dongamother. The do-gooder who had fixed her flyscreen and her air conditioner without any expectation of a thank you.

Till now she had written him off. Surely if he had done it, he would have mentioned it, boasted about it, held it over her head and used it as a means to flirt with her – as he did whenever their paths crossed. But now, after hearing his thoughts about Craig, she wasn't so sure.

The breeze whipped strands of his fringe into his eyes so he momentarily took off his hard hat to smooth it flat. The brief sight of the wind in his hair brought back that night on the hill. She pulled her gaze away and looked down at her hands. *Stop it!*

With iron-clad will she focused once more on the scene at hand. The giant red sleeve of the pile hammer was strangely silent. Her eyes ran over the massive claw that usually held a fresh pile over the side. It was empty. The men in the control room were currently sitting outside it having a cigarette.

'What's going on?' she asked.

'Nothing,' he grumbled. 'Absolutely nothing.'

'I can see that.'

'I'm having a bit of a bad day. My Norwegian boys never turned up.'

Her brow wrinkled. 'We're hiring some guys from Norway?'

The first sign of his mood lifting touched his face. 'A Norwegian buoy is an air bag apparatus that seals the ends of piles. We float them out from the land to the end of the wharf and the Norwegian buoys seal the ends so they don't sink to the bottom of the ocean. I ordered some and the bloody things never arrived.'

'Oh.'

'I've got two piles on the ocean bed and none in the hammer.'

'I'm sorry to hear that.'

'Me too.'

There was a momentary pause in conversation, then amusement lit his features. 'You still haven't told me why you've come to see me. Is there something you need help with?'

She hesitated. Had she been wrong to suppose that Gavin might actually give a damn about her as a person? He'd been very flirtatious so far. Except for today.

Today he seemed . . . preoccupied.

The favour she had to ask now seemed silly to mention. It was the kind of help you asked a friend you trusted. 'Actually, you know what?' She took her hands off the rail. 'Don't worry about it. It's nothing.'

'Wendy.'

A breath whooshed out of her at the gentling of his voice and the uncharacteristic use of her real name instead of the teasing 'Sarge' that usually dropped so easily off his lips.

'For goodness' sake, just say it.'

She turned around, wringing her hands. 'It isn't work-related.'

'I figured that.'

'I'm just looking for someone, that's all. And I thought you might be able to help me find him.'

'Who?'

'Your site supervisor, Hector Warner?'

He blinked. 'Yabber?'

That gave her pause. '*Yabber?*'

'Yabber was his nickname because he used to talk a lot. Bit of a chatterbox. Has five children all fully grown, so heaps to yabber on about.'

'Really? *Five* children?' She couldn't stop the inflection in her voice.

Five unknowns.

Five people who were connected to her.

Five shocks waiting to happen.

'You okay?'

She swallowed. 'Yeah fine.'

'Well, he's retired now. I'm afraid you've missed him.'

She bit her lip, almost too scared to ask the question. 'Did he leave a forwarding address?'

'Not with me.' Gavin shook his head. 'But maybe with one of the rest of the team. They were all good mates. He also hung around a lot with Fish's crew after knock-off.'

97

'Oh.' Her face fell as she looked over at the group of guys having a smoke on the barge. She was hoping she wouldn't have to ask everyone and thus put all her personal business on display.

'I can ask around for you,' he offered shrewdly. 'Then no one will know it's you who's looking for him.'

Her gaze flicked to his, gratitude quickly changing to caution. 'What's the catch?'

'No catch.'

'What do you want in return?'

'Nothing.'

She watched him cautiously. 'You sure?'

He paused, searching her face. She didn't know what he was looking for but he seemed to find it because he said finally, 'All right. How about that dinner?'

The thing was, that teasing look in his eyes wasn't there this time when he asked her.

'Really? That's all you want?'

'That's the only way you'll trust me, isn't it? If there's something in it for me?'

She stuck out her hand. 'Okay. I'll buy you dinner if you get me Hector Warner's address.'

He looked at her long white fingers, a strange expression on his face. 'I didn't mean for you to pay. Your company is enough.'

'I think it's necessary.'

Keeps it more like a business deal, she thought to herself, but said out loud: 'Now are you going to shake my hand or am I going to stand here looking like an idiot in front of your men?'

His lips twitched into that smile that never failed to take her breath away. 'All right, Sarge, I'm in.' Taking her hand, his fingers curled around hers, sealing the deal and somehow much more.

Chapter 8

'Information, Instruction, Training and Supervision.' Wendy drummed her fingers on her desktop.

'You've said that like four times now,' Chub commented from his side of the donga. 'Is it supposed to mean something to me?'

Wendy stood up and began to pace the floor, the back of her hand slapping her other palm. 'That's what we're supposed to be demonstrating to the client.'

'Demonstrating?' Chub queried vaguely. 'Demonstrating when?'

'In the safety audit in four weeks.'

That made Chub sit up. 'We're being audited?'

'Audited or shut down. One or both.' Wendy cringed.

'*We're being audited?*' Chub said again just to clarify.

'Yes! Aren't you listening to me?'

'Maybe you should say that part four times.' Chub dabbed a hanky across his beading brow and grabbed his comfort jar. 'Smartie?'

'What happened to the jelly beans?' Wendy absentmindedly took a couple.

'I ran out. Besides Smarties also provide positive verbal reinforcement. Let's face it, we need that right now.'

Wendy grinned. 'So you're on board, are you?'

'That depends.' He snorted. 'Have we got a plan?'

'Sort of.' Wendy sat down in her chair and wheeled it towards him. 'I think I'm going to have to prepare a Safety Presentation for all Barnes Inc staff and get everyone to attend during the next month.' She bit her lip. 'They're not going to like it, because it's going to pull them off the job. But it will definitely count towards us demonstrating the first three outcomes *and* also make good preparation for cyclone season.'

'It'll take some convincing.'

'Well,' Wendy spread her hands, 'isn't it better to be off the job for a day than for good? That's how we'll market it. They have to be made to see the bigger picture here, Cobber.'

'I'm starting to hear the word "we" a lot in your sentences.'

She returned his distrustful stare with a coy look of her own. 'You *are* going to help me with the presentations, right? It's practically your duty as the HR manager.'

He winced. 'Really?'

'Obviously if we're both running a session at the same time we can get through more people faster.' She paused, sensing she had to offer him something. 'I'll put donuts on the menu for morning tea.'

His whole face lit up. 'Done.'

She laughed and wheeled her chair back to her desk. 'I really gotta get these method statements finished.'

She had already spoken to Carl about them. After hearing the number of changes she wanted to make, he had advised her to 'make the fuckin' changes herself' rather than passing on instructions for the engineers to do so. This had been working quite well so far, except now she was down to Anton's method statements.

Anton seemed to run around doing all sorts of in-between jobs, like installing pipelines on the jetty, repairing existing wharf facilities and other miscellaneous stuff. Wendy had only met him a couple of times and was less than impressed with his cavalier attitude. But she supposed that's why he hadn't been given that much responsibility. His method statements needed quite a bit of work and she wanted to get started on them but Anton had gone on R and R and left the electronic files saved on his own hard drive. To access them, she needed his computer password. With the audit coming up, she couldn't see any other way but to disturb him on his break. She asked Carl's permission to call Anton and it was granted immediately. She knew that if Anton got mad about her calling, it was only going to make her reputation around site even worse. She could just hear the new rumours. *The Sergeant even tries to get you when you're on holiday.*

She bit her lip as she listened to the dial tone.

Anton's voice sounded groggy when he picked up the phone. 'H-hello.'

'Hi, Anton, it's Wendy Hopkins. How are you?'

'Did I meet you at the club last night?'

She cleared her throat. 'No, it's Wendy Hopkins from Barnes Inc. I'm the safety manager at Cape Lambert. We've met a couple of times on site.'

She heard a mad scramble as though someone had knocked over a lamp as they jerked to a sitting position in bed.

'Oh, right, yeah sorry. How can I help you?'

She smiled in relief. At least he seemed anxious to please rather than being angry.

'Just a small thing. I'm adding some safety notes to your method statements. I need your computer password to access the files.'

'Oh, er . . .' There was a heavy pause. 'Why don't you just write the changes down and I'll make them when I get back?'

Well, that's very generous, she thought. Since when did engineers make time like this for her?

101

'That's really great to hear, Anton. But, if it's okay with you, I think I'll do it myself this time. It's just that we're going to be audited in four weeks and I need to get these changes in the statement and redistributed as quickly as possible.'

'Are you sure I can't help you with it?'

Wow, this guy is great!

'Positive.' She smiled. 'Now, if you don't mind, can I have your password? I already have the log in box on my screen.'

'I, er, oh . . .'

'Anton?'

'How about I spell it out for you?'

'Okay.'

'It's all lower case. l-i-c-k-m-y-b-a-l-l-s. Did you, er . . . get all that?'

She bit her lip to stop the bubble of laughter in the back of her throat. 'Yes. Thank you. Goodbye.' She put the phone down. So much for being helpful! He just didn't want to tell her his password.

'What are you smiling about, little mate?' Chub rumbled from his corner.

Wendy shook her head wryly. 'Nothing much. Just another day in *this* office.'

Sunday morning finally arrived and, though Wendy didn't want to admit it to herself, she couldn't deny it any longer. She was looking forward to a day out with the girls. A day off from *Wendy Hopkins. Safety Manager. Keeper of the people. Protectress of the human workforce.*

Royal pain in everyone's arse.

Being treated like the town leper was starting to get really tiring. It was difficult to keep positive and friendly when everyone responded so negatively to her. It was hard keeping a reassuring smile on her face when she knew the man she was talking to was mentally reciting, *Die, woman, die.*

But Sunday, there would be none of that. She could just relax and be Wendy.

She slept in late, which really only meant till seven am so she could still catch breakfast in the mess. She was sitting on her own, munching on a slice of Vegemite toast, when a tray of bacon and eggs slipped into her field of vision.

She looked up to find Gavin grinning down at her as he took a seat.

'Hey, Sarge.'

'Gavin,' she returned drily, grimacing at his plate of oily fried food.

'I've got good news to report.' He opened his napkin and the gentle waft of his aftershave permeated her senses. She ignored it.

He picked up his fork. 'I've found Yabber.'

Her heart jumped. 'You have his address?'

'I have his address.' He cut off a piece of bacon and popped it in his mouth.

'What is it?'

'Ah,' his eyes crinkled in the corners, 'aren't you forgetting something?'

'Huh?'

'We were going to dinner, remember?'

'Yes, I know.' She flushed. 'I haven't forgotten, I just –'

'Have trouble having fun,' he finished for her.

She glared at him. 'I have a lot of fun, thank you very much.'

'Oh.' His voice remained casual. 'So you're not a work-aholic who punched the last guy who asked you out in the face?'

Her cheeks infused with heat. 'That was different. I thought you were going to attack me. Which you did, by the way.'

He moved his fork through his baked beans and said softly, without looking at her, 'What's got you so on edge you don't trust anyone?'

'Who cares?' she retorted crossly.

He met her gaze unblinkingly. 'I do.'

Her breath caught and it was an effort to push out her voice. 'Look, I said I'd buy you dinner and I will. But I'll take the address first. I need it.'

'Why?'

'It's important I talk to Yabber.'

'Why?'

She put down her own cutlery with a snap. 'None of your business.'

'All right, all right,' he sighed. 'I'll give you the address at dinner.'

'You're going to make me wait?'

'Not that long,' he assured her, that delectable smile of his holding promises she desperately did not want to think about. 'I just don't want you to, you know, back out because you got what you wanted.'

Nobody does anything for nothing.

Her temper got the better of her. 'I'm not going to double-cross you. I always keep my word.'

Another soft smile. 'So do I.'

Her skin broke out in gooseflesh and she tore her gaze away. 'Well good for you.'

He nodded as though the tension between them had been resolved. 'So I was thinking, how about we go to dinner in Karratha or Point Samson? What's your preference?'

She ground her teeth. 'As soon as possible.'

He laughed. 'Well, unfortunately this weekend is out. There's a shortage of good restaurants in town, so you have to book early. How about next Saturday?'

'A whole week away?'

'Absence makes the heart grow fonder.'

She lifted her finger. 'That saying was never used in this context. Besides, I'm supposed to be organising this dinner, aren't I? I'm sure I can get us into some place sooner than that.'

His eyes widened. '*What?* You think I just want *some place*. Sorry, Sarge.' He stood up and ruffled her hair as he walked past her. 'I think it'll be better for the both of us if you just leave it with me.' The brief touch caused both rage and, she hated to admit it, arousal. He was an arrogant, incorrigible beast who now held the one piece of information she needed.

'Hey, get back here!' She swivelled in her chair but it was too late. He was already too far away to still be in earshot without her shouting and attracting even more attention than their shared breakfast probably already had. She turned back to their plates and noticed to her surprise that while her plate was still full, his was empty.

When had he eaten all that? And why did she suddenly not feel hungry? The problem was, she couldn't keep her cool with Gavin. She just seemed to lose all sense of time and place. And worse, she over-reacted to everything. He was right. She was too much on edge. The day they'd met she'd hit him twice! He just seemed to push all the wrong buttons.

With a sigh, she shook her head and looked up, only to unwittingly catch the eye of the guy at the next table. He was winking at her.

'So, Sargent, you got a date with Gav, have you?'

Oh crap.

She knew denying it would just make him ask more questions so, resolutely, she stood up, pushed her chair in and left. She hadn't wanted that food anyway.

Thank goodness she was meeting the girls that morning. With her search for Hector at checkmate, she desperately needed to keep her mind off the futility of it all.

The girls met her in the car park at about ten am, both dressed in shorts and T-shirts with their bathers on underneath.

'So where are we headed?' she asked, infusing as much enthusiasm into her voice as she could muster.

Sharon grinned. 'Honeymoon Cove in Point Samson.'

The girls piled into her Nissan. After a couple of turns of the key, the engine (thank God) choked to life and Sharon gave her directions. It was actually quite nice to have a car full of cheerful voices as opposed to silence. The day was warm, humid and frankly perfect for a sunbake and a swim.

When they eventually arrived at the beach, Wendy thanked herself for taking this break.

It was perfect.

The crescent-shaped cove surprisingly sported golden sand as opposed to the red dirt she was used to seeing. It looked like the perfect texture to just melt your toes into. Both sides of the lonely stretch were framed by jagged rocks, black, red and grey rising up out of the ground in shards, as though they were defending this private little landing from invasion by the rest of the Pilbara. Gentle waves lapped the bank and she sighed with pure enjoyment of it all.

'The cove is protected by the coral reef,' Sharon told her. 'So it doesn't get rough here.'

Lena kicked off her thongs, picked them up and ran off down to the water's edge in bare feet. Wendy and Sharon laughed, following suit. They laid their towels out on the beach and then stripped off to enjoy a quick dip. The water was cool and refreshing. Wendy felt like she was washing off the last two weeks as she waded into what seemed like liquid sunshine, with the sun sparkling on the surface of the waves.

After fifteen minutes, they all got out and without drying themselves simply lay down on their towels.

Lena closed her eyes. 'This is the life.'

'What? The sand flies aren't bothering you?' Sharon teased.

'I got my sun cream and repellent on.' Lena flicked her hands up over her head. 'Besides there doesn't seem to be that many today.'

'It's the breeze,' Sharon informed her. 'A little too windy for them.'

'Feels perfect to me,' Wendy sighed.

'Doesn't it just?' Lena was silent for a moment. 'So what's this I hear about you and Gavin?'

Wendy's eyes, which had just started to close, flew open. She couldn't have heard about that *already*. Surely.

'Got a date in Karratha or something,' Lena continued unperturbed. 'When did he ask you out?'

Sharon sat up. 'You're kidding me.'

Wendy groaned inwardly. 'It's not really a date.'

'Then what is it?' Lena inquired.

Wendy searched the clouds for answers but they were singularly unhelpful. She couldn't prove the unromantic nature of her meeting with Gavin without revealing her search for her father. And as much as she liked these girls, she didn't want to put her emotional baggage on them. 'We're just friends,' she finished lamely.

'Not to him you're not,' Lena warned her. 'Trust me, Gavin's got a bit of a reputation. As long as you tug his line he'll chase you.'

'Really?' Wendy noticed to her chagrin that her voice sounded both small and disappointed. 'Have you seen him with a lot of other women?'

'Well, to be honest,' Lena sighed, 'he was after both of us at one stage. Don't get me wrong, he's very good looking and –'

'*And* I did fancy him like mad at one stage,' Sharon interrupted Lena, and Wendy's gaze immediately shot to her instead. Sharon's brow wrinkled. 'The problem with Gavin is, once you get to know him, you realise the only person he cares about is himself.'

'That's not true.' Defence jumped from Wendy's throat before she could stop it.

Lena sat up, folding her arms across her knees as she looked at her. 'Do you know something we don't know?'

The blue-tongue.

Craig's wife.

But she couldn't say it. These had both been private moments for Gavin. Even she was not supposed to have witnessed them. So she said nothing.

'I'm sorry,' Lena apologised. 'I didn't mean to offend you. I'm just trying to warn you, actually. I don't want to see you get hurt.'

Wendy averted her eyes. 'No need to worry about that. I'm not into Gavin that way.'

At least not most of the time. Luckily the conversation was interrupted as a wrinkled woman, possibly in her late sixties, wandered past them and then spread a towel nearby. As she left the towel and hobbled down to the water's edge for a swim, Sharon started the conversation again. 'So, Carl asked me to move in with him.'

It was a well-known fact that, unlike Dan, Carl chose not to live in the camp. It was thought that he wanted to give his men a bit of a breather from his presence. Dan, on the other hand, in true TCN style, wanted to keep his eye on his troops *even* when they were sleeping.

Lena turned to her quickly. 'Wow! What did you say?'

Sharon clasped her hands together. 'I said yes! Of course.'

'Oh shoot.' Lena stretched out her hand and squeezed Sharon's arm. 'I'm going to miss having you around.'

'I'm not moving that far. Just to Wickham.'

'But I won't get to see you at dinner.'

'You're always sitting with Bulldog anyway.' Sharon rolled her eyes. 'You won't even know I've gone.'

Lena looked at her hands and was silent for a minute.

'Uh-oh.' Sharon exchanged a glance with Wendy. 'What's going on?'

'Nothing really. It's just, well . . . it's Annabel George.'

'That crazy bitch!' Sharon said. 'Trust me, honey, you have nothing to worry about from her.'

'I'm not worried. I'm just annoyed.' Lena bit her lip. 'I asked Dan if he could please tell her to stop coming to see him all the time. And he told me he did but she just keeps coming. And he doesn't seem to want to be too rude about it.'

'Why not?' Sharon demanded.

'Well, he kind of feels like he owes her for being there for him when they were together.'

Sharon snorted. 'Isn't that what a girlfriend is supposed to do?'

'When were they together?' Wendy asked. 'To be honest, she doesn't seem like his type at all.'

'Thank you!' Lena shot her a look of gratitude. 'Apparently, it all started in high school. I saw this album she made for him. It's full of pictures of when they were together. Dan certainly looks like he was in love with her at one stage.'

'Of course he does,' Sharon said scornfully. 'He was probably sixteen and a virgin.'

'Well, she *is* gorgeous. You can't fault those perfect breasts.' Lena groaned. 'And she knows all this stuff about him that I don't.'

'Like what?'

'Like what his favourite muffin is. What music he listens to. That he worked at McDonald's for five years when he was going through uni.'

'None of that stuff is really that important, is it?' Wendy tried to reassure her. 'I mean, maybe she knew him well back then. But that's not what's relevant to him now. I still don't get why Dan feels he owes her.'

'Well.' Lena's eyes clouded as though she didn't want to reveal too much. 'He reckons she helped him when his stepmum was giving him hell.'

Wendy raised her brows. 'How?'

'Dan's stepmother thought of him as a remnant of his father's first marriage and treated him as such,' Lena responded bitterly. 'Dan moved out of home at seventeen because he didn't feel welcome there any more. Annabel and her parents let him live with them through uni.'

'Well, I suppose that was generous of her and her family,' Sharon conceded. 'But surely after living with her, Dan could see how incompatible they were.'

'Yes, but he didn't break it off for ages because he was living in her house and had nowhere else to go. He was young,' Lena shrugged, 'and he had no money and no support from his own family. Can you blame him for keeping quiet while he tried to get through uni?'

'I guess not,' Wendy said. 'But I suppose now he feels guilty about not being completely honest with her.'

'Yes.' Lena threw up her hands in frustration. 'And Annabel's milking it. Apparently she just moved to town, so Dan feels like he needs to help her find her feet because that's what she did for him back in the day.'

Sharon groaned. 'I can see where he's coming from but how annoying for you. I don't know what you can do about it.'

'Well,' Lena closed her eyes and put her forehead on her knees, 'I sort of went to see her myself to hint that I didn't like her hanging around my boyfriend too much. She works nights as a nurse at Nickol Bay Hospital in Karratha. Anyway, she basically told me that it was only a matter of time before she and Dan were engaged again.'

'Engaged!' Sharon squeaked. '*He was going to marry her?*'

'Apparently.' Lena nodded forlornly.

'Why didn't he tell you?'

'He said he didn't want me to freak out. He proposed just before he moved in with her, before he fell out of love with her.'

'Yeah, but the point is,' Sharon put her finger to her palm, 'he eventually did come to his senses, dumped her and moved on. She's the past, Lena. You're the present.'

'That's the thing,' Lena said dully. 'Like I said, he kept quiet, he didn't dump her. He waited till *she* dumped *him*. And now she reckons she's had a change of heart.'

'Oh, bollocks to that!' Sharon blew air into her fringe. 'It must be over fifteen years since they were together. Does she really believe he's been pining for her?'

'Well, she's certainly acting like it. I don't know what I'm supposed to do about her.'

'Maybe just give her a bit more time,' Wendy suggested. 'She might figure out Dan's lack of interest on her own.'

Sharon was about to add her two cents' worth when her mobile started ringing. She quickly fished it out of her beach bag and put it to her ear.

'Oh hi, darl, I'm good. Where are you?' A pause. '*Where?*' Sharon shaded her eyes and focused on a small fishing boat that was only just discernible in the distance. 'Oh yes, I see it . . . Nah, that's okay, I'll see you tonight.'

'Was that Carl?' Lena asked as she hung up the phone.

'Yes, he and the boys – Fish, Radar, Leg and Gavin – hired a boat. They wanted to know if we wanted to go for a ride. I said we were fine.'

Lena pouted. 'Why'd you do that? I want to go for a ride. It'd be awesome. Best offer I've had from the boys since Gavin put a shrimp on a fishing hook for me.'

Gavin had taken Lena fishing. Wendy experienced a jolt that was too much like jealousy.

Meanwhile, Lena was still talking. 'Can you call them back?'

'O-*kay*,' Sharon said with an indulgent laugh. But it seemed Carl must have left his phone below deck because he wasn't answering it. Sharon spoke to his voicemail and hung up. 'Why don't you try and wave them in?' she suggested to Lena as she put the phone back in her bag. 'The boat seems to be sailing closer.'

Wendy squinted at the horizon. It did too.

Lena jumped up, pulling a reluctant Wendy to a standing position. 'Come on, girl. You gotta help me.'

She began jumping and waving enthusiastically at the boat. Wendy couldn't help but chuckle at her eagerness and half-heartedly joined in. It seemed like the guys on the boat must have seen them because the fishing vessel was definitely coming closer.

'They can see us!' Lena waved even harder.

The boat continued to come in and just when Wendy thought it was definitely going to anchor, it made a sharp right turn and sped by adjacent to the coast. Leg, Radar and Gavin, who were standing on the bow, all dropped their pants and wiggled their bare bums at them.

Lena covered her eyes and screamed. Sharon was laughing so hard she was fit to break her sides. Wendy simply covered her mouth in astonishment.

The older lady who had been sunbaking on the beach beside them was delighted. Clearly, it was the most sexual excitement she'd had in years. She squealed and waved madly at the guys before asking Wendy, 'Are they friends of yours?'

'Er, sort of,' Wendy replied weakly.

'Those roaches!' Lena was indignant. 'Wait till I see them next!'

The mood of their afternoon somewhat unsettled, the girls decided to head off to the tavern in Point Samson for a seafood lunch. This venue was very casual and most patrons chose to sit outside at round plastic tables that had beach umbrellas inserted into the centre.

Lunch was by far the best fish and chips Wendy had had in a very long time. The Pilbara had a reputation for good seafood, so she wasn't surprised she was wowed by the simple meal. With a few more wedges of lemon, she could have eaten another plate, but decided still fitting into her bathers after lunch was more important. She doubted Chub would have showed this much restraint.

Just as they were finishing up, Carl and the boys arrived.

'I thought you'd be cooking your catches and eating them fresh.' Lena seemed surprised.

Carl's expression was decidedly grumpy. 'We ran out of beer.'

Wendy looked up as she felt Gavin's eyes unashamedly roving over her. Those brown portals seemed darker than ever and she wished she'd covered up a bit more like the other girls, who'd put their shorts and T-shirts back on. Her bathers were one piece so she'd simply tied a sarong around her waist. She hadn't felt at all self-conscious when she'd arrived. Now, it seemed like she was displaying an obscene amount of flesh.

To cut the line of his gaze, she got up and went into the tavern, claiming she needed another drink – which wasn't exactly far from the truth. Being in the same room as Gavin always seemed to give her a dry throat.

To her dismay, however, after a few minutes he followed her.

'So . . .' He leaned on the counter beside her as she waited for the bartender to come back with her drink. 'Maybe I was wrong. Maybe you do have fun sometimes. Did you enjoy the beach?'

'As a matter of fact I did.' The bartender set her Coke on a coaster before her. 'Until you guys broke the mood.'

'Come on.' Those eyes she couldn't trust twinkled at her. 'That was funny.'

She hesitated, sipping her Coke before looking up at him. 'Okay, it *was* funny.' Her grin curled around the straw between her lips.

'Now that's what I like to see.' The way he was looking at her made her heart throb painfully.

'I better get back to the girls,' she muttered. But as she turned to go a little devil sitting on her shoulder poked her in the neck. She stopped and looked back at him. 'Nice arse, by the way.'

She had meant to disconcert him – embarrass and unsettle him the way he constantly did her. But she should have realised that Gavin would be immune to such tactics. The gaze that locked with hers betrayed no trace of discomfort at all. Instead, he returned the compliment in all seriousness.

'You too, darlin'. You too.'

She whipped her face away, inwardly cursing herself for having said anything at all. Praying he wasn't looking at the subject of their conversation, she hightailed it out of there, clutching her drink to her chest. She was in such a hurry to leave, she almost collided with Carl as he and the other guys entered the bar to quench their thirst.

'Sorry,' she muttered at his startled expression and then crossed the threshold to the alfresco area to find the girls. She was thankful that in the meantime Sharon and Lena had finished both their drinks and their meals.

'You okay, honey?' Sharon looked her over with some concern.

'Fine.' Wendy drained her Coke and set it on their table. 'Actually I'm pretty tired. Do you mind if we head off?'

Sharon looked at Lena and the other woman shrugged. 'Sure.'

The drive home was uneventful and helped her to calm down a bit.

Unfortunately, however, when Wendy arrived back at her donga she found that the door was unlocked. Her heart jumped as she realised someone must have broken in. She cautiously pushed the door open and scanned the room. Her breath came short and shallow as she bit her lip while contemplating the scene.

Two things were very apparent.

The first was that someone had replaced her broken desk with a functional one and re-attached her wardrobe door to a new hinge.

The second thing was that whoever had done it couldn't possibly have been Gavin.

Chapter 9

You need to stop this now.

Gavin polished off his beer at the bar, not quite trusting himself to rejoin his friends outside where he knew Wendy would be.

Normally he was pretty good at choosing his targets. This time . . . not so much.

It had become quite clear after their first meeting that Wendy was definitely not casual fling material. She couldn't speak to him without her heart glowing in her eyes. Every time he resolved to keep his distance, however, he somehow found an excuse to stay within her orbit. There was just something about her that made him lose his head. He choked, wiping his damp lips on the back of his hand. No, he had his head. He knew that because every time he saw her it was like someone had taken a plank of wood to it. She made him forget the boundaries he'd set for himself.

You could really hurt her. Do you honestly want to do that?

It was clear the woman already had issues. Those big blue eyes spoke of pain, distrust and caution. Whatever baggage she had, it was big. If he were smart, he would back away.

Women who were damaged often ignored the rules of engagement, which numbered three:

1. No commitment.
2. No regrets.
3. No emotional intimacy.

Usually the odd fling on the job helped him forget the mess that was his own life. But this time, he couldn't help worrying that maybe Wendy would make that mess extra difficult to unravel. He had trouble remembering not to get too close, like asking too many questions about her personal life. Not that she wanted to answer them. He snorted in derision. She trusted him even less than he trusted himself.

So far, flirting with her hadn't even taken his mind off his own problems. In fact, it had made him dwell on them all the more – almost like rubbing salt into a wound, really. Talking to her only seemed to show him everything that he'd lost or could never have.

A jovial slap on his back broke his train of thought and he turned around. His smile didn't even slip a notch.

Man, I'm getting good at this.

It was Carl, with the others close on his heels. 'Fuck! I thought we'd never get in here.' His boss waved an authoritative hand at the bartender, who immediately hurried over. 'I'll have a round for my boys, thanks.'

Gavin grinned in acknowledgement. Carl wasn't big on fishing and had been complaining about his seasickness since they'd first set out that morning. He suspected this was half a lie but couldn't mistake Carl's genuine delight to be off the boat and on dry land. Fish, however, wore the expression of a man who had been short-changed.

'Damn it, Carl! You can't order a round. By the time the rest of us have a go, we'll have been here all afternoon.'

Carl's eyebrows waggled. 'That's the fuckin' plan. Now drink up and stop yapping. I've had enough of your fuckin' rods and reels, spear guns and bait boxes. I just want my peace.'

Radar seemed pleased and reached for a frothing glass with unabashed enthusiasm. 'I'll have a bit of your peace, Carl.'

'Me too,' Leg declared with a flourish.

Fish grabbed his own glass in resignation. 'I suppose not all is lost. We can still go crabbing in the evening.'

'Fuck that.' Carl firmly shook his head.

Fish turned to Gavin. 'What about you, brother?'

'So I'm your brother now?' Gavin toasted him in faint amusement. 'I don't know, mate. I don't think I have your stamina for the sport.' His mood had definitely been blighted by that run-in with a certain blonde too attractive for her own good.

Fish groaned at the ease of his defeat. 'Don't you want a nice big juicy mud crab for dinner?'

'Mate,' Gavin frowned, not really in the mood to argue the point, 'where will I cook it? It's not like the dongas are equipped with kitchens.'

'That's easy,' Fish said. 'You're going on R and R tomorrow, right? Just pack it in your bag.'

'No fuckin' way!' Carl was moved to interrupt before Gavin could reply. 'It'll fuckin' stink!'

Fish shook his head. 'Not if it's alive.'

Carl spluttered on beer froth. 'Are you fuckin' kidding me? You want Gav to take an angry mud crab as hand luggage back to Perth? Have you seen the fuckin' claws on those things? What if it escapes?'

Fish rolled his eyes. 'It's not very fast. And you just tie its clippers together and it'll be fine.'

Carl gawked at him. 'Don't tell me, you've fuckin' done this before!'

Fish regarded him as though his question was stupid and unnecessary. 'Carl, crabs don't make any noise, you know. They're not dogs. They don't bark!'

Carl raised his hand for the bar attendant to come back over. 'Fuck! I need another drink. I'm not pissed enough for this.'

But Fish had already turned eagerly towards Gavin again. 'So how about it? You want one?'

There was no way around it. He was going to have to tell Fish. 'I'm not going on R and R tomorrow. Craig is taking my leave instead.'

Fish rubbed his chin. 'Really? So it's just you and me holding down the fort? That ought to be interesting.'

Carl snorted. He already knew Gavin was skipping his R and R and had disapprovingly approved it. But it was news to Leg and Radar, as Gavin had known it would be. It wasn't long before Radar's nose was twitching and he was firing his first twenty questions.

'So what's with that? He got fatigue issues? The wife giving him grief?'

Gavin wasn't about to tell the site gossip anything and covered his silence with a sip of beer.

So why did you tell Wendy then? You were pretty open with her. It wasn't like him to use another man's business to impress a girl. If there was one thing he prided himself on, it was loyalty. Loyalty and the ability to keep a bloody secret. Wendy just seemed to provoke him. Provoke him to show her he was a better man. Funny how he didn't care what anyone else thought of him.

You're mad.

'Give it a fuckin' rest, Radar.' Carl frowned. 'And, Gavin, stop taking on everybody else's shit.'

Gavin took another sip of beer and remained stubbornly silent. Carl eyed him shrewdly. 'It's one thing to be a good manager, but they're not your fuckin' family.'

Yes, they are. 'So what are you doing tonight then, Carl?' Gavin made the move to change the subject. 'If you're not crabbing, that is.'

To his surprise, his boss's colour seemed to heighten. 'Picking up my missus and her suitcases from camp. She's moving in.'

Radar's eyes lit like bulbs. 'Really? That's getting pretty serious! You're going to have to hang up your bachelor hat soon.'

Carl grinned but added nothing further. Much to Gavin's chagrin, Radar immediately turned back to him. Though to be fair to the site gossip, Gavin had no one to blame but himself for his reputation.

'What about you, Gav?' Radar asked. 'You've always got something on the go. Maybe some local girl from Wickham this time?'

'Nah,' Fish snorted, a vengeful twinkle in his eye. 'He's sweet on the Sergeant. You remember that first engineers' meeting she called? Me and Anton weren't going to go and he came and fuckin' *collected* us!'

'Is that so?' Radar rocked back on his heels. Gavin groaned inwardly, wishing he could take a piece of masking tape to Fish's mouth. To his relief, however, Carl was equally unimpressed.

'And why the fuck weren't you going to go?'

For the first time, Fish seemed to realise that his ploy may have backfired. 'Oh . . . er . . . you know how it is, Carl . . .'

Carl's voice was dangerously quiet. 'Fuckin' enlighten me.'

Fish grew petulant. 'Well to be honest, mate, the Sergeant's not into safety so much as she's into nit-picking. She's as bad as Bulldog. Last week she told me she was thinking about introducing random drug and alcohol tests! Do you know how much disruption that's going to cause to our schedules?'

Carl didn't blink. 'I'm fully aware.'

Gavin put his glass on the counter with a snap. The mention of any sort of addiction, particularly drugs, never failed to get under his skin. 'I don't know about you, Fish, but I don't want anyone driving my equipment hooked on drugs or booze. Drugs are the most dangerous thing on a site like this. On any site really.'

Fish rolled his eyes. 'Yes, I'm not arguing that point, Gavin. But she won't let us use our own judgement. And you're hardly going to see my point of view, are you? Too bloody preoccupied with her blonde hair and her long legs. As for me, she could have three tits and I still wouldn't be interested. You'd need a kilo of Vaseline to lube that frigid bitch. There's only so much a man can take.'

'Got that right.' Gavin nodded, and then threw his fist into Fish's face, shocking everyone, including himself.

Fish reeled from the blow, grabbing his jaw as Leg and Radar grabbed his arms, holding him back so that he couldn't retaliate. Gavin watched Fish struggle as Carl pushed him away, his thick fingers digging into his arms.

'What the fuck is the matter with you?'

The white hot rage that had flashed like a lightning bolt across Gavin's vision cleared. He looked at Carl blankly, carefully weighing his options. He didn't care so much about losing this job as letting his men down. He gritted his teeth. 'I'm sorry, Carl.'

'You ain't sorry.' Carl nodded knowingly.

Gavin set his face, hopefully locking any emotion behind his eyes.

Carl's voice lowered to a growl. 'Don't get me wrong. He was out of line and Fish can be a dickhead sometimes but he's my best friend. You don't get to punch him like that without some sort of repercussion.'

'You want a free throw, Carl?' Gavin demanded, a bitter taste lacing his mouth. 'Go ahead.'

Carl released him, pushing him back as he did so. 'What I want is for you to stop living every day like it's your last. I'm over it, Gavin. And you should be too!'

If that was his marching orders, Gavin was happy to take them. Without a word, he left the bar, not sparing his companions a second glance.

That evening, Gavin wasn't in the mood to see anyone. For dinner, he grabbed a roll from the mess, stuffed it full of slices of roast beef and walked out. He'd rather eat alone on the front steps of his donga with a bottle of beer than have to endure the banter he was sure was going around by now. Radar would have had ample opportunity to get back to camp and spread the word about the bar incident. Not to mention the hecklers he'd passed on the way to the mess, who seemed to know about his upcoming dinner with Wendy. Someone must have heard the two of them talking. It just went to show that nothing was sacred on this job. *Nothing.*

He had to guard what he said more closely.

'Hey.' An unfriendly voice sounded from his left and had him looking up from his sandwich in resignation. To his surprise, it wasn't the usual suspects, but Mike Hopkins.

'Hey yourself, Mike.' He lifted his bottle to toast the older man. He hadn't had much to do with Mike, except maybe for one drunken ride in his ute the night of Lena Todd's birthday. Not his finest hour and definitely not a night that would have inspired any kind of admiration from this particular site super-visor, or indeed anyone for that matter. He hoped he would never be that depressed again. He took another sip of beer as humiliating images chased themselves through his head.

Mike broke his wayward thoughts. 'Don't get cocky with me. I'm only here to say one thing.'

Gavin raised his eyebrows and said, with a complete lack of interest, 'And what might that be?'

'My niece isn't in the market for a boyfriend.'

He suddenly remembered that Mike was also Wendy's uncle and a sigh rippled through him. 'Got your shotgun, Mike? You might need it.'

The older man tried to suck in a belly that was clearly beyond the point of being hidden as he straightened to full height.

'I don't want no louts messing with my family. She ain't here to get mixed up with the likes of you.'

Gavin slowly lowered his beer. 'So why is she here then, Mike?'

Mike stabbed a finger at him. 'Same reason you should be – to work.' He stalked away.

Damn it if the man wasn't right. Better to focus on work than trying to figure out some woman he had no business messing with. Wendy was a great girl, but he wasn't here to fight her battles. He had enough of his own to deal with. As though to illustrate the point, his phone buzzed in his pocket. A text message had come through: *Can I call you tomorrow around 7.30am? I have news.*

His fingers tightened around the phone as he punched an affirmative reply and then put it back in his pocket.

Good news, I hope.

By the following morning, Gavin had gained the wisdom that came with sleeping on it. He was deeply regretting his actions at the bar. Sure, Fish deserved to be taken to task. But he should have waited till his anger cooled and then told the man off privately. Instead, he'd made a bloody spectacle of himself. And that was the *very last thing* he should be doing.

He got to work early, took a file and waited in the donga meeting room for Fish to show up. They had their pre-start meetings in there every morning with their men, and today he knew that first up he had to swallow his pride and offer the deck engineer an apology. The project was his priority. He wasn't going to jeopardise the one thing in his life that stabilised him.

Luckily, Fish seemed to have the same idea. He walked into the meeting room five minutes early, a cagey expression on his face.

'Look, Gav, about yesterday . . .'

Gavin looked up from his file. 'Don't say anything, Fish. I should apologise first. I shouldn't have taken a swing at you.'

'Well you shouldn't have.' Fish shrugged. 'Not that I couldn't have taken you if I needed to.'

Gavin allowed his eyes to rake the other man's body before replying with a faint touch of amusement, 'Of course not.'

'It's just that I hate being henpecked. It gets my goat.'

Gavin struggled to keep his hackles from rising as Fish continued unaware, 'But if you're with her then . . .'

'It's not about whether I'm *with* her or not,' Gavin returned tightly. The conversation was once more teetering over into the path he didn't want it to take. 'Let's just focus on the job from now on, okay? Doing it well and staying on schedule. We've got a lot to get through today.'

Fish grinned. 'Speaking of stuff to do today, I had this great idea. Especially with Craig being away and everything. We spoke of it a while back.'

'What idea?'

But Fish was forced to postpone his reply as both their teams and Craig's filed in. There was scuffing of boots and the scraping of chairs as the guys all found seats, continuing to talk in loud jovial voices.

'Heard you two had a scuffle yesterday,' said Jack, nickname Spoon, who had a reputation for stirring. 'Gavin steal your bait, Fish?'

Laughter rippled through the group.

Thanks, Radar.

'It was more of a difference of opinion.' Gavin dismissed the remark before he flung an arm around his fishy friend. 'But, as you can see, we're all good now, and that's without even exchanging flowers or chocolates.' He took his arm off Fish's shoulders.

Fish coughed and rubbed his hands together. 'Right, so let's discuss today's tasks and issues.'

The meeting seemed to go all right although Gavin noticed his site supervisor, Marvin, barely said a word. Marvin was relatively new. He was Yabber's replacement and was finding it difficult to fill his predecessor's big shoes. Yabber had been beloved and trusted by all. Gavin knew the guys missed him but wished they would at least *try* to make Marvin feel more welcome.

'Another thing,' he said, as the meeting came to a close. 'I have a few important things to do in the office this morning so I won't be coming out to the wharf for a few hours.'

He was sure this wouldn't be an issue as they all had their morning workload pretty much set out. His presence wasn't really needed. In fact, Fish seemed to be mighty pleased he wouldn't be there. Gavin suspected it was because he liked being King Pin at the end of the wharf.

'So I got all three teams then?' Fish grinned as everyone stood up to go. 'Yours, mine and Craig's. Still trying to make it up to me, Gav?'

'You wish.' Gavin hastily left his side to catch his site supervisor before he exited the room. 'Can I talk to you for a minute?'

'Sure.' Marvin turned around. He was a slight man, thin of stature, with messy blond hair and bony fingers. His hard hat always seemed a little too big for his head – a circumstance that was definitely not in his favour.

'I just wanted to ask you how things have been going,' Gavin began cautiously.

'Oh fine, fine.' Marvin nodded, though his expression told a completely different story.

Gavin decided to cut to the chase because he knew he didn't have time to coax a confidence out of Marvin. 'Look, I know there have been some settling-in problems and I wanted to assure you that I'm aware of them.'

Marvin's eyes widened slightly but he said nothing.

'I just want you to trust me a little more, okay, and have a little more faith in yourself. We'll work this out. I think the guys just need time. But you can rest assured I'm not going to let the status quo continue unchecked.'

Marvin flushed. 'Er, thanks, Gav.'

Gavin slapped him on the back. 'No problem. I'll see you this arvo.'

Having said what he thought needed to be said to get his man through the morning, he went outside, which was the best place to receive private phone calls. It was seven-twenty-five and it was at times like this that he wished smoking didn't kill you. At least if he had a cigarette he wouldn't look so stupid standing out there, seemingly waiting for nothing. Plus, it might even calm his nerves. His fingers clenched and unclenched. He needed something to occupy his hands.

Like a cruel joke, Wendy stepped out of her office donga at that precise moment, looking as fresh as a flower that had just bloomed.

She didn't have her hard hat on, so he could see that those long, flowing blonde tresses of hers were confined loosely at the nape of her neck. And what a neck it was – as elegant as a swan's, with peach-perfect skin you just wanted to rest your face against. The outfit she was wearing left everything to the imagination – the loose-fitting shirt and long fluoro-coloured safety vest hid all her curves – but he'd had her in his arms once, not to mention the sight of her in her bathers the day before. He knew what his eyes were missing and it scalded him every time he caught a glimpse of her. Across the jetty, across the room, across the camp and now here . . . right in front of him.

His guilty conscience reared up and slapped him in the face, making him suddenly feel like a little boy who'd dared perve at the hottest girl in school.

Just at that moment Wendy looked up and saw him watching her. Her skin took on a delicious rosy hue as her step faltered. A hand went to the collar of her shirt, lightly brushing the merest fraction of exposed skin there. Turning his heat up like the dial on a gas heater. *Man! You are gone!*

'Hey, Sarge.' His mouth twisted in mockery of himself.

'I . . . er . . . didn't see you there.' She stopped. 'Are you looking for someone?'

There was a vulnerability in her eyes that touched him. She was lost too. Except, unlike him, maybe if someone helped her . . .

He shook off the thought. 'No,' he murmured in answer to her question and then, unable to stop himself, grinned invitingly at her. 'Just enjoying the view.'

'Okay.' She held both hands palm up. 'Clearly, you're in one of those moods, so I think I'm going to go now.'

She made as if to walk off but her words startled him and involuntarily he grabbed her arm. 'What do you mean? Those moods?'

She looked down at the hand that had halted her and he hastily disengaged it. The faint smell of either her deodorant or her shampoo wafted headily under his nostrils as she turned back around.

A frown marred her perfect features. 'You blow hot, you blow cold. You make fun of me, you flirt with me. But mostly you lecture me as though I'm a little girl. I don't need your assessment of how much fun I'm supposed to be having in my life, whether or not I'm a workaholic or if I'm too much on edge for your liking. As shocking as this might be, I wasn't put on this earth just to please you.'

Her eyes flared as she came to the end of this impassioned speech. With hands on hips, her body language was nothing but challenging.

'*Really?*' the devil in him drawled. 'Damn shame, that.'

But she wasn't fooled by his attempt at distraction. She'd adopted that fearless look that he loved more than anything else. She'd take him on if she could and then some. Her lips thinned. 'I mean, what's it to you what I do in my free time? Why do you even care?'

Good question.

A muscle in his jaw twitched and the words were out before he could stop them. 'Because I've limited my choices because I had to. You, you beautiful girl, don't need to bury yourself.'

His phone rang. It was seven-thirty.

The insistent bell was a stark reminder of his real obligations. Obligations so far from where he was standing right now it wasn't even funny.

'I'm sorry,' he said with difficulty. 'I must take this.'

It seemed mean to leave her standing there gaping at him. But he had to. Taking his phone out of his pocket he walked off, heading for the yard as he put it to his ear. It was safest to talk there in the wide open space where he could see anyone coming a mile off. Doing his best to put Wendy out of his head he spoke into his receiver. 'Janet?'

'Yeah, it's me,' came the courteous female voice that always seemed at odds with his raging emotions. 'How are you doing?'

'Fine, fine.'

'The job still okay?'

He thought about his run-in with Fish at the bar. But then banished it. That incident was sorted. 'Yeah it's all good. How's my family?'

'They are absolutely fine. Doing well, actually. Your sister wanted me to tell you that she got into medical school.'

The first genuine smile in weeks spread across his face. 'Really, that's great. Please tell her I'm really proud of her.'

'I will.'

'You, er, said you had news.'

'Not good, I'm afraid. A gang war has broken out in Sydney. It hasn't been released to the press yet but Eddie Marshall was murdered yesterday in his cell.'

Gavin closed his eyes and breathed deep. He could almost hear the sound of his own heartbeat.

'Are you okay?'

'His brother will blame me, won't he?'

'That's the other thing. Unfortunately, at the moment Eddie's brother is off our radar. I'm sure we'll relocate him soon. But since the incident, he's kind of disappeared. For this reason, I might be getting in touch with you more often, if you don't mind. Just to make sure you're okay.'

Gavin opened his eyes, rubbing his temple with tired, weary hands. 'Yeah, yeah, that's fine.'

'Look,' Janet said sympathetically, 'I know I've mentioned this since the beginning and you keep on turning me down, but we can provide you with therapy if you need to speak to someone.'

'No.' Gavin's tone was adamant. 'I can assure you that won't be necessary. I'm trying to keep my life as normal as possible.'

'And so you should.' The voice of his case officer was both soothing and unhelpful. 'It's the first aim for any participant in the Witness Protection Program.'

Chapter 10

Her clash with Gavin that morning pretty much fit with the rest of her day. It was definitely shaping up to be a bad one.

First up was a phone call from Dan's safety manager, Frank, to set a date for the audit. Having met the guy once before, she knew he was painful. She hadn't expected him to be quite so rude and short with her, though. He was all too happy to reveal his intentions, however, as their conversation came to a close.

'Just thought you should know that Neil was a good friend of mine. We went to uni together. I hope you can live up to his standards.'

She had a feeling the standards he was going to set had nothing to do with Neil's ability. Frank blamed her for his buddy's sacking and he was going to let her know about it during the audit.

Fantastic.

Her records couldn't just be clean. They had to be perfect.

She slowly replaced the receiver, chewing on her lower lip like it was a strip of dried jerky. Good thing she had a meeting with Carl that morning. In fact, she'd been on her way to this meeting when Gavin had done his usual 'suck the wind out of her sails' routine.

This time, more than usual. He'd seemed to be trying to tell her something but couldn't bring himself to. Frankly, she was over it and had tried to tell him so, but if anything it seemed to have made things worse. Gavin wasn't at all inclined to stop commenting on her personal business, give up Yabber's address without dinner or quit flirting with her.

She didn't like the way she always seemed to be in his cross-hairs, like he was keeping an eye on her or something. He wasn't like the other guys on site who heckled her. At times, there seemed to be more behind his words than just games but she could never be absolutely sure.

If only the man were a little uglier. It would just make him so much easier to deal with.

On this thought, she went to Carl with a stack of questions under her arm. They spoke for a good couple of hours. As it turned out, between 'fuck this and fuck that', Carl was very helpful. Even pointing her in a few directions she hadn't thought to look.

'He'll be checking everything, including individual people. Make sure everyone's licences and verification of competency tests are up to scratch. I don't want no fuckin' crane drivers being pulled off the job because they haven't been tested.'

'I'm on it, Carl.'

'And another thing, check we've got resumes for all the engineers.'

'Done that already.' She paused. 'The only person we haven't got a resume for is you.'

'Fuck! All right, I'll put my credentials together.'

They cut the meeting short so that he could go off and do this and she could finish off her changes to the engineering method statements. Unfortunately, she got stuck and needed to talk to Fish. Perhaps it was fate that intervened, or some other divine mystical power, otherwise she never would have gone out to the wharf that morning.

Sharon seemed reluctant to take her too. 'Don't you have a meeting with Carl or something?' she asked.

Wendy shrugged. 'It got cut short.'

'But surely you've got a heap of stuff you need to get on with in the office with the audit coming up.'

Wendy eyed her cautiously. 'I do but I need to see Fish.'

Like someone had just rung the death knell over her head, Sharon grimly slipped the bus into gear and faced forwards. 'All right. Hop on.'

Wendy boarded the bus, clutching her notes to her chest, wondering what on earth was going on at the end of the wharf that nobody wanted her to see. She couldn't help feeling just a little hurt too. Sharon was supposed to be her friend. She didn't think she'd be fighting this safety war with her as well.

Was no one on her side?

At first glance, nothing seemed to be out of the ordinary when the bus pulled into its usual bay beside a small donga office. The pile hammer was going, so she put two foam ear plugs into her ears before alighting from the bus.

BANG! BANG! BANG!

The sound of metal crashing on metal pounded her ear drums. She stepped out of the vehicle onto the trembling deck and several guys turned around and looked at her in horror before scurrying off like rats in a fire.

Something was definitely up.

She saw Gavin standing off to one side, talking sternly to one of his men. She vaguely knew his name . . . Marvin, was it? They appeared to be arguing about something but that wasn't her priority right then. She walked towards the railing to examine Gavin's piling barge. As she drew nearer, she could see the weight inside the hammer sleeve moving up and down as it powered the pile it was holding into the sea bed.

What was wrong with this picture?

'Wendy!' She felt a hand on her arm. But it was too late. She'd already looked down and seen what they'd been trying to hide from her. The blood went straight to her head as she yanked her arm out of Gavin's hold and spun around to face him. 'Stop that pile hammer *now*!'

To give him some credit, Gavin acted quickly and without protest. He grabbed the two-way radio receiver that hung over his shoulder and spoke.

'Stop the hammer. Over.'

'Okay, boss. Over.'

The hammer ceased.

Wendy took deep calming breaths as she watched the fishing boat she had only just managed to avoid boarding the day before bobbing on the waves a few metres from the pile they were driving. Fish, with all the gall of a man still in the thrall of his own genius, was busy scooping up stunned fish from the surface of the waves with a long armed net.

'How could you be so stupid?' Wendy whispered, not even daring to look up, the disappointment she felt was so deep.

'Wendy, I'm sorry.'

'Don't give me that!' She turned on Gavin like a hungry banshee. 'This is just the kind of schoolboy mentality I expected from you.'

Suddenly his mobile buzzed and he reached into his pocket and put it to his ear. 'No, Fish,' he responded tightly, 'the hammer has stopped because you've been made. No, I'm not kidding.'

'Tell him to get that boat to shore immediately and then meet me at Carl's office.'

Gavin nodded.

'And, Gavin, I want you there too.'

He nodded again.

Turning around, she was horrified to see Dan Hullog striding across the deck – just when she couldn't imagine things getting any worse. Deciding to face the music head on, she went forwards to meet him.

'What the hell is going on here?' he demanded as soon as she was within earshot. 'Is there a fishing boat down there?'

Her insides squirmed in humiliation. She glanced back at Gavin, who was still on his phone talking rapidly into the receiver. To her disgust, it looked like Fish needed some persuading to abandon his project.

'Answer me.' Dan's voice was brusque and stern like the tone of her boarding school's headmistress only much, much worse. 'Did that meeting we had last week mean *nothing* to you? I thought you were going to aid me in keeping Barnes Inc on track. Not watch idly as they break every rule in the book!'

She lifted her chin. 'I haven't been watching *idly*. I just got here.'

'And I guess that was only by lucky chance,' he retorted.

She clenched her jaw against the unfairness of it all, but couldn't resist just a hint of sarcasm. 'Yes, it was remiss of me not to put out the memo on "No fishing next to piles that are being driven".'

'This is not a joke!' He closed his eyes and rubbed his temple between thumb and forefinger. 'I think Barnes Inc has issued enough warnings to its people. You need to start taking some disciplinary action. I want to see these buffoons made an example of.'

'I will do my best, sir.'

'Make sure your best gets me results,' he fired at her, making her straight shoulders almost waver.

Almost.

'Tell Carl I'll be ringing him this afternoon to find out what's been done about this. Do you understand me?'

'Perfectly.' Gavin and Fish had as good as lost their jobs. What an absolute waste and all for a free lunch. What were they thinking?

Dan nodded roughly and then walked off.

'Wendy.'

She turned around to find Gavin watching Dan's retreating back, his brows drawn together over his dark eyes. 'Was he laying into you?'

She snorted. 'With good reason.'

'This isn't your fault.'

'Well you're right about that.' Her voice cracked. 'I'm not the one who's going to take the fall for it, am I?'

As much as she believed in her job and the fact that this was probably a fate that Gavin deserved . . . she did not want to see the man get fired. All the same she couldn't protect him. The question was, did she really want to? She had protected a man in the past and look where that had got her. Her best bet was to let Carl and Dan take control of the situation. She gripped her fingers together as though applying restraint.

I can't save him.

She looked up at his handsome face, still trained on Bulldog's back. A breeze made the collar of his shirt flick, though his broad shoulders remained stiff and unwavering.

He did a bad thing. He deserves what's coming to him.

His gaze returned to hers. 'Don't worry. I'll be fine. Let's go inform Carl and get this over with.'

She didn't know why he was reassuring her when he was the one about to stand in front of the firing squad. Without waiting for her, he led the way back to the bus.

'What's going on?' Sharon was still sitting in the driver's seat, nervously munching on a muesli bar.

'The fishing boat was discovered, not just by me but by Bulldog too,' Wendy sighed. 'But you'd guessed that already, hadn't you?'

Sharon choked on her bar. 'Look, Wendy –'

Wendy held up her hands. 'Don't say anything, Sharon. I wouldn't want you to incriminate yourself.'

Sharon's face lost colour. 'I didn't mean –'

'Sharon,' Gavin said warningly and then added, 'We need you to take the bus back now. We've got to see Carl ASAP.'

'Is anyone hurt?' Sharon asked in a small voice.

Wendy shook her head.

Luckily, the bus driver said nothing more and started the bus. There was no one on board but the three of them. They travelled in silence; the tension in the air was almost loud enough to create static.

When they arrived back at the Barnes Inc office dongas, Carl was not in his office and had to be summoned immediately. Fish had not arrived either. So Wendy and Gavin spent another excruciating twenty-five minutes waiting. At first they did not talk.

Gavin sat down in one of Carl's visitor's chairs, laced his fingers together, legs stretched out in front of him crossed at the ankles. She, on the other hand, paced the room like a jungle cat at the zoo.

How could he be so relaxed? Carl was going to be furious! Would he get notice when he was let go?

She had no idea.

How was Chub going to find two new engineers to replace them? It would take ages. Time they didn't have. They were going to fall further behind. Her name was going to be mud. Another two sackings to blame on the TCN spy. Gavin and Fish were well liked.

She was like stinky blue cheese on a perfume counter. Who would believe the decision had been out of her hands?

'Wendy, *sit down*.' The low timbre of his masculine voice plucked her last nerve.

She turned on him like a rattlesnake. 'What's wrong with you? Don't you care about your job? Why would you take a risk like that? It's ludicrous, senseless, just . . . completely dumb. And don't give me that look because I know you're smarter than you make out.'

'Your confidence in me is very reassuring,' he murmured.

'Urgh!' She put her hands on her hips as she paced. 'Take some bloody responsibility. Don't you care about your staff? The safety of your men?'

His mouth twisted as though he were mocking himself. 'My men, of course, come first. After all, I'd be no one without them. As for my job . . .' He paused. 'It means a lot to me . . . Keeps me sane.'

She stopped pacing, looking down on his deckchair-posed body with all the frustration of an artist studying a difficult subject. 'Then what are you going to do when you lose it?'

His face had that expression Wendy was beginning to recognise as the mask he used to cover up his real feelings. That 'chill out, sweetheart' eyebrow tilt and cocky 'what happens will happen' smile.

'There's a mining boom on and a shortage of engineers.' His tone was confident. 'It's not like people haven't already been trying to poach me, Sarge.'

'Oh, for goodness' sake, Gavin. It's a lot to risk for a dare or a bit of fun.'

He looked away, ignoring the statement. 'Don't worry if we don't have time for that dinner. I'll give you Yabber's address before I leave.'

She gaped at him. 'Why on earth would you think that's what I'm worried about?'

'Isn't it?' His head angled curiously at her as though he were momentarily distracted. 'It seemed like a pretty big deal last time we spoke about it. Like this guy has some kind of hold on you. You're not in trouble, are you? You can tell me.'

'*For crying out loud!*' She threw up her hands. Of all the bloody things to be asking when *he* was sitting in the manager's office about to be given the axe. 'This is not about me!' she flung at him. 'This is about you.'

Just then, the door burst open and Carl came storming in from the fray, his red face spoiling for a fight. He whipped off his hard hat and hung it roughly on the hook by the door. Gavin uncrossed his feet and sat up.

'What the fuck were you *thinking*, Gav?' Carl's eyes bulged from their sockets as he scanned the room. 'And where the fuck is Fish?'

'Here.' The sulky-looking ocean hunter had arrived seconds after him and was standing in the doorway. His chin came up defiantly when all eyes turned in his direction.

Carl jabbed his pointer finger at him. 'I've put up with you fuckin' off to your nets at lunchtime and buying bait during fuckin' smoko. I've even put up with you stinking up my fuckin' utes with your nightly fishing expeditions. But this time, you've gone too far!'

'Carl –' Fish began.

'Shut the fuck up! Just because we're mates, doesn't give you the right to fuckin' take advantage of me.'

'That wasn't what I was doing.'

'Then what the fuck do you call it?'

'It was harmless, Carl.' Fish reddened, closing the door behind him and advancing further into the room. Clearly realising that if he stood in the doorway he was making the entire office privy to this conversation, which was going much worse for him than he had expected it would.

'Harmless!' Carl barked. 'What if your boat had rammed into the pile because of the vibration in the water? What then?'

'I had complete control of the boat.' Fish straightened his shoulders. 'I ain't an idiot. Besides, no one was hurt.'

'That ain't the fuckin' point!' Carl slammed a fist into his palm. 'You can't just say, well fuck, I got away with it, so it's okay.'

'That's not what I –'

'We're trying to pass a fuckin' audit here! And you!' Carl turned on Gavin like a panther that had discovered a second chicken in his cage. 'You, I don't understand at all! How could you agree to this? Were you out of your fuckin' mind?'

Wendy could see Gavin's face close as though blinds were being pulled down before he opened his mouth to speak. 'Yes.'

That's it!

It was the only syllable he uttered by way of explanation and even Carl found it grossly inadequate.

'What the fuck?'

'Gavin,' Fish began desperately, addressing the piling engineer rather than Carl, 'you know that –'

'I knew what I was doing.' Gavin pinned Fish to the wall with his glare, cutting off in the process the other man's ability to speak. 'As I know what I'm doing now.'

'All we can fuckin' hope for is that Bulldog doesn't find out about this.' Carl marched to his desk, defeat written all over his face as he sat down. 'Fuckin' fat chance of that happening.'

'Er . . . Carl.' Wendy finally decided to speak up. 'He . . . er . . . he was there.'

Carl's face swung to hers as though he had just realised for the first time that she was present. And then, with absolute dejection, he dropped his head. It hit the desk with a bang. 'Oh, fuck!'

She swallowed. 'He wants this matter dealt with firmly.'

Carl swivelled his head to look at her, opening one eye just a crack. 'Of course he does. He wants their jobs, doesn't he? Very well. Fish, you're fired. Gavin, you're off with a warning. Wendy, inform the bastard and let's have done with this shit.'

Fish gasped in shock. 'You can't fire me. I'm your best friend.'

'Not today you ain't,' Carl grunted. 'And you'll have to move out of the camp too. You can't stay there if you ain't working on this fucked-up job. So you better make yourself some fuckin' plans.'

'But –'

'This far, none of your excuses have given me any cause to spare you.' Carl waved his hand. 'So don't fuckin' try to persuade me to give you another chance. It ain't happenin'.'

'I wasn't going to,' Fish replied sullenly. 'I was just going to ask . . . ' He paused, embarrassment clearly stunting his words.

Carl's eyes rounded madly. '*What?*'

'Could I stay with you for a few days – just till I'm back on my feet . . . ?'

'Of all the fuckin' –' Then Carl closed his eyes and gave up. 'Fine. Now fuck off the lot of you!'

What about Gavin? Wendy thought indignantly. He hadn't even tried to excuse his behaviour and just gets let off, scot free. It seemed incredibly unfair.

Fish opened his mouth to say something further and shut it again before yanking open the door to Carl's office and stalking out. Gavin rose slowly to his feet, shoving both hands deep into the pockets of his Hard Yakka pants.

'Listen, Carl, I was fully prepared to –'

Carl eyed him with contempt. 'Do you think I'm fuckin' stupid?'

'No, I –'

'Then fuck off!'

'But –'

'Next time you want to play hero, do it in your own fuckin' time.' Carl pointed at the door. 'Out!'

'Yes, sir.' Gavin turned and winked at Wendy. 'Guess dinner's back on, sweetheart.'

Her eyes widened as he turned and walked out, head held high, unscathed and untouched by what was supposed to have been the execution yard.

'What the fuck are you still doing here?' Carl demanded, and she pulled her gaze from Gavin and returned them to her manager.

'I, er, mean no disrespect, Carl. But do you think that was fair? Firing Fish but not Gavin when they were equally to blame.'

Carl snorted. 'Believe me, they weren't equally to blame. I wasn't about to screw up Gavin's life just because he decides to go all noble on my arse.'

'Noble?' Wendy repeated.

'You didn't fuckin' see that?' Carl waved his pointer finger to and fro in obvious surprise.

'See what?'

Carl shrugged. 'He was fuckin' protecting someone. I know Gavin: he's an arrogant bastard sometimes but he's loyal and he ain't gunna rat anyone out, particularly if he feels they don't deserve it.'

'So you're not even going to bother asking him?' Wendy demanded.

'His men love him. If they need to tell me who it was responsible, they will. It sure wasn't Gavin. Now is not the time to –' He shook his head. 'Look, never mind. Just tell fuckin' Bulldog that the ring leader has been dealt with and nothing like this will ever happen again.'

'What if he asks about Gavin?'

'Then tell him to fuck off, I don't care. It's time to move on. Now if you don't mind . . .'

She knew she'd reached the end of Carl's very limited patience, and nodded before hastily letting herself out. The outcome of the event didn't quite sit well with her, however. She didn't know how to feel about it.

Relieved.

Indignant.

Scammed.

Even if Gavin had been protecting someone, shouldn't they find out who that was and bring him to justice? She'd seen firsthand that feeling pity for people who did bad things didn't help them. It just made things worse.

'Hey, little mate, you're looking decidedly grumpy,' said Chub when she stormed back into their donga office.

'Hi, Cobber, just had the morning from hell is all. You're going to have to hire another deck engineer. Carl just fired Fish.'

'What?' Chub groaned. 'Do you know how hard it is to source a good engineer from Perth these days, especially to work out here? They're as scarce as hen's teeth.'

'So I've been told.' Wendy's lips pursed together as she remembered Gavin's overconfident remarks to her back in Carl's office.

'You know,' Chub broke into her thoughts, 'that's the second person you've had fired in just over a fortnight.'

She put her head in her hands. 'Would it help if I said I wasn't doing it on purpose?'

Chub winced. 'It's not me you have to convince. It's the rest of the site.'

However, persuading her co-workers was not actually that high on her list of things to do. She had a Bulldog to pacify, an audit to get through and, God help her, a date with Mr Subterfuge himself on the horizon.

The week blazed past in a plethora of meetings, milestones and mayhem. For starters, Wendy called the first meeting of the CMT, or Cyclone Management Team. They were short a member now because Fish had been fired, but Chub assured her that he and Carl were pulling a few strings with head office to get a new deck engineer as quickly as possible. The new man would replace Fish on the CMT as well.

This was the first announcement she made at the meeting, which comprised herself, Gavin, Lena, Carl and Chub. They all seemed to accept this information without question. She didn't think her second announcement, however, would be met with such easy approval.

'Now I know you guys might think that your roles in this only come into play in the event of a cyclone. But it's not true. There are some things you will need to set from now.'

There was no outburst about time deficiency or the usual communal groan, just an expectant silence. As she looked around this tight-knit little group she realised that she had not founded just a CMT but also a group of possible allies whom she might be able to count on in the future.

'Wendy, I have a question.' It was Lena. The young woman had raised her hand, which made Wendy smile. She could get used to this politeness.

'Go ahead.'

'I've heard around the traps that the camp dongas are only rated for a category-three cyclone. So, if we have a category four or five where do the troops go to wait it out?'

'Well,' Wendy nodded, 'that's actually one of the things I wanted to discuss with you guys. The reception and mess building is a permanent building but, as you all know, it's also about fifty years old. It was formerly a motel or something. A lot of it is pretty rundown. Although I think it is safer than the dongas, I wouldn't be confident putting any kind of cyclone rating on it.'

'So what do we do, Sarge?' Gavin asked. 'Fly everyone home?'

He was looking at her with respect, which warmed her just as much as his most flirtatious smile.

'There may not be enough time or enough planes. Airports can shut down at a moment's notice. We can't rely on them to stay open and functioning for as long as we'd need them.'

After a bit more discussion, it was decided that they would have to approach the Shire of Roebourne to organise an evacuation building their men could wait out the storm in. The shire might be able to suggest a school or community hall in Karratha that would be willing to function as a safe house should the need arise. Chub was put in charge of handling the details. In the meantime, Wendy spoke about running some practice evacuation drills with the engineers. There was absolutely no argument.

She was pleasantly surprised. Perhaps somewhere along the way, when she hadn't been looking, management staff had begun to notice that the work she was doing was actually worth something. Maybe it was the upcoming audit; maybe it was the fact that she'd put in more road signs, more bins and more memos on the notice boards than Neil had ever done. Or maybe, and this was what she hoped, the men actually felt safer under her watchful eye and frequent inspections. She didn't know. But they certainly seemed to have grown some faith in her since she'd started.

The knowledge buoyed her confidence and remained with her for a couple of days. Then, along with Chub, she started the safety induction sessions for the rest of the staff. And things went downhill from there.

They tried to focus these mini-seminars on preparation for cyclone season, which started in November. Given it was already mid October, the timing wasn't a moment too soon.

There was so much the guys needed to know, especially in terms of cyclone categories and warning systems. How to secure or batten down loose material, how to park their utes, when to evacuate, how to pack an emergency kit.

The list went on.

The boys were sulky at best when summoned to sit in what was usually their smoko donga for a few hours. She could tell they were sick of her after the first half hour and were just itching to get back to their posts. The smell of the room was also less than aromatic. She couldn't help but wonder if these guys washed their clothes every day. The donga stank of sweat, feet and smokers' breath. By the end of each session, she was also dying to get out for some fresh air.

Keeping her promise to Chub, she had teatime mid-morning. After one of these breaks, she came back to the donga to find that someone had graffitied her hard hat, which she'd left on the desk. They'd used the whiteboard marker to draw the blue checks often seen on white police cars back in the city. Obviously, it was some sort of crack at both her and her nickname. So the pranks weren't finished yet, were they?

Despite all her bravado, all this unnecessary resistance was starting to get to her. *How do I get them on side the way I have with upper management?* No answers immediately presented themselves.

Ignoring her hard hat, much to the chagrin of the group, who were obviously hanging out for a reaction, she continued with the lesson. The seminar ended just before lunch. She thanked them for their attendance, picked up her hard hat, put it on and walked out. As she was closing the door behind her she heard the room erupt in laughter, and some guy comment jovially, 'I thought I saw steam coming from the Sergeant's ears when she saw that hat. She's got great self-control on her, don't she?'

'You just watch yourself, mate,' a friend warned him. 'Or she'll take you out like she did Fish and Neil.'

With a sigh, Wendy stepped away from the door.

She walked back to her office where unfortunately Chub wasn't waiting for her. Taking off the hat, she turned it over in her hands. What should she do? Scrub this off, throw it out, get a new hat?

No, she'd wear it. And wear it proudly. It would be what they would least expect from her. If their prank had no effect then maybe they would give up.

Wendy was starving when she walked into the mess Friday evening for dinner. She was grateful to see both Sharon and Lena sitting at a trestle table near the buffet. Their conversation seemed to be fast and good-humoured when Wendy went to join them. Apparently, Sharon was having a few teething problems in her new home, especially concerning her new roommate, Fish.

Lena covered her smiling mouth with her hands. 'Oh no! Is three a crowd?'

'Oh *yes*,' Sharon groaned. 'But how come it's me feeling like the third wheel?'

Lena shook her head. 'Fish must be a real treat to live with.'

'Honey, he's sunshine on a cloudy day.' Sharon's tone was so rich with sarcasm that Wendy and Lena had to laugh.

'Is he at least looking for another job?' Wendy enquired.

'He's too busy fishing!' Sharon forked a piece of beef into her mouth with disgust. 'I'm sick of living in a house that smells like a fish market. Did you know, every night he comes home and guts his fish in my sink so he can freeze them. But he doesn't clean up. He just goes straight to bed. We get up in the morning to have breakfast and there's fish entrails still on the kitchen bench.'

Wendy gasped. 'Oh, that's gross.'

'Tell me about it. I mean, he cleans it up while we're at work. But I'd prefer not to have to wake up to it every morning.'

'Yuck!' Lena agreed.

To Wendy's surprise, Sharon turned to her and said, 'I suppose you think I got my just deserts.'

'What do you mean?'

'I know you think I was protecting Fish *that day*. But I wasn't. I was protecting Gavin.'

Wendy tried not to let her interest show. 'It's water under the bridge, or should I say under the wharf.'

'I don't want you to think that my loyalties are divided against you. I was the one who told Gavin to get in his ute and get on the wharf because Fish was up to no good. I didn't want him to get into trouble for not trying to stop things.'

Wendy's expression softened. 'You don't need to apologise to me, Sharon. I don't blame you for anything.'

Although Sharon didn't quite seem to buy this, she let it go.

That evening when Wendy was walking back to her donga she happened to see Gavin sitting on his own porch, beer in hand, talking to one of the men in his team. The man, Marvin again, was putting a carton of beer down at the base of Gavin's step. Gavin was shaking his head as if to decline. But his man seemed to insist before abruptly taking his leave. Feeling someone's eyes on him, Gavin looked up.

Wendy averted her gaze guiltily.

'Hey, Sarge, you wanna beer?'

Damn! 'No thanks.'

'You sure? I got plenty.'

'That much is obvious.'

'What's got you riled up this time?' He left his donga and fell in beside her as she continued to walk towards her own.

'Don't you think I know what payment for services rendered looks like when I see it?'

'Come on, Wendy, it's not like that.'

She stopped walking. 'You know, you better be careful. Even if your intentions are honourable, theirs aren't always. You will be sorry you did this.'

'Look, I know where you're coming from. Sometimes the actions we take can have repercussions that seem to last a lifetime. But other times you just need to go with your gut. This is one of those times.'

'You know what?' She threw her hands in the air. 'Don't worry about it. You're going to do whatever you want anyway.'

His voice seemed thoughtful. 'You don't trust anyone, do you? Who betrayed you? Was it a guy?'

I wish.

She glared at him. 'Didn't your mother ever tell you off for being too nosey?!'

'Nah,' he grinned. 'She thought my inquisitive nature was cute. I guess it doesn't work on you, huh?'

Gavin, cute? His personality was too potent to be cute.

She closed her eyes and willed her hormones to take a load off. What was it about this guy that unsettled her so much? She was usually such a controlled person. Her temper wasn't something she just lost at the drop of a hat.

For goodness' sake, change the subject.

Her eyes flew open to find him studying her mischievously and she asked him in her driest most no-nonsense tone, 'Are we still on for dinner tomorrow?'

'You betcha, Sarge. Meet me in the car park at seven. I'm driving.'

'But I was going to –'

He toasted her with his stubby before strolling off, as confident as ever that she would just go with his flow.

What choice do I have?

She let out a long breath, unable to decide what it was about him she found more annoying – the way he called her 'Sarge' with that cheeky grin of his or the undeniable zing that went up her spine every time he did so.

Despite the fact that it definitely *wasn't* a date, Wendy took at least an hour to decide what she was wearing that night. And then, having made the decision, reverted to her first choice, which she had previously dismissed as being too dressy. A white cotton skirt with a small lace trim on the hem, a sleeveless, V-necked pale blue top that fitted snugly over her breasts and curved outward where her waist met her hips. She had been going to pair this same top with her jeans. But after being in pants all day and with the warmness of the weather, she couldn't resist the skirt.

As promised she met Gavin in the car park. It was unfortunate that several other blokes on the way out from the gym also noticed her standing there waiting for him. They gave her a whistle.

'Hey, the Sergeant cleans up all right. You going somewhere, darlin'?'

'Nowhere special,' she murmured, but for the most part averted her eyes to discourage them from joining her. The youngest of them looked like he wanted to do so until Gavin came striding across the gravel.

She never thought she'd be grateful to see him nor that he too would have made an effort. A printed blue-and-white collared shirt and dark blue jeans that looked like the cleanest clothes she'd ever seen on him, or indeed on anyone in the outback, set off his manly physique. His hair was still wet from his shower, his brown locks curling over his ears in a way that made her fingers itch to smooth them. In a word, he looked delicious.

'What are you boys doing chatting up my date?' he scolded, making her cringe.

'It's not a date,' she made haste to inform the other guys, whose eyes roved from him to her with obvious interest. 'I'm just paying for his dinner.'

They laughed and she cringed again, this time at the ridiculousness of her own explanation.

'Sounds like a date to me.' One of them rubbed his prickly chin. 'A good one too, if the woman's paying. How'd you get her to do that, Gav?'

Gavin's lips twisted. 'Wouldn't you like to know?'

'Yeah, I would. That's why I'm asking,' the man persisted.

Gavin chuckled, jerking his thumb over his shoulder. 'Nick off.'

Wicked laughs faded as the group complied with his request.

'Wow,' Wendy commented, 'you've really got a way with words.'

'Thanks.' He grinned, unperturbed. 'Shall we go? My ute's parked right over there.'

'Listen,' she wrung her hands, 'wasn't I supposed to drive? I mean, I'm the one taking you out. That was the deal, right?'

'You seriously want to take all the fun out of this?' He raised his eyebrows. 'Come on, Sarge. What are you scared of? That you might have a good time?'

'I just think that . . .' She licked her lips. 'That wasn't the deal.'

'Well, I'm changing the deal.' Without her consent he took her hand. Large warm fingers closed around her smaller, more finely boned ones and tugged. He turned and started walking to his vehicle, unconcerned that she was tripping over her feet as she tried to keep up with him. Warmth spread up her arm and encased her heart.

Maybe I'll just go along with it. Just this one time.

'Okay,' she found herself saying. 'But I'll pay. Lena was telling me about this resort that she went to in Karratha –'

He grimaced. 'I know the one.'

'Yeah so, I thought –'

'The thing is,' he explained as he opened the passenger door of his vehicle so she could get in, 'I'm not going to let you take me off to some clinical run-of-the-mill restaurant in Karratha that you could probably find just about anywhere in the world so that you can hand over your credit card and pay for my information like I'm some sort of CI to your Sergeant.'

'CI?' she said indignantly, turning around.

'Confidential Informant.' He leaned over her.

'I know what a CI is.' She pursed her lips together, uncomfortable with his sudden closeness.

'It'll be much more fun to shell prawns under the stars, don't you think?' He grabbed her around the waist with two hands and lifted her bodily into the ute. Wendy had never fancied herself a featherweight. In fact, with her height and stature she definitely did not consider herself one of those waif-like women who looked like they would float away with the breeze if you blew on them. But one minute she was standing on gravel and the next she was sitting in his car. He grinned at her, not a puff or a pant on his lips. The deed had been effortless and now he was offering her the seat belt.

'Remember,' he winked, 'safety first.'

Oooooh! Her fingers twitched in her lap. She could easily slap him again. With iron will she restrained herself and snatched the belt instead. She could not resort to violence *every time* he disconcerted her.

After clipping the belt in place, she turned back to give him a stern piece of her mind but found the door slammed in her face. He was walking around the car to get in his seat. Frustration bubbled up her throat.

He didn't seem to notice. 'You'll love it,' he assured her as he started the engine. 'You haven't experienced seafood until you've had a meal at the Point Samson Yacht Club.'

'How would you know what I love? You don't even know me,' she said.

'Isn't that the point of this?' He reversed his car out of the bay and then rolled out of the car park.

'No.' She folded her arms. 'This isn't about getting to know one another. This is about Yabber and that address I need.'

'*Right*. Momentarily forgot.' He inclined his head. 'Won't happen again. So tell me about you. What makes Wendy Hopkins tick?'

'*Gavin*,' she said, half laugh, half groan.

'Wow, I love it when you say my name like that. And do I really make you tick?'

She rolled her eyes and looked heavenwards as though appealing to a higher power. 'I feel like I'm negotiating with a two-year-old here.'

'You can't blame a man for trying.'

'Oh yes you can.' She shook her head. 'I blame you.'

'Just like you blame me for the fishing-boat incident?' he asked, suddenly serious.

She sighed. 'No, actually I don't. I've kind of put two and two together since then. And while I don't approve, I don't hold it against you.'

He seemed to accept this. 'I have to say, that's good to know.'

'I know you think taking the blame for something you didn't do is very noble but don't you think it just exacerbates the problem?'

He took his eyes off the road briefly to look at her. 'You really need blood on this, don't you?'

'I need to make sure this site stays safe and having loose cannons walking around on the job makes me uneasy,' she shot at him.

His fingers gripped the steering wheel hard and then relaxed. 'Haven't you ever done something stupid that you wish you could just undo, start over, have a second chance at?'

'Don't you get it?' she sighed. '*This* is my second chance. And this time I don't want to do it wrong.'

'Oh.' He drew out the word. 'You're starting to make a bit more sense. So what was your big stuff-up?'

Her mouth pulled into a line as she looked out the window at the surrounding bush. She didn't need to tell him. But for some reason she wanted to. 'The last job I worked on there was this guy called Adam Booth. I knew he was an alcoholic and that he was often impaired on the job. I decided to take the issue to the project manager to have him fired.'

'And . . .' Gavin prompted.

She looked at her hands. 'He caught me before I managed to and hit me up with the wife-three-kids-and-a-mortgage guilt trip. He said he knew he had a problem and was on top of it. In fact, he had a sponsor and had been sober for a couple of days. He said he could only see himself getting better. Basically he begged me for a second chance.'

'And you gave it to him,' Gavin said softly. 'Why do I feel like this does not have a happy ending? The mutt didn't kill himself, did he?'

She bit her lip. 'He might as well have. He's a paraplegic now after falling off some scaffolding because he was half-cut a couple of weeks later. I was stupid to have believed him. You don't recover from something like that in a matter of days. It takes months, years!'

'That's true.'

'When I think about it,' she swallowed, 'I didn't just put him at risk. I put everyone on the job at risk. I still haven't forgiven myself for it. And I doubt his wife and three kids have either.'

He was silent for a moment. 'You had good intentions. You thought you were being kind. No one can blame you for that.'

'I can think of one person.' Her smile was bittersweet. 'So you see, that's why I can't afford to be lenient. I can't afford to just let people get away with things this time.' She turned back to meet his eyes. 'It's for their own good.'

He was silent for a moment. 'All right. I wasn't going to tell you, but I guess the full story might help you feel a little better about my situation. Do you want me to tell you what really happened that day Fish got fired?'

She hesitated, not wanting to admit to him exactly how damned curious she really was. But he didn't wait for a response, seeming to sense her mood anyway.

'Marvin, the guy who was actually there when Fish rocked up with his boat, is my new site supervisor. He replaced Yabber. I was in a meeting when Fish asked him to keep piling while he pulled the fish into his boat. This is Marvin's first job as a site supervisor and he's very keen to be liked. Everybody misses Yabber, he was such a character around here. Such a familiar face. I guess Marvin doubts the respect the boys have for him and wanted to lift his profile a little. Plus,' he frowned, 'Fish said that I was okay with it.'

'That still doesn't explain why you were so willing to take the blame.'

'Well,' Gavin shrugged, 'I wasn't exactly blameless, was I? To be honest, I knew that Fish was thinking about pulling a stunt like that; I just didn't know when. And I'd told Marvin only hours earlier to trust himself and me more. So you see, he's not dangerous or unskilled. He was just misinformed. It's my job as his manager to make sure that doesn't happen again and that the boys start toeing the line. You can rest easy, I'm definitely on it. Besides,' his smile was rueful, 'I couldn't let him get the sack for something that was partially my fault. Marvin's got a family and a mortgage too. What have I got?'

'I don't know. What have you got?' She turned and looked at him.

His mouth twisted and for a moment she thought he seemed a little philosophical but as quickly as the expression appeared, it was gone. 'I'm a very lucky guy. What I've got is freedom.' He grinned at her. But there was a hollowness in that grin that she was beginning to recognise. Considering his championship of the family, it seemed odd that he didn't want one of his own.

'Not looking to settle down,' she enquired slowly. 'Get married? Have a family?'

'Hold on there, Sarge.' He glanced at her archly. 'Are you proposing?'

'*No*,' came her gasp of frustration. 'Of course not.'

'Oh good.' He winked at her. 'Don't get me wrong. I love the company of women. But I'm not into that whole commitment thing, if you know what I mean.'

'How thoughtful of you to tell me,' she observed cynically.

'What is it with women and honesty? They want you to tell them the truth but when you do, they don't like it. What's a guy supposed to do?'

She laughed. 'Most of them lie.'

He pulled into a dark parking lot and turned to face her. 'You want me to lie to you, Sarge?' Those deep brown eyes were her undoing.

All of a sudden the cabin was too small, the evening too dark and the space between them much too scarce. Gavin Jones was a dangerous man. And what was worse, he freely admitted it.

'No.' Her voice sounded pathetically small. So much so that she immediately straightened her shoulders and tossed her head. 'Come on. Let's get this over with.'

And then opening her door, she jumped out herself this time.

Chapter 11

Wendy finally took a moment to take stock of her surroundings. Gavin had not taken her to some fancy restaurant in Karratha, that was for sure. The venue was nothing like any typical yacht club back in Perth. She squinted in the dark to make out what she could of the building, lit up from inside and by small spotlights outside. It was better described as a shack, sitting on red dirt in the middle of nowhere. An old sailing mast was shoved into the ground beside it.

'Welcome to the Point Samson Yacht Club.' Gavin waved his right arm before them.

As they approached the building, Wendy was able to tell that it was quite a popular little joint. The smell of fried fish and lemons filled her nostrils. She and Gavin looked around at the other guests, already tucking into platefuls of seafood, and at the people sitting in the alfresco area on wooden benches at wooden tables. They were attacking prawns, tucking into all sorts of shellfish, some she'd never seen before, and of course devouring the usual fillets of grilled or fried fish with chunky fries and overflowing salad bowls.

'Feel like anything in particular?' Gavin asked.

'I don't know,' Wendy murmured. 'It all looks good.'

'Well, I'm dying for some prawns. Shall I get us a bowl?'

'No, I'll get it.' She took her purse out.

'No, you will not.' He shook his head. 'Go sit down outside.'

He left her before she could protest. She glanced helplessly in the direction he had indicated. There was only one table left and it was far away from the others and not under the patio roofing. Wendy didn't mind though. How lovely to eat under the stars as he had suggested. Of course, she wasn't going to tell him that.

Gavin wasn't long returning. He brought with him a huge bowl of prawns, a bowl of salad and a bowl of chips.

Wendy's mouth watered. 'Wow! That looks like a feast.'

'Doesn't it?' He chuckled and put the food down on the table between them. 'So tell me,' he picked a prawn out of the bowl and ripped its head off, 'more of the story behind Wendy Hopkins.'

'Are we back on that again?' she groaned, munching on a chip.

'Come on.'

'I reckon I've told you enough: your turn.'

His lips twitched. 'Once upon a time there was a handsome prince –'

'Oh brother!' She laughed. 'You're not seriously going to go down that path, are you?'

'Okay . . . Since you aren't impressed, maybe not.'

He'd eaten the first prawn so he shelled another. She continued to nibble on her chip.

He paused and then said slowly, 'For the last five years I've been fly-in/fly-out. Doing a lot of jobs on the Pilbara and in Queensland.'

'You don't get lonely?'

He looked down. 'Sometimes.'

'What about your family? Are they in Perth?'

'No . . . I . . . I haven't seen them in a long time. Pretty much since I started this sort of work.'

'Brothers or sisters?'

He shook his head. 'Your turn.'

'I'm from Perth. No brothers or sisters,' she blushed, adding in a rush, 'that I know of. My parents supported me till I finished university and then I started working fly-in/fly-out pretty much straight away.'

'Seriously?' He gobbled another prawn. 'Not even a short city stint before you went bush?'

After boarding school, working away had been almost what she was used to. But she didn't want to bring up her freaky childhood with him so she let a light smile touch her face. 'I love the outback. Its rugged beauty, its endless expanses. To be honest I enjoy being a nomad, moving from one town to another, one job to another. One adventure to a new one.'

His eyes twinkled. 'Me too.'

They ate in silence and for a spine-tingling few seconds she felt like they were sharing a moment. It was ridiculous really.

'So are you liking this job at Cape Lambert?' he asked, forking a little bit of salad onto his plate.

'It was a rocky start but I think I'm starting to fit in . . .'

'You mean, all the practical jokes and stuff?'

'Among other things.' She cast a sideways glance at him, watching for signs of subterfuge. 'As you know, Ethel gave me that donga that was out of service. But I seem to have got a few mysterious donations.'

He lowered the prawn that was on its way to his mouth. 'What do you mean?'

'I mean, a desk, an air conditioner and a new flyscreen turned up without me or Ethel ordering them. Know anything about that?'

'I wish I did.'

'It doesn't matter.' She waved her hand. 'It would just be nice to thank the person, you know.'

He nodded. 'I'll keep my ears out.'

They ate in silence for a minute or two.

'What about work?' Gavin opened the conversation again. 'Is it what you were expecting?'

She took another chip. 'It's challenging. I mean, I love the work. It's just been hard getting everyone else to buy into my changes.'

He examined the prawn in his hand, as though wondering whether he should say something or not.

She rolled her eyes. 'Go on, everyone else has. I promise I won't get offended. Believe me.' She shook her head. 'I've heard it all before. But then, you know, I didn't take this job because I wanted to be popular.'

He looked up.

'Maybe not, but if you want a man's respect you need to involve him in the process a little.'

She paused to take a carrot, quietly munching as she considered his words. She hated to admit it but he had a point.

He shrugged. 'I'm just saying . . . with every pair of hands, you get a free brain. Might not be a bad plan to see what that's worth, if you know what I mean.'

She watched him closely as though really seeing him for the first time. 'You are absolutely right.'

That gorgeous head of brown hair moved in the gentle breeze and those eyes so dark had her wondering how many layers this man had. Her nerves buzzed as he returned her thoughtful gaze, unsmiling. Not really saying anything, just studying her in the same manner she was studying him.

He frowned. While she was wondering what was displeasing him, he took a prawn out of the bowl and shelled it for her. 'Here.'

'Oh, er, thanks.' She hadn't really intended to eat any prawns: it all looked rather messy. But the intimacy of his gesture raised bumps on her skin and she couldn't say no. Taking the shellfish from his wet fingertips, she bit into it.

Her eyes widened. 'They taste so fresh.'

'You see.' He smiled.

He took another from the bowl and shelled it for her, looking at her again in a way that made her insides squirm.

'You got something weighing on your mind, Sarge?'

She had a lot of things weighing on her mind. Not least of which was the fact that until she found her father she was unavailable for a relationship.

Not that Gavin was offering one. He'd made that perfectly clear. He wanted an after-work fling. A little romantic down time. That wasn't her – she couldn't do something like that. Once she let someone in . . .

She shook off the thought. It wasn't an option anyway, which was why it was so important for her to hold a man like Gavin at arm's length. He had *heartbreaker* written all over him.

'That actually reminds me of why we're here.' She reached for a napkin to wipe her hands. 'You were going to give me Yabber's address, remember?'

He waggled his eyebrows at her before reaching into his shirt pocket and pulling out a piece of paper.

She opened it and looked at the words scrawled in black masculine handwriting on the small notepad paper with a frayed top edge.

Red Rock B and B
Cossack Road,
Cossack WA 6720

'Cossack,' she repeated. 'That sounds familiar.'

'Should do. It's the nearest town to Wickham.'

'Really? What do they do there?'

He smiled wryly. 'Not much. It's a ghost town, full of historic buildings and old Japanese graves from back when they used to dive for pearls in these parts. Now that stop is mainly for tourists.'

Wendy frowned. 'Yabber is staying at a B and B there? How do we know he hasn't already moved on?'

'He's not there on holiday. He bought the B and B and is doing it up. Apparently, that's his retirement plan for him and his wife.'

'Oh.' She refolded the paper and slipped it into her handbag. 'That sounds about right, I guess.'

He sat back in his chair to devote his attention to watching her. 'Are you going to go see him?'

'Probably.'

'When?'

She shrugged. 'I'm not sure . . . maybe next Sunday. We have the day off, right?'

'I'm going fishing.' He rubbed his hands together.

She smiled. 'Of course.'

'Unless you want me to come along with you?'

She thought about it. Did she want a friend to lean on when she met her father for the first time, just in case he dismissed her and wouldn't answer any of her questions?

Of course.

But instead she shook her head. 'No, I'll be right, thanks.' She glanced at her watch. 'You know what, we should probably get back. It's starting to get late.'

He sighed. 'I knew I should have held onto that little bit of paper for another half hour.'

Wendy was excited to finally have Yabber's address in her hands. The unfortunate part, of course, was having to wait an entire week before she could use it.

Sunday was uneventful and Monday brought with it the very welcome news that Chub had managed to hire a new engineer for installation of the new deck. His name was Dimitri Chrysanthopoulos, his credentials were excellent and Wendy couldn't help but congratulate Chub on the speedy find.

'Wow, you got us a guy in a week! That's skill for you.'

'Oh yes.' Chub rubbed his knuckles against his generous chest. 'Turns out I'm not just eye candy.'

Dimitri arrived on Wednesday. His hair was dark and his moustache beautifully trimmed. His clothes seemed to be ironed every morning, a trait that definitely set him apart from the crowd. His personality was passionate enthusiasm, level ten, which never seemed to abate. He did a lot of finger-kissing, exclaiming and relaying of old stories on past jobs that seemed to lend some sort of vague wisdom to this one. Nonetheless, the men accepted him into the fold. And that was despite his most annoying habit of all – his tendency to invade personal space.

At first, Wendy thought it was just her, because she was female. But then to her amusement she started to notice he did it with everyone. He just stood too close to people when he spoke to them. And he'd suddenly grab your arm when he was making a point he felt was particularly fascinating.

'Men don't touch men,' Radar informed Lena and Wendy at dinner Friday night. 'You just don't do it; makes things damned uncomfortable.'

'Wow,' Lena turned and winked at Wendy, 'could it be possible that the guys are suffering from a little sexual harassment? Geez, I wonder how that feels?'

'It ain't sexual.' Radar rolled his eyes. 'The man's probably near-sighted, that's all. Needs to make sure you're still there or something. Who knows . . .?'

Wendy couldn't help but smile a little, though, at the meeting she called for the engineers. They were having some tea and biscuits afterwards to celebrate Dimitri's arrival. He was standing at the back with Carl, obviously too close for Carl's taste. Dimitri's hands fluttered about his face as he spoke. Wendy could see others watching the two in amusement also.

Dimitri took two steps forwards, Carl took two steps back. Dimitri took another step forwards. Carl's back was flat up against the wall, his eyes darting to the left for possible space. He jumped as Dimitri's hand suddenly whipped out and grabbed his arm, leaning in to impart the amazing climax of his story.

Carl's expression was one of terror. Wendy found it very easy to lip-read his response: 'For fuck's sake!'

'What's the matter, Carl?' one of the other engineers yelled across the room. 'Got a tongue in your ear, mate?'

The room erupted in laughter and Dimitri turned around and beamed. He didn't know what the joke was but was ecstatic to be part of it. Spreading his hands, he said, 'Such a wonderful team. I look forward to working here very much.'

While he was addressing the group, Carl managed to slip away and head to the door. 'What the fuck are you all still doing here?' he threw over his shoulder on the way out. 'Get back on the wharf!'

Wendy had an absolute stack of paperwork to get through for the safety audit. She didn't need another incident after the fishing one. Particularly when all the men were still sore about her firing Fish. Despite his rather eccentric habits, the guys had found him to be a good leader. He got the job done. Whereas Dimitri, despite all his enthusiasm, was still untested.

Perhaps that was why disaster struck Thursday morning, just as Wendy thought she was going to clear the week without any mishaps. She was out on the end of the wharf doing what Chub called her rounds. Every morning she visited each nook and cranny of the site to look for new hazards. Her chequered hard hat was now becoming a bit of an icon around site. The men loved that she hadn't swapped it for a new one, but instead continued to wear it proudly. It showed them that she didn't just want to be their boss but their friend as well. They began to joke with her rather than at her, which was a refreshing change.

On the skid, during one of her daily inspections, they did a mock line up and stood to attention asking her if she wanted to check out their uniforms as well.

'Feel free to give me a bit of a pat down,' Biro, one of the skid boys, encouraged her. 'I might be hiding something.'

She pressed her thumb and forefinger to her chin and considered him. 'You know what, you're absolutely right. Radar,' she addressed the saluting monkey next to him, 'pat him down.'

Biro immediately dropped his pose. 'Hey, that's not fair, you're playing dirty.'

'Get back to work!' Mike barked from across the platform.

Wendy looked up in surprise. He must have been watching the entire episode.

'Haven't you got more inspections to do?' he demanded.

She didn't grace him with a reply. Simply turned and left. She wasn't going to feed his rudeness.

This morning, however, she hadn't been to the skids yet but was still standing on the end of the wharf, transfixed by a school of whales frolicking not too much further out. Throwing their giant black bodies out of the water, they re-hit the surface with a massive crash that looked almost as severe as the pile hammer. She held her breath at the freedom they represented. Unlike her, these majestic creatures led a simple, carefree existence. Even this human wharf extension invaded but a tip of their enormous world.

'Whale-watching, Sarge?'

She recognised the voice immediately.

Sexy.

Confident.

Temptation personified.

He was like a box of chocolates someone kept waving in her face. She had tried without success to stop reliving some of the moments on her 'date' with him over the last couple of days. But it was difficult to get the man out of her mind, even though technically her personal obligations to him were over.

She braced and turned. 'How's the morning going?'

'Good.' Despite her preparation, her body still sang at the sight of him. 'We've got one pile in already. What about you?'

'Two hazard identifications and one minor incident.'

'Is that good news?' he asked wryly.

Her lips twitched. 'It means we are collecting a healthy file just in time for audit.'

His eyes flicked to her hat and then back to her face again. 'I like it. Do it yourself?'

She could only assume he was referring to the police checks. 'No,' she grimaced, 'it was a present.'

'Nice one.'

'Well, I better get going.' She turned to go. The bus had just pulled into the parking bay marked by a coloured zone on the deck. She saw Sharon hop out with a file of errands. It was good timing. The bus would be off again in fifteen minutes and she could hitch a ride. As she idly watched Sharon stroll away something seemed off. For some reason she couldn't fathom, because it had never occurred before, the back of the ship-loader crane seemed way too close to the bus.

This five-storey crane, which ran up and down the jetty on a set of rails, was mainly used by the wharf owners to transfer iron ore from the conveyor into the bellies of the ships that docked there. Sometimes, however, if there were no ships arriving, they let Barnes Inc use the crane for their own purposes – such as was the case today. It seemed Dimitri's men had taken charge of it for deck installation.

Wendy's eyes narrowed to slits as she tried to work out what was wrong with the picture. But it was Gavin who acted first.

'Sharon! Run!'

At the sound of his urgent call, the bus driver stopped dead. Her mouth dropped open in confusion. She looked around as though searching for the source of the voice. It was probably the worst possible thing she could have done. Gavin raced from the railing.

Then Wendy saw what was happening as though in slow motion. A cable tray that sat under the main body of the ship-loader crane had caught on the side of the bus. As the crane moved along the rails the bus tipped firstly onto two wheels and teetered . . .

'No! Stop!' The cry to the out-of-earshot crane driver was sucked from her lungs as she staggered forwards. She saw

Gavin yank on Sharon's arm to pull her out of range but at the urgency of his tug she dropped her files and tripped over them.

CRASH!

The bus fell.

Glass splintered as a few of the windows smashed.

Sharon let loose a blood-curdling scream.

Red dust on the deck whooshed into Wendy's face, causing her to choke as she raced forwards.

Oh God! Oh God! Oh God!

By the time she reached the scene Sharon had passed out on Gavin, who was kneeling on the ground under her. The lower portion of Sharon's left leg was caught under the top of the bus; the rusty, paint-peeling roof of the vehicle, normally hidden from them, was now a wall of steel on the deck.

Gavin looked up at Wendy, his face one of pain. 'I was too late.'

'No, you weren't.' She was surprised to hear her voice sounded strangely calm. Shouts were flying around the deck, expletives, exclamations, urgent instructions to the driver from ten different locations. Luckily, somehow one penetrated and the ship-loader crane stopped moving. Men were gathering around, terror in their faces. Slack-jawed and wide-eyed, they didn't know what to do.

'Oh fuck! What's Greg done?'

'He's ballsed it up.'

'Oh shit, it's Sharon! She must have been standing near the bus. Fuck!'

'Oh fuck!'

Wendy stood up and spoke to the man nearest to her.

'Go to the office donga.' She pointed at the one not three metres from them. 'Call an ambulance and the wharf owner's medic. Tell them all to get here now, geared for a major trauma.'

He jumped. 'Yes, ma'am.' And was away.

She turned to the next man. 'Sound the alarm. I want the wharf evacuated now. Get on the radio and make sure that all equipment is pulled over into the passing bays to allow the ambulance a free run.'

He nodded and was gone as well.

She looked at the third man, who immediately stepped forwards without hesitation. 'Get on the radio. And tell the gatekeeper, no further personnel are allowed on the wharf except for the ambulance and the medic. That *includes* the project manager and the client.' He scurried away.

She indicated to the last man to come closer. 'Call Carl. Tell him what's happened and try to keep him calm. Tell him not to come racing out here with a ute. The boom gate won't let him through anyway. Tell him he has responsibilities in the emergency procedure, focus on those – if that falls over this could get a whole lot worse.'

She turned back to Gavin. Sharon was still unconscious in his arms. Her friend's face was white, making her freckles stand out all the more, her lips a thin blue line. Cold dread raced through Wendy's veins.

She kneeled beside Gavin. 'We need to get that bus off her before the ambulance gets here and preferably before she comes to. You're the engineer. Tell me how to do it.'

He put a hand on her shoulder. His deep brown eyes enveloped her like hot chocolate. 'I'll do it for you.'

He eased out from under Sharon, laying the woman's head on Wendy's lap. She noticed a deep gash in his hand. Probably from the glass pieces scattered around them.

'Gavin, your –'

'It can wait.' He dismissed her concern brusquely and strode away, yelling orders across the deck. A few men staggered towards him, most backed away. Dimitri appeared, spittle spraying off his mouth in the effort to get words out quickly.

'What can I do? What can I do? This is my fault, yes?' His hands fluttered in front of his chest as he spoke.

'We'll assign blame later,' Gavin rasped. 'Right now we need to get the ship-loader crane to pick up that bus.'

He grabbed the other man by the arm and led him away towards one of the dongas where they stored supplies, slings and such. 'We need a plan.'

Wendy knew that picking the bus up off Sharon was going to be a tricky operation. Lifting any piece of equipment was never done on the fly like this. It was always worked out on paper first by engineers such as Gavin. You needed to work out the strong points on the load that you could lift from – you didn't want the object to tip or, worse, fall back if the part of it being gripped snapped off. You didn't want your load to swing out and knock something else as it was taken off the ground. You didn't want it to warp because of too few lift points.

Wendy swallowed. There'd be no paper today. Gavin had that look in his eye. He was going to do this by gut feel and gut feel alone.

Just then the evacuation alarm sounded and the men who were not with Gavin or Dimitri started moving towards meeting posts. Wendy's heart palpitated at the whining sound. She willed it to steady.

You must stay calm. Together. On track.

Lifting the hand that was not cradling Sharon, she clenched her trembling fingers into a fist to stave off the panic. It seemed to give her some comfort. She looked down and inwardly cursed. Sharon was stirring and on a moan her friend's eyes fluttered open.

'It's okay, honey.' Wendy tried for a smile. 'You just need to lie here for a bit.'

It seemed to take a moment for Sharon to work out where she was and who was speaking to her. Her wide eyes darted from left to right and then her voice pitched in panic. 'I can't feel my leg.'

'It's all right.' Wendy nodded. 'It's fine and we're going to get it out shortly.'

'Get it out from where?' Sharon muttered, trying to raise up on her elbows.

'Don't try to move, love.'

But Sharon had seen enough. She fell back.

'Oh shit. Am I under the damn bus?'

'Sort of.' Wendy tried to keep her tone light. 'Do you want to speak to Carl? I can call him. I have my phone on me.'

'I don't know.' Sharon's voice was breathy and weak. 'Should I? I might start crying and he'll just worry . . .'

'Honey, you're under a bus. He's worried already. If he hears your voice it might calm him down a bit . . . and keep your mind focused on something else.' Wendy took the phone from her pocket.

Sharon nodded and Wendy dialled the number, clutching the phone to her ear. Carl picked up after two rings.

'Wendy!' his voice panted. 'I'm at the gate! Tell them to let me on the fuckin' wharf! *Now*!'

'No,' she returned calmly. 'You can't do any good here. Besides you're not in your right mind.'

'I need to fuckin' be there.'

'The ambulance and the medic only,' she returned firmly. 'Everyone else is coming off the wharf now so I suggest you get back.' She glanced at Sharon. 'There is someone who needs to talk to you though.'

Before he could reply she passed the phone to Sharon. The woman's voice wavered as she pressed the phone to her ear, her head still in Wendy's lap. 'Carl, it's me.'

Sharon closed her eyes, obviously listening to a tirade of emotion from her partner. Wendy looked up and saw that some men were attaching slings through the broken windows of the bus. The ship-loader crane was edging back.

Suddenly Gavin was by her side again. 'We're not going to attempt to fully lift the bus off the ground. It's too dangerous. We're just going to tip it up on its side wheels so that you can slide Sharon out.'

She hoped she was strong enough. Of course she was strong enough. Sharon was about her size.

Just focus. You can do this.

She felt his hand on her shoulder again. 'It's okay. I'll be here to help you.'

'Sharon,' she looked down, 'I need you to hang up the phone now and lie still.'

The next few minutes seemed to pass in a blur of shouts, creaking steel and straining slings. Some time during the operation, the medic arrived. He had a stretcher and other equipment.

With the bus groaning on two wheels, Wendy, with Gavin's help, transferred a gasping, shocked Sharon quickly to the stretcher. Her injured friend turned the colour of paper during the ordeal, her eyes rolling back into her head. At first Wendy thought she might have passed out and clasped her hand. 'Sharon, are you still with us?'

'Just barely.' Sharon's voice was scarcely audible as the medic took over and Wendy scrambled up to get out of the way.

Gavin's crew lowered the bus again. The useless vehicle lay there like the carcass of a dead animal on the deck: all it needed was a swarm of flies.

After that, things seemed to progress more easily. Wendy was happy for the medic to take charge – get Sharon back to shore where the ambulance had chosen to wait. As soon as the medic's vehicle sped away, the enormity of what had just happened struck her, closely followed by the realisation of what she had to do next.

She needed to report this event to the Mines Department and get an inspector out. The scene needed to be preserved so that the incident could be investigated. The ship-loader crane had to be tagged and put out of service until cleared for structural damage by the mines inspector. The unions! They'd be on her back like a sack of potatoes: when could the men return to work safely, and what to do about a new bus and the remains of this one? Her mind reeled.

There was so much to do.

She put a hand to her temple and swayed unsteadily.

'Wendy.' Gavin's calm voice. 'Are you okay?'

'I need a second.' She held up a hand as she crossed the deck to the toilet dongas, only just making it into the room before her breakfast came up into the bowl in front of her.

She sensed the light go on and the door close silently behind her. But she gave it no more thought before vomiting again.

As it turned out Sharon had broken her leg in three places. She was going to need surgery, after which she could not put any weight on her leg for at least six weeks. The most important piece of news, however, was that she would make a full recovery. It was a great relief to Wendy that Sharon's disability would not be permanent.

'I'd never forgive myself,' she told Chub on Saturday morning.

'Well, that's a stupid statement if ever I heard one,' he snorted. 'Nothing at all to do with you. It was a combination of bad moves, nothing more. You could not have predicted this.'

'I was right there.' Wendy ground her teeth. 'I didn't even notice something unsafe was going on until it was too late.'

Too busy watching whales and Gavin's gorgeous smile.

She winced with guilt.

'You stop that, you hear me!' Chub shook his finger. 'I heard you were fabulous out there. The men are saying they've never seen anyone act with such a clear head.'

Wendy snorted. 'Then they couldn't have seen me throwing up in the toilet for ten minutes after the medic left.'

'Perfectly understandable.' Chub shrugged and then glanced at her with quick concern. 'You did eat something later though, didn't you?'

'I kind of wasn't hungry.'

'I always eat when I'm worried.' He paused. 'Actually, I just always eat.' He sighed. 'This week, though, I'm on a health kick. No jelly beans, Smarties or anything sweet during the day.'

'Good for you.'

He reached across his desk and grabbed a giant orange packet of savoury snacks. 'Burger Ring?'

She laughed. 'Sure.'

'Much better.' He grinned at her lifting mood.

She cast him a suspicious look before taking one of his Burger Rings. 'Thanks, Cobber.'

'No worries.'

She spent the rest of the morning talking. Firstly, she had assembled all the different work teams to tell them what had happened, as the truth could easily get exaggerated with the Chinese Whispers. She gave them an update on Sharon's condition and told them she was going to be fine.

As for the teams that worked on the wharf, she allowed the skid team and the berthing dolphin team to return to duty. But Gavin and Dimitri's teams could not resume their work until the Mines Department inspector had been out to investigate the scene.

The site operated under the Mines Act and was therefore subject to the Australian government's Mines Department. She hoped they wouldn't take forever in clearing them and the ship-loader to perform its normal duties. The wharf owner was furious at the delay.

She then began her own investigation, talking to the ship-loader crane driver and various others in Dimitri's team, including the man himself.

It soon became apparent that the fault lay with the ship-loader crane: it had overrun its safe working area. These limits were set and marked on the rails but there was no barrier or stopper in place to prevent overrunning. Wendy was surprised it hadn't happened before. This, combined with a new crane driver who didn't know the rules and a new deck engineer, Dimitri, who couldn't instruct him otherwise, had led to the incident. She spoke to many of the men who had witnessed the accident and took notes on their suggestions on how another could be prevented. They were actually really forth-coming with their thoughts and Wendy remembered the advice Gavin had given her in Point Samson.

She returned to the office for the afternoon, trying to get through the paperwork she'd let slide the day before. Swivelling in her chair to face Chub, she asked, 'What do you think about a suggestions box, Cobber?'

'A box of what?' He looked up eagerly.

'Suggestions.'

'Oh,' his face fell, 'you got me excited.' He shrugged. 'Suggestions from whom?'

'Anyone, anytime. We could put them in our sessions for people to add to and in the smoko rooms.'

'You seriously think the men are going to willingly put a safety suggestion in one of your little boxes?' Chub snorted. 'They might as well volunteer to have their balls cut off by their mates.'

'It'll be anonymous.'

'Still not worth it.'

'Okay . . . how about every week, one random suggestion maker gets a carton?'

Chub grinned. 'Now you're talking. Hell, I'll put in a few suggestions for that. But where are you going to get the money? Not sure that Carl will shell out with this project currently running at a loss.'

'I'll look at our budget.'

If there wasn't enough cash she'd pony up the dough, at least for the next few weeks. She wasn't saving for anything except a little peace of mind. She was tired of having to follow men around like a lion trainer with a whip. She wanted their respect, but more importantly she wanted them to invest in their own well-being.

At least Sharon's accident had shaken the men up. Maybe she could push this to her advantage – get them to take a little more notice of her and her ideas. The audit was still about two weeks away. She had some time to make a few big changes . . . if the guys would just get on board.

That evening she went to visit Sharon in hospital in Karratha. The Cape Lambert bus driver looked rather pale and small in the adjustable stainless steel bed. Both Carl and Lena were in the room with her when Wendy arrived and so, coincidentally, was Annabel George.

Her presence was completely warranted, Wendy noted, given she worked there and was in her nurse's uniform. On first inspection, she also seemed to be acting extremely professionally too, fluffing pillows and giving Sharon her pain medication. Nonetheless, everyone else in the room looked relieved when Wendy poked her head in.

'Well, if it isn't my guardian angel.' Sharon smiled, trying to sit up. 'Come in, come in.'

'Now don't overdo it with the visitors,' Annabel tutted. 'I don't want Daniel ringing me complaining that I mistreated his staff.'

'Sharon doesn't work for Daniel, I mean *Dan*,' Lena corrected her. 'She works for Carl. I'm sure he won't be ringing you.'

'No?' Annabel mused. 'I suppose not. He's never been one to express his feelings much, has he? Even when he proposed he didn't say it. He simply put a diamond ring in some chocolate mousse and I was left to connect the dots.' She laughed fondly at the memory with a hand over her heart. 'It was such a magical night, let me tell you.'

'Please don't,' Wendy intervened as she watched the expression on Lena's face morph into murderous. She didn't want another two injured women on her watch. 'I mean, I don't think we need to know the details.'

'Not a worry,' Annabel responded cheerfully and then said to Sharon, 'I'll be back in a couple of hours to check up on you. Your visitors must be gone by then.'

'Thank goodness,' Sharon whispered as the door shut behind the nurse. 'I love hearing about her past with Dan as much as Lena does.'

Wendy came towards the bed and took Sharon's pale hand. 'I'm so sorry this happened to you.'

'Yeah, because it's *your* fault,' Sharon returned sarcastically, then smiled. 'Honestly, you take too much on your shoulders, Sergeant.'

It was the first time one of the girls had called her by her nickname. But instead of the derogatory ring when the boys said it, it conveyed Sharon's admiration. She was touched.

To cover her embarrassment, she rattled off a little about her investigation that morning and some of the suggestions made by the men that she was now thinking of implementing.

'How's my bus?' Sharon asked.

Wendy's lips curled. 'In bad shape, I'm afraid. But nothing a panel beater can't fix.'

Sharon grinned. 'Well, I suppose I'm on holidays now, aren't I?'

Lena patted her hand. 'That's a good way to think about it – a well-deserved break.' She covered her mouth when she realised what she'd said. 'Whoops, you know what I mean.'

Sharon laughed but Carl growled, getting up from his silent vigil by the bed and running rough hands through his dark hair. 'There's nothing fuckin' good about this! Nothing! I could have fuckin' lost her yesterday!'

'Honey.' Sharon stretched out her hand and he came unsteadily towards her, engulfing her fingers in his large paw. 'You're never going to lose me. I promise.'

He turned her hand over in his and said, without looking up, 'I suppose we should get fuckin' married then.'

Everyone in the room stilled. Expectation filled the air. Even Wendy's own heart seemed to beat in her ears. Carl half looked up, his colour a deep red, his eyes squinting at his sweetheart's face.

'Carl Curtis, are you asking me to marry you in a hospital while I'm laid up in bed with a broken leg?'

'Fuck it!' Carl leaned over and kissed her forehead. 'You look beautiful. Besides, I thought all women wanted to get fuckin' married. Don't you?'

Sharon tilted her head up and grabbed his face between her palms. 'Not to anyone but you.'

Wendy and Lena stepped slowly back from the bed to offer the couple a little space.

'I guess sometimes when you know you just know, right?' Lena said tentatively, a strange expression on her usually perfect features.

'I suppose so,' Wendy said slowly, knowing that Lena was thinking about Dan, and Annabel George and that horrible chocolate mousse story.

Wendy put her hand on her arm. 'Lena –' She had been about to say something like, 'Don't let her get to you,' or 'That was years ago,' when Sharon broke their moment.

'What the hell are you two doing cowering at the back of the room? Come over here and congratulate me!'

Lena's face immediately lit up. 'Congratulations!' She came forwards, arms spread wide. 'I'm so happy for you both.'

And the moment to speak was lost.

Chapter 12

It was fortunate that Sunday was already scheduled as a day off. The mines inspector still hadn't made it out to the wharf and half the men could not return to active duties. The inspector had promised he would attend the site first thing Monday morning, for which Wendy was actually grateful – at least she wouldn't have to cancel her plans to go to Cossack to see Yabber. It was a visit that had been simmering at the back of her mind all week and to have to put it off now would have been awful.

She was both nervous and excited about the prospect of meeting Yabber. This could be the end of her search – the possible beginning of a new relationship and the final chapter in the book that was her identity.

She would know the full truth and the knowledge couldn't come soon enough.

Sunday morning she was up in time to catch breakfast at the mess at seven but decided it would be best not to surprise Yabber before nine o'clock. She went for a jog to kill a little bit of time. She was on her way back when she saw Gavin sitting on the front porch of his donga. On impulse, she decided to go talk to him.

They hadn't really said anything to each other since the accident. And after everything they'd been through together, she felt like she needed to at least acknowledge it. He had been very brave. And, as much as he was a rascal, when it counted, he'd been there.

Her feet slowed down as she approached him because she noticed for the first time he was actually on the phone. She had been about to walk away when something stopped her. Perhaps it was his expression.

She'd seen teasing on Gavin's face before. Mischief. Arrogance. Even disdain.

But affection ... genuine love ... pain ... they were emotions she'd thought would never crease that brow or soften those eyes. She couldn't tear her gaze from him. It was one of those weird moments, like the incident with the blue-tongued lizard, when she felt that she was catching a glimpse of a man nobody else knew existed.

As she got closer, she could hear what he was saying. 'Yeah, no problem. Um ... I don't know, what do you recommend? Okay, orchids it is. Yeah, a whole bunch ... Can you deliver it tomorrow? A card ... Um, can you write, *Dear Kate, There was never a doubt in my mind that you could do it. Love you and miss you.* No, she'll know who it's from. Okay, thanks. Bye.'

He clicked the phone off and sat there silent for a moment looking out unseeingly at the line of dongas before him.

Who the hell is Kate?

'So, Sarge,' he drawled, 'you going to say hi, or creep away?'

Her skin went hot with embarrassment. She coughed, searching frantically for words that were now stuck in her throat.

'I just wanted to ask you how your hand was,' she finally spluttered. 'After the accident, things all got a bit carried away and I didn't know if you went to the medic or you got stitches or something.'

He held up a bandaged palm that didn't look too serious. 'A couple of stitches. Nothing more.'

'You were really brave.'

His smile was tentative as though he wasn't used to receiving compliments. He said finally, 'So were you.'

For some reason she wanted to prolong the conversation. 'I, er . . . I thought you were going fishing today.'

'I thought you were going to see Yabber.'

'Just heading off now.' She nodded, feeling like he'd snubbed her.

'Hey, Sarge.'

She looked back. 'Yeah?'

His brows were knitted together and his eyes were twinkle-free. 'Good luck.'

She smiled, bizarrely buoyed by his well wishes. 'Thanks.'

Cossack was only fifteen minutes' drive from Wickham, sitting right at the mouth of the Harding River. The town itself was little more than a village and mostly deserted. It had an eerie, nostalgic feel to it that instantly put Wendy in the mood to explore. There were a number of historical buildings that stood out on the flat rocky red earth that was sparsely populated by shrubbery. A two-storey courthouse with white stone pillars and a wide verandah spoke of a place that had been influential in its day, though the stone jail and police quarters next door certainly implied a rough society.

There were several other historical buildings in the main part of town. A post office, telegraph office and school. Wendy strolled through these killing time before she made the 'must see' trek to visit the cemetery, one of the focal points of the town's history.

It was divided into two separate areas, one for the European settlers and the other for the Japanese pearl divers who either were lost at sea or drowned while diving. In the European cemetery, she saw the grave of a ten-year-old girl who had died from tetanus after treading on a nail.

It reminded her of the reason she was there.

To discover her own history.

She got into her car and drove back up to the entrance of town where she had seen Hector's ramshackle B and B on her way in. It was certainly in need of doing up. The old shed next to the main house looked like it was still recovering from the last cyclone that had swept through these parts. The main brick house seemed sturdy enough but it was probably as old as Hector himself.

She stepped gingerly out of her car, awash with nerves. Was he her father? Would he be angry to see her? Disappointed?

Or just plain shocked?

Until this point, she hadn't stopped to consider how she could be affecting his life and the lives of his family. If finding out she had brothers and sisters was a shock to her then it would be to them as well. And also perhaps to his current wife or partner.

She had absolutely no desire to cause problems for another family. She knew firsthand how much destruction revelations such as this could cause. Gripping her fingers together she resolved to keep her cards close to her chest when speaking to him. She didn't need to reveal anything until she was sure.

Slamming the door of her car, she shoved her hands in the pockets of her jeans.

Grow a spine and just do it.

She threw her head back and walked determinedly over the pot-holed driveway to the front door. It was unlocked, with a sign hanging from a nail on the front of it.

We are open. Please come in.

She opened the creaky flyscreen and walked into what was obviously a reception area. There was a long wooden counter, an ancient desk fan blowing ribbons and a bell displayed prominently in place of an attendee with yet another sign: *Please ring.*

Again, she complied, killing the urge to bite her fingernails.

A woman immediately popped out of the back room, wiping her hands on a tea towel as though she had been in a kitchen. All smiles and a generous bosom, she could have been Mrs Claus but for those tight wiry black curls.

'Hello, love, looking to rent a room?'

'Er, no thanks,' Wendy responded. 'I just came to see Hector. Hector Warner. Is he in?'

'Indeed he is.' Her pink cheeks seemed to colour up even more. 'He's out back having a smoke. And who might you be?'

'I'm . . . I'm . . .' Wendy firmly swallowed her nerves. 'I'm from the camp in Wickham. I'm working on the wharf at Cape Lambert. My name is Wendy.'

The woman's eyes lit. 'He'll be pleased to get news from the jetty. I expect you know how much Yabber loves to chew the fat. Not that many people to talk to around here apart from me, I'm afraid.'

'And you are . . .?' Wendy prompted cautiously.

'His wife.' She beamed, holding out her hand. 'Linda Warner, pleased to meet you. Do you want to follow me?'

'Yes.' Wendy was glad for a reprieve from conversation in order to gather her wits. The older woman led her through another door and straight down the guts of the house to the backyard. She could see that there were parts of the house they had started doing up and other sections they hadn't got to yet. As she exited the rear sliding door, she saw a man with his back to her, seated on an old park bench under the shade of a tall gum. His feet were crossed under a wooden coffee table that had a steaming mug on it.

She gazed out over his red, ramshackle backyard, littered with shrubs and pieces of renovation debris. She couldn't help but reflect how much the lack of order resembled her life. No clear patterns or path. Just confusion.

As she came closer to Yabber, the first thing she noticed about him was that he had ginger-coloured hair streaked with grey. She was not expecting that. He looked up when his wife walked down the uneven stone path that cut through a weed-ridden lawn.

'Hey, darl.' Linda was the first to speak. 'Do you know this girl?'

He winked at Wendy. 'Wish I did. What's your name, lass?'

She wasn't expecting a strong Scottish accent, especially since Linda seemed definitely Australian.

Wendy cleared her throat. 'I'm Wendy. You don't know me,' she began slowly. 'We've never met but I, er, heard about you while I was working at Cape Lambert.'

'Did you now?' Hector raised interested eyes. 'What exactly did you hear?'

'Well . . .' She took a deep breath. 'When I heard your name, it sounded familiar and I thought you might have known my mother.'

His wife stopped in the process of leaving them.

Yabber was non-committal. 'Really? What was your mother's name?'

'Helen. Helen Padbury was her maiden name.'

Yabber frowned. 'Doesn't ring any bells.'

'It's just that,' Wendy glanced at his wife, 'she spoke about a Hector she used to know, er, quite a number of times.'

Yabber shook his head. 'I'm sorry, when did we know each other?'

'About,' Wendy licked her lips, 'twenty-nine years ago.'

His wife turned on Wendy, hands on hips. 'Did she work in a pub in Edinburgh?'

'Edinburgh?' Wendy was momentarily thrown. 'My mother lives in Perth, always has.'

Linda seemed to breathe a sigh of relief. 'Then you definitely have the wrong man. Yabber's only been in Australia for fifteen years. We got married in Scotland, had all five of our kids there. Then I decided I wanted to show my kids my homeland, so we moved here.' She smiled fondly at the

180

thought. 'It was only supposed to be for a spell, but Yabber fell in love with the place – decided he didn't want to go back.'

'Hang on a minute there.' Yabber sat up straight. 'What's going on? What do you mean, I'm the wrong man?'

Linda rolled her eyes. 'Oh, for goodness' sake, Yabber. Can't you see this girl thinks you're her father?'

'I . . .' Wendy began, startled by the older woman's perception.

But Yabber grabbed hold of his ample belly and roared. A deep throaty laugh that started at the pit of his stomach and worked its way up through his lungs.

'I'm so sorry, love,' Linda excused her husband. 'He's always been this tactless.'

Yabber stood up and came to Wendy, putting a hand on her shoulder. 'I must tell you, though, I find your theory very flattering. Beautiful thing like you. Who wouldn't want to say the lass is mine? I'll be telling this one at dinner parties till I die.' His belly shook again on a low rumble.

A party trick? A good laugh?

Wendy looked down as a wave of nausea threatened to overcome her. Her eyes focused on his feet which, she noticed for the first time, were encased in thongs. All ten toes were there. No sign of the injury her mother had spoken of . . . Tears bit painfully at her eyes. She did her best to blink them back. Disappointment wasn't the only thing she felt – there was definitely a mixture of relief in there as well. All the same, she had no desire to break down in front of either of them.

'I'm sorry to have interrupted your morning.' She shuffled awkwardly on the spot. 'Look, I'll just get out of your hair.'

'Oh, darling,' Linda protested, 'you look like you could use a hot drink. Shall I go get it?'

'No, no.' Wendy waved her hand in protest. 'I'll just get going.'

'I'm really sorry, love. I didn't mean to –'

She could hear Yabber's voice behind her as she stumbled back down his garden path. But her only thought was to get out of there as quickly as possible.

She'd come here to discover the truth. And the truth was, she'd discovered nothing.

She got back out to the street, her whole body trembling in the aftermath. Fumbling with her keys she made it into her car and slammed the door shut. Biting down hard on her lower lip, she fiercely pushed the keys into the ignition.

The car choked briefly and then died.

No, not here.

It seemed too symbolic that she'd lost both the thread of her journey and the battery of her car in the same ghost town.

She got out, leaned against the car roof, closing her eyes and lifting her face to the sun. She breathed deeply until that panicky feeling in her chest dissipated and her heart rate slowed. Yes, she'd had a setback but it didn't give her permission to fall apart on the side of the road. She took her mobile out of her pocket, pleased to see that her fingers were no longer shaking. She had Chub's and Carl's numbers in it. Both calls went to voicemail. She imagined they were both probably still sleeping in.

There was really only one other person around that she could ask for help. With a sigh, she headed back to Yabber's B and B.

'I'm sorry, lass, but my truck is in for servicing.' Yabber spread his hands apologetically. 'Is there anyone else I can call for you from the camp?'

'Do you have Lena Todd's number?'

'Not Lena's.' His face brightened. 'I probably still have Gavin's number in my phone though.'

Wonderful.

Gavin would take full advantage of this situation.

'Do you have anyone else's?' Her brow wrinkled.

He frowned. 'A few people's office numbers. But there will be no one in the office dongas today if you've all got the day off.'

Wendy nodded with resignation. 'You're right. Could I have his number? I'll call him myself.'

He looked up Gavin's number on his phone and called it out to her. She typed it into hers, thanked him and then headed back out to her car. She half prayed Gavin wouldn't pick up, but on the fifth ring he did.

'Hello.'

'Gavin, it's Wendy.'

'Well, hello there, Sarge.' The usual drawl, which had her glancing heavenwards. 'Miss me already? You've only been gone a couple hours.'

She gritted her teeth. 'I've sort of got a bit of a problem out here.'

To her surprise, his voice lost its teasing note. 'Are you all right? You're not hurt, are you?'

She almost said yes just so she could hear his reaction, but stopped herself. She was allowing his outrageous personality to bring out the worst in her.

'No, I'm fine. It's my car. It won't start.'

'Battery finally died, did it?'

'Yeah. I was wondering if you could come and pick me up? I'll fill your tank up with petrol or something for your trouble.'

'For my trouble.' His voice was a low, sexy murmur, making the phone tremble next to her ear at the sound of it.

'Yeah, seems the least I could do.'

'What is it with you and this whole nobody-does-anything-for-nothing mentality?' he demanded crossly.

Because nobody does. A kind of helplessness rippled through her, only compounded by the lack of success in her mission that day. Tears smarted in her eyes again and a lump grew in her throat. *Oh crap. What a time to get misty! Pull it together, girl.*

'I don't know what you're talking about,' she choked, desperately trying to push words out before the dams broke.

'Look, Wendy,' Gavin's voice was gentle again. 'I'm coming right now. You're at Yabber's B and B, right?'

'Yes,' she whispered but he had already rung off. She slowly lowered the phone. *Oh to hell with it.*

She let herself cry. Sobs, unflattering gulps and tears that ran down her face.

But it helped. She felt lighter for it and was grateful, at least, that no one had caught her in this weak moment.

After about twenty minutes, Gavin drove up and parked beside her. His concerned expression and tall, manly figure alighting from the car put a longing in her heart that she couldn't quench.

She walked around to meet him. The softness of his hair on his forehead made him seem so approachable she almost wilted where she stood.

'How're you doing?' was his greeting.

'Okay,' she shrugged. 'It's a beautiful day and you were very quick.'

He was looking at her strangely, though, and it suddenly occurred to her that her eyes might still be red from crying. *Damn!*

'You sure, Sarge? You look a little –'

'Oh that.' Her voice squeaked as she waved a finger from her left eye to her right. 'It's the hayfever. It can hit me suddenly sometimes.'

Gavin's mouth twisted; he was clearly dissatisfied with this explanation but willing to let it go for the moment. 'I thought we might try jump-starting your car. I've got some leads in my ute.'

'Okay.'

He cracked open both bonnets and grabbed the leads from his ute. She watched him silently and gratefully. With furrowed brow he connected his battery to hers. 'You know, Sarge, you really should have changed this out months ago. Why didn't you?'

'I don't know . . .'

'But you've been having trouble starting your car for some time now.'

'Yes, but it just never seemed urgent enough.' She shrugged.

Everything else going on in her life seemed to come first. She was always on the brink of identifying her father or finding her feet at work or visiting Sharon in hospital or just too damn tired. The car was something that could wait till after. Or so she thought.

He turned his ignition and then tried starting her car. The engine revved slightly, giving her hope for all of two seconds before giving up the ghost again. After several tries, they both had to concede defeat. He undid the leads, winding them around his arm as he walked towards her.

'Sorry, Wendy, I'll have to go buy a battery and then come back and install it. I know a place in Dampier that'll be open today.'

'I couldn't possibly ask you to do that.'

'You didn't.'

She wrung her hands. She didn't like being beholden to people. It made her vulnerable, and she couldn't have that. Especially not today when she felt lousy enough.

'Wendy, what's the matter?'

She looked up with a smile that she hoped wasn't too fake. 'There's a service station just out of town. I'll fill your tank.'

He came up to stand next to her, flinging the leads in the back of his ute beside them. 'My tank is already full.'

'Then I'll buy you lunch. How about a sandwich?'

'Just ate.'

'Okay, what about a carton?' she murmured desperately. 'We could swing by a liquor store.'

'Marvin just gave me a stack of beer.' Half the mischievous twinkle in his eyes she hadn't seen for a full hour was suddenly back.

She folded her arms and looked at the ground. 'What do you want, Gavin?'

He was silent for a second and then, with a sigh, he put both palms on her cheeks and gently tilted her face up, so that she had no choice but to meet those bottomless dark eyes. For an awful, crazy moment, she thought he was going to kiss her again. Her heart leaped straight to her throat. Her eyes widened as her hands flew to cover the ones tenderly cupping her face.

'No,' he whispered, 'that would be too easy.'

He released her and announced with all the flare of a circus ringmaster, 'I want your opinion on some artwork.'

'What?' she faltered, rocking unsteadily on her feet. 'You . . . w-what?'

'Do you have an eye for colour?'

'No.'

He dusted his hands. 'Neither do I. That's why I like my drawings in all the same shade.'

'*What are you talking about?*'

He folded his arms. 'Are you going to compensate me for my trouble or not? It's on the way to Dampier, so we're heading in that direction anyway.'

She studied his face but it was unreadable. 'I . . . I *guess*.'

'Well, come on then.' He stepped back and opened the door to his ute. 'I haven't got all day.'

She rolled her eyes. He was obviously enjoying her confusion so she cleared her face of all expression. 'Fine.' She climbed into his ute and laid her hands on her lap. 'I'll have a look at this artwork.'

'No worries.' He slammed her door shut and then walked around the vehicle to get in himself.

Dampier was only an hour away by car, so she wasn't too worried about not making it back to camp in time for dinner. It was a gorgeous day. The landscape flew past her window, the wheels of the ute eating up road, calming her somewhat.

He had placed his phone in a pocket built into the car dash. It buzzed briefly and she glanced at it, noticing he had a text message from someone called Janet.

He saw her looking at his phone, reached over and turned it off.

She averted her eyes back out the window, wondering how many more women Gavin had in his life that she didn't know about. For goodness' sake, she knew he was a flirt, but this was ridiculous.

Flowers for Kate.

Text messages from Janet.

Did he have a wife hidden somewhere too?

'You've gone all disapproving again,' a dry voice chuckled. 'I wish I knew what was going on in that head of yours.'

She looked at him, studying the strong masculine profile. Perhaps he had love interests all over the state. Gavin was such a rascal and, according to Lena and Sharon, he'd hit on every single woman around here. Maybe this was just his thing. Maybe . . .

'Will you stop looking at me like that?'

She jumped. 'Like what?'

'Like you want to gut me and feed me to the seagulls.'

'Not a bad idea,' she murmured.

'Geez, Wendy,' his fingers tightened on the steering wheel, 'you've got a real chip on your shoulder.'

'So do you.'

'Good point.' He paused. 'So who's Yabber to you?'

'Nobody.' It was the truth. He couldn't fault her for lying.

'You're going to have to give me more than that.'

'I thought we might be related,' she sighed. 'But turns out we're not.'

'I see.'

He saw *nothing*, but she wasn't about to enlighten him. Instead, she shifted the conversation to a safer topic – his work history. He glanced at her briefly, with amusement, but obliged her with tales of jobs he'd done in Tom Price, Paraburdoo, Port Hedland and Marble Bar. Gavin had certainly fast-tracked and streamlined his career in the last five years, picking his jobs carefully and working his way up the ranks quickly. He'd be a Carl in a few years and probably even more unbearable by then too. She smiled at the thought.

'Hey,' she interrupted him, 'the sign says Dampier is that way.'

'The artwork is down here,' he informed her.

She eyed him doubtfully. 'It is?'

'You'll see.'

They turned up Burrup Road and seemed to be heading out on a peninsula. He stopped the ute by a beach and she looked out the windscreen in awe.

'What is this place?' She'd worked at Parker Point wharf two years ago and hadn't even bothered to come down this way.

It was such a contrasting landscape. Deep blue sea and white sand worthy of any island paradise. But then rising up all around the shoreline were gently sloping hills covered in rocks of varying shades of red. From that deep iron ore tone to a subtle peach. Like God had taken a handful of boulders and sprinkled them across the land in little piles. Interspersed between these sharp edges was the occasional shrub that seemed to struggle to sprout beside the barren rocks.

'It's a sacred Aboriginal site. Some people say this is Australia's Stonehenge,' Gavin told her.

As she walked from the car towards the rocky hills, she could see wallabies jumping up jagged stones that she would find difficult to climb. These marsupials pounced in little packs like miniature kangaroos dyed a mousy brown.

'Come on,' Gavin urged, taking her hand. 'Let's go for a walk.' She didn't resist as he pulled her away from the shore and down a small valley between two hills. It looked like they were walking on a dry creek bed. The rocks were polished and smooth and the sand between them fine.

'Look at the rocks.'

Gavin directed her attention to the slopes either side of them and she finally realised what artwork he had been wanting to show her. The red rocks were covered in hundreds of chalklike markings. So many Aboriginal petroglyphs telling a history of their very own. Etchings of lizards, kangaroos and snakes. Pictures of feet and hands, both human and animal. Then there were images of Aborigines with spears, some presented individually, some in groups. They walked further up the dry creek and the stories and memories continued in images upon the rocks.

'It's beautiful.' She was completely in awe.

A wry smile turned up his mouth as he watched her. 'I thought you might like it.'

She turned in a full circle, her eyes following the movement of the artwork. 'You come here often?'

'Whenever I need peace.'

Understanding dawned. 'And you thought that's what I needed today?'

He shrugged. 'Yeah.'

Today she had gone back in time twice. Firstly at Cossack when she'd re-walked the first steps of the first foreign settlers. And now here, amongst this rich archaeological collection of rock art, where the natives had created their own visual record of times almost forgotten.

She hadn't discovered her own history but she had discovered something else.

Life went on.

With or without her.

She could hide. Or she could be part of it and let go of a past that didn't want her anyway. Her gaze returned to Gavin. He had given her something she didn't think was possible. She walked towards him. He stood perfectly still, watching her through half-closed lids. Without a thought. Without a smidgen of caution. Just pure instinct. She pushed her palms up his chest, over his shoulders and joined them behind his neck. Her body swayed into his – every curve fitting itself into his hard planes, like two cogs locking together.

'Thank you,' she said as she closed her eyes and sealed her mouth to his.

Chapter 13

Gavin did not think.

He merely responded.

This kiss was utterly different from the one he had so shame-lessly stolen. Not a prompting of lust. Or the act of a man in desperate need of a distraction in his life. This was a woman, pouring every ounce of her soul into the action.

She wasn't holding back. He could feel her trust and tender-ness wrap around him as surely as her arms did. She wasn't scared. She wasn't worried. Her body arched into his, length-ening their contact from chest to thigh.

God forgive me.

He was powerless to resist so honest a gift, even though more than a week ago he had vowed to hold her at arm's length.

Arm's length be damned!

He drew her closer. Their mouths tumbled over each other in desperation to give and take. He pushed the tips of his fingers into her hairline as he grabbed hold of her face to steady their feverish desire, gentling the caress till his heart and body ached with need.

I can't do this.

He pulled away, still holding her face, watching her eyes slowly open, like the sun rising on the dawn of a new day.

'What is it?' she whispered, her mouth turned up slightly into that sweet, shy smile. 'Did I do something wrong?'

His voice was a husky rasp. 'No.'

The problem was that she was way too *right*. Too perfect in every way. He'd been mad to think that he could just have a fling with this woman and then move on unscathed and unscarred.

Wendy wasn't your walk-in-the-park relationship. She was a keeper and he knew that if he put even one foot in that direction he'd be lost. That's why he had to let her go. It was, ironically, for her own safety.

Had she but known it.

He released her, and surprise mixed with hurt glimmered in her eyes. It killed him slowly as he disentangled his body from hers. And with that damned cocky mask he liked to hide behind back in place, he took her hand and raised the back of her palm to his lips. 'Come on, we should get that battery of yours.'

Before she could respond, he was leading her back over the rocks, past the Aboriginal figures that had once given him comfort, but now seemed to jump out at him like accusing pixies. They cleared the dried-up river and the beach and arrived back at the car.

'Gavin, not so fast.' Wendy's voice was breathless behind him.

His feet slowed but he didn't turn around to look at what would no doubt be her panting and flushed countenance. He was in full retreat mode. He had to get this done.

Come on! It was just one little kiss. Get a grip.

Opening the door to his ute, he released her hand. 'Get in.'

She glared at him but complied as he walked around the vehicle to his own seat. Once he was in, however, she immediately opened the conversation. For the first time that day he wished he wasn't sitting with the woman of his dreams in the middle of nowhere.

'You said I didn't do anything wrong.'

'You didn't.' He started the engine.

Her voice was small. 'Am I that bad a kisser?'

His foot jerked uncontrollably on the pedal as the car took off in a cloud of dust.

'No.'

'For goodness' sake, Gavin, talk to me. You're freaking me out here.'

'I just don't think,' he said slowly, 'as colleagues . . . that it would be a good idea for us to get together.'

Although he didn't look at her, he could sense she was gaping at him.

'*This* from the man who's been flirting with me since I arrived in town? I don't get you. What's changed?'

Fuckin' everything. He coughed and then found refuge in his usual defence. 'I'm just sensing that you don't get the rules.'

'What rules?' Her voice was a vulnerable caress that was almost his undoing.

'What do you want, Wendy? Do you want to have sex?' The words grated on his tongue but he pushed them out, cruel words that she had to hear. 'A few good tumbles in my donga or yours till I get bored of your body and we resort to avoiding each other on the job?'

'*What?*'

''Cause you know I don't do commitment. And I certainly don't do relationships.'

'I know . . . I just –'

'What?' He gripped the steering wheel, in his head begging her, practically screaming for her not to say it.

'I just thought maybe,' she struggled and then swallowed, 'things were different now.'

'Why would they be?' he demanded, challenging her to lay her feelings bare. Tell him that he was mad. That there was something there between them that he couldn't deny. More than a fumble in the dark. Not a one-night stand or a meaningless fling but something real and tangible and so special that even thinking about it made his skin tingle.

Don't rise to the bait, Wendy.

To his relief, she turned her face to the window so he couldn't see it. 'Never mind.'

Good girl.

If there was one thing he could count on with Wendy, it was her self-respect.

His fingers tightened on the wheel. He should be relieved, satisfied that she was safe. Yet all he felt was anger and disappointment in himself.

There were things in life he could never have. And now she was one of them. He gritted his teeth till his jaw ached.

At Dampier, he waited in the car while she got out and bought her own battery. He figured she needed the space. He was sure that if it were physically possible to get home before dark, she would have got out and walked. Thank goodness for small mercies.

Her eyes seemed a little red on her return, but the glare she gave him was as vibrant and as feisty as ever. She wasn't going to roll over and play dead.

It tore a smile from him. 'Man! You're beautiful when you're angry.'

'Wow!' She slammed her passenger door shut. 'That's an original one.'

'Come on, Sarge –'

'*Shut up, Gavin.* Just drive!'

They completed the rest of the journey to her car at Cossack in stony silence. When they arrived he got out and installed the battery for her. She watched him with a cold and critical eye, making him feel like the snail in her lettuce patch. Then when he finished the job, she whipped out her purse and pulled out a hundred-dollar bill, which she must have withdrawn from an ATM in Dampier. She presented it to him.

'Wendy.' He held up his hands in protest. This was too much. He wasn't going to let her pay him.

'Take it,' she rasped, jiggling it at him.

'No.'

'I said take it!' she choked desperately. 'I don't want to owe you anything.'

'You don't owe me anything.'

'I owe you this.' She shoved the note into his shirt pocket. And despite the emotional turmoil between them, the brief slide of her fingers against his chest was enough to render him speechless long enough for her to get away.

'*Wendy!*' he called as she strode away, blonde hair whipping behind her.

She neither turned nor acknowledged his existence as she got into her car and drove off, leaving him to watch her cloud of dust.

Feeling like a right arse, he returned to his ute and got in. Ripping the note from his pocket, he looked at it. What the hell was he going to do with it? Spending it was out of the question. He shoved it in the coin compartment of the car and started the engine. He also turned his phone back on. It buzzed almost instantly.

There was another message from Janet.

She was probably wondering why he hadn't responded before. He pulled out his phone and opened the text. *Urgent! Please be available to speak tonight at 7.30pm. Confirm.*

He typed in *Confirm* and sent the message.

It would be more news regarding Peter Marshall, no doubt. Surprisingly, the mere thought of his nemesis no longer made his adrenaline pump. Even seeing the druglord on the news no longer gave him the urge to switch off the television and heave. It was this man who had made his life hell, and was continuing to do so. But he wasn't afraid of him any more. In fact, he hoped Peter Marshall would find him someday. He'd love to have a face to face and an excuse to smack the living daylights out of the son of a bitch. All this sneaking around had given him a taste for an open match.

He had been in witness protection for five years now. Every year grew harder and harder. He longed to return home or just to visit his family, who had also moved cities when this whole debacle occurred. But he didn't dare put their lives at risk too.

Instead, he tried to focus on his men. They were his surrogate family. His sole responsibility. If he could just stay honest to them and to this job, he was safe. The people he loved were safe.

He couldn't afford to bring Wendy into his life.

Getting close to anyone was too dangerous.

As long as he was in this program, attachments to people and places were always temporary. He took a job, did the work and moved on. And that's what he had to keep doing again and again and again.

He backed his ute out of the car bay and sped out of Cossack.

The problem was, he couldn't see an end date in sight. When would Peter Marshall give up? When would that man stop hunting him?

Certainly not now. Marshall's brother Eddie had been murdered in jail. If the guy had wanted revenge before, he'd be spitting for it now.

As Gavin drove into the camp car park, he tried to put Peter Marshall out of his mind. He still had a few hours to kill before he had to deal with that phone call. It would be better if he didn't dwell on what Janet may or may not say.

He did his laundry, read a magazine, took a jog, then had a shower and his dinner. In between he spoke to a few of the guys and allowed himself to feel normal. Then, at seven-twenty-five pm, he returned to his donga to receive what he hoped was good news.

It wasn't.

'We re-located Peter when he attended his brother's funeral with the rest of their family in Darlinghurst,' Janet reported. 'He's been plotting, Gavin. Not just revenge for his brother but for a number of friends and family who have been killed in this year's gang war.'

'How many deaths have there been?'

'Four we know of. He's not happy. I'd say he's also a target himself, which is why he went underground for a week.'

'But he's visible now.'

'He's not just visible.' Janet coughed. 'I'm afraid that's the bad news. He's booked a flight to Perth. We're not one hundred per cent sure but we think he's looking for you.'

'But if he's taken that many losses . . .' Gavin began.

'None as important as his brother. He still blames you for having put Eddie in jail in the first place.'

Gavin clutched the phone tightly. 'So he's looking for me again . . . in earnest.'

Bring it on.

Janet misinterpreted his tone.

'Don't panic,' she said. 'Like I said, we can't know for sure. I just wanted to make sure you were on alert. Just keep doing what you normally do, but be extra cautious with who you talk to and who you involve in your life.'

Like Wendy.

Stay the hell away from Wendy.

'No problem,' Gavin agreed.

'Okay.' Janet seemed ready to go. 'I'll call you again if there're any more developments. And if you need to reach me, don't hesitate to make contact.'

'Sure.' Though when she rang off Gavin felt strangely bereft.

He cursed that day he'd witnessed Brayden's murder, as he cursed it every time he was reminded of how trapped he was.

Back then, he'd been as carefree as a teenager with a licence and probably not much more mature, despite being in his late twenties. He hadn't needed to be. He was a well-paid young man with no dependants. He had worked a couple of engineering jobs overseas, made a stack of money and decided to return home to Sydney to enjoy an easier life. A Friday night after work had meant three things for him. Mates. Girls. And a couple of drinks . . . maybe more.

That critical night, it had been a friend's birthday. His usual crew were out on a pub crawl celebrating. They'd just finished a drinking session at a flashy joint called Pulse. Everyone was waiting on the bus. Brayden said he was out of cash and needed to go to an ATM. When he didn't come back soon enough, the others started to get annoyed. Gavin volunteered to go find him and jumped out of the bus. He'd taken those back streets off the main road to get to the 7-Eleven faster. The ATM was supposed to be located on the corner next to it.

But he found Brayden before reaching the ATM. His friend was having what appeared to be a disagreement with another man Gavin didn't recognise – swarthy, scarred and dark-haired with tattoos on the backs of both hands. Gavin naively approached the scene, still intending to speak to Brayden, when unexpectedly a gun went off.

'Hey!' he yelled, increasing his pace to the scene. But as Brayden crumpled to the pavement and the shooter spun around, brandishing the weapon like someone who had used it many times before, Gavin knew he was done for.

'What the hell?' the tattooed man said. 'What are you looking at?'

As Gavin took a step back, the murderer lifted the weapon to take aim. Gavin spun around just as the gun exploded again. Pain erupted in his shoulder, making his vision blur, but he had enough momentum to stumble on. He heard footsteps behind him and knew the gunman intended to finish him off.

Gasping with pain but high on the need to survive, he clutched his shoulder and ran as fast as he could, which was more of a swaying stagger, towards the lights of the busy main road. He could see the bus and fell into the arms of a bouncer standing out the front of the club he'd been drinking in not half an hour ago.

'What the fuck?' the stocky man cried as his hand came away from Gavin's shoulder wet with blood.

'Behind me,' said Gavin before passing out.

He didn't know what transpired next because he was unconscious and didn't come to until he was sitting in a hospital bed, the bullet having already been removed. His mother, father and sister were sitting by his side and a police officer was standing at the foot of the bed.

He'd given a statement and for a while that had all been enough. But then using his description and their knowledge of the area's drug gang, they went and caught the bastard.

His name was Eddie Marshall.

Brother of Peter Marshall, reigning drug dealer in Sydney's most powerful organised crime ring and owner of Pulse.

Basically, he was a prince as far as criminals went.

That notoriety alone should have set off alarm bells in Gavin's head. But he'd just had a bullet removed from his shoulder and one of his best friends was dead. When the police came knocking for his testimony at trial, he didn't say no. Like a cocky young hound, he'd been hungry for justice and sure that he could get it for both Brayden and himself. If the thought that the Marshalls would not play fair had occurred to him, he probably would have dismissed it. Perhaps he still would even now. Somebody needed to bring Eddie to justice. If only there wasn't such a steep price.

But for his testimony, Eddie Marshall would never have been jailed for life.

And but for his testimony, Peter Marshall never would have come after him.

For the next few days, Gavin's mood remained foul. Not because he knew a psychotic druglord was after him but because one of his men was holding up his end of the project. The job was the only thing keeping him sane – between avoiding Wendy and staying off Peter Marshall's radar. It was something else to focus on and he needed that distraction.

However, he couldn't get on with the job unless he had a faulty pile repaired. Bloody Spoon was demanding confined-space training before he would do the repair welding.

Working in a small or confined space was often considered more dangerous than working in the open. There were many hazards associated with working inside tanks, or down mines or in any space that was restricted, mostly to do with not being able to get out quickly if there was an accident, or having to work alone without supervision. Sometimes, if the space was very small, it might also be poorly ventilated, thus increasing other risks.

Gavin was fully on board with all the issues. But the so-called 'confined space' that Spoon was talking about was inside the end of a pile. Piles were one and a half metres in diameter – so definitely wide enough for a man to stand inside comfortably. The repair work Gavin wanted him to do was only forty centimetres from one end. If Spoon just stuck his hand out straight, he'd be waving it outside.

It was ludicrous to suggest that he needed confined-space training for this, especially as it would take him off the job for at least a day.

And that wasn't the worst thing about it. The worst thing was he knew he'd have to get Wendy involved. He'd been so successful in avoiding her all of Monday and Tuesday. But today he was just going to have to go and see her because she was the only person who could sort this issue out once and for all.

At two-thirty in the afternoon, he left to the sound of guffaws and teasing remarks. His men had all noticed his bad mood and one of them shouted at his retreating back, 'I think Gav needs another visit from his Norwegian boys!'

Ever since he'd been overheard saying to his supplier, 'I need those Norwegian buoys and I want them today,' he'd been the butt of a number of gay innuendoes. Normally he'd be the first to see the funny side.

But not today.

Every time he saw Wendy, it was like ripping off a Band-Aid. He knew this afternoon would be no different.

He knocked on the door of her office donga and then wished he hadn't. Nobody did that! They just walked straight in.

While he was still cursing himself, the door flung open and Chub filled the threshold. 'Damn it, Gavin, you made me get up. Do you know what an effort that is?'

Despite himself, he couldn't help but grin. 'Got your exercise for the day, mate. You should thank me. Is the Sergeant in?'

Chub eyed him a little too shrewdly for his taste. 'Come a-calling, have you?'

Gavin shuffled from his front foot to his back. 'Something like that.'

'Well, you're welcome to try.' Chub stepped aside. 'She's been on the phone all day.'

Gavin removed his hat and entered the donga, immediately seeing Wendy seated at her desk. She gave him a tentative smile of acknowledgement. 'I'll just be five minutes,' she mouthed and then continued to talk on the receiver cradled between her ear and her shoulder. He stood there awkwardly, hat in hand, watching her, soaking up the view like a desert mirage. She was leaning all the way back in her chair, boots up on the desk, crossed at the ankles, like she'd been at this conversation a long time.

His eyes couldn't help but wander up those long legs, so prominently and beautifully displayed. His attention flicked to the elegant fingers impatiently twirling a hair lackey band. She must have taken it out of her hair at some point because those long blonde tresses were caressing her cheeks and shoulders in that mussed 'just-got-out-of-bed' look he'd never get to see for real.

A low chuckle sounded just above his ear. 'Do you need a cigarette with that, mate?'

'Er . . .' He turned around to find Chub watching him with interest.

He cleared his throat. 'Could you tell her, I'll wait in the smoko donga till she gets off the phone?' He ran a hand through his hair, embarrassed. 'She looks like she's going to be a while and I could do with a coffee.' *Or something stronger.*

'No problem.' Chub grinned. 'I'll let her know to come and get you.'

Grateful for the reprieve, Gavin got out of there, hoping that he'd sufficiently disguised the fact that he was fleeing the scene.

He was so hell-bent on his escape, he didn't realise that the smoko donga wasn't empty until he was halfway through making himself a cup of tea. It was a rather pathetic sounding sniffle that had him looking up as he was about to add milk. Standing at the far end of the long donga, with a box of tissues, was Lena Todd. She had her back to him but he could hear her pulling tissue after tissue from the box, clearly as unaware of him as he had previously been of her.

Is she crying?

He couldn't leave because he'd asked Chub to tell Wendy to come here. And there was no way he was going back to Wendy's hot legs and her smug donga mate.

Haven't you got enough damsels in distress in your life?

With a sigh, he withdrew a second mug from under the counter and added a tea bag to it. *What's another one over a cup of tea?*

Lena jumped as the hot beverage was placed in front of her. 'Gavin. I thought nobody else was in here.'

'Me too. So what's the problem, Madame E?'

'What makes you think there's a problem?'

He indicated her face with a casual wave of his pointer finger as he sunk his nose into his mug for a sip. 'You've definitely looked better.'

'Thanks.'

'No charge.'

She sighed. 'You're a real arse sometimes, you know that?'

'Somebody's got to be.' He shrugged. 'Craig's the nice one, Dimitri's the foreign one, Anton's young, Carl's wise, Tony's efficient and so on. So I'm the arse. It's what I do best.'

Despite herself, she cracked a smile. 'So what am I?'

He paused. 'You're tough. You've put up with a lot these past few months but you managed to get through it all with your enthusiasm intact.'

His words seemed to have the opposite effect to what he was aiming for as her face immediately crumpled. 'Really? If I'm so bloody tough, why am I letting this psycho rattle me so much?'

'Psycho?'

'Annabel George,' she sniffed, drawing the mug he had put on the table towards her. 'Dan and I went out to dinner last night and right in the middle of it she calls him on his mobile for advice.'

Gavin raised his eyebrows. 'Advice about what?'

'Apparently she has a leaky tap in her bathroom and she was wondering if he could recommend someone who could fix it for her.'

'Sounds harmless enough.'

'Maybe.' Lena sipped her tea. 'Until I found out she makes calls like this to him all the time. She's acting like he's her husband or something.'

'What does he think about it?'

'He says he's just being a good friend and thinks I'm being ungenerous. He said she's not confident with things like that the way I am and sometimes just needs a little help. That's when we had our first fight.'

'Oh.' Gavin nodded, understanding dawning on him. 'Let me guess, Bulldog doesn't understand why you can't trust him. Particularly when he has told you that he's not interested in her.'

'Yes.' Lena glared at him. 'But it's not about trust. It's about respect. Annabel doesn't respect our relationship. She doesn't respect me. She's just taking advantage of Dan's good nature and his inability to turn his back on a helpless woman ... urgh!' Lena groaned. 'I don't know how else to explain it.'

'No, no,' Gavin agreed thoughtfully, 'I get it.'

'Oh good.' Lena looked at him eagerly. 'Can you explain it to Dan?'

Gavin gave a bark of laughter. 'Are you kidding me? You want me to go to talk to Bulldog about his relationship with you? That's one way to get my balls cut off, I suppose.'

Lena sunk her chin into her hands. 'Then what on earth am I supposed to do?'

'Well,' he began slowly, 'if you want this woman to stop going after Dan then maybe you need to find her a replacement.'

'A what?' Lena dropped her hands.

'You've told her to back off and she hasn't done it.' Gavin tried not to sound patronising but it seemed to come out that way. 'I know her type. She's the kind of woman who needs someone to take care of her. Dan's done it before and she obviously wants him for the job again. Believe me, I can smell clingy a mile away. How do you think I know when to run?'

'Did I say you were an arse before?'

He grinned. 'You certainly did.'

'Well, I rest my case.' She sniffed but it was obvious his idea had given her pause because she added, 'But who would want to go out with *Annabel George*?'

'Well, she's not bad looking and very eager to please. For some guys that's enough.'

'Okay.' Lena nodded decisively. 'I'll give it some thought.'

'You do that.' He polished off his tea and stood up to take his mug back to the kitchen.

Lena stood up too. 'Gavin.'

'Yeah?'

'Thanks. I mean for the tea and the advice and everything. Maybe you're not such an arse after all.' To his surprise, she threw her arms around his neck, delivering him in one impulsive movement a quick hug and a peck on the cheek.

'Er . . . no problem.'

And then a new voice broke through. 'Am I interrupting something here?'

Lena dropped her hands and they both spun guiltily towards the door, just like there was something to hide.

Damn!

'No,' he said.

'*Wendy?*' said Lena.

The blonde safety manager looked stern. 'Gavin and I have a meeting.'

'Oh,' Lena waved, 'I'll just get out of your way.'

Wendy leaned her hip on the desk, arms folded, as she watched the young engineer leave the room. As soon as the door shut behind Lena, she turned blue eyes on Gavin.

'Wow! Her too?'

'*What?*'

'That'll be three all up that I've counted so far . . . apart from myself. *If* I can count myself, which given our last moment together – you know, the one before you started avoiding me – clearly I can't.'

'Three what?' Gavin demanded.

'Women!' Wendy's eyes shot daggers at him. 'But your evident prowess with the opposite sex can't possibly be what you came to see me about.'

He watched her in shock, not knowing how to respond. He knew what he wanted to say. *Don't be ridiculous. You're the only woman I want to be with. I can't sleep. I can't eat. I can't concentrate on my job because you're forever in my head.*

But, of course, he couldn't say any of that. It would only lead to complications that could possibly endanger her life.

So instead, he blinked twice and said baldly, 'You're right, Sarge. It's not what I came to talk to you about.'

He'd never seen anyone look so cross about being right. His lips twitched as he quickly outlined his problem with Spoon and the demand for confined-space training. 'So . . .' he drawled when he was done, 'is it really warranted or is he just being silly?'

For a moment she was silent, obviously tossing up whether she should have allowed him to change the subject so easily. Finally she responded, tight-lipped. 'There are several criteria that need to be met before a work area can be classified as a confined space. I can do a formal risk assessment before he starts work but just from what you've explained to me, I don't think this is a confined space.'

'So he doesn't need the training?'

'Not from a specialist, no. But let me chat to him for half an hour or so about some small risks associated with this job.' She paused. 'We would also be wise to apply some other controls too, such as making sure that there is adequate ventilation. Maybe put a fan behind Spoon to disperse any fumes out of the pipe.'

'Okay, that sounds good.' He wanted to stay and say something more. Her body language shrieked both contempt and unfinished business. But he knew to bring up the subject he had just successfully managed to avoid would be disastrous. Even now he wanted to kiss those soft lips into a smile. Envelop that rigid body in his arms and whisper sweet words in her ear.

Go now!

He walked towards the door and picked his hard hat up off the kitchen counter. 'Thanks for the advice, Sarge. I'll see you around.'

Sitting on the steps of his donga that night, Gavin tossed back a beer and wondered if his life could possibly get any worse.

And then Mike showed up.

'Why hello there, Hopkins,' he greeted the bald-headed skid supervisor. 'You seem to be making a habit of stopping by. Would you like a beer?'

'No.' Mike's expression was anything but friendly. It was clear he intended his visit to be a short one because he was dressed for the shower. Having removed his uniform, he wore a white undervest, a towel around his waist and thongs. In one hand, he carried a toiletries bag that looked like it had been around the world and back again at least six times.

'A shame that.' Gavin tipped back another mouthful.

'I thought I told you to stay away from my niece!'

'Did you?' Gavin leaned his forearm on his knee. 'Damn! I knew there was something I forgot to do last week.'

He wasn't a big drinker but he'd already downed three that night because of his mood. Definitely more than his usual quota and on an empty stomach the alcohol seemed to be going straight to his head.

Mike looked positively murderous. 'This isn't a joke.'

'No, you're absolutely right.' Gavin tried to nod with sincerity but his head jangled a little too much so he stopped. 'This week you have my word that I will do everything in my power to avoid her.'

'Oh really? What did you do?'

Gavin chuckled. 'Nothing you wouldn't have done if you'd been in exactly the same situation.'

Mike took a swing at him. But Gavin caught the fist before it hit the side of his face. The action, however, sobered him. He had seen that light in someone's eyes before.

Wendy's.

'Now why the hell would you go and do that?' He threw Mike's fist away and stood up, the alcohol fumes clearing from his brain.

'Do you think I don't know trouble when I see it?' Mike hissed.

'What?'

'I've been you, Gavin. And I know exactly what you're doing.'

Gavin folded his arms, unable to disguise the contempt that crossed his face. 'Oh yeah? And what exactly would that be?'

'You're running.' Mike's eyes flicked over him in disgust. 'And you're going to keep running until whatever's chasing you tires or gives up.'

'For fuck's sake –'

But Mike interrupted him. 'Do you want me to start digging?' he threatened. ''Cause I will. I have no qualms in exposing you and whatever game you happen to be playing, legal or illegal.'

This time Mike had his attention. But Gavin didn't say anything, merely waited for what was obviously coming next.

The price of the negotiation.

'Stay away from my niece: she's not going down that road with you. She's been through enough.'

'Are you threatening me?'

'Damn straight I'm threatening you.'

Gavin's eyes narrowed. Mike was panting slightly from the toll the conversation was taking on him. He wasn't afraid. If anything he both pitied and respected Mike for taking such a firm position about his niece. He wondered if Wendy knew of her uncle's protective nature.

Probably not.

'So, Mike,' he put his beer down as his eyes ran over the gentleman's portly figure, 'just out of curiosity, from one man to another . . . What were *you* running from?'

Mike's face flamed red. 'None of your damned business!'

Gavin's eyes lowered and noticed for the first time a rather interesting aspect of Mike's bare feet. 'Must have been a pretty hard jog,' he commented thoughtfully.

'Don't underestimate me,' Mike spat at him. 'If you try me, Gavin, I'll bring whatever's chasing you here faster than a bolt of lightning from a black cloud. Do you understand me?'

Gavin held up his hands in mock surrender. 'Perfectly.'

Chapter 14

It had been a kiss to cast all other kisses in the shade. Soft but firm, arousing but tender, and wholly and woefully shake-your-bones-out-of-your-body powerful.

And no wonder.

It was delivered by one of the most experienced playboys on the Pilbara. Gavin had not one, not two, but *three* women on the go. He was unashamed. Unfaithful. And unapologetic.

In fact, the only thing he *was* concerned about was her complicating that state of affairs.

She swallowed hard. *Thank your lucky stars.* At least she had escaped.

She should be grateful that he had sensed her inexperience. It was probably clear from the clumsiness of her kissing or perhaps the way she'd thrown herself at him that she was starving for that sort of attention – and not interested in anything casual. There was no other reason that she could think of for his sudden and immediate withdrawal from a courtship that *he* had started. He must have realised that she wasn't his equal in the sexual games he liked to play. She knew she should be feeling relieved, but it was humiliation that stained her cheeks crimson. She tried to focus on the files in front of her.

The audit was tomorrow. The culmination of four weeks' work and late nights stressing. She'd actually had to skip her R and R to be in town for it. *Just think, you could be lazing on a beach right now instead of sitting here feeling pathetic.*

After catching Gavin embracing Lena, she'd kept mostly to herself. She didn't think the two were involved. Lena was too in love with Dan for that. Gavin was probably being his usual flirtatious self. Taking what he could, when he could.

And as for Lena, she was young and impulsive. She had Annabel George circling her boyfriend like a shark. Perhaps she wanted to show Bulldog that she too was in high demand – make him jealous enough to be firmer with the loony stalker.

Who knows?

Who cares?

She just had to remember who she was and what she was there to do rather than get involved in other people's love lives or, worse, caught up in an affair of her own.

For the last five days she had worked solely on preparing herself for the audit – trying to concentrate all her energies into this task. That actually wasn't as easy as she hoped.

For starters, they'd just hit November. The tropical Cyclone Season Outlook had been issued by the Bureau of Meteorology, which was basically a prediction of the likelihood and frequency of cyclones in the coming season due to global weather patterns and other relevant statistical information. She didn't like the look of their predictions this year. It seemed they could be expecting some nasty storms quite early in the season. Yet another issue to worry about.

Secondly, perhaps not as important but equally as stressful, word had been spreading around site that she and Gavin had been on a few dates. The rumours were now a full-blown love story that the guys liked to quiz her about whenever they got the chance.

'He treating you right, Sergeant?'

'You tell me if he ain't toeing the line.'

Apparently, a couple of men had witnessed Gavin getting her call on Sunday and watched him run off hot foot to rescue his 'sheila in distress'. Compounding that was the fact that he had been missing for the rest of that day. Everyone just assumed they were an item now.

Even when she denied it. Which she did. *All the time.*

Chub was quick to realise something was up. For someone who was always protesting his inability to understand women, he seemed to be all-seeing when it came to this debacle.

'So you sure those rumours about you and Gavin aren't true, little mate?'

'Would I lie to you, Cobber?'

'Well.' Chub sighed as though picturing a romantic scene in his mind's eye. 'It's just that when he came in here last week he was looking at you like you were a bowl of hot wedges served with sour cream and sweet chilli sauce.'

She rolled her eyes. 'I would think that highly unlikely.'

Chub reluctantly pulled himself from the pleasant daydream. 'Little mate, if there's one thing I *never* make mistakes about, it's bowls of hot wedges with accompanying dips.'

'Good to know.' She smiled.

He eyed her thoughtfully. 'I just don't want you to do something dumb, like save yourself for me.'

'*What?*'

'I didn't want to be cruel. But I'm sorry, love. It's just not going to happen.'

Wendy put her hand over her heart. 'OMG! Why not?'

'You're not my type.' He lowered his voice to a whisper. 'You eat like a stick insect on a diet. Who does that?'

She laughed. 'All right, you've convinced me to give up hope. I won't save myself for you.'

He turned back to face his computer but said seriously, 'No point in saving yourself period. Life starts now, little mate, not ten years from now. Trust me. I know.'

She looked at him for a moment. 'Cobber, what *do* you look for in a woman?'

'Mostly a pulse.'

She laughed. 'Don't say that. You're a great guy. Any woman would be lucky to have you take an interest in her.'

'You think?' For once she thought he lost some of his cockiness. 'I'll keep that in mind.'

She didn't quite know what else to say to him so decided for a subject change. 'Have you got a hard copy of everyone's resumes? 'Cause Frank will want to flick through them definitely.'

Chub seemed relieved. 'Yep, all here.'

'And Carl's?'

'Just added it. Did you know before this job he worked in Indonesia for five years?'

'Yeah, I read it over last night. He's got a tonne of experience in the field, hasn't he?'

Chub nodded. 'Then we're all set.'

'Great, I'm going to start working on the bookshelf.'

She swivelled in her chair to look at the piece of furniture behind her. The day before she'd had a couple of the guys move a large but empty bookshelf from the main office donga to sit in the space behind her desk. Now she was going to arrange her files of carefully ordered records and documentation into an easily accessible library of information. Frank could demand any bit of paper for any section on site he wanted. She would just be able to reach behind her and pull it out as efficiently as possible.

Despite her preparations, Wendy was still nervous as hell the next morning. Unable to eat, she skipped breakfast and went into work half an hour early just to double check all was ready. Carl, on the other hand, was actually pretty relaxed for a man who ordinarily seemed to be constantly at the end of his fuse.

Wendy figured that betrothal must agree with him.

Frank and Dan turned up at precisely eight and were escorted into Carl's messy office by John Lewis, who seemed put out at having to contaminate himself via association with the client.

Wendy was already seated in the visitor's chair and had been discussing with Carl some of the things that TCN might focus on. She quickly cut off her words as Dan's intimidating stature filled the room, closely followed by his sly-looking henchman. If tension had a Richter scale, in that moment it hit ten.

Even Wendy found it difficult to keep her hackles from rising and she knew the whole 'client is the enemy' culture on the job must be starting to affect her.

'Good morning.' Even Dan's bland greeting seemed to indicate the onset of battle.

Wendy had put two more chairs in Carl's office earlier and indicated for their visitors to sit down. 'Would you like a coffee?'

'No, no. I'm fine, thanks.' Dan waved her offer aside.

But Frank – who appeared to be more keen on the idea of being waited on by Wendy than actually quenching his thirst – immediately nodded imperiously. 'Yes, of course. White, three sugars. Lots of milk please, but not so much that you've made it cold. I like my coffee just above lukewarm. Like around forty-one degrees, if you don't mind.'

Wendy momentarily toyed with the idea of giving him a still boiling black coffee with no sugar *in his lap* but then decided spite was not the answer to a quick and painless audit. With clenched jaw, she nodded politely and left the room.

When she returned, arrows were already being fired across the desk in quick succession. Carl was bracing himself against the onslaught, knuckles white as he clutched the edge of his table. He looked up gratefully when Wendy walked back in.

Frank was talking loudly. 'Now, of course, I will personally want to peruse all your files. I want to see your licences, your competency certificates, your training schedules, your registers, your daily inspection reports, your risk assessments, your JSAs, your hazards reports, your . . .'

Luckily, Bulldog interrupted him. 'Frank, I'm sure they don't need to be read a catalogue.'

Frank's mouth grew mulish but he accepted this criticism and shut his notebook. 'I just wanted to be specific.'

'Here.' Wendy held out his coffee.

His expression turned smug. 'Well done,' he said, rather than 'thank you' – as though impressed her puny brain had *actually* managed to achieve something.

She ignored the dart and drew up a chair next to him, trying to focus instead on what Dan was saying.

'Frank will definitely be staying on well into the afternoon to examine your files and your diligence in these various areas. But this morning I wanted to talk about two specific incidents.'

'Extremely hazardous incidents.' Frank sipped his coffee. 'I'm still stunned there wasn't more damage or injuries.'

Wendy ignored him. So did Carl.

Dan continued to speak. 'Namely, the incident with the fishing boat – what I would call a near miss. And the incident with the bus – not so happy an ending.'

Carl spread his hands. 'What do you want to know? We haven't hidden anything from you in either case.'

'Are you sure?' Frank asked. 'I'm certain Lance must have had some help with that boat of his.'

'Lance is an accomplished fisherman,' Wendy put in stonily. 'He didn't need any help.'

Bulldog turned a militant eye upon his henchman, whose trap immediately shut, and then turned back to Carl. 'We are not accusing you of hiding anything. I just wanted to personally go through your files on both these incidents and make sure that you have completed all follow-up – and future prevention procedures – to my satisfaction.'

'Not a problem.' Wendy stood up. 'I'll go get them.'

'I'll help you.' Frank also stood up quickly, as though if Wendy was left unsupervised she might try to tamper with the documents.

'Fine,' she mumbled.

They retrieved both files and brought them back to Carl's office. Dan began flicking through the papers immediately.

'So it says here you had the mines inspector out Monday.'

'Yes.'

'And it all went well?'

'Because I've noticed the ship-loader crane was back in service pretty quickly,' Frank butted in before she could respond. 'Was that cleared for use?'

'Absolutely.' Wendy didn't hesitate. 'There was no damage to the crane and as soon as we put the stopper on the rails we were right to go.'

Dan continued to flick through the file. 'And what of Dimitri and the crane driver?'

'I did a detailed debrief with both of them, and indeed all the men,' Wendy responded. 'You can see the reports right there.'

'And what of prevention measures?' Frank demanded. 'How can you be sure this won't happen again?'

Wendy directed her reply to Dan. 'Well, the mines inspector had a long talk with the men involved and made some suggestions. But I did my own report and we have tightened up our procedures for use of the ship-loader crane and, of course, that stopper is in place now.'

'Just so you know,' Frank said contemptuously, 'a stopper doesn't fix everything. Your people need to be thinking about what they are doing.'

'For fuck's sake,' Carl barked at Frank. 'You eat a bowl of beans last night or something? Your arse is flapping faster than your mouth.'

Frank turned the colour of the red kidney variety as his eyes shot to Carl in shock.

'I can only assure you that ever since that fuckin' incident with the bus – an accident that nearly took my fiancée's life, by the way – we have been treating the scene like a war zone. There is no measure that could be taken that hasn't already been taken.'

Frank, who had regained some of his composure, opened his mouth to say something but Carl held up his hand for silence.

'And as for the fishin' thing. There has been no other incident like it on or under the wharf either before it occurred or since. Fish, or should I say Lance, was a loose cannon who has been dealt with.'

Wendy also gave her explanation. 'Lance was fired because he went fishing on company time, placing himself and potentially others at risk. We have removed both him and his influence from this site. There is no further problem.'

'But –' Frank began.

'Yes, I agree.' Dan closed the file and stood up. 'I think I will leave Frank here to complete the audit. My main concerns have been addressed. I would like to commend you, Wendy, on the changes that have been made on the job. I've seen many improvements just walking around on the wharf.'

'Thank you.' Wendy beamed.

'Well, we haven't seen your files yet,' Frank added huffily. 'You don't need to worry, Dan. I'll go over everything with a fine tooth comb.'

Dan looked at him in some amusement. 'I wasn't worried.'

Carl tried not to look too relieved as he stood up, holding out his hand. 'Good to see you today, B– Dan.'

'Good to see the back of me, you mean.' Dan shot him a knowing grin. 'Congratulations, by the way.'

'Oh.' Carl ran a self-conscious hand through his hair. 'You heard . . .'

'It's hard not to.'

Carl clicked his tongue. 'I keep forgetting about you and Lena. Telephone, telegraph, tella woman, right?'

Dan's mouth hardened, but he said nothing more. Carl coughed, clearly wondering what he had said wrong. The client manager stalked out the door, leaving Frank to eye Wendy up and down like a chicken whose neck he was about to snap.

'I would be happy to take a look at those files now.'

She lifted her chin. 'No problem.'

Frank followed her back to her office, where Chub was working quietly.

'So what would you like to go through first?' Wendy asked.

'Everything.'

I had a feeling you'd say that.

Frank trawled through every file on her fancy new book-shelf, studiously taking notes and photocopying some for his own records or more detailed inspection later. Sometimes, he also checked electronic files that she hadn't printed. They broke the day up with a walk along the wharf and in the yard. He stuck his twitchy nose into every possible nook and cranny he could find. He asked her and the men a deluge of nit-picky questions and just seemed to get angrier and more aggressive as the day progressed.

Wendy knew why.

It was because he couldn't find anything seriously wrong with their work practice.

And every time he said 'Ah-hah!' she would withdraw a new file and kindly point out that the problem had already been identified and was being fixed in accordance with proce-dure as detailed by the documentation.

He stayed late.

Very late.

It was nine pm and Frank was still going through files. Everyone had long since gone back to camp. Wendy's stomach grumbled. She knew that she had missed the mess dinner and was going to have to run into town to get something. If there was anything still open.

From her vantage point in the kitchen, she bobbled her tea bag in her seventh cuppa that day and watched him flicking, for the second time, through one of the huge files of resumes.

She watched him pause, finger to the page, and a slow smile spread across his slimy froglike lips. He whipped one resume from the file and went to the photocopier to make a copy. There was only one word to describe his expression at this point. Gleeful.

Uh-oh.

She set her cup down on the kitchen counter and walked over to him. 'Is everything all right?'

He looked up as he shoved the sheets of paper into a file he had been compiling for himself. 'I think we're done here.'

Finally!

'So did we pass?' she asked.

His expression grew increasingly smug. 'To be honest, I can't say for sure at this point.'

'I beg your pardon?'

'There are just a couple of things I need to go over.' He patted his file. 'And I'll let you know in the morning.'

Great! Thanks for the sleepless night.

She watched him walk towards the door and let himself out before glancing down at the resume file he had taken his last bit of information from. The file was open and exhibiting the resumes of two men.

Carl Curtis on one side and Gavin Jones on the other. She sat down.

Which one did he take?

She tried to think back over the scene and couldn't recall which side of the file he had removed papers from. She had read Carl's resume recently because he'd just put it together for them last week. She couldn't think of anything that could possibly be wrong with it. Carl was an engineer and project manager experienced both locally and overseas. But Gavin's resume, she hadn't really seen before.

Biting her lip, she withdrew the thin document from the sleeve and scanned the contents. Compared to a lot of resumes she had seen, Gavin seemed to have put in the minimum amount of information. There were no extra notes or those little personal details that people sometimes added to make themselves look more interesting or likeable. Like a list of hobbies or referees. He had stated his date of birth, giving him at least six years on her. Funny, she hadn't thought it was that much. His marital status was blank.

Of course.

But so was the university and high school from which he had graduated. He had merely written BE (1st Class Hons) and BSc beneath his name, indicating he had two degrees – a first-class honours in a Bachelor of Engineering and a Bachelor of Science. She'd always known the man was smart. That wasn't a surprise.

What *was* a surprise was the employment history located further down the page. He had only included projects he'd worked on in the last five years. From the high-responsibility roles he'd held on these jobs, it was clear he must have also had an extensive work history before it. Why hadn't he listed it?

He struck her as a man who had at least ten to fifteen years' experience. But he hadn't bothered to mention the early milestones of his career on paper.

She sat back in her chair and thought over the various conversations she'd had with him. And a simple truth dawned on her.

I don't know anything about Gavin that happened more than five years ago.

Her eyes flipped back to the front page of the resume and scanned the top for an address. A house in Perth. Number 3 Northberry Road, Leederville, just up the road from her adoptive father's pub. She tested her memory. Gavin had told her that he took his R and R in Perth but not that he was from there or born there.

She was probably just being pedantic. What did it matter anyway? Frank couldn't shut down Barnes Inc's operation just because Gavin hadn't given his full employment history and place of birth. The information he had provided was adequate though sparse. Frank had no case here.

She shut the file and frowned.

Unless I'm missing something.

She locked up the donga and left site. In the end, she had some fruit from her fridge for dinner and went to bed early. Not that she slept much. She was too worried about what Frank might try to pull out of his hat the next morning.

And the sleep she did have was peppered with dreams of Gavin. Quizzing him about his past amidst sordid kisses on rocky sandy beaches.

She awoke to the sound of her screeching alarm, feeling like she'd only been under for two minutes.

BEEP! BEEP! BEEP!

Clutching her throbbing head, she jolted to an upright position. *Oh yeah! Today is going to be a great day.*

Neither Carl nor Chub seemed at all perplexed that Bulldog hadn't called that morning to let them know whether they had passed the audit.

'That man is just putting off the inevitable,' Chub assured her. 'He doesn't want to pass us. But he has to, so he's taking his time about it just to torture us.'

'You don't understand, Cobber,' Wendy bit her lip, 'Frank's got it in for me. He's Neil's best friend.'

'No wonder he's such a dick. Don't worry, little mate, we'll get that phone call before ten o'clock. You mark my words.'

But they didn't get a phone call at ten o'clock. Instead, Frank turned up personally. If self-satisfied was a smell, he would have reeked of it. He demanded an immediate meeting with Carl and Wendy.

The three of them congregated in Carl's office. Carl sat behind the desk, Frank in one of the visitor's chairs. Wendy shut the door, too nervous to sit down.

'So,' Carl folded his arms, 'what do you have for me?'

'It appears,' Frank stated grudgingly, 'that the majority of your work procedures are acceptable. So we will not be shutting this operation down.'

'Well, that's a fuckin' relief.' Carl grinned at each of them as if he had known it all along.

'I haven't finished.' Frank lifted his chin haughtily and Carl's grin disappeared. 'We will not be shutting this operation down so long as one problem I have identified is rectified *immediately*.'

Carl glanced at Wendy and then frowned. 'What problem?'

'You, Carl.'

Carl's gaze swung back to Frank. 'What the fuck?'

Frank opened his file and withdrew what Wendy could now see was not Gavin's but Carl's resume. 'It has come to my attention that you do not have a driver's licence.'

Carl stood up. 'Of course I have a fuckin' driver's licence. Had one for years. Got it when I was fuckin' eighteen years old. So maybe I had to sit the fuckin' test six times but I still got that shitty little piece of paper.'

Frank remained seated as he revealed the guts of his diabolical plot. 'According to your resume, the last job you worked on was in Indonesia. Apparently, you were there for four years. During that time, you acquired an Indonesian driver's licence but you allowed your Australian one to lapse.'

'So I didn't pay a few fuckin' bills. Big deal.'

'It *is* a big deal.' Frank closed the file with a snap, making Wendy's heart sink. 'It means you are not legally allowed to be driving in this country, let alone cruising around in a ute on a highly hazardous construction site. Which is why . . . Dan and I are requesting your immediate removal from the project until such time as you have fixed the problem. It is simply too unsafe to have you here.'

'My removal?' Carl was momentarily speechless.

Frank glanced at his watch in a businesslike manner, as though he had something more pressing to do after this arse-kicking. 'I shall personally escort you to the gate, where you will have to arrange for *someone else* to drive you home. You are welcome, if you like, to correspond with site via telephone from Wickham but under no circumstance are you to set foot at Cape Lambert until you have a legitimate Australian driver's licence.'

'But that could be weeks, depending on how many government departments we get bounced through,' Wendy protested. 'What about the project?'

'That is our request.' Frank shrugged. 'We shall, of course, expect Barnes Inc to keep up with its proposed schedules and other work practices in the meantime. Your company has by no means lost any of its responsibility to its contract, despite this slight mishap.'

Slight mishap.

She could just kill him.

'I ain't fuckin' leaving.' Carl stabbed a finger at him.

'I'm sorry but –'

'Shut the fuck up, you arse-faced little shitbag.'

Frank's jaw dropped open.

'There is no fuckin' way that I'm leaving my men just so you can get high and mighty on a fuckin' technicality. I can't leave the project now. I'm fuckin' running it.'

'Well, you'll just have to get someone else to run it for a while.'

'It's my project, my responsibility, my baby. I'm not going to let you fuckin' kick me out. You've got no right. Anybody with two brain cells to rub together can see I can fuckin' drive.'

Wendy had actually witnessed Carl tearing around in his ute and several times nearly backing into someone or something, but decided this was not the time to bring that up.

Frank nervously licked his lips. 'I don't think you quite see my point. What you're doing at the moment is not just against site regulations. It's against the law.'

This statement only seemed to incense Carl further. 'Tell you what, fuckface! When I actually give a shit, you'll be the first person I give it to!'

Frank stood up, clutching his file for support. 'Mr Curtis,' he tried to infuse authority rather than fear into his voice, 'why don't we just make this simple and you accompany me to the gate now?'

'I'm not going anywhere with you. And if you try to fuckin' make me, I'll snap your puny little neck with my bare hands.' Carl viciously mimed doing so.

Frank swallowed hard and then in desperation turned to Wendy. 'You have one hour to escort this man from site. If he is not gone within that time, I am shutting this operation down. I mean it. I am shutting you all down!'

On this cowardly threat, he stalked from the room, slamming the door behind him.

Carl began to pace the floor, anger vibrating from every fibre of his being.

'Carl –' Wendy began tentatively.

'Shut up,' he snapped. 'I'm fuckin' thinkin'.'

But after pacing for five minutes he still hadn't said anything more.

'Carl, if I may –'

'You may not.'

'I know it's a pain in the arse but we've only got,' she glanced at the clock on the wall, 'fifty-four minutes before that idiot shuts Barnes Inc down. Please let me get you off the premises before that happens – at least till we can get you a licence or figure something out.'

'I'm not going.'

'But you know there is nothing else we can do.'

He turned on her contemptuously. 'You just had Neil and Fish fired. Do you honestly want to escort the project manager off site now as well? How do you think that's going to go for you?'

She recoiled like he had slapped her. All this time, she had thought Carl oblivious to the rumours circulating about her, or at the very least indifferent to them. Perhaps she needed to credit him with a little more awareness, despite his apparent 'she'll be right' attitude towards everything.

After wringing her hands for a few moments she said, 'I don't care what people think of me, and neither should you. We both know you wouldn't be leaving the project to prove Frank right. You're doing it for the good of everyone else. Just stop for a minute, Carl, and look beyond your own pride.'

He finished pacing to glare at her, opened his mouth and then shut it again. For a second she thought she might have got through to him, until he lifted his arm and pointed to the door.

'Out!'

'But –'

'*Out!*'

Knowing that no further words were going to make a difference, she quickly made for the door, which he slammed shut behind her.

What am I going to do now?!

She hurried back to her office, trying to ignore the looks of curiosity from the others seated in the main office donga, who had also just witnessed Frank fleeing the scene. She sat down at her desk and put her head in her hands.

'I take it it didn't go well,' Chub's faintly amused voice sounded in front of her.

She groaned and looked up. 'We have fifty minutes before TCN shuts the Barnes Inc operation down.'

'What?' Chub started. 'Why?'

Wendy quickly outlined Frank's evil plan.

'That weasel.' Chub frowned. 'I hadn't attributed him with so much creativity.'

'Well, I don't know how to get Carl off the premises, Cobber,' Wendy cried, throwing up her hands. 'He simply won't go.'

'Seems to me what you need is some muscle.'

She looked up at him hopefully.

'Yes, yes, I have an incredible amount of upper body strength.' He proudly lifted his girth and then dropped it. 'There's, er . . . just one problem.'

'What's that?' she demanded.

Chub's mouth twisted into a pained expression. 'I'm chicken. Always have been. You know when I was at school I used to wet my pants, literally, whenever there was a fight in the playground. And most of the time I wasn't even involved.'

'Urgh!' Wendy moaned in frustration. 'Who else can I ask? Nobody is going to want to help the TCN spy escort the project manager off the job. Apart from the fact that everybody hates me, Carl would no doubt offer to fire them on the spot if they so much as touched him.'

'Good point.' Chub examined the fingernails of one hand, then said without looking up, 'You could ask Gavin.'

'I *am not* asking Gavin.'

'Why not? He is the next senior person on site. On those rare occasions when Carl is sick or on R and R, he's supposed to be the acting project manager. Almost seems like his right, really.'

'I don't see how it's his right at all,' Wendy snapped, feeling like she was fast losing control of the situation.

'And,' Chub nodded seriously, 'he's got muscles. That fella is built like a brick shithouse. Have you seen him with his shirt off?'

'No.' Wendy choked.

'You should,' Chub nodded thoughtfully, 'you'd like it.'

'*Cobber.*'

Chub lifted his palms up in surrender. 'I'm just saying.'

She was silent for a moment as she glared at him. His lips twitched under her murderous stare before he shot a quick look at his watch. 'Well, I guess you've got all of forty-five minutes to think of something else. I'd get onto that if I were you.'

'*All right*,' she cried, 'you win! I'll get Gavin on the phone.'

Chapter 15

The phone rang twice before he picked it up.

'Sarge?'

'Hi, Gavin.' She infused what she hoped was a business tone into her voice. 'I need your help. Can you come to my office?'

'Er, sure. Could you just give me an hour? I want to stay till this pile is driven.'

'It can't wait an hour. *I need you now*,' she pleaded and then realised maybe she should have used a different turn of phrase. 'I mean, I need your muscles.'

Geez, girl!

'You need my *what*?'

She slapped her palm to her forehead and closed her eyes. 'Did I say muscles? I mean that in the context of your whole body –'

'You need my *body*?'

'Look, can you just get down here and stop asking stupid questions?!' She slammed down the phone and jumped away from it like it was a tiger snake.

A snort from Chub came from her right. 'Well played.'

'Oh, shut up.'

Gavin arrived not ten minutes later, throwing the door open and leaping into the room like Batman minus the mask and cape.

'G'day, lead foot,' Chub murmured. 'Do you think you could have got here any sooner?'

Gavin ignored him and turned to Wendy. 'What did you say you needed?'

'Offering your services, are you?' Chub's lips twitched. 'Somehow I'm not surprised.'

Wendy stood up, wringing her hands and biting her lower lip. 'TCN is going to shut us down in thirty minutes if you don't persuade Carl – perhaps physically – to leave site.'

Gavin stuck his pointer finger out. 'You see, I never would have guessed you were going to say that.'

'Really?' Chub seemed amused. 'Wasn't it obvious?'

Wendy glared at the HR manager, who appeared to be enjoying himself far too much. 'Will you be quiet? Can't you see we're going through a crisis here?'

Chub lowered his eyes. 'Sorry.'

Wendy quickly filled Gavin in on all that had occurred at the audit that morning. 'We're down to twenty-seven minutes.'

'Trust me.' Gavin grinned. 'We're not gunna need that long.'

Chub threw Wendy a smug look. 'What did I tell you?'

But she ignored him, holding the door to their donga open. 'Then let's get this show on the road.'

Wendy and Gavin headed over to Carl's office, reaching him just in the nick of time. The project manager had donned his hard hat and safety vest. It was apparent he was just about to step out – no doubt to resume his usual duties.

'What the fuck is this?' His jaw slackened as Gavin walked in, followed by Wendy, who meekly shut the door behind her and leaned back against it, holding the knob for support.

'Call it an intervention,' Gavin informed him.

Carl took one look at him and then turned to Wendy. 'You've brought this pretty boy, who can't hammer a nail in straight let alone a fuckin' pile, to get me out?'

Gavin grinned. 'Always great to get a little feedback on the job – lets a man know how he's doing.'

'If you think he can talk me into fuckin' leaving you're mad.'

'Who said anything about talking?' Gavin scoffed. 'I was just going to knock you out and drag your body to the kerb.'

Carl's attention finally swung back to Gavin with a growl. 'I'd like to see you try.'

Gavin shrugged and took a step forwards, just as Carl's fist caught him on the side of the jaw.

The piling engineer's head turned with the force of the punch and Carl's fist immediately dropped as though he was stunned at what he had just done.

Gavin looked back at him. 'You know, I was actually joking about hitting you. But now . . . *now I'm not.*'

He threw his fist into the fray but Carl blocked. So he launched another one that hit home.

Wendy's hands went to her face. 'Guys! Stop! I thought I could do this but I can't.'

They ignored her. A chair overturned. Boots marked the vinyl.

'This isn't right!' she cried.

You're supposed to be the safety manager! Instead you're in here encouraging two men to brawl! Are you crazy?

Without thinking she threw herself into the skirmish, intending to pull their arms apart. If she had thought about it, she would have realised that such a tactic would have been useless against the strength of two bulls with their horns locked together, but she wasn't quite thinking clearly.

She was thrown aside and as she hit the side of the desk and then the floor she felt a strange popping sensation in her shoulder before pain erupted, engulfing her like lava from a crater in the Bunya Mountains.

She screamed.

'Goddamn it, Wendy!' Gavin yanked away from Carl and threw himself on the ground, crawling to her side. He half-picked her up, holding her to his chest.

His heart beat like a gong against her flaming cheek. She moaned in pain.

'I think she's dislocated her shoulder,' he threw at a panting Carl, who was now sagged against the back of a chair.

The door burst open. John Lewis and several other staff in the immediate vicinity came in, stopping dead in their tracks at the damage wreaked by the struggle. Carl's torn safety vest, overturned furniture, Wendy cocooned in Gavin's arms with a shaking body and deformed-looking shoulder.

'Where's the site medic?' Carl rasped.

'He's on the wharf,' John said quickly. 'Some guy fainted this morning. Dehydration or something . . .'

'Fuck! Couldn't he have passed out tomorrow? Dickhead!'

Wendy vaguely heard his voice through the pain. Tears poured down her face.

'It'll be quicker to drive her into Wickham than to wait.' Gavin stood up, lifting Wendy off the ground easily, as if he was picking up a baby. 'We need to get a doctor to put it back in immediately.'

But through the throbbing mist, Wendy remembered something.

With effort she lifted her head from the comfort of Gavin's chest, choking out the words with bull-headed stubbornness.

'I . . . I'm not going anywhere without Carl.'

Carl looked at her in shock until his mouth slowly eased into a grin. 'Fuck, Wendy! If I didn't know any better I'd say you fucked your shoulder on purpose. Rest easy, girl! I'm coming with you. In fact, I'll drive.'

'No!' she and Gavin said at the same time.

He held out his arms. 'Then let me take her.'

'You're not touching her,' Gavin spat at him. 'And we're going in my ute.'

The rest of the staff gave Gavin a wide berth as he stalked from the room carrying his burden.

'Guess I'll be leaving for a while then,' Carl said gruffly to John. 'Will you ring Bulldog and tell him that I've left site?'

'Sure, Carl.' John nodded and watched stunned as he followed Gavin and Wendy out.

Wendy looked up into Gavin's worried face, fascinated by both the guilt and the concern she saw there. His hair was a mess from the fight and his shirt pocket torn. But he looked undeniably and irrevocably scrumptious. If she wasn't in so much pain she would try to snuggle in further.

'Tell me,' she murmured, 'did we make it?'

'Make what?'

'Make it on time?' She gasped as her shoulder twitched.

'Wendy, don't talk, you're aggravating it.' But he glanced up at the donga clock as they left the building all the same. 'With two minutes to spare, Sarge.'

'Thank goodness.'

Gavin drove Carl and Wendy to Wickham Health Centre, which was a little more than five minutes from site. Carl's brash voice and loud demands soon made their case an urgent one and Gavin carried Wendy into the office of a middle-aged male doctor.

The doctor wasn't at all thrown to be confronted by two anxious and roughed-up men and one groaning female. Wendy suspected patients in fluoro vests must be a common sight in these parts.

'A dislocated shoulder, I see.' He rubbed his hands cheerfully as he examined her. 'Doesn't look too bad. I can pop that one back in place myself.'

After administering Wendy with a local anaesthetic to the injured area he lifted her arm and, bracing her shoulder, manoeuvred the bone back into place. She felt the popping sensation again but this time no pain – though that was hardly surprising, considering her whole shoulder was now numb.

The doctor arranged her arm in a sling and told her she would need to go immediately to Nickol Bay Hospital in

Karratha to have some X-rays done, just to ensure the bone really was back in place and she hadn't fractured it or any other part of her shoulder.

Wendy thanked him and then allowed the boys to escort her back out to the car with the doctor's referral in hand. She leaned heavily on Gavin, protesting when he offered to carry her. She didn't want to seem like a big baby when the injury was her own impulsive fault.

Forty minutes later they found themselves in another waiting room in Karratha and Wendy could see that guilt was really starting to catch up with Carl.

'Listen,' Carl ran thick fingers through his dark hair, 'I'm real fuckin' sorry about your shoulder, Wendy. I didn't think it would come to this.'

'You should be fuckin' sorry,' Gavin growled.

She reached over and squeezed Gavin's knee with her good hand. 'Don't start. I'm going to be fine. I'm just glad that it's not you two lying in beds in here instead. I thought you were going to kill each other.'

'Could have, should have,' Gavin agreed.

'Would have,' Carl added with a challenging sparkle in his eye.

'Oh, for goodness' sake,' Wendy rolled her eyes. 'If you must, take it outside this time.'

'No.' Gavin's attention returned to her, guilt in his voice. 'Here I am trying to protect you and you get hurt anyway.'

'Protect me from what?' She glanced at him in surprise.

He looked away and didn't quite answer. 'This is my fault.'

'It ain't your fuckin' fault,' Carl reprimanded him. 'You were only trying to do what's best for the project.'

'Knocking Wendy across the room?' Gavin shot at him derisively.

'I think you both knocked me,' Wendy corrected him. 'If it was anyone's fault it was mine for being so stupid as to try and break you up.'

'Well, I'm not going to fuckin' split hairs over blame,' Carl sighed. 'I just want to put this shit aside and move on.'

'Then you'll have to work from Wickham until I can get your licence sorted.' Wendy glanced at him sternly.

'I can't do everything from fuckin' Wickham.'

'I'll do the rest.' Gavin nodded determinedly.

Carl snorted. 'And why would I put you in charge?'

The cocky smile was back on Gavin's face. 'Come on, Carl. I've always had a fancy to be project manager.'

Carl looked heavenwards. 'I wish to fuck I had better options.'

'So you agree then?' Gavin said quickly though Carl didn't look at him. Instead he turned to Wendy.

'You keep an eye on him. His fuckin' ego is likely to take up too much space!'

'Wendy Hopkins?' A nurse came out to collect them.

Wendy raised her good hand. 'Right here.'

After the X-ray was done and Wendy was cleared to leave, Gavin drove them to Carl's house in Wickham to drop him off.

Sharon met them in the living room, her leg encased in a giant blue plastic boot.

'Oh no! What's happened?'

Wendy couldn't resist: 'I got in a fight.'

'With *who*?'

'Carl and Gavin.'

Sharon's gaze swung straight to Carl. 'What did you do?'

'Why do you always assume I've fuckin' done something?' Carl replied sourly.

'What were you doing fighting with Wendy?'

'I wasn't fighting with Wendy. I was fighting with fuckin' Gavin!'

'Who threw the first punch?'

'What the fuck has that got to do with anything?' Carl flushed.

Wendy put her good hand on Sharon's arm. 'Let him be. There was a bit of an ultimatum from the client. Carl took offence, Gavin and he got into a fight and, dumb idiot I am, I thought I was strong enough to break it up.'

Again, Sharon's gaze zoomed in on a sullen-looking Carl. 'What was so bloody offensive?'

Wendy quickly apprised Sharon of the full situation. 'So you see, Carl can't come back to site until he's got his driver's licence.' She glanced around the room as though searching for a missing child. 'Where's Fish?'

Sharon's face clouded. 'I kind of kicked him out yesterday.'

'Still leaving his fish guts in the sink?'

'Worse,' Sharon pulled a face, 'much worse. Yesterday he caught this huge mud crab. He wanted to catch some more but this really big one broke the net. So he came home to get another net and put the captured mud crab – still alive, mind you – in our bathtub for safe keeping.'

Wendy covered her mouth and gasped. 'He didn't!'

'Do you know what his defence was?' Sharon did a very good imitation of Fish's voice. '"Well, how was I supposed to know you hadn't had a shower yet?"'

Wendy choked back her laughter.

'I take it your shower is over your bath,' Gavin drawled.

'Yes,' Sharon confirmed. 'I nearly broke my other leg trying to get out of the tub before the snappy little thing nipped my ankles off.'

'That ratbag,' Wendy exclaimed.

'It was so humiliating. Definitely the straw that broke the camel's back.'

'I don't blame you.'

Gavin looked around at the group. 'Sorry to interrupt,' he rubbed his hands together, 'but now that I'm acting project manager, I think we should make a plan for the future.'

'Oh, you do, do you?' Carl eyed him in annoyance.

'Yes,' Gavin said decisively. 'Carl's working from here, I'm returning to the wharf and I think Wendy should go on R and R.'

Wendy's head spun around fast. '*Why?*'

'Well you're overdue, aren't you, because of the audit? Now you've got a sore shoulder . . . perfect time to take a break.'

'But there's so much to do.'

'Not that I can see. Take the leave and rest up. You need to.'

She glared at him. 'My arm is fine. I'll take the day off and tomorrow –'

'You'll fly home.'

'I will not.' She turned fully to him this time, her unslung hand on her hip.

'You know,' Sharon said thoughtfully, 'I'm with him on this one.'

'Yeah, he's right,' Carl nodded. 'You're fuckin' done, Wendy, at least for the moment. You need a break. Look at you. Your right arm's fucked. You're not fit to do shit.'

'But I've got follow-ups from the audit to deliver and cyclone prep stuff to do.'

'Which will all still be here when you get back.' Gavin smiled at her, making her fingers itch to slap him. 'Come on.' He put his hand in the small of her back. 'I'll take you back to your donga so you can pack. Chub will book the flight.'

'See you, Wendy.' Sharon waved cheerfully.

'You did that on purpose,' Wendy accused Gavin when they stepped out of the house.

'Did what, Sarge?'

'Ordered me off site in front of witnesses, so you could get a three to one vote.'

'Okay, so I'm guilty of a little subterfuge.' Gavin gave her his killer smile. 'Did you only just notice that about me?'

'Oh, good one.' She rolled her eyes as he helped her into his ute, his hands on her elbow and waist, sending a buzz up her spine that had no business being there.

He walked around to his side, got in and started the car. 'I just wanted to make sure that you rested,' he said seriously. 'Skipping R and R is not good for your health.'

It was so much of an echo of her own words that she had to gape at his audacity.

'Wow. That's pretty hypocritical considering you're more overdue than I am.'

'How do you figure that?'

'You skipped your leave because of Craig and since he's come back you haven't shown any signs of heading off to Perth.'

He grimaced. 'It's not a good idea for me to go to Perth right now.'

'Why?' There was a weird expression on his face. Gavin did cheeky, sexy, mischievous and teasing very well. Dark and mysterious stood out like a gold button on a black coat.

His expression lightened suddenly, however, as he glanced at her with a grin. 'Because the fish are biting at Exmouth not Perth. I was thinking of going there instead for my next break.'

'Then go.'

'I can't leave now. I've just been made project manager.' She couldn't mistake the glee in his voice. 'My career is on the rise, Sarge. You don't turn your back on that.'

'Hmm, don't let it go to your head.'

He laughed.

'What?'

'Nothing. Just you.' He pulled the car to a halt and she realised they were back in the camp car park. The air in the cabin suddenly seemed a tad thicker.

But as she went to open her car door he put a hand on her arm. 'Well, I hope you have a good break and get to see your friends and . . .' his expression was wistful '. . . your family.'

Yeah, because that's going to relax me.

He saw her frown. 'Did I say something wrong? Is this about the guy back home who hurt you? He's not going to be around, is he?'

She shook off his hand as she stepped out of the car. 'You're wrong, Gavin. You've always been wrong. The last guy who hurt me wasn't a boyfriend.'

'Then who was it?'

'My father.'

Her impulsive admission to Gavin shocked her. So much so that she hadn't allowed him to question her further. After avoiding the eye contact he was obviously trying to make, she had excused herself and continued to her donga alone. Her discomfort stemmed mainly from the fact that it was the first time she'd said that to anyone *including* herself. Admitting that her father's desertion at birth had caused her pain had seemed silly before. He'd never even known her. Perhaps he thought he was giving her a better life . . . she couldn't know for sure.

On the other hand, he had impregnated a woman he supposedly cared about but hadn't even stuck around to see what his son or daughter looked like. It seemed like rejection of the highest order.

Sitting on the plane the next day, she had ample opportunity to reflect on the discoveries and dead ends that she'd encountered on her journey to find the man who'd abandoned her. Being away from site and on her way home, the place where it had all begun, seemed to trigger that restless feeling in her again.

The *need* to know.

By the time the flight ended, she was resolved to at least question her family again. Not so much her mother this time though, as her adoptive father. She'd catch him alone and see if she could get further information out of him. Parry Hopkins was a withdrawn, shy man who tended to hide in his wife's shadow. She was sure he knew more than he was letting on.

She allowed herself three days to rest, shop and read. It was an absolute pleasure to be dust free and able to sleep in till midday if she desired. Unable to stop the workaholic in her, however, she did do a little sorting of the hoarded junk that had been lying around the house for years. Her shoulder seemed to be improving markedly but the doctor had told her to keep the sling on for one to two weeks.

There wasn't a day that went by when she didn't think of Gavin, or wonder how he was faring with his newfound power. *Probably loving it.*

Or his three or more love interests. *Probably loving that too.*

Why was it that women were always attracted to bad boys? Why was Mr Quiet-Shy-Dependable always such a lame duck? The one who had a sensitive side and enjoyed the odd chick flick every now and then was rarely the guy to make your heart race, your skin burn and your fingers tingle.

It's probably adrenaline. Your body recognises the danger. It's your brain that thinks it's love.

Love?

How did that word get stuck in there? Surely she wasn't that delusional?

It was actually a relief to have a goal in place to distract her brain from such confusing thoughts. She planned to see her father on Monday. It was the least busy day at his pub, The Grunt. It was the one place her mother didn't venture often. The best time, Wendy figured, was about four o'clock – after lunch, before dinner.

Parry was very surprised to see her, as she knew he would be. They were not close. Ever since she'd learned to drive, contact with both her parents had seemed unnecessary and sadly unwanted by either party. Nonetheless, he came out from the kitchens to greet her, kissed her on the cheek and invited her to sit down at one of his empty tables.

'What happened to your arm?' His eyes went immediately to her sling. 'Are you okay?'

'Oh, it's nothing. I dislocated my shoulder. It's on the mend.'

'You put too much on yourself.'

He was a small man, shorter than Wendy, with a thinning head of black hair. For a cook, he was surprisingly thin. He had sad eyes, a drawn face and the mark of duty stamped quite firmly on his lined brow.

'Can I get you something, Wendy? Coffee? Cool drink? Something stronger?'

'No thank you.' She waved away his offer with a slight smile. 'I just came to talk.'

'Really?' He looked wary. 'About what?'

'I think you've got an idea.'

When he continued to stand there, while she sat at his table, she sighed. 'Is it that hard to talk about this with me?'

'I don't want you getting angry and upset again.'

'Believe me, I'm past angry and upset. I've been through enough these last six months. I've realised that getting emotional about the past is a waste of time because you can't change it.'

He finally sat down at the table. Setting his tea towel aside, he placed one hand over the other. 'You certainly can't.'

'But just because you can't change the past,' she licked her lips, 'doesn't mean you can't learn from it.'

'What do you want from me, Wendy? I've already told you everything I know.'

'Not everything,' she said carefully. 'Do you love my mother?'

His gaze jumped to hers. 'Yes, God help me. It's why I have stayed with her. Hoping, praying things would change. Maybe it's time to let go.'

'Is that why you forgave her when you found out I wasn't yours?'

'I forgave her because I loved both of you. I still love you both.'

She shook her head. 'You tossed me out when you found out I was another man's child.'

'Is that what you believe?' He reached out to grab her hand. 'I know I have handled this badly, my dear, but I never stopped loving you. I just felt like I no longer had the right to.'

'That isn't an excuse.' Wendy's lips pulled in a straight line. 'Do you know how ostracised I felt being packed up and sent away as though I had done something wrong?'

He withdrew his hand. 'Things were a mess here too. It's better that you didn't have to witness the fighting that went on while you were away, especially in those first few years.'

'Fighting about what?'

His eyes flicked to her briefly. He hesitated. 'I wanted to find your biological father and tell him that a mistake had been made.'

She leaned forwards in shock. 'Did you find him? Did you tell him?'

'No, I didn't tell him,' he said with some difficulty. 'Helen was against it and so was my mother.'

'Grandma?'

'Both your grandparents, actually. Dad was alive back then and they were opposed to changing the status quo and dirtying the family name.'

Wendy could believe that. Her grandparents were both of the previous generation's mindset – traditional and conservative. Her grandmother, in particular, was very Italian and very Catholic. The last thing they would want is a bastard child in the family for people to gawk at. Particularly one they had claimed as their own for the last six years.

'Also we knew that . . . your father . . . was married. There was the other woman to consider. We didn't know what would happen if we told them.'

'Wait.' Wendy's eyes narrowed. 'How did you know that Hector was married?'

'His name is not Hector,' Parry practically spat. 'That's just a fantasy your mother likes to live to make herself feel better.'

Wendy blinked. 'I don't get it.'

He answered bitterly enough. 'I think your mother thought he would return after you were born. Maybe to claim you and her . . . Who knows? She kept tabs on him. But just before you turned one, he married someone else, thus severing the possibility of a relationship. He made his intentions clear.'

Wendy nodded. 'And that's when you came back on the scene and offered to marry her yourself?'

'Yes.'

'Did you know she was keeping tabs on my father?'

'Yes.' He gritted his teeth. 'Because I was keeping tabs on him myself. I wanted to see if he would come back for you. And when he didn't, it seemed proof you were mine. Can you tell what a fool I was?'

'Not a fool,' Wendy said quietly. 'You just wanted to believe my mother was telling the truth because you loved her.'

'Exactly. I didn't realise she was using me to make another man jealous. Hoping he would come back to stake his claim. It all makes sense in hindsight.' His voice turned bitter. 'She only accepted my second proposal after her other lover got married. But I didn't see that. I was just too eager to believe that things could go back to the way they were before everything got messed up for me and Helen.'

Wendy felt ill.

It seemed her mother had used Parry as much as she had her daughter, but not just for the reasons Wendy had previously thought – money, power, a roof over her head.

She'd used her to get back the man she really loved.

Until, of course . . . it was just too late.

Chapter 16

Overwhelmed by the information she now had to digest, Wendy left the pub in a daze and didn't realise until she was halfway home that she had forgotten to ask one crucial question.

If Hector wasn't her father's real name, then what was? She was sure now that Parry knew. In fact, he probably even knew the man's last name if he'd been keeping tabs on him for a year after she was born. She turned her car around and headed back to the pub. But when she arrived Parry had left.

'He was feeling unwell,' one of the bartenders told her. 'Said he'd take the afternoon off and come back for dinner.'

She assumed he'd gone home; her mother would be there too. But that didn't matter. She'd confront both of them together.

She got back in her car and drove out onto the main road. After driving about a kilometre, she noticed a turn-off. Northberry Road.

Why was that familiar? And then with a jolt, she remembered that Gavin lived in that street. Curiosity got the better of her and she turned her car into the small street. She couldn't remember his house number, only that it was a small single digit number. This clue didn't help her particularly in locating his residence but her knowledge of him did.

All the houses in the street, with the exception of one, had immaculately tended front gardens – pristine lawns, trimmed bushes and flourishing beds of flowers or other native flora. House number three, however, was a wasteland of weeds, dead trees or shrubs in desperate need of trimming. It was a gorgeous day, and so many of the other houses had their windows or front doors open. Number three had windows shut and curtains drawn – and there was a dusty old Holden parked in the driveway. It clearly hadn't been used in a while because there were dry leaves collecting around its wheels and its back boot displayed splotches upon splotches of bird poo.

Charming.

She turned her car into the driveway and cut the engine, taking in the details of the house like a detective searching for clues. Of course, she couldn't be sure it was his house. For all she knew, Gavin employed a gardener to come once a week to make sure his Perth home was ready to receive him whenever he decided to come home.

Yeah right.

Why did this man fascinate her so much?

He was just like this house. Difficult to read and all locked up. She couldn't make up her mind as to whether he was a nice guy or a bastard. He had all these wonderful giving moments, where he helped people and really felt for their plight. But as quickly as fog sweeps into a field he could become distant and unreachable.

She knew nothing personal about him. Like even if he had family, a brother, a sister? Where did he go to school? Had he ever been in love? Maybe some woman in his past had destroyed his faith in love.

Who knew what went on behind closed doors? As she squinted at the metaphor before her a *rat a tat tat* on her side window made her jump so violently that if not for her seat belt she would have slammed her head into the roof.

With a hand on her heaving chest she turned to see a man bent double, looking in at her. He seemed vaguely familiar but she couldn't quite match a name to his face.

He was tall and slim but well built. His hair was blond and his skin a little weathered and wrinkled, making his age impossible to estimate. He looked like the kind of man who worked hard and partied harder. Honestly, he could have been anywhere from early thirties to late forties. A simple spherical silver stud graced his right ear.

He waved his pointer finger indicating that she should wind down her window. His smile was friendly enough but she still put the window down only a couple of inches.

'Can I help you?'

'Have you seen Gavin Jones recently?'

So this *was* his house.

'Er . . . yes,' she answered cautiously.

He scratched his head. 'I, er . . . just wanted to know when he might be coming home?'

'Why? Who are you?'

'My mates call me Skinner.' His grin broadened. 'Hasn't he mentioned me? Gav, me and my brother, we go way back. But at the moment I'm just the guy who collects his mail.'

'I beg your pardon?'

'He asked me to do it. You know,' he nodded, 'while he's out of town.' He held up some envelopes, all addressed to Gavin Jones, as though to prove it. 'I've got a whole stack now and just wanted to know when he's coming round to collect. I think a few of them are bills . . . and you know it would be a bugger if his phone got cut or something.'

She relaxed slightly. What was she thinking? There was nothing suspicious about this man. Gavin, being his usual carefree 'unconcerned about the little things' self, had clearly just forgotten all about him.

'I'm sorry, you know the last time I spoke to him about going on R and R, he said he wasn't coming back to Perth – said he wanted to go to Exmouth instead for the fishing.'

'That'd be Gavin.' The man nodded ruefully. 'When's he going on R and R?'

'I don't know.' Wendy shrugged. 'He's pretty busy at the moment. Maybe in a week or two?'

'I see.' The guy put his forearm on the top of her car, as though settling in for a long conversation, which didn't enthuse her much. 'Who are you anyway?' he continued. 'His girlfriend?'

Tell-tale gooseflesh started to appear on the back of her neck. 'No, no, no. I'm a colleague – the safety manager at Cape Lambert.'

The man's grin stretched further. 'Definitely need a safety manager at one of those out-of-the-way places up north. So what are you doing here today?'

His question threw her. What could she say to that?

Came out for a perv? I'm a stalker. I'm not his girlfriend but I want to be . . . This guy definitely wasn't the dodgy one. *She* was.

'I . . . er . . . was just in the area.'

'In the area?' he prompted.

'My father owns a pub around here.' She licked her lips. 'I knew Gavin's address so just thought I'd drive by his house.'

'Really?' His tone seemed to indicate that he understood more than she was saying. She felt her skin heat.

Why do you allow yourself to get into these messes? He was probably going to report right back to Gavin that he'd seen her parked outside the front of his house, gazing adoringly at the door just like your average neighbourhood psychopath.

Great!

He leaned in closer to her window and said with a grin, 'I won't tell if you don't tell.'

She jumped, not realising till now that she'd lapsed into her own thoughts again. 'But what about the mail?' she asked softly. 'Don't you want me to check with him about it? Tell him to contact you?'

'No need to mention me at all.' He waved his hand good-naturedly. 'I'll contact him. I was just accosting you because I was lazy . . . and could never resist a pretty face.'

She looked away sheepishly. 'So you've got his number?'

'Yes.' The man straightened. 'I got his number.'

Ten minutes later, Wendy pulled up outside her parents' place. The front door was yanked open before she even knocked. Her mother stepped outside and closed the door, which seemed to indicate immediately that Wendy was not going to be admitted.

'Hi, Mum.'

'What did you say to him?' Helen demanded without greeting or preamble.

She was shocked to see the pain in her mother's eyes as the older woman looked up, tight-lipped and pale. It was the most animated and real she'd ever seen her proper English mother.

'What? What do you mean?' Wendy faltered.

'You know exactly what I mean? Dragging up the past again! What is with you?'

'Nothing is *with* me!' Wendy tossed at her, fists clenched by her sides. 'All I want is the truth. If you just told me, I wouldn't need to, as you say, *drag it up again.*'

Her mother began to pace on the front porch. 'I don't know how to convince him that he's seeing this all wrong. How can I make him stay?'

'Stay?' Wendy's fingers loosened. 'Parry's leaving?'

'He wants a divorce, thanks to you! I want to know exactly what you said about me.'

Wendy gasped. 'Nothing. We hardly spoke about you at all. It was more about me – about what happened when I was sent away to boarding school.'

Helen Hopkins ran trembling fingers through her blonde hair. 'He thinks I don't love him.'

'Well, you don't,' Wendy returned frankly. 'At least not as much as . . . the one who got away.'

'*You said that to him?*' her mother cried.

'I didn't have to. He knew it already,' Wendy snapped. 'He's just been putting up with it all these years because he loves you and loves me and hoped things would change . . .'

Helen deflated slightly. 'But they have changed! They've been changed for years. How can I convince him? Why does he think I stayed with him?'

'Well, considering you guys have kept me in the dark for most of my life I don't know why you're bothering to ask me now!' Wendy said crossly. 'He did say that you and Grandma always seemed to side with each other. Maybe he thinks you were pressured by the family.'

Helen snorted. 'All this family has given me is grief. Made me feel like an outcast they can't cast out. I can't change a mistake I made so long ago.'

'Well, all I've got from this family is indifference.' Wendy glared at her. 'Since the day I was born. Did you know I ran into Uncle Mike in Karratha? Just by chance, mind you, didn't plan it. And he told me to get lost and go home. If that doesn't just sum it all up, I don't know what does.'

Her mother's head jerked up. 'Yes, well, he's never . . .' she faltered '. . . taken much of an interest in you.'

'Well, I've ended up working on the same project as him. Not that he wants anyone to know we're related.' Wendy shook her head derisively, not realising the true depth of her hurt until now. 'I told him he could rest easy on that score, considering we aren't even biologically connected after all.'

Her mother's hands stopped their wringing. 'How did he react?'

Wendy thought back to that day at Karratha post office where she had accidentally run into Mike. He was paying a bill and she'd called in to ask about PO boxes for any men called Hector. Of which, of course, there were none.

She'd recognised him and gone over to say hi, just as a courtesy of course, because they were family. No surprises that he'd been distant and dismissive.

'What are you doing here anyway?' His grouchy expression seemed to cloud even further. 'Last I heard, you were wasting money trekking across the globe.'

'I'm looking for my father actually.'

'You're *what*?'

'Oh, didn't you know?' she had uttered sweetly, glad to have finally taken the wind out of his sails and wiped that self-satisfied expression off his face. 'I thought everybody except me knew. Parry Hopkins isn't my father.'

He'd looked at her for a long time then. Eyebrows drawn together, dark eyes running over her as though taking in some detail he might have previously missed. 'Who told you that?'

'Mum. But she claims not to know where my real father is. So I'm off to find him myself.'

He snorted scornfully. 'I think that's the dumbest thing I've ever heard! What a colossal waste of time. More aimless and foolhardy than backpacking.' He stabbed a finger at her. 'What you need to do is get a job and stop gallivanting. Bring you back to earth a bit, I think.'

She glared at him. The very last thing she had expected was a lecture. After all, she wasn't a child. Even her own parents didn't comment on how she was living her life any more. They were just happy to be informed. She turned away, intending to leave. Uncle Mike clearly wasn't even worth politeness. It was no wonder he was the black sheep of the family.

'Hey, I'm talking to you.'

Her eyes drew together as she turned back to him. This time though she didn't bother to mask her annoyance.

He took a breath. 'Come to the Point Samson bar tonight. I think I know someone who knows someone who can offer you a job.'

She wished she could have thrown the suggestion back in his face. But the fact was, at the time, she had been looking to settle in the area and rebuild her funds. It would have been shooting herself in the foot to turn him down.

So that's how she'd first connected with Bulldog and subsequently turned up for her first day at work. Her lips twisted at the humiliating memory.

'Wendy, what is it?' Her mother's voice was weak and breathless, bringing her back to the present.

'You asked me how he reacted, didn't you?' She shook her head, contempt lacing her tone. 'He reacted by embroiling me in a blackmail scheme he had going. He's a user. Just like the rest of you. You know that advice you gave me last year about no one doing anything for nothing? Well, it was spot on.'

Her mother paled. 'I don't know why you want to find a man who is not interested in you. Never has been. It's just a recipe for heartbreak! Trust me, I know.' She came over and grabbed her daughter by the shoulders but Wendy shook her off.

'You can't know that he's not interested in me.'

'He has never come back for you. He has never called me to talk about you. He has never asked for proof he is not your father. After I got pregnant he didn't set foot in this city for two years. Doesn't that tell you something?'

'All it tells me is that you know more than you're letting on,' Wendy returned bitterly. 'And if this is how you plan to hold onto Parry, with this half-baked honesty, then good bloody luck because I don't think it's going to work.'

Helen stepped back like Wendy had slapped her. And for the first time in the entire debacle, Wendy had to question whether she had gone too far.

Without a word, Helen spun on her heel and went back into the house. Wendy heard the key turning in the lock. Letting her know, beyond a shadow of a doubt, that she would not be seeing her adoptive father again that day.

*

After the disastrous run-in with her mother, Wendy tried several times to waylay Parry at his pub but had no luck. It seemed he'd taken some time off work and was not coming back for an indefinite period. She had no idea whether he had moved out of the home he shared with her mother. Helen would not take her calls, nor answer the door to her any more. It seemed that the final cut from her family she had thought they were not capable of giving had finally come. She really was on her own.

It was almost therapeutic to get on the plane that Friday morning and get the hell out of town – leave all the angst behind her. Being subject to some ridicule and rumours at Cape Lambert seemed like a walk in the park compared with her emotional slap at home.

It was Lena who picked her up from the airport. The young engineer was positively beaming from ear to ear.

'Wendy, I'm so glad you're back. I need you for Operation AGM.'

Wendy blinked. 'Operation AGM?'

'Annabel George Management. I'm fixing her up with somebody else.'

Trepidation gripped Wendy. *Please don't say it's Gavin.* 'Er, who?'

'I don't know, *somebody*. That's one of the technicalities I'm still working on. The point is, I've managed to persuade Sharon to persuade Carl to have another Barnes Inc/TCN public relations function at that pub in Point Samson, Friday after next. We're going to tell Annabel about it and have Dan as bait.' She clapped her hands gleefully. 'She'll come for sure.'

Wendy breathed a sigh of relief that was closely followed by a new kind of worry. 'So if Dan's the bait, how are you going to get her to meet other guys?'

'We'll introduce her round. Me, you and Sharon.'

I was afraid you were going to say that.

'Annabel won't know it, but she'll be on a speed-dating adventure.'

'Sounds foolproof,' Wendy returned dryly.

'I know, right?'

As they left the airport car park in Lena's ute, Wendy noticed the pavement was wet and the red gravel off the side of the road seemed darker and richer. The air was heavy with smells of metals and earth.

'Has it been raining?'

'Yeah,' Lena said. 'The season is certainly turning.'

'So how's the project going?'

'Good, actually.' Lena smiled but kept her eyes on the road. 'Gavin is really holding his own as the project manager. I think he's surprised everyone, and unfortunately put poor Carl's nose out of joint in the process.'

Wendy grimaced. 'I take it the new driver's licence hasn't showed up?'

'Not yet.'

'I'll have to see what I can do to move that along.'

'Might not be a bad idea.'

'So how's Sharon?'

Lena swatted her hand. 'Oh, she's good. Fish has left town. Apparently, he's lined up some great job at a coal terminal in Queensland. We won't be seeing him for a while. So Sharon and Carl have been having *a lot* of quality time.'

'And how about those wedding plans? Have they set a date?'

'It's in April next year,' Lena confirmed brightly. 'I'm going to be a bridesmaid.'

After everything Wendy had been through on R and R, Lena's cheer was starting to get a little too glarey. So she was relieved when they lapsed into a comfortable silence for the rest of the journey to site.

As they were turning into the dirt road that led to the Cape Lambert wharf, Lena did mention one last thing. 'You know, Gavin's holding a meeting for all the engineers in about an hour. You should sit in on it – would get you up to speed real fast.'

Wendy couldn't argue with this, so after a brief catch-up with Chub and a few others, she entered the meeting room to find the usual crew assembled around a speaker phone and Gavin sitting at the head of the table.

He looked up and took in her face with a slight curl of the lips.

'Welcome back, Sarge.'

'Thanks.'

For a second they were the only two people there, encased in a perfect, private, sound proof bubble. And then it popped.

He clapped his hands and she was back in the real world. She turned away red-faced as he addressed the group. 'All right, guys, let's settle down and get this show on the road. Do we have Carl on the line?'

'Not yet.' Craig grinned and stood up to dial. Carl picked up the phone after only two rings.

'You're fuckin' late,' he grumbled.

'Your clock is fast, Carl,' Gavin grinned. 'We're exactly on time.' Everyone at the table quietened down and shuffled in their seats as though settling in for the long haul. 'Okay, let's start with progress reports. Who wants to go first?'

They went around the table and each engineer discussed the status of his section of the job. A man called Harry, the project planner, also added whether this was before or behind schedule. If it was behind, the group would discuss how any issues or problems that existed could be addressed.

It was efficient. It was all inclusive. And it was very, very effective.

It was Gavin.

Wendy had to hide her smile several times as Carl tried to butt in to exert his power. His efforts were futile and met with a good deal of humour rather than respect. The truth was, while Carl was a good project manager, a fair leader and a man who tended to tackle problems head on, Gavin's more quiet, loyal and dedicated management style seemed to be just

251

as successful. While Carl went hell for leather, Gavin seemed to hold the reins lightly, but was still more than ready to pull in hard should his horse wander off the track.

Wendy remembered the advice he had given her at the Point Samson Yacht Club. *With every set of hands, you get a free brain.* It was exactly his style and watching him in action deepened her admiration for him.

Unfortunately, Carl had not taken to this cavalier treatment. Wendy could feel his frustration building over the airways and knew his enforced exile was starting to get to him. It came round to Lena's turn to speak and it was clear she had been having a few issues that week. None of them good.

'We can't afford to have what happened yesterday under the wharf happen again,' Gavin said carefully. 'I don't think we should install any more trusses from the land.'

'Now hang on a minute there,' Carl interrupted, clearly sensing his moment to shine. 'You can't just fuckin' stop one method of installation, it'll send us further behind.'

Gavin sighed. 'With all due respect, Carl, we started installing from the land to speed things up, but now it's just getting too dangerous.'

'I'll be the fuckin' judge of that.'

'I'm sure you would be if you were here.' Gavin frowned. 'But you're not so I have to make that call.'

'I want a second opinion.'

'What about mine?' Wendy jumped in because she could feel a fight spoiling. 'If it's a safety issue, then I could be of some help.'

'What a good fuckin' idea,' Carl said immediately. 'Lena, give Wendy a report on what happened and email me a copy. We'll go with Wendy's opinion.'

It was apparent that all he wanted to do was take the decision out of Gavin's hands.

'If you say so, Carl.' Gavin kept his voice level, but over the top of the phone he winked at Wendy – clearly unabashed by the usurping of his power. She sighed with relief. All she had been trying to do was help him avoid another fight with Carl, after all.

There were a couple of sniggers that echoed around the room.

'Who's fuckin' laughing over there?' Carl's voice cracked.

The sniggering degenerated into coughing.

'All right, then,' Carl's voice was indignant, 'I think we're done here. You boys and ladies should get back to work!'

The men looked to Gavin and he nodded silently around the room. There was the scraping of chairs as they murmured their goodbyes and Carl rang off.

When it was just Wendy and Gavin left in the room, his eyes twinkled at her, making her heart do flips. 'You know, Sarge, I'm a big boy, I can take care of myself.'

'I know,' she shrugged, 'I just don't want you and Carl to become enemies over this. It's not worth it. His isolation isn't going to be for much longer.'

He leaned his hip on the desk. 'It doesn't mean you need to jump between me and Carl every time he throws a punch my way.'

She blushed as his eyes ran over her body.

He frowned. 'How's your arm? I see you've taken it out of the sling.'

'Oh yeah,' she agreed, glad for a change of subject. 'It feels much better. I don't think I need the sling any more.'

'The doctor said two weeks.'

'*One* to two weeks,' she corrected him. 'And I'd rather not make a spectacle of myself. It'll just be more fuel for the rumours that you and Carl aren't getting on.'

'So it's about protecting me again?'

She crossed her arms and grimaced, wishing that for once she could be as unreadable as he was. Instead, she attempted damage control. 'It's not anything to do with you, Gavin. I just want what's best for the project. Isn't that what you want too?'

He gathered up his memos and files and said grimly, 'Yes. Yes, of course.'

Chapter 17

Gavin returned to Carl's office, closing the door and slamming his files on the absent project manager's desk. It would help if there were a pill or something he could take for unwanted feelings. A special antibiotic for bugs of the heart.

It had been so good while she was gone. Things had been back to normal. He'd started to enjoy his new role. The threat of Peter Marshall was a worry at the back of his mind but not a debilitating fear.

Okay, so maybe he'd thought about her every day. But at least her presence hadn't been a constant drain on his emotional reservoir. He didn't have to be concerned that she was too close to him – that she might get caught in the cross-fire – that his feelings for her might grow in ways they just shouldn't.

Seeing her again for the first time today had been like a shot of adrenaline to the temple. And then when she'd jumped in like that at the meeting as though to 'rescue' him again, it seemed like proof she felt the same way.

You need to get a grip, man. You don't want *her to feel the same way, remember?*

He glanced at the wall clock. Nearly time to speak to Janet. He got his phone out of his pocket and placed it on the desk. Sitting down in Carl's chair, he willed the bloody thing to ring.

All things said and done, it was kind of nice having his own office. At least he didn't have to take these calls outside any more. Of course, things with Carl were deteriorating at a rate of knots. He wasn't quite sure how to fix their relationship or assure the guy he wasn't trying to take his job. Carl had always been a good boss. Fair to a fault. But even sometimes the tallest of giants suffered a fall that took them a while to get up from.

The phone rang, jolting him from his reverie, and he snatched it up.

'Hello?'

'Hi, Gavin. It's Janet.'

'Any news?'

'Not good I'm afraid. There's been a leak in the department. We think your alias and Perth address have been compromised. Now would be a good time to take your R and R.'

'That's just not possible.'

'Why not?'

'I've been put in charge of the project.'

'I thought I told you to keep a low profile. Peter Marshall has been seen at your house in Perth. In fact, he's stealing your mail.'

'That's all right.' Gavin shrugged. 'I don't have anything of importance sent there. He's not going to get anything from that.'

'All the same, we do feel he is narrowing his search. I've alerted the authorities in Wickham and would like you to call this number if you feel you're in trouble.'

He took down the number she read out.

'In the meantime, we will continue to keep our people on him and will let you know if there are any movements in your direction. Are you sure you can't go on R and R? Somewhere that's neither Perth nor Wickham.'

'I was actually thinking of Exmouth . . .'

'Perfect.'

'But like I said, it's just not possible right at the minute. I'll leave when you tell me he's on his way here.'

'Cutting it fine, Gavin.' Janet sounded worried. 'Cutting it very fine.'

The following day, Wendy came to see him about Lena's report. He didn't really need her to brief him on what had happened because he'd already heard the story from various sources. But the temptation to have some alone time with her was a little more than he could resist.

'So apparently the tide came in a little early, soaking the ground under the jetty,' Wendy explained. 'They had two cranes parked there, one almost in the water, when the semi-trailer turned up with an eight-tonne truss on the back of it.' She rolled her eyes. 'You know what happened, don't you?'

He grinned. 'It got bogged.'

'So they thought they'd use one of their cranes to pull it out of the mud.'

Gavin already had an image of the scene in his mind's eye. Fieldmouse and Radar chattering away like two little monkeys with a plan. Lena had been on the skids frames. She had no idea they were going to attempt a lift without her advice or her input. His mouth twisted. 'They attached to a weak point.'

'Exactly.' Wendy flicked Lena's report against her palm. 'Radar looped a sling around the roo bar of the bogged semi-trailer and when the crane started pulling the thing just popped off the truck like done toast, only it was accompanied by this almighty *bang*! They basically created a sling shot with the roo bar as the cannon ball. I am gobsmacked that the bar landed safely in the dirt without hitting anything.' Wendy folded her arms. 'You know, I leave you guys for a week and you forget everything, *everything* I say to you. You know, what's a girl got to do to get noticed around here?!'

A slow grin spread across his face as he thought of myriad possibilities, all wholly unsuitable to voice in a place of business.

She seemed, however, to be aware of the direction in which his thoughts were travelling because she lifted her index finger and choked out, 'That was a rhetorical question. Don't you *dare* say anything.'

He gave his most innocent shrug. 'Whatever you say, Sarge.'

'Well,' she sighed, finally pulling back the chair in front of his desk and sitting down in it. 'The roo bar incident aside, I did a JSA on just installing trusses from the land. Assessing the risk with our matrices, I don't think with the weather turning that it's safe any more.'

'Hey,' he spread his hands, 'I'm on your side. Have you forwarded your opinion to Carl yet?'

'No, I thought I'd run it by you first.'

'Well, go ahead.' He nodded. 'I'm sure he'll have exactly the same verdict when he hears what you have to say. As long as,' his lips twitched, 'you don't tell him what I said first.'

'Gotcha.' An awkward silence fell and then she leaned forwards as though about to stand up again to leave. After all, there was nothing more to say. She should go, right?

'How was your R and R?' he quickly burst out, stalling her. *You fool.*

Her brow furrowed. 'Er, good.'

'You don't sound very enthusiastic.'

She closed her eyes and shook her head. 'Oh you know, I just had a lot of family stuff going on.'

He remembered she had told him that it was her father who'd had the crippling effect on her private life. His imagination began to create scenarios. All of them angered him.

'Did you see your old man?'

'Huh?' Her eyes widened.

He hesitated. 'Perhaps it's none of my business. It just seemed from your expression that maybe he might be giving you a hard time again.'

'I wish.' She turned her face away. 'The truth is, Gavin, I don't know where my father is. I've never met him.'

He did a double take. 'But I thought you said –'

'His crime was abandoning me before I was born. I didn't find out about his existence till about a year ago. And I know this might sound lame, but it's really screwed up my sense of identity. I've been searching for answers ever since . . .'

'It doesn't sound lame,' he said quietly. 'I can see how something like that can be a real betrayal of trust.' *It's no wonder you won't rely on anyone.*

A few other puzzle pieces clicked into place for him. 'Oh shit, you thought Yabber was your father?'

Her grin trembled on her lips. 'For a little while . . .'

'If you'd confided in me I could have told you he wasn't.'

'I didn't trust you.'

You don't trust anyone. A fist squeezed his heart tight and he licked his lips. 'But apparently, you trust me now.'

She seemed amused at her own weakness. 'I guess so.'

'What do you know about this guy?'

'My father?' She blinked. 'Nothing much. He was a drifter who liked the outback, a welder by trade, he has an injury on his right foot that scarred him for life, he's married . . . I thought his name was Hector too but that turned out to be wrong. Anyway,' she slapped her palms briskly on her lap and stood up, 'it doesn't really matter.'

'It clearly matters to you.'

'It did.' She nodded thoughtfully. 'But when I look back on what I've been through this last year – all those ups and downs, broken relationships, fighting with my family, unable to work because of this obsession – I think this search has taken more from me than it has given.'

She walked towards the door, indicating that the time for confidences was at an end. But then, like a druggie addicted to the one poison, he stalled her again. 'You going to the shindig Lena's planned at Point Samson next week?'

Wendy rolled her eyes. 'I think she'd kill me if I didn't.'

'It'll be good for you. Get away from all that family stuff and just focus on friends. There are many people who like you, Wendy.'

'Yeah right,' she scoffed. 'I'm the TCN spy, remember? I've got a long way to go around here.'

'You're also the girl who pulled Sharon out from under that bus, the woman who protected everyone's jobs by getting us through the audit – and the only reason we're prepared for cyclone season is you. Don't sell yourself short.' He looked down at his hands and said tightly, 'You bring a lot to this project.' *And to me.*

Her hand had been resting on the knob of the door and she turned a gorgeous shade of pink that made him want to kiss her silly. 'I do huh? That's certainly a compliment coming from you.'

He looked up and grinned. 'You'll only hear it once, Sarge, so don't let it fatten your ego.'

She cocked her head to one side as she looked at him – a strange, wistful expression staining her features. 'I'll get that report to Carl,' she said huskily and let herself out.

He stared at the closed door probably far longer than necessary. It was the most honest he had ever been with her and it felt good.

After that, it was off to the wharf. The difficulty with being project manager was he still had to hold down his other role as piling engineer as well. Sometimes there just weren't enough hours in the day.

But he was resolved to keep a low profile from then on. And he did, staying out of Wendy's way and focusing as much as he could on the project.

Another week passed and this was working out quite well for him until on Wednesday evening when he opened his donga door and noticed that someone had pushed a newspaper under it so that it rested on the floor of his quarters.

The sight wouldn't have been such a big deal if the newspaper hadn't been pre-opened to a particular page and story. The headline read: *Peter Marshall Seeks Revenge for Deaths During Gang War*. He hastily crouched and picked it up.

Closing his door behind him, he turned on the light and looked around the messy room to see if anything had been taken, moved or touched. The disarray, however, seemed to be a result of his own untidiness rather than invasion. Also his window was locked and the knob on his door didn't appear to have been tampered with.

He looked at the paper again. What was this? A warning? Was Peter here?

He grabbed his mobile and headed to the car park for good reception. When he was sure no one was watching him, he dialled the emergency number of his case officer.

'Hello, Gavin. Is something wrong?'

'You still have your sights on Peter, right?'

'Yes, of course.' Janet was immediately concerned.

'He's still in Perth?'

'Yes, staying at the Hyatt with a couple of his cronies.'

Gavin felt his heart rate slow.

'Why, what's happened?'

Gavin glanced at the paper, knowing that if he told her about it, she'd have him out of there immediately. He couldn't go yet. There was too much to do and Carl still wasn't ready to take the reins back. Besides, she'd said it herself: Peter was still in Perth.

'Oh, it's nothing.' He forced his voice to be even. 'Paranoia, I guess. I just thought I might have missed a call from you or something.'

'Well, there's no sense in staying in Wickham if you're worried. I've got a house for you in Exmouth ready to go.'

'Not just yet.' Gavin paused. 'I'll let you know.'

He rang off, looked at the paper again. If Peter wasn't here, could he have sent one of his men instead? Under any other circumstances he would have thought so. But he'd had the pleasure of meeting Peter after Eddie's court sentencing. About a week after his brother was put away, Peter had been waiting for him on his doorstep. He'd stayed in the shadows until Gavin had stepped out of his car and onto the drive.

'Geez, you work late,' were the first words out of the druglord's mouth.

It had taken Gavin a few seconds to figure out who the person addressing him was. He'd seen Peter in court but he'd always looked somewhat tidier in a suit and tie. In jeans and a T-shirt, he could now make out all the tattoos on the criminal's arms.

'That's right.' He nodded just as Gavin connected the dots. 'I'm Eddie's brother, Peter. But you can call me Skinner. You crossed the wrong family, mate, and it's time you paid your due.'

'My due?' Gavin had taken a step back.

'Come now, don't tell me you had no expectation of repercussions.' Peter cocked his head to one side. 'Believe me, your punishment is so important, I wouldn't trust anyone else with it. I'm the only person who can get it right.'

Gavin withdrew his mobile from his pocket. 'I'm calling the police.'

In hindsight, it had been a dumb move. Peter had slapped the phone out of his hand, so that it ricocheted off his car and onto the driveway, smashing into pieces.

As Gavin was still processing the destruction of his phone, there was a flash of steel and then a knife entered his chest, luckily on the wrong side of his heart.

He felt no pain. No doubt it was all thanks to shock. As Peter withdrew it, he murmured, 'Twenty cuts for twenty years.'

The knife was yanked out, sending him staggering back, but it came back all too quick, this time just below the ribs.

Survival instinct must have kicked in then because as the knife came out, Gavin brought his fist up and smashed it into Peter's face. The man fell back laughing. But it was enough time for Gavin to stagger to his car.

This time the pain was unbearable.

He knew he had but seconds before another wound would take him. His vision was blurring yet somehow he held on to his faculties and was in the car, pushing the central-locking button with not a millisecond to spare.

Peter's right fist was pounding on the window and he was yanking on the door handle with his left hand. His lips were snarled back against his teeth as Gavin fumbled desperately with the keys.

Come on. Come on. Come on.

The window smashed.

The glass against his face felt like rice confetti compared to the agony in his side but in the same moment the engine roared to life. The sound was like cavalry horns to a dying man who could no longer hold his fort. Shoving the gearstick down in reverse, he accelerated and the car jerked back. Peter, who had his hand through the window trying to grab the steering wheel, was thrown off balance and landed on his arse as Gavin reversed like an L-plate driver out of the driveway. The last glimpse Gavin had of Peter was in his rear-view mirror. He saw the blurred image of a man with a red fist staggering across the front lawn in an effort to get to his own car, parked down the street.

Gavin didn't attempt to drive to the hospital. His shirt was soaked to the skin with his own blood and he was fighting nausea. He was going to pass out. He could feel it coming. He made it instead to the nearest petrol station, where a terrified teenager screamed at her manager, 'Come quick!'

Gavin still coudn't believe that the jury at the following trial had failed to find Peter guilty beyond reasonable doubt for the knife attack.

After that, his family had packed up and moved to Melbourne and he'd packed up and moved to Perth. The Witness Protection Program had seemed like salvation. Five years on, it was more of a prison.

But at least he knew one thing. Peter wanted this revenge for himself. He wouldn't be sending anyone if he could help it. So what was with the paper? Who had shoved it under his door?

Mike?

To be honest, he hadn't really given the old man or his threats much credit. After all, he was being protected by the federal government. How was a sixty-year-old with one foot out the retirement door possibly going to breach their walls, find out who he really was and then summon Peter Marshall to the Pilbara? It was a bit of a joke really.

Still, no other explanation immediately presented itself. He wondered if he should show the story to Mike and gauge his reaction, just to be sure. Not bothering to change out of his work clothes, he left his donga once again with the paper in hand.

A quick drop-in to reception and a short chat with Ethel apprised him of Mike's donga number. There was no guarantee, of course, that the older man would be in. But he'd try all evening if he had to.

Mike's donga looked a little rundown. His flyscreen was full of holes, which he'd covered over with duct tape. As luck would have it though, he opened the door first knock.

He didn't look pleased to see his project manager. 'What are you doing here?'

Gavin grinned at him. 'I missed you. You haven't been by in a while.'

'Cut to the chase, Gavin.'

'Thought you might have dropped something.'

He held up the paper as Mike stepped out of his donga, leaving the front door wide open. The site supervisor had his boots off but was otherwise also still in his work gear. A car magazine lay open on his unmade bed. Snatching the paper from Gavin's fingers, he read the headline with a frown and then turned the paper over as though looking for a punchline. It wasn't there. He shoved the paper back in Gavin's hand. 'I don't get it.'

Gavin raised his eyebrows. 'Not yours?'

'No.' Mike snorted. 'Look, I don't know what game you're playing and frankly I don't care, as long as you stay away from me . . . and my family.' He turned to head back into his donga and Gavin was just about to turn away when he noticed something about Mike's room.

His desk was broken. One leg was bent out of shape.

Gavin's eyes flicked quickly to the air conditioner, which was askew in its hole in the wall and not plugged in. Clearly indicating Mike had never used it.

Faulty, perhaps?

Gavin's gaze jumped back to the man's bare feet. Two toes missing. Wendy's voice jogged his memory. 'He has an injury on his right foot that scarred him for life.'

Aw, man!

He jumped up the step to Mike's threshold and wedged his foot against the door before Mike could close it.

The older man started as the door jammed. 'What now?'

'That's why you're so protective of her, isn't it?' Gavin's voice was breathless. 'That's why you fixed up her donga for her. And that's why you're scared to bloody death of even looking her in the face.'

'I don't know what you're talking about,' Mike growled. 'Take your bloody foot off my property.'

'Welder, aren't you?'

'What?' Mike shook his head, as though trying to clear the buzzing of annoying insects. He pushed the door against the force of Gavin's boot.

But Gavin didn't budge and continued speaking, unperturbed. 'Originally, you were a welder. I met your wife once. No kids though . . . at least not with her.'

The splotches on Mike's skin seemed to stand out all the more as his face lost blood.

'Get out of my donga, engineer.'

Too late.

Gavin was already seeing puzzle pieces he hadn't realised he'd been collecting clicking into place. And the sight of the picture they made was boiling his blood. 'Do you know what hell you've put her through this year trying to find you? She's an emotional train wreck. Doesn't know who she is. Doesn't want to trust anyone any more. Did you know she gave me a hundred bucks to change her car battery because she couldn't believe that anybody would do anything without an ulterior motive?'

'I'm warning you! Go away!' Mike seemed desperate now.

'I think you've done enough warning and not enough explaining,' Gavin shot at him. 'And I'm not buying it. You need to tell her. She wants to know. She needs to know. And at least if she has the truth, she can stop fretting about it. Because, believe me, you are not worth fretting over.'

'I know it!' Mike burst out. 'That's why I don't want her to know. I have no excuse, you see. I'm just a lousy human being.'

'*Really*? I could have told you that.'

'I slept with my brother's fiancée!' Mike let go of the door and stepped back, hard, callused hands clutching his bald head. 'How do you come back from something like that?'

'You need to tell Wendy. You need to make it right for her.'

'You don't understand.' Mike spread his hands. 'I didn't actually know she was my daughter. Like *really my daughter* until she told me a couple of months ago.'

'So what?' Gavin could feel his impatience rising. 'You should have told her then if that were the case.'

'I'm never telling Wendy.' Mike's tone was adamant, his features set like plaster.

'Why the hell not?'

'It would just be bad news. Why upset her?'

'You should tell her because it would be the unselfish thing to do.' Gavin glared at him. 'You can't keep it a secret because you're too ashamed. I'm sure she's not going to try and force you to be part of her life if you don't want to be. She just wants to get her identity straight. I mean, you obviously care about her.' He waved a hand at the mess that was Mike's donga.

Mike looked away, a muscle flexed in his jaw. Gavin could see that the man was torn. And he really should have butted out at that point. After all, this was a family matter and not his family to boot. But he just couldn't help himself. 'Okay, mate, I'll give you a chance to figure this out. But if you don't come clean soon, I'm going to start dropping some serious hints.'

Mike's face swung back to his. 'You wouldn't. It's nothing to do with you.'

'Wendy's happiness is everything to do with me.'

'Why?' Mike's eyes narrowed on him.

'Because,' Gavin finally unwedged his foot and took a step back from the door, 'I love her.'

Over the next couple of days the weather deteriorated as did both Gavin's mood and patience. Thanks to his big flapping mouth, Mike now knew his most closely guarded secret. The only thing saving him from humiliation was that he also knew Mike's.

She was an unspoken bond holding them both at check-mate. A condition Gavin definitely didn't like being in.

On Friday he received a call from Carl, who gleefully announced that he had just received word he should have his Australian licence back by Tuesday. As piling seemed to be running on schedule too, there was no point in delaying his R and R any longer. Particularly not for a gorgeous blonde with long legs he had no business looking twice at. So he began to set in motion plans to fly out to Exmouth the day Carl got back to work. He knew his case officer would be pleased that he was finally thinking about taking care of himself. He called her to let her know his intentions. In return he learned that Peter Marshall had made no attempt to fly out from Perth since they had last spoken and, in fact, was busy meeting and doing business with some of his Western Australian connections.

There was just one ordeal left to get through – Lena's morale-boosting gathering at Point Samson pub. Carl had been all for it, especially when he heard it wasn't Gavin's idea. Not that it was a bad plan. He knew the men loved Lena's excursions and social functions and he couldn't fault the girl for her enthusiasm. It was just that the last function he'd attended at that particular pub had been a disaster for him. He was sure this one would be equally bad.

Why?

Wendy would be there.

No doubt dressed to the nines and the target of every pick-up line ever invented. He knew his men and was under no illusions. They would recognise an opportunity when they saw one. Particularly considering he'd been protesting for the last month that he and Wendy were not an item. It was going to be difficult to keep his fists in his pockets all night. Then, of course, there was a possibility far worse than that. He almost couldn't bear to contemplate it.

What if she met someone nice? He could hardly complain if some decent bloke decided to try his hand and she went along with it. After all, wasn't her happiness what was most important?

As acting project manager, he had to at least show his face or it would be bad form. He definitely had no intention of drinking heavily though or staying long. After a quick dinner and a couple of hours of small talk he'd be out of there. Dressed carelessly in jeans and a collared short-sleeve shirt, he took his own ute to the venue so that he'd have a quick getaway.

The Point Samson pub was quite a large facility, set up with both indoor and outdoor bars. For drinking, the outdoor bar was much more popular because it was set on a large balcony that overlooked the ocean. He walked in and took in the scene at a glance.

Carl was in high spirits and had clearly hit the grog hard. He was dressed in a Hawaiian shirt, also known as his party shirt, and was ordering a jug. Surrounding him was Dimitri, Chub, Craig and a good many others Gavin easily recognised. Sharon, one leg still encased in a large plastic boot, was standing further down the bar with a cocktail in one hand, chatting excitedly to Lena and . . . Wendy.

His roaming eyes had to pause.

The safety manager looked breathtaking in a simple dark blue evening camisole with a scooped neckline. She'd dressed it down with a pair of jeans and black boots. But of course, her hair was out, her skin was glowing and that curve between her neck and shoulder looked so bloody kissable he had to consciously bite his tongue. She lifted a hand and waved to him. He returned the greeting but turned away, clenching his jaw. There were already several local men eyeing the tight-knit little group of women, weighing up their chances and their courage.

This was going to be much harder than he'd thought.

He leaned on the railing of the balcony and drank in the black ocean. Suppressing emotions he knew he shouldn't feel before he threw himself into the fray. The lights of the pub twinkled on the glassy surface of the sea. Black shapes and a gentle splash told him there might be a couple of dolphins frolicking out there.

Half their luck.

Shaking off his mood, he pushed back from the railing and went to join Carl's group. Chub greeted him first.

'Not a bad turn-out,' the large man commented jovially. 'But I'm thinking I might go inside for some seafood. There seems to be nothing but booze out here.'

Gavin and Dimitri laughed appreciatively as he left the group to sate his appetite. Carl seemed to notice Gavin there for the first time and eyed him warily. After a strained silence, he relented, slapped Gavin on the back and said, 'What the fuck are you doing standing there empty-handed? You waiting for me to buy you a fuckin' drink then?'

'Just settling in, Carl.' Gavin leaned back on the bar. 'Scoping the scene out, so to speak.'

'For fuck's sake,' Carl rolled his eyes, 'stop being such a wanker.' He yelled at the bartender, 'Get this man a drink!' He looked shrewdly at Gavin. 'I suppose you think I owe you one after the way I've been treating you.'

Gavin tried to look innocent as the dark-haired man passed him a frothing glass. 'Your conscience pricking, Carl?'

'Shut your trap and hit your piss,' Carl instructed him. ''Cause you ain't getting no fuckin' apology out of me.'

Gavin accepted this in the apologetic spirit in which it was obviously intended and with a secret smile politely changed the subject. 'So I don't see Bulldog about.'

Carl's face clouded. 'Just as well. The girls are hatching some scheme and I don't like it.'

Gavin glanced again at Wendy, Sharon and Lena and noticed for the first time how they kept looking at the door like they were expecting someone. And then, as if on cue, Annabel George walked in, pausing on the threshold to scan the bar.

She was over-dressed for the occasion, not that any man would find fault with her taste. All male eyes turned as one to the mauve halterneck cocktail dress that was both a little too low on the neckline and a little too high on the hem. Her dark curls were piled sensuously on top of her head and her expressive eyes were heavily lined, making them look bigger than normal. If she intended to allure or impress, she would have absolutely no trouble doing it tonight. The odd part of the picture, though, was what she was carrying. A large glass bowl of chocolate mousse, topped with cream and cherries, the presence of which seemed to be causing a stir across the room.

He glanced at the girls. Wendy and Sharon looked worried. Lena looked furious.

'I think the show has just started, Carl,' he drawled, indicating the scene unfolding before them.

Lena walked over to Annabel and was clearly talking rapidly to her, pointing at the bowl and putting her hands on her hips. Annabel was just as clearly *not* listening. She was certainly smiling, but kept trying to glance around Lena as though she were looking for someone else. After a while, things seemed to escalate. Lena put both hands on either side of the glass bowl of mousse and Annabel finally met her eyes squarely. But she wasn't happy with what Lena was suggesting. She was shaking her head.

Then Lena was trying to tug the bowl of chocolate mousse out of her hands. It seemed oddly like watching a Bugs Bunny cartoon, as the bowl moved dangerously from one girl to the other.

Mine.

Yours.

Mine.

Yours.

And then Lena let go.

A bit of cream slopped out onto Annabel's gorgeous mauve cocktail dress. The tension in the room escalated as men paused, some mid-drink.

'Oh fuck!' said Carl as Annabel scooped a handful of mousse out of the bowl and threw it in Lena's face. It hit with a splat like wet mud. Lena squealed, dipped her hand in the bowl and threw some back.

A cheer erupted from the crowd.

'Fight! Fight! Fight! Fight!'

Sharon tried to pull Lena back but there was fury in her eyes. Annabel looked crazed as she flung another sloppy missile while trying to keep the bowl out of Lena's reach.

Wendy tried to step in but was pushed viciously aside, almost overturning the chair she crashed into behind her. As she was righting herself, her eyes met Gavin's again across the room. The silent message she threw at him was louder than any shout.

Please help me.

While he had been content to watch the show, he was not immune to that face or that message from her. With a sigh, he put his beer on the counter and walked over to the skirmish. Many guys booed him but under Wendy's grateful gaze, he put a hand on each of the girls' shoulders, holding them easily apart with his superior strength.

'Listen, ladies, as much as everyone is enjoying this, I think it's time to break it up.'

To his horror, they both turned on him like two angry cats, simultaneously scooping handfuls of mousse from the bowl and slapping it into the front of his shirt and splashing it on his face.

'Bloody hell!'

Thankfully, just at that moment an authoritative voice boomed beside him. 'What the hell is going on here?'

It was Bulldog, jaw clenched.

His presence seemed to have a calming effect on both women. They both sagged in defeat. Gavin released his grip.

'Daniel,' Annabel reached imploringly towards Bulldog. But the TCN project manager immediately went to Lena, his right hand tilting her chin up so he could examine the damage wrought in chocolate on her face.

'*Are you crazy?* What are you doing?'

Lena winced. 'Er, defending your honour?'

When he did nothing but glare angrily down at her, she reached up and ran her finger down her cheek and then put the chocolate-loaded tip in her mouth. 'Revenge never tasted so sweet.'

'Stop that,' he warned, half laugh, half groan, and then taking her hand turned around. 'I'm taking Lena back to camp to get cleaned up.'

'Daniel,' Annabel implored again, 'what about me?'

Several men immediately jumped to her aid. Each one looked sleazier than the last. Bulldog's eyes passed over them. Finally, he chose someone who hadn't actually volunteered.

'Chub, will you drive Annabel home?'

Chub, who had been carefully weaving his way through the crowd carrying a large bowl of deep-fried prawns, looked up in annoyance at being suddenly called upon.

'Seriously?' His eyes travelled to a chocolate mousse-covered Annabel. '*Now?* A man needs dinner before dessert.'

Annabel gasped in outrage, a hand pressed against her heaving brown bosom.

Wendy touched Chub's arm lightly. That pleading expression was back again, making Gavin feel jealous it was no longer directed at him. 'Please, Cobber?'

He hated the intimacy he heard in her voice when she spoke to the HR manager. *Why doesn't she talk to me like that?*

'All right,' Chub sighed. He looked over at Annabel. 'Come on then. But we're eating these first.'

Bulldog turned to take off with Lena, so Annabel reluctantly made haste to follow Chub, leaving Gavin standing there looking at Wendy.

She put a hand on his shoulder. 'I'm so sorry.'

His insides twisted at her touch and he looked down at the mess on his shirt to cover how much she affected him. 'Guess I should go back to camp too.'

'No,' she protested immediately, 'I'm not going to ruin your night as well as your shirt.'

'Seriously, Sarge, it's no trouble.' It's not like he'd wanted to come in the first place. What a great excuse to leave.

'Come on,' she tugged on his arm, 'I've got an idea.'

'But –'

She didn't allow him to speak, pulling him through the crowd with determination. They went inside and straight towards the toilets.

'Er, Sarge.' Gavin dragged his feet. 'Are you aware that this is the ladies' room?'

'Yes.'

'Are you also aware that I'm a man?'

'Very aware,' she nodded softly as she turned to meet his gaze. 'Don't worry, there's no one else in here.'

It was quite impossible to slow his erratic heart now that they were alone and she had so much more skin on display than usual – all creamy, curvaceous perfection. His eyes devoured her as she put her hands on her hips and said, 'Take off your shirt.'

Something in his face must have given him away because she laughed – a glorious gurgle that made him think of precious gems being scattered across a velvet display case. 'Relax. I'm not going to rape you,' she said.

'What a shame!'

She blushed, holding out her hand. 'I can rinse that area of your shirt and dry it under the hand dryer. We'll be done in minutes.'

'All right,' he finally agreed, willing his body to stop buzzing as he unbuttoned his shirt. Perhaps, if he hadn't been so focused on controlling the rush of blood to his loins, he would have realised the extreme foolishness of this seemingly harmless move.

Chapter 18

Wendy could hardly breathe. After bending down to splash the cream and chocolate off his face, Gavin stood up straight again, torso exposed, steadily regarding her, the very image of masculinity. Broad-shouldered with a gorgeous pair of pecs and a double keyboard set of perfectly formed abdominal muscles tapering beneath. His upper arms were a sculpture of easy contours.

His jeans hung low on his hips, revealing the waistband of red underwear that had the word 'Spiderman' repeated around the circumference of his waist.

Belatedly, she realised he was still holding out his shirt to her and tore her gaze from his underwear to the checked cotton. She snatched it from his grasp and immediately turned towards the sink to spot-clean it. Hot water flowed freely from the tap and, relaxing a little, she looked up to watch him in the mirror.

'So,' she injected what she hoped sounded like cool indifference into her voice, 'what's with the Spiderman underwear? Got a fetish you want to tell me about?'

She saw him grimace in the mirror. 'It was a practical joke

that I haven't had the heart to throw out. My sister, Kate, bought them for me a couple of Christmases ago.'

Kate!

Her eyes jerked to his in the mirror. The woman he had been sending flowers to was his sister. The knowledge took one sandbag off her heart. Not only was Gavin ten points less promiscuous, he'd also just given her the very first ever piece of personal information about himself. It was a step in the right direction.

'You have a sister?' She tried to preserve the indifference in her tone.

'Yeah.' To her disappointment, he didn't elaborate. In fact, his face clouded as though he'd realised he'd said too much. She sighed. They weren't getting emotionally closer despite the fact that she had now seen him practically naked.

Her gaze dropped from his face to his shoulder to his perfect collarbone to his . . .

'Hey, what's that?'

'What's what?'

She draped his shirt over the dryer and, wiping her hands on her jeans, went towards him in a kind of stupor. Of their own volition, her fingers reached out and touched the round indented scar just under his collarbone. His skin was warm and supple under her fingertips and she couldn't resist prolonging the touch. His pec muscle jerked as she explored the damaged skin.

'If I didn't know any better I'd say it was a bullet wound.' She had said it as a joke, not really believing for a second it was true. After all, where would Gavin have come in contact with an angry gunman?

But the way his body stilled and the awkward silence that followed gave her pause.

'Not that I've seen one before,' she mumbled. 'I just watch a lot of crime shows.'

'It's nothing,' he rasped. 'It's just nothing.'

Like a surveyor discovering new terrain, her eyes moved further down his chest to another scar below that. It was more of a wide slash than a round scar this time. He sucked in a breath as her fingers followed the trail of her eyes.

'Shit, Gavin, what have you been doing with yourself?'

Her eyes widened as she spotted yet another scar just under his ribcage. Her fingers began a path diagonally across his chest towards it, until he startled her by snatching her wrist.

'Will you stop that?'

'Sorry, I –'

'Don't apologise, just don't do it.'

'O-*kay*.' It was hard not to hide the hurt in her voice. He searched her eyes furiously for something she couldn't fathom and then released her wrist. 'No harm done,' he ground out.

She swallowed. 'I was just curious, that's all. It looks like you've really been through something.'

Instead of responding, he took his shirt off the dryer and held the wet patch under the nozzle.

She watched him curiously. 'Have you?'

The dryer continued its drone. He bent his head to his task. The muscles in his back bunched attractively as he turned the material over in his hands.

She cocked her head to one side, trying to play the card *he* normally dealt *her* – teasing voice, innocent smile. 'You know, you're always talking about how I have a chip on my shoulder. But you definitely have one. Plus a couple of notches taken out of your torso too. I hate to wave the word hypocrite around . . .'

He turned. 'But you're going to anyway.'

'You know,' she said, 'you said to me once that if I were in trouble I could tell you and you'd help me. Well, same goes for me. I'll help you, if you need it.'

He put his shirt back on. She was sure it must still be a bit damp but he didn't seem to care. He looked down at her, his expression completely unreadable. No smile, no mask, no provocative twinkle in those bottomless eyes. Just a darkness she couldn't fathom. A muscle clenched and unclenched just above his jaw like he was frozen in his own mental prison. 'Thanks for the offer, Sarge. But I'm not in any trouble.'

'I don't believe you.'

'You don't know me.'

'You're right,' she said bitterly. 'I've practically told you my life story and it's only today I find out that you've even got a sister. Why so secretive?'

He didn't reply, merely closed what space was left between them to deliver a paralysing kiss that effectively silenced whatever questions she might have. She felt his thumb slide up her cheek and his fingers cross her hairline as he cradled her face. She knew it was a stalling tactic, but even so her body instinctively swayed towards his. He scooped her to him hungrily with his other arm and the air whooshed out of her lungs.

'Knock, knock.' They broke apart at the sound of another female voice. Wendy spun around, colour flooding her face. Sharon was standing just in front of the doorway, eyes wide.

'Sorry, I didn't realise. I –' She put a hand to her temple and looked down. 'Should I go?' She shook her head and then said with more finality, 'I should go,' and began to back away.

'No.' Gavin's voice was like a stranger's. He stepped around Wendy, refusing to look at her as he sauntered towards Sharon. 'This is the ladies' room after all. I'm the one who should be leaving.'

He walked out without a backwards glance, leaving a lump the size of a golf ball forming in Wendy's throat.

Sharon must have misinterpreted her expression. 'Wendy, I'm sorry, I didn't know. I just came to check on you guys, make sure everything was okay.'

Wendy waved her hand, wanting to reassure Sharon that she hadn't done anything wrong. But her voice wouldn't come, at least not without tears first. She bit down desperately on her trembling lower lip to keep from completely losing it.

Sharon was not fooled. She came towards her. 'Wendy, what's wrong? That arse hasn't led you up the garden path, has he?'

'On the contrary,' Wendy hiccupped, 'he's been completely honest. Told me that he's no good for me and kept his distance.'

'Gavin, a gentleman?' Sharon mused. 'Who would have thought?'

Wendy rubbed her eyes, not trusting herself to speak. Sharon didn't give her much time to recover, however, before asking a much more difficult question. 'So if you and Gavin are not an item, what did I witness just now?'

'Nothing.' Wendy gritted her teeth. 'It was a mistake. He was actually angry because I was getting too personal. It's all on me.'

'Things like this are never all on you, honey.' Sharon rubbed her arm. 'Trust me. Don't beat yourself up. Just think of it as a bullet dodged.'

Wendy averted her eyes and her voice seemed to shrink even in her own ears. 'Only I don't think I've dodged it.'

'What do you mean?'

Wendy hiccupped nosily, unable to hold back any longer. 'I think I've already fallen in love with him.'

'Oh, honey,' Sharon said, immediately throwing her arms around Wendy's sobbing frame. 'I know how that feels.'

Despite Sharon's obvious sympathy, there was little she could say to make Wendy feel better. The next day, Saturday, it became obvious the bus driver had made mention of the incident to Lena because the young engineer also tried to cheer her up by suggesting another girls' day out the next day – their Sunday off – perhaps they could go see the famous Red Dog statue, just for a laugh? Wendy agreed, more to make Lena feel like she was helping than because she really wanted to go. With her disastrous love-life and the emotional chaos she'd left back in Perth she was finding it very hard to get enthused about anything.

When ominous news hit Saturday afternoon, she began to wonder whether she should go out and get herself a rabbit's foot or a four-leaf clover. Anything to stem the bad luck that seemed to be following her around like a stray dog.

It all started when Dan called just before four o'clock. 'Good afternoon, Wendy.' His tone was professional but not upbeat. 'I don't know whether you've been following the news . . .' She hadn't, not with everything else taking up so much space in her head. 'But TCN has just received word from the wharf owners, and also from the Bureau of Meteorology. We are officially on blue alert.'

Wendy's personal issues dropped off her shoulders like mud sliding off a pig's rear. Her position and responsibility suddenly came into sharp focus. 'What category?'

There was a pause. 'Four.'

Four was bad. Not as bad as five obviously. But, at this stage, she wasn't expecting a cyclone worse than three. 'It's not even December,' she protested.

'Yes, the bad cyclones are more likely late in the season. But it doesn't mean they can't and won't occur now.' Dan cleared his throat. 'It's still a tropical low off the coast but the bureau has started watching it closely. We might be lucky. It might change course or reduce in strength to a category three or two.'

'Or it could get worse.' Wendy shut her eyes and rubbed her temples between thumb and forefinger.

Dan's voice grew gentle. 'We will cross that bridge when we come to it. Don't let this get you down, Wendy. Not yet. I've read your cyclone plan. Barnes Inc should be well equipped to deal with the next forty-eight hours. You just need to put into action all your preparations and we'll get through this. Get a good night's sleep because you're going to be super busy tomorrow.'

Wendy opened her eyes and sat up straighter. 'Thank you, Dan. I'll let the project manager know and we'll start rolling out prep for the cyclone.' She put down the phone.

'Did I hear the word cyclone by any chance?' For once, Chub was not addressing her from his seat but had come to hover over her desk. She looked up at his worried face.

'We're on blue alert for a category four.'

'I was afraid you were going to say that.'

She glanced at her watch. 'We haven't got much time left today but we should at least try to make a start on getting the word out. Can you get on the airways?' she asked. 'And draft a memo to all staff to put on notice boards and hand out to supervisors. I'll start calling anyone who is on R and R and tell them they are not to come back to site until we are through this.' She bit her lower lip. 'But first, I've gotta go see Gavin.'

'No worries.'

Wendy rubbed her cold hands together to stop them trembling as she made her way to Gavin's office. She was very lucky to find him there when she walked in. She was worried she'd have to call him and wait for him to come back from wherever he was on site.

His eyes registered her with surprise. He pushed his chair out a little and put his pen down. 'Wendy.' His use of her real name was telling. No doubt, he was still feeling embarrassment from their last encounter. Not that she wasn't. It just seemed to fade in importance to what she had to tell him now. 'Hi, Gavin.'

He cleared his throat. 'Yesterday evening at the pub I –'

'If you're about to give me the "it was a mistake" speech, save it.' She waved his words aside. 'I'm already fully aware and am not here to talk to you about that.'

'O-kay.' He raised his brows.

'The client just called. We are on blue alert for a category-four cyclone.'

'Right.' Standing up, he put his hands on his hips and looked at the floor, brain already ticking over. 'Have you contacted the people on R and R?'

'Chub's doing it.'

'You'll also have to cancel the R and R of anyone who was due to fly out Monday or Tuesday, including myself.'

She reluctantly made the offer: 'You could go earlier before the airport closes. We all know you're overdue.'

'And leave you dangling in the wind?' He grinned at her. '*Literally*. Surely you don't think I'm that cold-blooded, do you?'

She shook her head.

'No,' he rubbed his chin, 'all incoming R and R ceases now. All outgoing ceases tomorrow evening. We will stick with the cyclone plan.'

Wendy nodded. 'We've got to get our evacuation centre in Karratha ready.'

'But not yet. We've got a lot of prep to do before evacuation.'

'Of course,' she agreed. 'I'll call a meeting of the Cyclone Management Team for first thing in the morning, shall I? What time suits you?'

'Early as possible,' he answered. 'Six am. This is our priority from now on.'

'No worries.' She turned to go but he called her by name again.

'Wendy, we'll be okay. Do you remember Cyclone Vance back in '99? That was a category five and there was no loss of life because everyone did what they were supposed to do. We're well prepared.'

As organised by Wendy, the Cyclone Management Team gathered first thing the next day in the main office meeting room. Dimitri looked petrified and his accent seemed more pronounced. Wendy imagined it was because he'd never really believed that he would have to do anything serious. She was glad to have him though. If Fish were around, no doubt he would be researching how the cyclone might adversely affect the movements of mud crabs rather than smart evacuation procedures.

Wendy looked around her table of infantry. The first line of defence against the beast coming in off the coast. Gavin, Lena, Chub, Dimitri, and Carl on speaker phone.

'All right.' Gavin stood up at the head of the table. 'We have about thirty-four hours before the cyclone hits. We need to start preparing this site for gale-force winds. All other duties are to be abandoned in favour of cyclone preparation.' He addressed his attention to the phone in the middle of the table. 'Carl, I know you still can't come on site but you can help Chub prepare our evacuation centre in Karratha.'

'Glad to be fuckin' useful,' Carl barked.

Wendy looked at Chub and added, 'We could be waiting out this storm for hours. So we need plenty of food and blankets, which can be moved from the camp with the help of the staff there.'

'As for the rest of us,' Gavin continued, 'we need to start tying down and putting away. Lena, I want you in charge of everything on land. All plant and equipment is to be de-mobi-lised. Any task not critical or essential deferred. Dimitri, I want you in charge of everything on the wharf. Any at-height work locations are to be cleared of materials and equipment. Please make sure that anything that can be blown away is packed away.'

'And what the fuck will you be doing, Gavin?' Carl's voice crackled on the speaker.

Gavin gave a slight smile. 'You'll be happy to know that I'll take care of the big stuff. All the crane booms need to be secured and the vessels, like my barge and the tug boats, need to be relocated to the safe moorings within the next twenty-four hours.'

'How long will that take?' Dimitri asked.

'All day,' Wendy frowned, 'if not longer, given a round trip to the moorings is about thirteen hours by tug.'

Gavin nodded. 'I might not see you all again till tomorrow. In the meantime, Wendy, can you hold the fort here?'

'Sure,' she agreed and then looked around at the group. 'We've all got our checklists. But I've got a master and I'll be coming around to triple check everything about five pm this evening.'

'What about our staff?' Lena enquired. 'Ever since we went on blue alert some of the men have been asking to be flown home.'

Gavin gritted his teeth. 'I'd love to be in the position to fly everyone who lives out of town home, but you know that's just not possible. Not just because the airlines might not do it but because there are just too many of us. So if we can't do it for everyone we're not going to do it for a few. It's not fair. As long as everyone does exactly as they are told we should be safe at the evacuation centre in Karratha.'

Lena sighed. 'I thought as much.'

'Get your personnel lists ready too,' Wendy advised. 'Before we evacuate we'll need everyone on the job to be accounted for.'

'Sure.'

After taking a few more questions, Wendy returned to her office. She could already feel the adrenaline filling her veins. Shaking her tingling fingers, she forced herself to take a couple of deep breaths and walk to the kitchen instead of her desk. A cup of hot tea might help her think calmer and clearer. They were still in the early stages. Chances are this cyclone would get downgraded or it would move away from the coast. After all, it was only the last week of November.

Surely they'd be all right.

The next fourteen hours unfolded in a blur of checklists and monitoring. Wendy kept the radio on, constantly listening out for updates. And Bulldog also kept her apprised of anything new that came in from the Bureau of Meteorology and the Fire Emergency Services Authority. Most of the time, however, she already knew. The bureau and FESA's websites were both very informative and she could monitor the cyclone position off the coast via an internet tracking map. The damn thing remained on course and continued to intensify.

She was still at work at seven that night. It was getting dark out and rather windy. There was nothing more she could do for that day and she knew she had to get back to camp, but she couldn't seem to leave Cape Lambert until she'd heard from Gavin.

Even as she was considering the thought, the door to her office donga swung open and he walked in.

'You made it back from the moorings.' She smiled with relief. 'Everything all ship-shape?'

'Fine.' He didn't look pleased. 'What are you still doing here?'

Waiting for you to get back. 'Oh, just a few last-minute things,' she returned vaguely. 'I'm ready to go now.'

He put his hand on his hips. 'You bet you are. Wendy, it's dark out there. You should be back at the camp, looking for a good book for when you're locked up in Karratha tomorrow.'

'That's what you think I'll be doing?' She rolled her eyes. 'Reading a book? I doubt very much I'll be able to concentrate with gale-force winds throwing pieces of buildings, possibly ours, around outside.'

His face relaxed somewhat. 'Sorry for snapping, I'm just tired.' He ran a hand through hair she longed to neaten. 'I doubt I'll be reading a book either.' Some of the teasing Gavin returned. 'Tell you what, I'll bring a set of playing cards. We'll play poker to get your mind off things.'

She eyed him doubtfully. 'I don't know how to play poker.'

'I do.' His lips turned up in that smile that always got under her skin.

She had no doubt he did. Although the specific rules of the game were unknown to her, she knew what a poker face was and Gavin had one of the best in the business. If they played for money he would no doubt fleece her dry. 'We'll see.'

'In the meantime,' he placed a hand in the small of her back, 'go back to camp. Like I said, there is nothing more for you to do here.'

'No worries,' she agreed. 'But what about you?'

'I've got to secure all the office donga doors and windows and turn off the power and water. Then I'll leave.'

He picked up her bag and took her by the hand, practically dragging her to the door.

'Gavin.' She tugged at his hand in protest. 'Do you mind?'

'Yes, Sarge. Very much.'

'All right, all right,' she agreed. 'You win, I'm going.'

She passed a restless night, finding it initially very difficult to fall asleep. When she awoke, it was to the wailing of the emergency warning signal. At first it was loud and then grew softer as the speaker moved away. No doubt it was mounted to an SES vehicle being driven through the town. She glanced at her digital bedside clock. It was just before four.

The siren was the signal that they were just about to broadcast more information on television and radio regarding the cyclone. She had no doubt that they had just slipped into yellow alert.

Twelve hours before impact.

Dan confirmed this when he called her mobile at four-thirty.

It was time to prepare the camp for evacuation. They had already put the word out there the day before that an evacuation would be called at five-thirty in the event of a yellow alert and that all men were to be in readiness. The camp had its own sirens that would be sounded when the time came. All personnel were to gather at muster points to be accounted for. After that, they were to leave in buses and utes to the Barnes Inc evacuation centre in Karratha.

Wendy left her room at five and headed to the mess for a speedy breakfast. It was unusually full. Some of the guys who normally skipped breakfast had decided to gather there. Not for food but for news. Someone had put a radio on in the hall and turned it up. The men were eerily silent as the announcer droned in monotone over the subdued clinking of cutlery against plates.

'News just in from the Bureau of Meteorology suggests that Cyclone James is due to cross the coast in less than twelve hours. James will likely impact the town of Wickham the most with its destructive force. Locals are urged to make preparations as per advice provided by the bureau and FESA. At this stage, the bureau has predicted winds as high as two hundred and ninety kilometres per hour and so have upgraded James to category-five cyclone. Luckily, the storm will hit during low tide so storm surge or intense flooding is unlikely, though not ruled out. Locals have been urged to batten down, secure their windows and doors and, if they feel their homes are not built to withstand these conditions, retreat to welfare centres provided by the Shire of Roebourne. To find out more information FESA asks locals to please refer to their website. Personnel from FESA are currently conducting inspections of the town to ensure all residents are prepared.'

Wendy's ribs tightened around her heart. An upgrade in the cyclone category was definitely not the news she'd been hoping for.

A full tray of food appeared across the table from her. It contained four slices of toast, some cold meats, a bowl of Coco Pops, fruit salad, yoghurt and two buttered pancakes with a cup of coffee.

'Tell you what, little mate, I'm so nervous about all this, I've completely lost my appetite.' Chub's expression was dirty as he pulled out a chair and sat down opposite her. 'And they don't help matters putting on that depressing radio in here.' He lifted two slices of toast, shoved a piece of ham between them and took a bite. 'You know, with this ordeal in store, we should all be keeping our strength up, not fasting.'

Wendy's eyes looked down at her half-eaten slice of toast and a smile tickled her mouth. 'I'm glad you're managing to eat something, Cobber. No matter how meagre.'

'Well you know,' Chub nodded modestly, 'I'm doing my bit for the team. Same as any man here.'

'How are things going in Karratha?'

'We're all set.'

'And Carl?'

Chub's mouth twisted. 'He is by far the bossiest person I have ever met. But I suppose he's managed to kick things along nicely. I just wish he wouldn't make it so obvious how much he's enjoying using me as his punching bag.'

'He's been missing being in contact with the site.' Wendy's smile deepened. 'I'm sure he's loving having some of his power back. The main thing is that you haven't had any problems.'

Chub shook his head. 'After breakfast, the camp kitchen staff are moving more supplies there. We've got heaps of tinned foods and ready-to-eat meals if the school cafeteria kitchen no longer functions during the storm, which in all probability, it won't.'

'And what about clothing and bedding?'

'Well, as per the cyclone plan, we sent out a list yesterday about what everyone was to pack for the evacuation.'

Wendy ran a hand across her temple. 'Oh crap, I haven't packed yet.'

'Did you get the list?'

'It's probably still in the inbox on my computer at Cape Lambert.'

'It's only four items anyway,' Chub reassured her. 'Spare set of warm clothes, your pillow, your blanket and any valuables you don't want to lose that could fit in a backpack.'

She polished off her orange juice. 'I can do that.' She drummed her fingers on the counter, worried that with so much going on she was going to forget the little things that made so much difference.

'Oh damn, what about torches?' Trembling fingers fretted their way through her messy hair. 'And mobiles. I forgot to tell everyone to charge their mobiles and put fuel in the utes. We've gotta find a safe place to park them, Cobber. Oh shit. There's still too much to do.'

'Wendy.' Large hands grabbed her by the shoulders and gave her a gentle shake.

Her face flicked up. 'Sorry, Cobber.'

'You just go back to your donga and pack. Torches and mobiles are already sorted but I'll go talk to people with utes now. I need you to calm down and take a load off. Do you want me to call Gavin to help you?'

She allowed her hand to drop from her hair. 'No. Why would I need you to call Gavin?'

'Just a thought,' he returned cryptically, regarding her with his double chin buried in his chest. 'Look, I know you fancy yourself captain around here, little mate. But there's absolutely no need for you to go down with the ship, so to speak. You take care of yourself this morning, you hear me?'

'Loud and clear.' She shot him an affectionate smile.

'Good.'

Mustering the men for evacuation turned out to be a relatively quick and painless procedure. For once, the men did not question her authority or the instructions meted out through various key personnel. Everyone was accounted for, ready and prepared to go, their faces a mixture of fear and hope.

The Cyclone Management Team personally saw everyone to a vehicle, ticking names off lists. Soon there were only five people left standing in the car park. Wendy, Gavin, Chub, Dimitri and Lena.

They split up and walked through the camp, making sure everything was secure. All the donga doors and windows were shut so that the cyclone had the least chance of damaging them. Although Wendy wasn't holding her breath, given the rating on the dongas was only category three.

At seven am it was nine hours till impact.

They re-convened in the car park, where two utes were parked in readiness to go. They were just about to hop into the vehicles when a car turned into the car park and three men alighted from a dark green Mitsubishi. One man was familiar to Wendy.

The man she knew as Skinner strode across the wet, windy car park towards them, leaving the other two leaning against the vehicle. He winked at Wendy. 'Hey, love.'

She felt intensely guilty as Gavin shot her a quick look before turning around to greet the man, saying, 'I thought you were in Perth.'

The out-of-towner cocked his head to one side, a teasing grin stretching across his not-so-teasing face. He was still wearing that silver stud, Wendy noticed, and his longish blond hair was slicked back with some sort of styling gel. 'And here I was thinking you'd forgotten all about me.'

Something was wrong.

It wasn't just the weather putting a chill in the air any more. She couldn't lay a finger on what it was exactly, but something was creeping her out.

'Excuse me, sir.' It was Chub who interrupted the awkward silence. 'But in case you hadn't heard, there's a cyclone coming. It's going to hit town in less than nine hours. We all need to get some place safe.'

Skinner's gaze flicked briefly to him before returning to Gavin. 'I was hoping to have a little chat with Gavin here first.'

'A *chat*,' Chub repeated, affronted. 'No offence, mate, but this is no time for a catch-up.'

Wendy watched the way one of Gavin's fists clenched and unclenched at his side. She thought it odd that there had been no handshake at this reunion of old friends. While she was still trying to figure it out, Gavin turned around to face them. 'You guys all go in Chub's ute. I'll follow later.'

'What?' she whispered.

'Are you sure, Gav?' Lena demanded, also casting Skinner an annoyed gaze. 'I think we should stick with the plan.'

'I'll stay here till Gavin is ready to leave,' Wendy immediately volunteered. 'You guys go in Chub's ute.'

'No!' Gavin's tone was so fierce that for a moment all they could do was stare at him. Skinner came up behind him and clapped him on the shoulder. 'Come on, mate, if the little lady wants to stay, she can stay. I don't mind.'

Gavin shrugged his hand off and looked sternly at Wendy. 'This is a family matter. It's private. I don't want you here.'

Skinner cleared his throat. 'It's a family matter all right.'

There was a pleading look in Gavin's eyes. 'Can you please just leave? I'll be fine.'

More secrets. It was the story of their relationship. Should she really be surprised? He didn't want to confide in her. Wasn't it about time she gave him the distance he demanded? But her feet wouldn't move.

Gavin turned to Chub and the others. 'Take her, will you? I'll meet you guys there. Come on. You're running out of time.'

Dimitri clasped his hands. 'Well, I for one do not want to stand around arguing while the weather gets worse. No?' Without further ado, he hopped into Chub's ute, waiting for the others to follow. With a shrug, Chub got into the driver's seat.

Wendy felt Lena's hand on her arm. 'Come on, Wendy. Obviously he wants some space. He's got the other ute and he's with his friend so . . .'

'Are you sure you'll be okay?' Wendy asked again. Her eyes flitted once more between Skinner and Gavin.

Gavin's face crinkled into a reassuring smile. 'Just go, Sarge, and find a pack of cards. We're playing poker as soon as I get there.'

She watched his carefree wave as she allowed Lena to push her into the back of the ute.

Poker, huh?

She was afraid their game had already started.

Chapter 19

As soon as Chub's vehicle was out of sight, Gavin spun around. He could feel his blood pulsing in his brain as he faced the man who had been the horror in his nightmares for the last five years.

'Where's your knife, Peter?' he shot at him. 'Aren't you here for the other eighteen jabs?'

'You want to get right into it, do you?' Peter regarded him with the admiration of a hunter who had finally caught a particularly wily fox. 'I thought you'd at least thank me first for letting your friends leave without a scratch.'

'Not really interested in small talk,' Gavin shrugged. 'Given I've been expecting you for the last five years. What took you so long?'

Peter's expression hardened. 'Cocky little bastard, aren't you? You do realise I have two guys with me. Your odds of surviving this meeting aren't exactly good.'

Gavin knew that as surely as he'd known he had to get Wendy and the others away as quickly as possible. All the same, he wasn't going to lie down and play dead.

'Really?' He peeled his lips back from his teeth. 'Still not seeing that knife. What about a gun then? Your brother wasn't a very good shot. But who knows? You might be able to aim straight.'

Peter's fist whipped out and caught him on the side of his jaw. Gavin didn't need much more provocation than that. Fuelled by fear and adrenaline both his fists shot out, catching his enemy once in the face and once in the gut.

Peter doubled over, laughing. 'Is this because I invited your girlfriend to join us?'

'She's not my girlfriend.'

'Still,' Peter mused, 'I would have loved her to be here for this.' He rammed Gavin, throwing both fists into his belly.

But Gavin's fury protected him. He felt almost no pain. A man possessed, he hit back without even stopping to consider his own injuries. He punched Peter across the car park until he had the man on his back, groaning and looking up at him.

'I think it's time for me to go.' Gavin turned and hurried towards his ute. Maybe he could make it while Peter was down.

Just before he reached the car, he felt two kicks to his calves. Even as his legs folded and he sank to the bitumen on his knees, the blow to his nose came out of nowhere. His cheek hit the ground. He lay there not knowing whether the wetness on his face was a result of his own blood or the fact that it had started raining. He could see Peter sitting on the ground and realised it must have been his men who had taken him out.

Peter rested his arms on his kneecaps. 'We haven't finished our conversation yet.'

A booted foot placed itself on Gavin's cheek, preventing him from getting up. He was forced to lie there and look at Peter's gleeful expression.

'You see, last time,' Skinner explained, 'I didn't think things all the way through. I came to your house in anger. I acted without precautions. It was actually good you got away. The thing is,' Peter spread his hands as though he were addressing a rapt group of students, 'I don't want to be done for murder.

Knives, guns, they give a man away too easily. Why should I be punished for something you did?'

Gavin said nothing. Not that he could have even if he wanted to with his mouth squished painfully against jagged edges of red gravel, the metallic smell of soil and blood filling his nostrils.

'Rope,' Peter explained, 'on the other hand, can be purchased anywhere. It's such a common commodity, so much harder to trace.'

Peter's man removed his boot from Gavin's cheek and he was yanked to his feet and held fast.

'You're going to hang me then?' Gavin demanded derisively, spitting blood and dirt as he spoke.

'Oh no,' Peter said dismissively. 'Then the fun's over too quickly. You'll be pleased to learn that I've decided that I'm actually not going to kill you at all.'

Gavin felt no relief. Time had obviously cooled Peter's anger to the point where death simply was not enough.

'Why should I?' Peter asked with all the satisfaction of the Cheshire Cat. 'When Mother Nature can do it for me?'

Gavin realised for the first time what Peter intended to do to him. For two stunned seconds he did not resist as Peter's faithful dogs began to push him towards his ute. Then he began to thrash about and a roar erupted from his throat. But against three men he was unfortunately no match. Every time he managed to get out of one person's grip the other two would hit him until the first man had recovered. It wasn't long before they had him tied to his own windshield. His arms were stretched wide and taut, each wrist held tight by rope that was then wound around the side mirrors and pulled through the windows into the car. They tied the two ends together inside the car. His legs got the same treatment, both pulled straight and spread-eagled across the bonnet. They held fast his ankles with rope that knotted several times around the roo bar.

'What do you suppose Mother Nature has in store for our Gavin?' Peter whistled as he worked. 'A good flogging no doubt. I hear the rain hits as hard as a nail gun and the sand rips the first layer of skin off. The screaming of the wind is so loud, prolonged exposure can burst your eardrums. Of course,' he mused, 'you won't be able to see anything with all that sand and debris blowing about. And if it's a big bit of debris that hits you, it could take your head off, but with any luck it'll just be your arm or your leg. Or maybe both before anything that drastic happens. Did you know,' he taunted further, 'that if you leave the windows or doors of a donga open, the air pressure generated inside can sometimes literally lift the box off the ground and fling it somewhere?' He finished the last knot and came over to pat Gavin's cheek affection-ately. 'I wonder if it's the same with cars?'

They drove his car further into the camp so that it couldn't be seen from the main road and left the windows of his ute open.

After they deserted him, he struggled till his wrists and ankles were burning and bleeding. But it was to no avail. He could do nothing but wait. And pray.

Chapter 20

The entire drive to Karratha, Wendy was deeply unhappy with Gavin's departure from their plan.

I shouldn't have left him. I should have stayed with him.

Then I would know he was safe.

Skinner didn't exactly look like a responsible individual. Maybe Gavin knew him well enough to ask him to collect his mail. But that didn't mean he was smart enough to do what Gavin told him before the arrival of James in now under eight hours. He certainly wasn't local. Would he know how to handle himself? Wendy hoped Gavin wouldn't get messed around by his friend's ignorance.

Her concentration was down when she reached the evacuation centre but luckily Carl and Chub had done a great job with preparation for their arrival. They were using the central block of the school: a gymnasium surrounded by classrooms on three sides and a cafeteria on the final side. At red alert they would close and lock up this entire block. But as people were still arriving most of the main doors and windows were open. There were people setting up camp in the gymnasium. She could hear the buzz from a hundred different portable radios. People were sitting on their blankets, propped up by pillows, playing cards or following the storm on TVs and radios stationed around the room. She wondered how long they'd have reception. It was good to see torches and gas lamps everywhere for the inevitable power failure.

The thing about cyclones was, once they started, it was mostly a waiting game. After it passed, and FESA gave them the 'all clear', then they could go outside to survey the damage.

The camp chefs were preparing a proper lunch in the cafeteria. It would probably be everyone's last hot meal for a while. There were also a few televisions on in various classrooms around the place where people were avidly watching and chatting.

Barnes Inc was sharing this safe house with their major contractors and TCN, so there were many faces that Wendy didn't recognise. She did see Bulldog come in though, and also Frank.

For the next couple of hours, she did her final checks, welcomed the newcomers and continued to pace the floor with one eye on the main doors. Her worry escalated as Gavin's absence continued. She tried calling him several times but his phone rang out.

Where the hell is he?

At ten she heard the wailing of the SES sirens again, both from outside the building and echoed in the various radios and televisions switched on around her.

They were on red alert.

Six hours to impact.

And still no Gavin.

Everyone knew that at red alert, preparation should be over. It was time to get to shelter and lock up, no matter what. Wendy sat down in the chair nearest to her as the orders to secure the building were shouted around the gymnasium. She looked down at her hands; they were trembling. She clenched and unclenched her fingers. The shaking wouldn't stop.

She felt a hand on her shoulder.

'Wendy, what's wrong?'

She started, unaware that anyone had been watching her. Her eyes flicked up and she said weakly, 'Lena.'

The young engineer was accompanied by Sharon, Carl and Chub.

'You want something to eat, little mate?' Chub sounded worried. 'You've been running around all morning and you've starved yourself again, haven't you?'

'You do look fuckin' pale,' Carl commented. 'Chub, go get her some tea.'

Her large friend nodded and moved away to fetch it.

'It's Gavin,' Wendy said, 'he's still not here.'

'What the fuck is the bastard doing?' Carl demanded. 'Where is he?'

Lena turned quickly to the project manager, wringing her hands. 'Just before we left camp, some of his friends from out of town turned up to see him.'

'The man's fuckin' entertaining during a fuckin' cyclone!'

'Well, it was yellow alert back then,' Lena reassured him. 'And it seemed like he wouldn't be long. He said he would catch up. We did leave him a ute.'

Wendy winced. 'I'm thinking we shouldn't have left him at all.'

'He told us to.' Lena shook her head. 'In fact, he looked bloody desperate that we go – something about a private family matter. Don't worry, Wendy, knowing Gavin he's probably taken up shelter with those mates of his and in typical inconsiderate style has just forgotten to tell us about it.'

'Call his mobile, honey,' Sharon suggested to Wendy.

'I have. It's switched off.'

'Dickhead.' Carl rolled his eyes. 'I can't send someone for him now.'

Just then Dan joined their little group. 'Are you talking about Gavin Jones?'

Wendy turned to him eagerly. 'Yes.'

'I just received a message from a friend of his. Apparently, he's taking up shelter with them.'

'There you go.' Lena smiled, patting her shoulder again. 'I told you. Nothing to worry about.'

But he said he was going to play poker with me.

Twice.

It just didn't seem right.

'I don't know.' Her brow wrinkled. 'I know this may sound dumb, but I've just got a bad feeling.'

'Wendy,' Carl warned, 'we can't send anyone to go look for him now. It's too dangerous.'

'Well there's no need to,' Dan nodded, 'he's fine.'

'I know.' Wendy got up from her plastic chair, which was normally some kid's seat in Science class, and moved slightly away from the group. Her friends began to chat quietly between themselves about other things, throwing her the occasional look of concern.

She went to the window. It didn't look too bad yet. The wind was brisk but trees weren't bending or breaking. She went to the television where an anchor was showing the progress of the cyclone and where meteorologists predicted it would hit first. Chub brought her a cup of tea and she watched the TV for a little bit, but was unable to quieten the warning bells in her own head, let alone the ones on the television.

There's got to be something else on apart from just weather reports.

She started flicking channels just as her Uncle Mike walked into the room.

'I've been looking everywhere for you, girl. Why aren't you in the gymnasium?'

She took in his sudden concern with a shrug of annoyance. 'I wanted some place quieter.'

'Well, the gymnasium is the centre of this structure. It's the safest area in the building.'

'Relax,' she sighed. 'The storm hasn't even hit yet.'

'All the same –' Mike began.

'I think I'll stay here.' She cut him off. It was mightily forward of him to start playing protective now when the entire lead-up to this storm he hadn't given a crap about her. She turned back to the TV and changed the channel again. Her body froze as a familiar face suddenly came on screen.

Something shrivelled and died inside her as she took in the image in horror.

The hair was a different style and colour, and he was wearing a short-sleeved T-shirt that revealed tattoos on his skin that had not been visible to her either of the times they'd met. But there was no mistaking that heavy silver stud or that twisted grin that seemed to take delight in her sudden and overwhelming fear.

She turned up the volume.

'Wendy,' Mike started again.

'Shut up,' she hissed. 'I'm trying to listen.'

'. . . a warning to North West residents. Police Media advised this morning that they believe disgraced Sydney businessman Peter Marshall has left Perth in a stolen vehicle and is heading towards Karratha. A warrant for Mr Marshall's arrest was issued out of New South Wales last week where he allegedly engaged in organised crime activities. Mr Marshall made the news five years ago following his brother's conviction and sentencing, with open remarks against the witnesses in his brother's case. Mr Marshall's brother, Eddie Marshall, died in custody on 29 August this year. Members of the public are advised not to approach or deal with Mr Marshall. It is believed he is armed and dangerous. Anyone with any knowledge of Mr Marshall's whereabouts are urged to contact Crime Stoppers.'

'Oh God!' Wendy dropped the remote.

It hit the vinyl floor with a resounding *THWACK* as scenes flashed past her eyes in quick succession like the highlights of a movie she hadn't realised she'd been watching.

Gavin complaining about the lack of fun in her life. 'Because I've limited my choices because I must. You, you beautiful girl, don't need to bury yourself.'

Gavin outside his donga. 'Look, I know where you're coming from. Sometimes the actions we take can have repercussions that seem to last a lifetime.'

Gavin in the car. 'I don't do commitment. And I certainly don't do relationships.'

Gavin at the health centre. 'Here I am trying to protect you and you get hurt anyway.'

Her own fingers trailing down his gorgeous chest. 'If I didn't know any better I'd say it was a bullet wound.'

She had been so naive.

So foolish.

So clueless.

Then she remembered one last thing that sent a chill through her bones.

The memory of Peter Marshall leaning close to the window of her car. 'I won't tell if you don't tell.'

She stood up on shaky feet, whispering, 'I led him right to him. He never would have found him if it weren't for me.' She clutched the desk beside her for support.

'Wendy, *Wendy*,' Mike was saying urgently. 'What's going on?'

Her eyes flew open. 'I've got to find him.' She turned unsteadily.

'You're not going anywhere.' Mike reached out and grabbed her arm.

'Let go of me.' She tried to yank herself out of his grip.

But for a balding old man he was mighty tenacious.

'No bloody way.'

'What the fuck is going on here?' It was Carl. The conversation in the group across the room ceased as eyes turned to her struggle with Mike.

'I've got to get to Gavin,' she rasped. 'Now! Something dreadful has happened or is happening to him.'

'Wendy,' Lena came towards her, a hand reaching for her shoulder, 'we've just been through this.'

'Look.' She drew Lena's attention to the television, where the druglord's photo had flashed up again to close the report. 'That's the man we left him with, right?'

She allowed the room to fall silent as the rest of the group came closer to observe what was going on. It didn't take Lena more than thirty seconds to grasp the situation. 'I'm coming with you,' she announced.

'Over my dead body,' Dan growled. 'I'll go with Wendy instead.'

'No way,' Lena protested. 'We'll both go then.'

'If Lena's going, I'm going,' Sharon announced.

Lena shook her head at Sharon. 'You've got a broken leg. It wouldn't be a good idea.'

'It's only half broken now.' Sharon patted her boot but Carl threw her a stern look.

'You're fuckin' staying here. I'm the project manager, I'm heading up this rescue.'

'Nobody should go,' Mike growled. 'Not for that waste of space. This is ludicrous, all of you risking your lives for just one man.'

Silence fell as they all turned incredulous eyes on Mike.

'Fuck,' said Carl after a moment. 'Forgot he was still here. Why don't you just take yourself off, Mike? Have a fuckin' Cuppa Soup. It'll make you feel better.'

'I'm not going anywhere,' Mike growled. 'And neither is Wendy.'

'Oh fuck off, Mike.' Something in Wendy's brain snapped. 'You don't own me.'

All this arguing was just giving her a headache and frankly wasting her time. She wanted out of there *now*! And she didn't care who followed and who didn't.

'Fine.' Mike gritted his teeth. 'But you can't go alone. Somebody has got to go with you and it might as well be me.'

'He's right, little mate.' Chub, who had been silent so far, finally stepped in. 'You're going into a war zone. You'll need a plan of attack and of escape. It's nearly five hours till impact. What are you going to do exactly?'

'I'm going to search Wickham for him.' Wendy threw up her hands in frustration, wishing they'd all just get out of her way.

'What's to say he's in Wickham?' Chub demanded. 'They could have brought him to Karratha. After all, they need to get out of the weather too.'

Wendy pushed her fingers into her hair, scrunching it at the roots. 'I don't know. What do you think is more likely?'

'You need more people on this.'

'Dan and I will search Karratha,' Lena offered.

'Okay,' Wendy agreed eagerly. 'And I'll search Wickham and Point Samson. We're looking for a green Mitsubishi parked in someone's driveway.'

'All right, I'll go with Wendy,' Chub announced. Then another thought seemed to occur to him. 'But what happens when we actually find this green Mitsubishi parked in someone's driveway?'

'What do you mean?' Wendy asked.

'Well,' Chub's expression was dubious, 'what do you want me to do? Go knock on the door and say, "Hey, Mr Druglord, you know that guy you've taken hostage? We'd like him back?"'

'Yes, Cobber,' Wendy hissed, her fist smashing fiercely into her palm, 'that's exactly what I want you to do. The alternative of just doing nothing is not an option.'

Chub took a hanky from his pocket and mopped his beading brow. 'I was afraid you were going to say that.'

'You should take some weapons,' Sharon put in helpfully. 'For the confrontation.'

'Of course, that'll improve our odds of success dramatically.' Chub's face seemed to be going slightly green.

'I saw some cricket bats in the gymnasium,' Lena offered.

'Fuck, that's good,' said Carl. 'You should take those.'

'Oh yeah,' Chub added, 'bloody foolproof.'

'Chub, stop being so negative or you can stay behind,' Wendy shot at him. She knew he was just trying to be the voice of reason. But reason played no part in what they were doing. If it did, they wouldn't be going at all.

'Sorry, Wendy.' Chub rolled his heavy shoulders and set his teeth. 'Just thinking too much.'

'I'll be in charge of our cricket bat,' Dan told Lena dryly. 'And I'll do the knocking if it comes to that.'

Chub nodded. 'So I guess I'm batting for me and Wendy, God help us! But just one more practical question, if you please. Suppose we hit the Sydneysider on the head and make off with Gavin. Lena and Dan can come back here but what if Wendy and I don't have enough time to make it back to Karratha?'

'It's not safe to stay at the camp during the storm,' Carl interrupted. 'But you could go to our place in Wickham.' He shared a look with Sharon and she nodded in agreement.

'Then that's what we'll do,' Wendy said shortly, itching to be off. All she'd been doing the whole time they were planning was watching the clock. The precious minutes seemed like hours. Deep down she knew she was making decisions like a mad woman.

But it was Gavin out there. She'd served him up to his enemy on a silver platter and now she had to fix this.

Or die trying.

But her friends . . .

'Listen,' she started desperately, 'I know how dangerous this is. You guys don't have to join me.'

'Okay, little mate,' Chub held up his hands for silence, 'stop talking or you might just persuade me.'

'I left him behind too,' Lena said quietly. 'I want to go.'

Wendy dusted her hands and headed for the door. 'Then let's do it now!'

She couldn't afford to waste another second. Unfortunately her uncle had different plans. He braced himself inside the door-frame, preventing her departure. 'This is a suicide mission. You can't go.'

'Nobody asked you to join us,' Wendy snapped. 'Just move out of our way.'

'No.' Mike's blunt refusal made her want to slap him.

'Fuck, Mike,' Carl shouted, 'this is nothing to do with you. Piss off!'

'Wendy is my family.' Mike's eyes were wild as they darted about her group. 'I'm not going to let her place herself in danger.'

'I thought I made myself perfectly clear to you months ago.' Wendy's voice shook. 'There is not one drop of your brother's blood running through my veins. You are not my uncle.'

'No, I'm not,' he croaked. 'I'm your father.'

Wendy's mind reeled. For a second she couldn't compre-hend his words. Couldn't take them in. Not when she had so much else going on in her head.

'I had an affair with your mother. I'm your biological father,' Mike blurted out.

'You're telling me this *now*?!' she yelled at him, feeling as if her circuit breaker had just hit overload. It was too much.

'I know it's a lot to take in,' Mike babbled. 'But stay, I'll explain. We'll talk about it.'

A lot to take in!

Her brain nearly melted.

'Shut up!' Her stomach flipped and she had to press her hand there.

'I'll tell you anything you want to know,' Mike continued. 'Right here. Right now. It's what you want, isn't it? What you've been searching for all year.'

'You insensitive *bastard*!' She spat out the words, tears smarting in her eyes. Her heart was too full for her ribcage and it beat against her bones, making it difficult to breathe.

Mike paled at her words but he persisted. 'I'll explain every-thing. I'll tell you what happened. When it happened. Why I left even though it broke my heart.'

'Wendy, what is he talking about?' Lena asked.

'Nothing,' Wendy retorted. 'Nothing I want to know about any more. Let's go.' She didn't know where the strength came from but she managed to push him aside and walk through the doorway.

'Wendy!' She heard him calling her name. The pleading in his voice did nothing to bend her will.

If he did indeed have something to say to her, then he could wait on her convenience. After all, he had not breathed a word to her about their relationship until it suited his purposes. Perhaps her mother had been right. Perhaps she should never have tried to find him.

Chub, Lena and Dan caught up with her. And in silence they marched through the gymnasium, collected a couple of bats, and a few other bits and pieces from the main hall, like torches and first-aid kits.

Then they were outside.

The wind whipped into Wendy's hair, somehow refreshing her rather than scaring her. The storm outside was nothing beside the one now raging under her skin. Beating her blood like an ice-cream milkshake.

Anger made her senses sharp. An unstoppable energy infused her nerve endings. Worry fuelled her adrenaline. No one was going to stop her from saving the man she loved.

Not even Mother Nature.

Chub and Wendy wished Lena and Dan luck before hopping into their own ute and making for the main road.

The streets were deserted and wet.

The sun had already slipped behind the clouds. It was getting darker. The air was heavy with moisture and expecta-tion. It felt more like six o'clock in the evening than twelve forty-five in the afternoon. In this light, it was usually common to see families of kangaroos by the side of the road. The dumb things had no sense of danger. But this time there were none to be seen.

Wendy tried to sit calmly in the passenger seat. It was an effort to keep her hands still. Her nerves felt live, like wire that hadn't been earthed properly. She was sure if anyone touched her they'd receive a shock. There was just too much churning around in her body to suppress.

'Want to talk about it?' Chub asked as their vehicle moved onto the main road.

'No.'

'Are you sure?' he prompted. ''Cause you look like you're about to explode.'

'I don't want Uncle Mike distracting me from Gavin.'

'Well, we're stuck in this car for the next forty-five minutes or more, depending on how bad the weather gets. You might as well get some of it off your chest while there's still time to kill.'

'I just don't understand it,' she burst out. 'He had an affair with his sister-in-law. Or his almost sister-in-law. It's disgusting. I'm an episode of *Dr Phil* waiting to happen.'

'Well, you know,' Chub shrugged, 'maybe that's why he was so hell-bent on keeping it a secret. He was probably ashamed.'

'Oh, the whole family was ashamed!' Wendy threw up her hands. 'I realise that now. My mum, my adoptive father Parry, my grandparents. Particularly my grandmother, who is a traditional Italian Catholic. They've all wanted to bury me in a hole since my conception.'

'I'm sure that's not true.'

'No,' Wendy sighed, 'you're right. Mum had them all fooled till I was six years old. And then Parry found out I was actually . . . his brother's. I think that was the beginning of the end for everyone, including me.'

'Why do you say that?'

'Well, I got sent off to boarding school while they fought amongst themselves.' Wendy thought back to her conversation with Parry. All the pieces were starting to slot into place. 'Parry wanted everyone to tell Mike.'

'Did they tell him?'

Wendy frowned. 'No.' She slapped a palm over her mouth. 'I told him, when I ran into him in Karratha. He must have put two and two together when I said I was looking for my father.'

'Wow. That would have been a slap in the face.'

'For who?' Wendy demanded bitterly. 'After he knew the truth he wanted to know me even less.' She clenched her fists. 'He needn't have worried. I wasn't going to ask him to become involved in my life. I just wanted some answers.' She shook her head. 'And now I have them. Mike doesn't have any children. My unknown family stops with him. Thank God!'

A sudden thought struck her. 'Do you suppose he was just lying to stop me from going after Gavin?'

'Sorry, love,' Chub said. 'Only a father's conscience would have made him go to so much trouble.'

'But my mother called my father Hector. Why would she do that when his name is Mike?'

'To stop you from finding out the truth. Wait –' Chub grimaced. 'You said your mother's name was Helen, right? And Mike's brother is Parry.'

'Yeah.'

'I think I know why she called him Hector.'

'You do?' She turned her gaze from the road to look at him.

'Well, it's just a theory,' Chub shrugged, 'but you ever heard of Helen of Troy, the woman who caused that whole Trojan horse thing to be built?'

'Vaguely.'

'She had the two brothers fighting a war over her. Their names were Hector and Paris.'

'My mother was just trying to make it a romantic story all about her,' she groaned. 'Typical.'

'Well, you know,' Chub shrugged again, 'people will do and say almost anything to make themselves feel better.'

Wendy frowned as her eyes shifted back to the scenery outside her window. It was starting to get a little rougher. Trees were bending in protest. The weaker branches had already come off. She pointed to some of the ones that had blown onto the road. 'Just be careful. We might need to drive a tad slower.'

Chub slowed down a little and she had to fight the urge to bite her tongue at the cautious pace she had just told him to take. In that instant, Mike and all the problems attached to him and the family that had done her no favours receded.

Gavin was her priority right now. She had to get to him before it was too late.

They went to Point Samson first. There were more hotels there. If a tourist wanted to find a safe place to hibernate during the cyclone, it would be there. After searching the car parks of all the accommodation sites for signs of a green Mitsubishi, they were forced to admit that this theory had been wrong. Twice they were scolded by hotel staff, who ran out to tell them to find shelter, *immediately*.

They agreed rather than explaining their situation and moved on. It was just easier.

After that, they drove through the residential housing section and even went into a caravan park that had definitely been evacuated. No sign of that beat-up green Mitsubishi there either.

The phrase 'needle in a haystack' kept popping into Wendy's thoughts.

She bit her fingernails. 'Come on. Come on. Come on.'

Chub sensed her mood. 'We still have a couple of hours till impact. Shall we head for Wickham?'

'Yes.' It was a struggle to talk at all without throwing up. She glanced at her phone again, hoping for a text message from Lena or Dan saying that they had found him.

Nothing.

They drove to Wickham in silence. She could feel the wind pushing under the car, rocking it slightly as they drove –

almost taunting them with its power. Red pebbles spitting against the doors were becoming louder. She rubbed her neck because it had started to ache from sitting so stiffly. But she couldn't relax. Sitting in a car made her feel so useless. She'd been coiling her adrenaline like the spring in a Jack-in-the-box. Something had to open that lid soon.

They drove past the camp first as it was at the entrance to the town. The car park was completely empty. No sign of a green Mitsubishi. So they carried on and made their way slowly through every street in the small town. It was raining again and visibility was getting harder with the sky losing more light. Chub had his wipers vigorously dashing water from their windscreen but the pace was still slow.

And also fruitless.

Wendy felt panic tickling the underside of her ribcage.

'I don't know what to tell you, little mate,' Chub said softly after half an hour. 'It might be best if we just headed to Carl and Sharon's now.'

Wendy clenched her fingers together. 'I want to go back to the camp. That was the last place we saw him. Maybe the fools are all in the mess or something. The building is old but it looks sturdy enough.'

'All right.' She could hear the doubt in Chub's voice but resolutely chose to ignore it.

She wasn't giving up until there was absolutely no time left.

Back at the camp, they parked their ute in the car park and exited the vehicle. Wind tore at her clothes and hair. Rain pelted her face, mixing with her tears. They had neither raincoat nor umbrella but Wendy couldn't allow these circumstances to affect her. In any case, they would be useless against a cyclone. They ran straight to the mess. Wendy got there first and Chub puffed up shortly after. But he was also carrying the bat.

Wendy walked the perimeter of the mess, gazing in windows. Gavin was not inside.

And then she turned the last corner by the back entrance and spotted it. Not the green Mitsubishi.

But Gavin's ute.

She ran forwards, hoping that it would present her with some clue to its owner's whereabouts. She didn't expect to find Gavin strapped to the hood, pale and soaked with blood and water, like a corpse that had been left to rot after execution.

She almost dropped where she stood, but something kept her going.

Oh God! Is he dead?

A wail escaped her lips. Her fingers feathered about on his wrist, looking for a pulse.

His eyes flew open. 'Wendy?' he croaked.

'Gavin, oh Gavin. Thank God. Thank God.' Blood was roaring through her head with both relief and the urgency of the situation.

Chub lumbered up behind. 'Shit! What have they done to him?'

'I don't care, we've got to get this rope off,' Wendy cried.

Both Wendy and Chub tried to loosen the knots, but the rope was wet and pulled so tight. It was obvious from the cuts on his wrists that Gavin had been struggling earlier and his efforts had only tightened his bonds.

Wendy's fingers were bleeding. The wind was getting louder. She had to shout to get Chub's attention. 'We can't do this. We need something to cut it.'

'The mess.' Gavin jerked his head at Chub's bat. 'Smash a window.'

Chub ran to the hall's entrance, where the front double doors had glass window inserts. He brought the bat up and then followed through. Glass exploded and unfortunately blew back on him when the air pressure from inside the hall whooshed out – he received a few small cuts to his face.

'It's all right,' he yelled, giving them both the thumbs up before sticking his arm through the window and unlocking the door from the inside.

He disappeared into the building and Wendy turned back to Gavin.

'Why didn't you tell me how much danger you were in?' she demanded, gripping his arm with both hands.

A crooked smile twisted his now blue lips. 'Never seemed like the right moment, Sarge.'

His explanation was so wholly inadequate that she didn't bother to question him further. It was growing more difficult to talk over the howling wind and she would rather save her breath.

She could feel gravel spitting against her jeans. It wasn't too painful yet, but she knew that it wouldn't be long before each of those stones would strike like tiny bullets against her calves.

Chub seemed to be taking an age. She gripped Gavin's arm even tighter, trying to give and receive reassurance at the same time.

'You shouldn't have come, Sarge!' he yelled at her. 'You should have stayed in Karratha.'

'We'll argue about that later,' she yelled back.

Chub returned with two long carving knives in his hand. He wordlessly handed one to Wendy. They began to work again on Gavin's bonds. This time the process was much quicker. Pretty soon he was sitting up rubbing his wrists while they were working on the ties holding his ankles. As soon as they were done, he slid down off the roof of his car, groaning at the impact of his broken body hitting the ground.

Chub pointed at his vehicle but he shook his head.

'They took my keys.'

'It's all right,' Wendy yelled. 'We'll all fit in Chub's ute.'

It was less than an hour till impact. They had to get to Sharon and Carl's as quickly as they could, which shouldn't be a problem, given it was only a five-minute drive away.

'Come on.' Chub gestured for them to follow and started marching back towards the car. Now that Gavin was safe, some of Wendy's other senses were coming back online.

Her clothes clung to her skin, wet and cold, chilling her to the bone as wind battered her with invisible fists. It was hard to walk. It hurt to walk.

She could barely see in front of her as they made their way back to the Barnes Inc ute, to the accompaniment of groaning dongas and the high-pitched whistling of the wind.

They made it to the edge of the car park. Chub's ute was in sight.

Then it came out of nowhere.

A narrow sheet of corrugated metal – maybe a piece that had ripped off the roof of one of the dongas – flew through the air before them, almost as though it had been hurled by a giant knife thrower. It skilleted Chub's ute cabin like a kebab stick, shattering glass and burying itself in the head rest of the driver's seat.

Wendy, who had been running towards the vehicle, stopped so suddenly she fell back, landing on her bum. Her hand flew to her throat, as if it too had just been sliced. Her eyes bulged from their sockets as she studied what had been their only ride to safety.

She felt rather than saw Gavin bend down beside her to help her up. Her eyes remained fixed on the ute sitting out in the open car park unshielded by surrounding dongas and buildings. Now that the front and side windscreens were smashed it was an easy tipping target for Mother Nature. The vehicle crashed onto its side and whatever windows had survived the corrugated iron now lay disintegrated on the gravel.

Without a word, Chub turned around and ran back the way they'd come. Gavin tugged on Wendy's hand and she tore her gaze from the scene to run after him. But where to?

They caught up with Chub back at the mess. He was through the double-door entrance and standing in the main hall, heaving and pale as a ghost. All the trestle tables had been folded away and put at the back of the room, so it was just a huge empty space, surrounded by windows. Wendy saw each of these portals as a threat. Anything could fly in. They needed to shield themselves behind concrete or something.

So much sand and dirt had blown in through that small hole Chub had made in the door already. They'd shut it behind them but it was rattling ominously. The sand that blew through stung Wendy's face. Her wet clothes clung to her like a robe of ice.

'We can't stay here,' she told the others as they moved as far from the damaged door as possible. 'This building isn't safe. This *room* isn't safe. Can we still make it to Carl and Sharon's?'

'You're not suggesting we walk, are you?' Chub demanded. 'Did you see what's floating around out there? We'd never make it.'

As if to echo this sentiment, the window next to the door that was rattling imploded.

'Get down!'

Gavin pushed her body to the floor, covering it with his own. When the sound of glass ceased, Wendy looked up at the damage. She didn't know if something had hit the window or if it had simply given in to the air pressure or the rain pelting every surface. The streaks of water that came in behind the glass were horizontal. Water was entering elsewhere too – through joints and gaps around other windows that had seemed airtight until this moment. She put her arms up to shield her eyes as the wind blew another deluge of glass, sand and water halfway across the room. Luckily, only the dregs reached them but it wouldn't be long before they'd be standing in the line of fire.

'How much time do we have before impact?' she cried desperately.

Gavin squeezed her shoulders. 'Wendy, I think James is already here.'

Chapter 21

'If we hadn't created an opening, this space might have lasted longer.' Gavin's eyes darted over the walls. 'But now the air pressure in here is going to go crazy. We don't have much time.'

Even as he spoke an acacia tree standing near one of the windows, and bending so far backwards you'd think its trunk was made of rubber, finally gave way. Its roots ripped up out of the ground and the tree keeled over, smashing into another mess window. One of its branches was now protruding into the hall, giving them the surrendering wave of a dying soldier.

The eaves of the building groaned.

Wendy could hear plaster bursting and cracking. Sand whipped around the room scalding her arms and legs as more debris powered in through these new openings. She covered her eyes.

'The roof is not going to hold,' Gavin yelled over the ever-increasing noise. Even though she wasn't the structural engineer in the group, she probably could have told him that.

'Come on.' He pushed them out of the mess into the kitchen and shut the door. The building shook and trembled. The kitchen was smaller than the mess hall, but the tops of the walls were still lined with windows – the kind that let in light but couldn't be opened. Wendy hoped this made them stronger.

'All right.' Gavin walked around the room. 'Do any of you know this building? I only use the mess. Got no idea what else is behind the reception room. Is there a toilet or a bathroom? We need to get into the smallest room in the place, hopefully a room with no windows or very small windows. It'll be the strongest room.'

'The only other room I know of is the games room, which is a mirror of the mess.' Wendy groaned.

'Wait,' Chub lifted a finger, 'there are two storerooms behind reception. They're tiny, like walk-in wardrobes, no windows.'

'And they have shelving?' Gavin demanded.

'Steel-framed shelving attached to the wall on one side.'

'Perfect.' Gavin licked his lips. 'Lead the way.'

Wendy heard a distant explosion as she walked through another door – this one leading into reception.

She tried not to think about what it might have been.

The two storerooms were side by side. Chub flung open the door of the first. It was full to the brim with food. Packets of biscuits, bottles of coffee, cans of every vegetable and fruit you could think of, bags of rice, long-life juice and boxes of cereal.

Gavin pushed open the second door. It was full of blankets and linen.

'Okay.' Chub's eyes widened. 'I bags that one. You guys take the linen.'

He walked into the food storeroom, his bulk practically filling the space.

'But don't we want to stay together?' Wendy asked. 'Won't you get scared in there all by yourself?'

'Little mate,' Chub held up a hand at her protest, 'do you know what I do when I'm scared?'

'What?'

'I eat. Trust me, I'll be fine. Besides,' he shrugged, 'we won't all fit in one. Not comfortably anyway.'

Gavin walked into the linen cupboard, grabbed three blankets and a few sheets. 'We'll swap you linen for food.'

Chub took the pile of bedding and stepped out to allow Gavin in to choose a few bits and pieces.

Wendy shivered as she waited, her eyes darting to the windows across the other side of the reception room. It was so dark outside. She couldn't see more than a few metres in front of the window.

'Okay.' Gavin deposited the food in the second storeroom and came back out to shake Chub's hand. 'Good luck.'

'You too, mate.' Chub squeezed Wendy's shoulder and reluctantly she tore her gaze from the windows.

'Don't come out for any noise, all right,' Chub warned. 'Stay put until you hear the sirens.'

He kissed her on the cheek and then, as though slightly embarrassed, turned quickly and walked into his cocoon, slamming and locking the door behind him.

Gavin and Wendy walked into the other storeroom and shut the door.

It had been dark outside, but the storeroom was pitch black with the door closed. Not a single iota of light penetrated their senses.

They stood in the centre of the room, their wet bodies pressed together. Wendy shuddered as another distant explosion crashed overhead. The building trembled. She began to quake. Tears rolled down her face. The storm roared outside like a jet engine. It was overwhelming.

Almost.

She felt two hands on her shoulders and Gavin's lips spoke close to her ear so he wouldn't have to shout over the blare of the cyclone. 'We should strip down to our underwear and wrap ourselves in blankets. We could be here for a few hours and it would be better to be warm. What do you think?'

She nodded, before she realised he couldn't see her body language in the dark. At her silence his hand moved up her shoulders and she felt his thumb against her cheek, wiping her tears away. She nodded again with his hands on her face, knowing he would feel it, and then moved away, not wanting him to realise how undone she really was.

With trembling fingers she unbuttoned her shirt. It felt so good to rip that thing off her clammy skin. Her jeans were next. Wet as they were, it was like peeling off a pair of tights. A blanket flew around her and suddenly she was enveloped in warm wool. A little scratchy against the skin, but dry was better than wet.

She said, 'Thank you,' but, because she hadn't shouted, didn't actually hear the sound of her own voice in the darkness.

His hands were suddenly in her hair, undoing the clip that kept it up. He turned her around and started drying her soaked locks with a sheet.

She felt like a child. A helpless, lost, vulnerable little child.

She wanted more from this man than these polite gestures. The silent darkness in this room was like a wall between them. Devoid of his teasing grin and mocking voice, she felt so bereft.

A loud *BANG!* shook the building, followed by the squeal of tearing metal. Followed by another *BANG!*

It sounded like they were losing the roof over the mess, or maybe it was the games room. Who knew?

Who wanted to know?

She fell back against him, her breathing short and shallow as she began to tremble violently.

'Hey, it's all right. We'll be okay, Sarge.' She felt his lips against her ear lobe and shuddered. Not from fear this time but from a building awareness that was curling through her body like the flame of a growing fire. He drew his blanket around her shoulders as well. She turned in his arms, letting her blanket slide off her shoulders and pool at their feet, happy to take the warmth of his body instead.

She felt his chest spasm at the sudden feel of her skin against his. She laid her ear against his heart. The steady, if accelerated, beat was a welcome change from the racket going on outside. His arms tightened about her, his lips kissing her hairline.

The shelving rattled as another *BANG!* erupted somewhere in the building. She lifted her face up to gasp or cry out but he moved his head and his lips were on hers.

Like a shot of morphine, relief was instantaneous. There was no cyclone.

Except the one raging inside of her.

They kissed like they were being chased, devouring each other with feverish abandonment. She pressed her body into his, her hand at the base of his neck, feeling the sudden leap of his pulse.

Something pelted a wall behind them, like shots fired from a machine gun.

BANG! BANG! BANG!

She pulled him closer. Their mouths did not break contact.

He tied the blanket in a loose knot behind her neck so his hands could roam down her back and undo the clasp of her bra. It fell away, along with all inhibitions. She slid her undies down with one hand and kicked them off.

A *CRASH* sounded in the kitchen. The tumbling of pots and pans. Had the shelving torn down?

She didn't care.

Her fingertips feathered over the contours of his abdomen, over his chest. Glorying in all that was male, in all that was Gavin, in all that was hers.

Metal drew hard against metal. *Creeeaaaaakkkkk!* It wailed in desperate protest. No doubt the building was under attack from stray sheeting.

His long strong fingers curled around her bare bottom and then under her thighs. She felt herself leave the floor as he pulled her legs up around him. She hooked her ankles behind his thighs, her arms about his neck, grazing her chest against his.

BANG! BANG! BANG! CRASH! SMASH!

His lips slid down her throat as her back hit the wall behind them. She grasped him tighter, welding herself to him till she didn't know where her body ended and his began.

CRASH!

SMASH!

Her fingers curled desperately into his hair as she moaned with the storm.

CREEEEEEEEEEAAAAAAAAAK!

Wendy's eyes flew open as she cried out.

Fireworks burst overhead.

Rocks hurled, shards pierced, glass shattered, walls collapsed. The shelving rattled till she thought the joints might give way.

CREEEEAAAK! BANG!

But still no burst of light penetrated their dark cavern. The walls had not caved in. The roof had clung on. The rain had not snuck in through the cracks. She closed her eyes as her forehead fell to his shoulder. His lips were on the curve of skin where her neck met her shoulder. His body went limp.

The storm continued to rage outside. But as far as Wendy was concerned, it was already all over.

Chapter 22

Wendy awoke to the sound of a FESA siren.

This one at least was good news. The cyclone had passed. They were giving the 'all clear'.

She had absolutely no idea what time it was, but felt like they had been trapped for hours. Probably all night.

She and Gavin had eaten a few biscuits and things around what she assumed was dinner time. They'd spoken sparingly as it was difficult to hold a conversation over the noise.

Then they'd noticed the storeroom was starting to flood: a circumstance that was possibly even more scary than being out there in the raging storm.

Luckily, the water in the storeroom rose only a few inches before stopping. Gavin pulled out one of the steel shelves and leaned it against the wall so that they could actually sit on the shelving and take their feet off the floor. They laid blankets on the shelving and around themselves. For the longest time, they sat side by side on a steel shelf, hands clasped, backs against a cold wall.

Some time during their vigil, she must have fallen asleep. They were no longer holding hands, but his arm was around her, and her head was on his shoulder. As the wail of the siren faded, an eerie silence fell.

She slowly lifted her head, feeling her neck cramp. It was still pitch black in their safe haven. But they were unhurt. A smile tickled her mouth.

We're alive!

She felt his thumb rubbing up and down her bare arm and wondered if he had slept too or had been awake the whole time. He certainly didn't sound groggy when he asked, 'You okay, Sarge?'

'Fine. You?'

'Perfect.'

'Have I been asleep long?'

'A few hours. I was glad – you needed it.'

A thought occurred to her. 'Chub!' She flung off the blanket that had been around her and started to ease forwards.

'Easy now,' he warned.

She landed with a splash on the ground in front of the shelving.

'Oooh gross.' She swore. 'It's so cold and I can feel things floating in it.' She rolled her shoulders. Her limbs were sore and aching from sleeping in an awkward position.

She heard Gavin's dry chuckle in the darkness. 'Forgot about the moat, did you, Sarge?'

'Well, we should try to get out now, don't you think? Check if Chub's okay?'

'You might want to put some clothes on first.'

'Yes.' Her voice croaked. She was glad it was still pitch black so hiding her embarrassment was super easy.

'They're probably still a bit damp though,' he said, suddenly sounding a little breathless.

'Well, we don't have much of a choice.' She was surprised that her voice didn't tremble on the words.

She felt the shelves, searching for the place where she'd left her shirt, until her fingers touched material. It was a little wet but she could bear it.

Where the hell is my underwear?

Heat infused her cheeks as she remembered the circumstances of their removal. Her bra was probably floating somewhere in the swamp at her feet.

So she decided to do without. She slipped on her shirt and then felt around for her jeans. They were definitely not dry and grated against her skin when she sat back on the edge of the shelf and pulled them on. Wet and tight, they were about as pleasant to put on as freshly mixed cement.

She heard Gavin getting dressed next to her and fought the urge to ask him, *Did last night mean something to you?*

Because it meant something to me.

But that conversation had to wait, especially with Chub possibly seriously injured next door.

She cleared her throat. 'Should I try the door?'

'I'll do it,' Gavin said.

A splash as he jumped down to the door and then the click of the lock releasing. The door opened about two inches before jamming.

'Damn,' Gavin muttered. 'Something has fallen on it.'

The two inches, however, was enough to let in a shaft of light. It was definitely the next morning.

'Little mate?' a third voice called. It was Chub, and Wendy breathed a sigh of relief. She waded gingerly over to the door.

'Cobber,' she called through the space. 'Are you all right? We're fine but we can't get out.'

Suddenly, a portion of Chub's face appeared in front of hers. 'Yep, out and about over here. Looks like you got some sort of metal beam leaning on your door. It's wedged against the wall in front of the storeroom. Hang on, I'll see if I can move it.'

'Be careful,' Gavin warned. 'You don't want to disturb anything else.'

They heard Chub grunting and then the clang of metal bouncing on concrete. The door to their storeroom flung wide.

Wendy's arm immediately rose up to protect her eyes from the sudden burst of sunshine.

'Well, aren't you two a welcome sight?' came Chub's jolly greeting.

She slowly lowered her arm.

Oh my God!

It looked like a war zone. The building was not even a shadow of its former self. It wasn't even a building. More like a mass of brick, steel, rubble and smashed furniture. Of course, not all the walls were down. But much of the roof was certainly off. She looked up and saw no ceiling, just clear blue sky.

'Frankly, I think it's an improvement.' Chub rubbed his hands together. 'Always thought this building needed a facelift.'

'I think it's had a little more than a facelift.' Gavin's head tilted back, his eyes squinting at the clouds. 'Nothing like being chewed up and spat out by the Pilbara.'

Wendy rubbed her cold, damp arms. 'Do you suppose we can get out of here?'

Chubb nodded. 'Not a bad idea.' He stepped over a fallen roof beam and around the reception desk, which looked like it had been cut in half. The windows were all smashed. If he'd been smaller, he could have crawled out through one of them. Instead, he stepped cautiously through the debris to the far wall, which was still standing, and unlocked the door there.

He stepped out of the building. Wordlessly, Gavin took Wendy's hand and led her carefully in Chub's wake. When they stepped through what felt like the 'portal of life' Chub noticed their joined hands. But his eyes flicked away and, to Wendy's relief, he said nothing.

In any event, it was good to be breathing fresh air even though she was chilled to the bone. As they stepped out onto the car park bitumen, a squeal erupted a few metres away. Wendy looked across the debris-littered tar and spied Carl and Dimitri standing in front of Chub's upturned ute.

Carl looked positively green as his gaze ran over the savaged vehicle.

There were two FESA officers beside them. A FESA ute and a Barnes Inc ute were parked side by side further back. The car park flooding was pretty minor, though the rest of the camp didn't look like it had fared as well. Some dongas were still standing, but at least half were tipped on their side.

The squeal, however, had not come from these four men, the cars or the camp, but from a small brunette who had started picking her way across the risky terrain towards them. Annabel George was dressed immaculately in a blue dress, full make up and black wedges, wholly unsuitable for walking around in this sort of hazardous environment.

Wendy stared at her for a stunned second. *How does she do it?*

Stumbling over fallen trees to get to them, Annabel's face was flushed with delight.

'Annabel, calm down,' Chub called.

But she didn't break pace. When she reached him, she leaped into his outstretched arms, throwing all her limbs around what she could of his ample form. '*You're okay!*' she cried. 'I was so worried. I didn't know what to do.'

'Just upgraded my safe house, that's all.' Chub patted her back awkwardly. 'To something a little cosier.'

'Don't joke about this.' Her voice was muffled against his shoulder. 'It's not funny. You know, I'm supposed to be at work, but I couldn't go. I had to come with them to see what had happened to you. But I must say –' she lifted her head to eye 'them' over her shoulder '– they were very insensitive. They wouldn't drive me. I had to go in the FESA vehicle!'

'Really? How inconvenient.' He kissed her swiftly and then placed her back on her feet.

'I'm seeing it but I ain't fuckin' believing it.' Carl eyed the couple, aghast, as he also joined the group.

Chub looked up quickly over Annabel's head and cleared his throat. 'How're you going, Carl?'

'A lot fuckin' slower with your bloody girlfriend in tow.'

Chub turned an interesting shade of pink.

'Girlfriend?' Gavin murmured, slapping his large friend on the back. 'You've been busy.'

Wendy tried to catch Chub's eye but he refused to look at her. By which time, Dimitri and the FESA personnel had also walked over so she couldn't question him.

'You folks all right?' one of the FESA guys asked and they all nodded.

Carl jerked his thumb over his shoulder. 'We had to get them to escort us here. The roads are fuckin' under water or covered in debris. We couldn't go the usual way.'

Wendy nodded. 'I'm just glad you came.'

'Good to see you too, mate.' Carl held out his hand to Gavin. 'There's been too many people fuckin' worried sick about you.'

Gavin shook his hand. 'Thanks, Carl.'

'So where were you hiding?' Dimitri asked. 'The mess looks almost completely destroyed. Don't tell me you were in one of these dongas.'

'The storerooms behind reception, actually. They held,' Gavin explained. 'How about your school?'

'Absolutely fine,' Dimitri responded. 'A few classrooms were flooded but nothing to be alarmed about. In fact, the men are getting restless. They're dying to get back here and salvage the rest of their belongings.' He grimaced. 'Not that I think they'll find much.'

'What about the town?' Wendy asked.

One of the FESA guys stepped forwards. 'Not good, I'm afraid. Wickham was the worst hit and has been pretty much flattened and flooded. Karratha and Point Samson are not so bad. The cyclone lasted about seven hours, the eye taking almost forty minutes to pass over Wickham.'

'Geez.'

'So far, though, we haven't received word that there has been any loss of life, which is very good news – seems like the locals took all the right precautions. 'The FESA man's tone seemed positive enough. But when he mentioned the word 'locals', something jarred in Wendy's brain.

'Did Lena and Dan make it back to the school okay?' she asked.

Dimitri and Carl exchanged a look. Carl cleared his throat and Wendy had an awful feeling in the pit of her stomach even before he spoke.

'No.'

She felt Gavin squeeze her hand before he asked, 'Why were they away from the school?'

'They were looking for you too,' Wendy quickly told him. 'In Karratha. We were trying to see if we could find Skinner's green Mitsubishi. Thought it would lead us to where he was holding you.'

Gavin was pale. 'I hope they never found it.'

An awful silence fell. It was Chub who finally broke it. 'Well, let's go look for them.'

'We already have FESA people and the police on the job,' one of the FESA guys informed them.

'That doesn't mean we can't fuckin' look for them too.' Carl nodded to Chub.

The FESA guy protested. 'It's not really safe for you to be out touring the area.'

'When I start fuckin' touring, I'll let you fuckin' know,' Carl snapped at him and then turned to Wendy. 'I want you and Chub back at the school though. I need people there to organise post-cyclone procedures. Craig and Sharon have made a start but they're not up to speed with what you had planned.'

'Not a problem,' Wendy agreed, even though she would rather be out looking for Dan and Lena too. After all, it was her fault they were missing. They never would have embarked on this risky adventure if she hadn't opened her big mouth and told everyone what was going on.

Gavin released her hand. 'I'm going with Carl.'

She could have predicted he was going to say that. But the implications of his words still had their bite. They had just come through the cyclone together, miraculously safe and sound. So now he wanted to go off chasing murderers.

Wonderful!

Not to mention the fact that last night she had given herself to him body and soul and they still had not spoken one word about it. *Maybe he doesn't* want *to speak about it.*

After all, what had changed? He'd been telling her for months he didn't want to go down that road. Maybe he was keen to pretend it never happened. She looked away guiltily as Carl addressed Gavin again.

'I could definitely do with the company and maybe a bit of an explanation.'

Gavin inclined his head. 'Sure. I should also give my case manager, Janet, a call.'

Janet!

To her further shame, the relief she felt at hearing this woman's position was greater than when she'd heard the FESA 'all clear' sirens.

If nothing else, at least she was the only woman in Gavin's life.

'You've got a fuckin' case manager? A *police* case manager?' Carl gawked. 'Mate, you've got a lot of explaining to do!'

'I'll do it in the car.'

It was soon agreed that the FESA vehicle would escort them all back to the school in Karratha. From there Carl, Gavin and Dimitri could drive off to search Karratha – at their own risk – for Lena and Dan.

Chub, Wendy and Annabel got into the back of the FESA vehicle. Neither Chub nor Wendy seemed inclined to talk much but Annabel was more than happy to give a running commentary about Cyclone James and all that had transpired since he had arrived.

Wendy felt every minute of the monologue. Particularly with the rolling picture of devastation and destruction out her window to illustrate it. Several times where the road was blocked with debris or flooding, they had to pull off and drive around the obstacle. Wendy began to bite her nails. The off-road journey was very hard going and she was surprised they hadn't burst a tyre yet. Perhaps they should listen to the FESA guys. Should the boys really be combing Karratha now?

You'd rather leave Lena and Dan out in the cold? When they helped you look for Gavin?

No, that wasn't an option either.

They finally reached the school and the FESA vehicle drove away as soon as it dropped them off. The state emergency staff had much more pressing matters to attend to than construction workers who wouldn't listen to reason.

Carl wound down the window of the Barnes Inc ute to wish Wendy and her companions a brief goodbye. The men weren't even getting out of the ute before taking off. Wendy resisted the urge to stall them. What for? To throw her arms around Gavin's neck for another desperate hug? Better not to slow them down.

It didn't help that as they drove off she turned around to find Chub also wishing Annabel goodbye. Passionately. They finally broke apart and Annabel tripped happily off to her car, which was parked not too far away. She was off to Nickol Bay Hospital to assist with the injured.

About bloody time.

'Something you want to tell me, Cobber?' Wendy demanded as Annabel's car left the scene.

A red stain flooded Chub's face. 'What can I say?' He winced. 'That night at Point Samson when I drove Annabel home she invited me in to try one of her ANZAC biscuits.' He held up a hand in reverence. 'They are to *die* for! Honestly, I must have eaten five or six of them. Didn't leave her place till after midnight.'

'Midnight? It took you that long to eat six biscuits?'

'Well, she'd also just bought this new TV but didn't know how to set it up. So I stayed and did that for her.'

'Ah-hah.'

'I didn't mind.' He shrugged. 'Didn't mind when she called me the next day because she needed some help hanging a painting either. She made me tiramisu afterwards.'

Wendy raised an eyebrow. 'So I take it that was the second date?'

'I guess so.' Chub rubbed his chin thoughtfully. 'On the third date, I mowed her lawn for her. We had the most gorgeous lemon slice together when I was done.'

'You do realise she's just using you as her on-call handyman.'

'Yes,' Chub agreed with a sigh. 'But I'm determined to build on that. Turns out we have a lot in common.'

'*Like what?*' Wendy's tone was disbelieving.

'You know, brownies, pancakes, shortbread, muffins, scones, cake, biscuits. She loves to cook 'em and I love to eat 'em. We're a match made in heaven. She had me at "coffee or tea?"'

'Seriously?'

He grinned. 'Look, I know you think she's a fruit. But I like fruit. Especially mangoes dipped in caramel. Delicious!'

'You could do better.'

'Maybe. Maybe not.' His expression turned serious. 'Wendy, she needs me and is willing to go to great culinary lengths to keep me around. She's kind and beautiful and seems to like spending time with me. Plus,' his blush deepened, 'she's a nurse. She's been talking about exercise – you know, so I can keep eating but get a bit healthy. She really cares. That's enough for now. I'll work on the other stuff later.'

'If you say so, Cobber.'

They entered the school gymnasium to a deluge of questions from all directions. Wendy wished she had a loud speaker so that she could just talk over the top of them because they basically all wanted to know the same thing.

'When can we leave?'

The thing was, she didn't want to release busloads of men only to destroy vehicles and score more injuries through their own eagerness to get back to a camp which in itself was riddled with unsafe areas. Sure it needed cleaning up, but that would be done in a safe and orderly fashion. She glanced at a clock on the wall. It was eight am. The men had been cooped up for a while now since the 'all clear' had been given.

Sharon and Craig came stumbling forwards.

'Man, is it good to see you!' Sharon exclaimed. 'I don't know if I'm on my head or my heels. Are you okay? Where's Gavin? Did you find him?'

Wendy quickly gave them an update on everything that had transpired. While she was doing so an idea occurred to her. 'Does this school have a PA system?'

'I think so.' Craig pointed at a couple of speakers high on the walls. 'The mike's probably in reception.'

'We'll have to break it to the boys that they're not getting out any time soon,' Wendy explained. 'But I also want to give them some good news. Let's go talk to the chefs.'

It turned out the school cafeteria had no power, but the chefs did have several portable gas-burning barbeques and crates of sausages. The boys would be getting hot dogs for breakfast. That, at least, would cheer them up.

The phone lines were dead too. But another representative of FESA turned up about an hour later with a map of the district. He showed Wendy the most significant areas of damage. Places to avoid at all costs. He also told her that the airport would be re-opening the next day, so if she wanted to fly some personnel home, that would soon be an option.

As it was very unlikely that everyone would be able to go back to the camp, and it would be a while before work started on the wharf again, it definitely seemed like a good plan. The school couldn't accommodate this many men indefinitely. There was no news yet on the state of the wharf. She guessed at this stage no one was game enough to visit the work site when they were still salvaging their homes.

The FESA representative stayed for about an hour, talking with her about plans for the town's rehabilitation. It was information overload but she tried to retain as much as possible – taking notes on her own maps.

It was very difficult to concentrate when her mind was never far from Gavin and what he may be doing. Had they found Skinner? She hoped they had notified the police first. Perhaps taken a few officers with them. Her chest tightened every time she pictured them meeting the druglord again.

In the meantime, however, she had her own dangers to counter. She sent men around the building to check for gas leaks. There were some classrooms behind the gymnasium that had flooded. She asked the guys to remove any appliances from these rooms, such as televisions and radios, and put them outside to dry or throw them out if they seemed dangerous.

Chub came to see her while she was still issuing orders. 'Little mate, where are your things? You should get changed into some dry clothes before you get pneumonia.'

She glanced down and realised how terrible she must look. With everything going on, she had completely forgotten about something as mundane as clothing. 'You're right.'

She found her bag in the gym where she'd left it what seemed like eons ago, and headed for the ladies' toilets. They were now being used by men as well.

One of the guys standing in the line saw her approaching and yelled out, 'The Sergeant's here. Stand aside, guys.'

They nodded wordlessly at her and, to her surprise, one man held the door open for her butler-style as the two occupants quickly finished up and scooted out. Perhaps she *had* climbed a long way in their esteem since she'd arrived.

She changed into a fresh pair of jeans, new underwear and a shirt. The dry clothing against her skin made her feel like a million dollars. It was almost a luxury.

As she stepped out of the toilet she thanked the guys and was about to move back to the desk she'd set up at the back of the gym when a shadow crossed her path. Its owner was the very last person she wanted to see.

'Mike.' Her acknowledgement was tight and unwelcoming. She refused to attach the word 'uncle' to his name. '*Now* is not the time.'

'I just want two minutes,' he pleaded. 'Two minutes to explain.'

'I have too much to do.'

'*Please.*'

Something in his voice stopped her. Desperation perhaps – the sound of a man on the verge of tears. He pointed at a sports equipment storeroom near the toilets. 'We'll have some privacy in there.'

Reluctantly, she inclined her head. They walked into the room and the smell of worn rubber assailed her senses. Surrounding them were several plastic bins of balls, mitts and bats. They didn't close the door because there were no windows in the room and so no light. But it was enough to keep them away from prying eyes and ears.

'Talk quickly,' she said flatly.

'Firstly I want to say how glad I am to see you.' A hand reached towards her, which she quickly stepped back from. 'The cyclone was so bad. I . . . I thought I'd lost you.'

Wendy lifted her chin. 'You lost me twenty-nine years ago, Mike, long before there was any cyclone in the picture.' She sighed. 'My mother was wrong about a lot of things but she was right about you. You've never been interested in me. So why guilt should suddenly prick you now is mind-boggling.'

'I was trying to do the right thing by my brother. I wanted to ease the pain I had caused him,' Mike said tightly, his bald head beading with sweat. The man did look rather sick with his own self-loathing. It was the only reason Wendy waited impatiently for the rest. 'I didn't want to complicate his life any further. I'd done a very, very selfish thing and I was trying to make up for it by exiling myself.'

'What about me?'

'I didn't allow myself to think of you. In my mind, you were not my child. You were his child. It didn't matter about DNA. I had no right to you, as I had no right to Helen. It wasn't personal.'

'You know what,' Wendy tapped a finger to her palm, 'I just don't get it why the lot of you think that once you've revealed to me that I was just a bargaining chip in your little love triangle that that's supposed to make me feel better. Am I supposed to say, no worries, guys, it wasn't personal, you were too busy fighting amongst yourselves to be bothered about me.' She gritted her teeth. 'I'm a person, damn it! And I've been pushed from pillar to post my whole life because the three of you couldn't stop playing your stupid mind games. I have never felt wanted or loved or special to anyone . . .'

She hung her head. *Except – maybe – to Gavin.*

His name resonated with the beat of her heart. But she firmly pulled her thoughts away from that can of worms and refocused on Mike. 'It's over now. I don't want any of you in my life any more. This time, *I'm* moving on.'

'But you don't understand,' Mike rushed out. 'I realise all that. I realise that what we did was wrong. Shameful in fact! That's why I couldn't tell you I was your father. I knew you would shun me like this. But please, if there is any chance –'

'There is *no* chance,' Wendy cried, before grasping at what self-control she still had. 'Now, if you don't mind, we're in a state of emergency here. And I know you don't care about anyone but yourself, but I do.'

Fury shot up her throat like an electric current as she exited the storeroom. It was a full five minutes before she regained the ability to think straight.

As it turned out, that was not a second too soon.

The men were just finishing their hot dogs when the front entrance of the gym burst open again and in walked Carl, Gavin, Dimitri, Lena, Dan and three police officers. It took all Wendy's strength not to do an Annabel George and race across the room to throw herself into Gavin's arms.

'Is everyone all right?' she demanded, noticing that Lena was limping. Dan was supporting her.

'Fine.' Lena smiled at Wendy reassuringly. 'Just a slight accident.'

Wendy came over and quickly embraced her friend. 'Where were you? Why didn't you come back to the school?'

Bulldog grimaced. 'We sort of got stuck in a bathroom. But it held. So we were lucky.'

'A bathroom?' Before she could ask them anything further Carl interrupted.

'Is that fuckin' hot dogs I smell? Where is my fiancée?'

After these questions were answered, it didn't take him or Dimitri long to excuse themselves.

'Ma'am,' one of the police officers addressed Wendy, 'is there a private room in this building where we can take witness statements from this couple?'

'Um . . .' For a moment Wendy's mind went blank and then she remembered the storeroom. 'Yes, the storeroom. Take a couple of torches with you.'

She grabbed two red ones that were lying on the far side of her makeshift desk. Lena and Dan hobbled away with the law enforcers. She was finally alone with Gavin.

He grinned at her. 'I thought they'd never leave.'

This time, Wendy did not resist the urge to throw her arms around his neck. 'Thank goodness you're back. I've been worried sick. I'm trying to do my best here but I can't concentrate with my mind still on you and that man . . .' She swallowed hard. 'Skinner.'

He gently pulled back a little and said softly, 'Well, I had to come back, didn't I? That game of poker is long overdue.'

She dropped her arms and put some distance between them. 'I'm not playing games with you any more, Gavin. I'm done. I want the truth. All of it. Now.'

He scratched the back of his neck. 'It's difficult to know where to start.'

'How about your real name. Or did your case officer, Janet, let you keep that?'

'My real name is Gavin Rusman. We only changed my surname to Jones.'

She leaned back on the desk, arms and legs folded, waiting for him to continue.

His lips twitched. 'I've been in witness protection for the last five years because I put Skinner's brother away for murder. He's been after me ever since. You can understand why I had to keep that a secret, right? I signed an agreement with the government.'

Her limbs loosened a little. 'Okay, so you weren't just being an arse with all those secrets on purpose.'

'Thank you for the concession.' He inclined his head. 'I take it it's not a very large one?'

'You've been nothing but a ratbag since I met you!'

'I was actually trying to protect you. I didn't want you to get messed up in all my problems. Look at what happened to Dan and Lena.' Some of the bravado left his face. 'They found that green Mitsubishi, you know.'

Wendy's hand covered her mouth. 'You're kidding.' Thank God she already knew they were safe. Still, her stomach flipped over. 'When we all went off to find you, none of us were thinking straight. *Especially me.* I just knew I had to get to you and I put everyone in danger. How could I have thought a cricket bat would be any match against a *druglord*?'

'Well,' Gavin conceded, 'turns out Bulldog didn't actually go with your plan.'

'He didn't?'

'Not that it was a bad one.'

'Get real, Gavin.'

'All right,' his eyes twinkled, 'it was shocking. But who am I to complain?' He came towards her, cupping her cheek and causing a full-body tingle. 'You and Chub saved my life.'

She pushed his hand away. 'Stop trying to distract me from this story. What did Bulldog do?'

'The Mitsubishi was parked outside a house, a rental property, I assume. Dan and Lena had all their PPE in the back of the ute. So they got fully kitted out, took a couple of clipboards and went and knocked on the door.'

'Okay,' she frowned, still not quite sure where he was going with this.

'When one of Skinner's men opened the door, Bulldog said they were contracted by FESA to check the safety of the property before the storm hit.'

Clever.

'So they went in and pretended to check the property while looking for me. In fact, everything was going really well until one of Skinner's men who was at the camp recognised Lena in the garden. She was calling my name softly.'

A chill ran down Wendy's spine. 'So then what happened?'

'They decided to take them hostage and locked them in the bathroom.'

'Aah, *the bathroom.*'

'Skinner's guys thought it would be uncomfortable, but as you know it's the strongest room in the house.'

'And . . .'

'The rest of the house . . . wasn't so strong.' Gavin shrugged. 'When the police got there they found two bodies in the living room. One was Skinner's and the other – one of his men. The third man, I believe, got away. Lena and Dan were still in the bathroom and absolutely fine. Lena actually hurt her ankle tripping on debris on the way out.'

Despite the fact that there was definitely no love lost between her and Skinner, Wendy couldn't stop her throat closing up. Having just been through the cyclone herself, she knew his death must have been awful. And yet still, she had to ask: 'What happened?'

'They didn't have cyclone shutters on the windows. The ones in the living room imploded and basically they got glassed. Looks like Skinner was fatally wounded in the neck by a huge shard.'

Wendy cringed and looked away. 'You know, I almost feel sorry for him.'

'But not quite?' It was a question more than a statement.

'No.' She looked back at him, suddenly shy. 'After what he did to you . . . I can't even forgive a dead man for that.'

He watched her silently for a moment, hands buried in the pockets of jeans that had long since dried.

He looked a mess. The shirt he was wearing was crushed and dirty. The buttons were out of sync, so that one side appeared to be longer than the other. His hair was not just tousled, some of it was standing on end, and the shadow along his jaw showed how badly he needed a shave.

All in all, he looked delicious.

Bloody delicious.

Nothing could ever disguise Gavin's healthy virility or the sparkle in his eye that was always her undoing. A lump formed in her throat as the moment she had been dreading finally arrived.

'Listen, about what happened in the storeroom last night . . .'

She pushed off the desk, hoping to give herself more strength by standing rather than slouching. Still, she couldn't resist trying to stem some of the coming pain. 'Look, don't worry about it. It's all right. You don't have to explain. I get it.'

'Giving me a get out of jail free card, are you?' he asked quietly.

'Well, I wouldn't put it that way exactly.'

He ignored this remark. 'What if I don't want one?'

'I don't understand.' Her voice faltered.

'I haven't told you the truth yet. At least not the truth I've owed you for a long time,' he began, a certain vulnerability she had never heard before suddenly entering his voice. 'You're right. There should be no more games between us.'

'No more games.' She nodded, not daring to say more.

'The truth is, Wendy,' he lifted his eyes to hers and they blazed like fire, 'I love you.'

Her heart stopped.

'I think I loved you from the moment you slapped me in the face. You were a real wake-up call for me in every way.' He grimaced. 'Not that I didn't fight it.' His head bowed as he struggled with the explanation. 'I will admit my original intentions weren't exactly honourable, but it didn't take long for things to change. Of course, I knew we couldn't be together, at least not like that.'

'Why not?' Her voice was a breathless whisper.

'I didn't want you to be in danger by being associated with me. Turns out, I did a very poor job of protecting you.' He looked away. 'Can you forgive me?'

She stared at him for a moment and then, licking dry lips, said, 'Already have.'

'Really?' He met her eyes quickly, his expression hopeful.

'Oh, for goodness' sake!' She laughed, holding up her arms. 'Just shut up and kiss me.'

There was that cocky grin she knew and loved. 'I thought you'd never ask.'

He put both hands on her waist and pulled her to him, taking her mouth as soon as their bodies met. Her arms wrapped around his neck and she soaked him in like sunshine, glorying in the peace that she only found in Gavin's arms.

He pulled back just a breath. 'You do love me, right?'

'What do you think?'

He groaned and kissed her again. For a moment they were lost in their own little world. Nothing else mattered except the fact that they'd both finally found home.

The sound of a throat clearing cut through the magic. They broke contact but only enough to turn their heads towards the intruder, cheek to cheek.

It was Chub, eyebrow raised, foot tapping. 'Something you want to tell me, little mate?'

Wendy grinned at his impersonation of her from earlier, and shrugged. 'What can I say? Turns out we have a lot in common.'

Epilogue

The days that followed were difficult but Wendy's heart was not heavy.

While the destruction around her was mind-boggling, she was up to the challenge of setting everything to rights. In fact, she was up for anything.

Gavin's presence by her side gave her a buzz that wouldn't abate. Their courtship had been so fraught with uncertainty that to have his attention with no hidden agendas was like walking on clouds. She didn't want to lose the feeling any time soon.

Barnes Inc flew most of its men home, retaining a small staff to assist with the reconstruction of the camp. Damage to the wharf and surrounding plant was actually fairly minimal as it had been designed to withstand the worst a cyclone could throw at a structure. The site offices had not fared so well but repairs were already underway.

Bulldog and Lena got engaged – a circumstance that surprised no one. And Fish sent them a postcard from Queensland, wanting to know if any fish had washed up on the bank because of the cyclone. And if so, did they collect them?

Nobody bothered to reply.

Though both Wendy's Perth parents called to see if she was okay, neither of them made mention of each other and she didn't care to ask. Her conversation with Parry was awkward. She told him that she knew the truth about Mike. He seemed relieved to hear it but he also asked for her forgiveness for not telling her the truth. It gave her hope that one day they would repair their relationship.

A few days after the cyclone, Gavin and Wendy were lying on a blanket at Honeymoon Cove, drinking in a star-streaked sky and a bottle of wine.

'You know I can't believe everything that's happened to me since I got here,' Wendy mused. 'I feel like a coin that's been flipped.'

'Really?' Gavin's voice seemed cautious so she rolled onto her side and propped herself up on her elbow.

'What?' she prompted. 'Do you know something I don't?'

'You can read me that easy now, Sarge?'

'It's an art I'm perfecting.'

He paused. 'There is still one thing I haven't told you. Not because I didn't want to but because I was waiting for someone else to do it first.'

She frowned. 'Someone else?'

'Mike Hopkins, your uncle.'

She allowed herself to re-settle onto her back. 'You mean my father.'

There was a sigh beside her. 'He told you.'

'You *knew*?'

'I kind of put two and two together when I discovered your broken air conditioner in his donga, along with your damaged window and broken desk. The clincher was his foot. Not many guys can boast an accident like that.'

'*He* was the one who fixed my donga? My fairy dongamother?'

'Yep. Told me to stay away from you too when the rumours were doing the rounds. Said he'd make me sorry. Didn't want a loose cannon like me messing with his daughter. Who knows?' His expression was incorrigible. 'Maybe he was justified.'

She ignored this attempt at a joke too. 'He *threatened* you?'

'I guess so.'

'But you're twice as big as he is.' She frowned. 'Not to mention, twice as young and . . .'

'Twice as good looking.'

She snorted. 'And half as smart.'

'Okay, okay,' he chuckled and she finally smiled.

'I think the point is that,' Gavin continued solemnly, 'in his own way, Mike does care about you.'

She was silent.

'You don't think so?' His voice was tentative.

'It's just hard, you know . . .'

'To trust again?'

'I guess it's something to think about,' she answered after a moment.

And she did for a month or so. She had time. Mike had flown home with the first lot of men sent back to Perth while Wickham recovered from Cyclone James.

The next time she heard word of him, it was from Chub. The man had tendered his resignation and was staying in Perth. The news didn't sit well with her so she gave him a call.

'I heard you're not coming back, Mike.'

There was a heavy pause down the phone. He said finally, 'I thought you might like some space.'

'I don't need that much space,' she assured him. 'Don't resign on my account.'

'Are you sure?'

'Yes.'

'All right.' His voice sounded lighter. 'I'll see you in a few weeks.'

'Yes, you will.'

It was only a small step, but it was something.

As she was hanging up the phone, Gavin walked into her office donga looking positively buoyant.

'What's up?'

'Well, I'm finally going on R and R and, as we discussed, I asked Carl whether you could have some time off at the same time.'

'He said . . .?'

'That I had a lot of fuckin' nerve,' Gavin grinned. 'But he agreed anyway.'

'Oh great!'

'I was thinking,' he offered tentatively, 'instead of going to Perth, would you like to come to Melbourne with me? I'm dying to see my family and would love to introduce you.'

Her heart filled. 'I'd love that.'

He sat down in the visitor's chair opposite her desk. Tapping his fingers on the edge, he studied her carefully. 'There's just one thing you kinda need to know first.'

'Oh?' She braced herself. 'What's that?'

That cocky lilt curled his mouth as he pulled a pack of cards from his pocket. 'How to play poker, Sarge.'

Acknowledgements

When I think about all the people who have come to my aid in helping get this book finished by deadline, I count myself extremely blessed.

When I agreed to write *The Girl in the Hard Hat*, I was not only a full-time mum to three children under five but I had just found out I was pregnant with my fourth baby. There was no way, short of a miracle, I could have written this book without help.

In particular, I would like to mention my wonderful mother, Juanita, who has sacrificed so much in life so that I might embrace any opportunity that comes my way. She did the lion's share of the babysitting so that I could get this book done at the expense of her own very busy schedule. Secondly, I want to express thanks to my aunt and uncle, Moira and Richard, who were there every Monday morning to help out with the kids and the housework – whatever I needed really. Their support was very generous. And thirdly, to my wonderful husband, who did his best to give me every Sunday to spend with my characters while he took over the family duties. His belief in my work and my journey as a writer has always been strong since the beginning.

I want to convey my gratitude also to my mother-in-law, Shirley, who came to stay with us for three weeks as the deadline was looming closer. The extra concentrated time she gave me to write and also to recover from being sick with the flu was a real lifesaver to me.

Without the love and care of these people, *The Girl in the Hard Hat* never would have been written.

I must also recognise those people who helped with the technical side of this book. Rob Doy, an old friend and colleague from my Cape Lambert days, was very generous with his time and advice regarding the role of a safety manager on this site. I was very lucky to be able to tap into his extensive occupational health and safety knowledge banks and also his willingness to read short extracts of the book to see if I was on the right track. If there are any mistakes to be found, rest assured they are mine – his eyes never saw them.

Other industry professionals I consulted included Carmen Hermann and David Grenfell.

Two big hugs must go to my dedicated critique partners, Marlena Pereira and Nicola E Sheridan, who have been with me every step of the way. Their fresh eyes, insight and ideas were invaluable to the strength and quality of this story. I also want to thank my back-up team, Kym Brooks and Cath Ryan, who also helped boost my confidence in this manuscript when it was faltering.

Thank you to my agent Clare Forster for her enduring faith and patience with me. And also to Beverley Cousins, my enthusiastic publisher, who has been such a pleasure to work with. The team at Random House has, as usual, pulled out all the stops. Thanks to everyone who worked on this book.

To all my friends and family, who have put up with my bad moods, my illness, my whinging and my complete lack of energy, especially in the final stages of pregnancy. You know who you are. I send you all my love and gratitude.

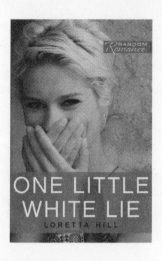

If you enjoyed *The Girl in the Hard Hat*,

look out for Loretta Hill's hilarious romantic novella

ONE LITTLE WHITE LIE

When one little white lie turns into a red-blooded reality . . .

What do you do when your best friend is the serial match-maker from Hell?

Single girl Kate Dreson knows that her friend Lisa is not going to leave her alone unless she tells her that she is happily dating someone.

Who knew that one little white lie could so blatantly backfire?

Because the imaginary boyfriend she described so lovingly to her friend has suddenly walked into her life and started making himself comfortable in it.

Trapped by her lie, poor Kate is powerless to stop him. But the real question is, does she really want to?

Available as an ebook from February 2013.

Read on for a taster.

Chapter 1

'So, baby, did it hurt?'

Kate Dreson choked. 'I beg your pardon?' she spluttered, lowering her glass of lemon, lime and bitters and pressing a hand to her throat.

'You know.' The man next to her cocked his head to one side and winked rakishly. 'When you fell from Heaven?'

Kate shut her eyes. *Please disappear, please disappear.*

But when she opened her eyes again he was still there, draped all over the bar and grinning at her like a gambler with a winning ticket.

Why me? Why does this always happen to me?

The guy was the physical embodiment of a hangover-in-waiting. The only thing currently holding him up was the stool he was sitting on. She knew what he wanted. It was written all over his face. And his eyes! They couldn't stay above her collar bones for more than five seconds. Her grip on her glass tightened. She really couldn't handle this for much longer. Where was Lisa? Was that girl *ever* going to come back?

Wait a minute . . .

A sudden dread filled her. Knowing her best friend's track record, she was probably staying away on purpose. Kate's suspicions solidified as she remembered Lisa's cryptic remark from earlier that evening.

'Wouldn't it be great if you met someone tonight?'

That sneaky little –

The man beside her recalled her attention when his hand started edging its way across the bar towards hers. 'I was thinking,' he flicked his head, indicating the exit over his shoulder, 'maybe I could show you my place.'

O-kaaay. Kate put her drink down and firmly pushed it away from her. *The camel's back is now officially broken.*

What on earth had Lisa been thinking anyway? Of all the men she could set her up with . . . *this guy?* Did she honestly believe she would like him? It was beyond a joke. No, actually, it wasn't a joke. It was an embarrassment.

'Look,' she began as he nodded knowingly at her silence. 'I think –'

He put a finger to her lips. 'Don't fight it, honey.' He leaned in towards her. 'It's okay to want me.'

Kate's skin crawled. Was this guy for real?

I mean, seriously!

Part of her wanted to laugh hysterically. Instead, she reached up and pushed his hand away from her mouth. He was invading her personal space. Being polite wasn't cutting it anymore.

'You know what?' she said as she swivelled off her bar stool and shoved it under the counter. 'I'd love to see your place.'

'You would, baby?' He seemed so hopeful that Kate almost felt sorry for him.

Almost.

'Sure I would . . . when hell freezes over.' She spun on her heels and moved into the crowd that covered the dance floor.

She didn't turn around to see if he had reacted to her jibe, not wanting to waste precious getaway time. She had to put as much distance as she could between them before his liquor-befuddled mind kicked into gear and he realised that he'd been rejected. The last thing she needed was a sleazy drunk turning into an angry one.

After a minute of pushing through the crowd, she allowed herself a glance over her shoulder. She could see nothing but dancing people. The crowd had closed in around her and she was lost in a sea of groovers, none of whom was her drunken admirer. It looked like he hadn't followed her. She breathed out slowly. Thank goodness! She hadn't been as lucky last time when Lisa –

Lisa! That girl had a lot to answer for! How many times was she going to have to extricate herself from an awkward situation of Lisa's making?

Her best friend had to be the worst serial match-maker that ever lived. Kate began weaving her way through the crowd again. This time, however, she had a new purpose – to find Lisa and give her a long overdue piece of her mind.

Tonight was supposed to have been about them and their friends. Just a group of mates hanging out with each other, having a good time – plain old-fashioned no-hidden-agendas fun. But Lisa, as usual, had turned it into yet another set-up opportunity. Half an hour after Kate arrived she had left her alone with a man they'd only just met, who wasn't even Kate's type. No, that was being generous. Of the guys who weren't her type, take the bottom guy on the list, dip him in crap and then you got the guy she'd left at the bar.

Kate shuddered and supposed, cynically, that she should be grateful that Lisa hadn't given him her number like she had with the last guy. After a full week of fighting off Sydney's biggest psycho, she was looking forward to putting her phone back on the hook.

The problem with Lisa was that her intentions were all good. She thought she was being helpful. She thought she was doing something imperative to Kate's happiness. Every time

Kate tried to explain to her that her efforts weren't wanted or needed, Lisa refused to believe it. She thought Kate required someone to move her life forward.

'I *am* going forward,' Kate continually protested, only to experience the 'pregnant pause' and the look that only best friends can give.

OK, so maybe she hadn't been on the 'social scene' much lately, preferring to stay in with a chick flick and bowl of popcorn, rather than have a night out at some noisy club. But it was hard when your ex was still in your social circle, and every time you wanted to hang out with your friends you had to make small talk with his lovely wife. Not that she had anything against the poor woman. Hell, she was good and welcome to Mark, who she was sure hadn't changed at all. It's just that their breakup wasn't the kind where either party benefited from staying in touch. And even if they had wanted to do so (from a strictly sadistic point of view), wasn't that what Facebook and Twitter were for?

As for meeting men . . .

Kate rolled her eyes. She wasn't interested in meeting someone new. After everything Mark had put her through she was definitely better off without the drama. Wasn't she entitled to a little down time?

She could almost hear Lisa's voice in her head: 'Two years is over-kill!'

Geez! Judgemental much?

All she was doing was being cautious – taking care of herself first. Before she entered into any sort of relationship again she wanted to be able to stand on her own two feet.

She was still a student with meagre scholarship funds as her only source of income. But this year she was finishing her PhD. Next year, she'd be working and the year after that . . . maybe she would have paid off all her debts. When she entered into a relationship again, she didn't want to be vulnerable, especially financially, to her partner. When she'd dated Mark she had trusted him so much. She had believed they were a team – equal partners. She had never imagined that in his mind the scales were tipped his way.

They were *engaged*, for goodness' sake. To her that meant commitment. Stupidly, she had put all his needs first and had allowed her own identity to slip through the cracks.

Never again.

To give Mark some credit, he had managed to teach her a few essential home truths. Don't trust anyone. Don't rely on anyone. And certainly don't ask anyone to love you uncon-ditionally because that's just way too much to expect. Kate's wavering convictions firmed up. It was better to just stay clear of the whole dating – aka getting your heart ripped out of your chest – game.

At least for a while anyway.

Lisa had to be made to see this. She had to be made to see that Kate had far more important things to do than get hurt again.

I'm happy being single. Kate lifted her chin. *In fact, I need to be single.* She was just too busy to be in a relationship. What with her PhD to finish and her . . . her PhD to finish, there was just no time.

Kate was so caught up in her internal tirade against men and interfering best friends that she failed to notice the stranger whose broad-shouldered back suddenly blocked her path. So she walked straight into it.

Thrown back by the impact, she probably would have fallen over if he hadn't turned around and caught her by the elbows to steady her. She looked up to catch a glimpse of his face just as a strobe light flashed behind him.

Kate saw stars instead.

The subtle scent of expensive aftershave filled her nostrils and the warmth of the hands on her elbows seemed magni-fied beyond all reasonable perception. For a moment Kate couldn't move. She just stood there stunned by her unexpected awareness of him and the tribal-like beat of the club that seemed to be drawing them together.

And then, as suddenly as this new feeling grabbed her, he let go. She fell back, blinking stupidly.

She shook off the irrational stupor and said 'Sorry' to his feet, then turned away, needing to get out of there before she embarrassed herself further. With the bright lights behind her again, her vision returned and she was able to make her way through the crowd.

Poor guy. Kate winced as she passed another circle of dancing friends. *Hit by a human missile mid-conversation.* Involuntarily, she wished she had seen his face. Maybe apologised properly . . . maybe . . .

She caught herself before she finished the thought.

Where are you going with this? I thought we just decided you weren't interested in meeting anyone new anytime soon.

Her thoughts returned to Lisa as she spotted her friends. They were sitting in a red booth laughing over some blue cocktails. But Lisa wasn't with them. Thankfully neither was Mark. He and his wife hadn't been able to make it tonight.

'Hey, Kate.' Her old high school buddy Casey gave her a wave. 'Where've you been?'

Kate grimaced. 'I'm looking for Lisa. Have you seen her?'

'I think she and Andrew went outside,' Casey's boyfriend said.

Kate turned around and headed for the back door. Lisa's disastrous match-making had to stop. Kate squared her jaw. And it was going stop tonight.

'Tom, I don't like this place.' Henry Carter looked around at the crammed dance floor, the rotating lights and the large booming speakers. 'It's too noisy.'

Tom cupped his ear. 'What did you say?'

Henry wished for about the hundredth time that he hadn't made the fatal mistake of taking his brother into his confidence.

It had been a stupid slip. A slip that had got him dragged off to a club he never frequented and didn't even like. He wasn't prone to male bonding sessions usually. He could bluff with the best of them. But he'd been sitting there staring at his computer with not an ounce of inspiration when his brother, Tom, had showed up at six o'clock that evening. It was Friday and Tom's law firm had finally shut its doors for the week.

'Man, I need a drink!' his brother said. 'Shall I call us a cab?'

As Henry had looked up and seen him standing there, all lawyer, in his black Armani business suit and Italian shoes, holding up his super-flash Smartphone, he'd had an epiphany.

'Tom, what do you want out of life?'

'I beg your pardon?'

'I mean really, what are we all doing here?'

Tom pocketed his phone. 'Writers!' He shook his head. 'I knew this would happen one day.'

'I'm serious.'

'So am I. You think too much. Way too much. And don't get me wrong. I love your ideas and so does half the world. But when you start philosophising about the meaning of life, that's when I gotta ask myself the question.'

Henry blinked. 'What question?'

'Can I deal with you going mad?'

At any other time, Henry would have laughed at such a comment. Tom had always been the joker of the family and could pull Henry out of the sullens at the worst of times. But not that day. Not after eight hours of writer's block.

'You know, I've just realised that I've got nothing in my life but my writing and today . . . not even that.'

'Rubbish,' Tom scoffed. 'Look around you. You live better than the Prime Minister.'

He had pointed at the large wall behind Henry. It was all glass and looked straight out at the Sydney Opera House and Harbour Bridge.

'I mean, anything of value,' Henry corrected himself.

'Last time I checked that view was worth a buck or two.' Tom cocked an eyebrow at him. 'Not to mention the yacht you got parked in the harbour tht you never use.' His eyes brightened. 'Listen, if you don't want it, I'm happy to take it off your hands.'

Henry sighed. 'Go for it. I was going to take Fiona out on it this month. But I guess that's out of the question now.'

'*Oh*, so you broke up.' Tom looked far from sorry. 'I was right about her, wasn't I?'

'There's no need to look so damn pleased about it.'

Tom rubbed his hands together as though his score on an electronic counter had just gone up. 'I knew the minute she threw the words "trust" and "fund" into casual conversation that she was just with you for the money.'

'Thanks a lot.'

'Come on, Henry. It's not your fault women are shallow. It's in their nature.'

'They can't all be,' Henry protested, although he was beginning to doubt the strength of his convictions.

Tom sat down on the arm of the couch. 'Isn't Fiona the fourth girlfriend this year who's turned out to be a gold-digger?'

'I wish you wouldn't use that phrase. But yes.' Henry nodded glumly. 'Although, I only went out with Donna three times, so I guess she doesn't really count.'

'I remember her.' Tom nodded with a sudden burst of recollection. 'She was the actress hoping you would connect her with the people who are making your latest book into a movie.'

Henry shut his eyes. 'What is wrong with me?'

'I think the question you're actually looking for is, what isn't?' Tom grinned.

But Henry wasn't listening. 'It's like they don't care who I really am. All they want is H. L. Carter.'

'Well, he's quite a catch,' Tom mused. 'Rich, famous, *mysterious*, not as good looking as me but then, you know, you can't have everything.'

'Will you shut up and be serious for ten seconds?' Henry stood up angrily and began pacing the floor. 'Besides, I'm not going to be mysterious for much longer.' He frowned, as he thought about his upcoming engagements.

'What do you mean?'

'It's my publisher. The media has been hounding them and they don't want to keep me a secret anymore.'

'How loyal of them.'

'They made me sign a publicity agreement to promote my next trilogy. Book one is coming out in March.'

'Publicity agreement?' Tom gaped at him. 'But you hate that sort of thing. What have they got you doing?'

'Everything,' Henry moaned. 'Radio, print and television.'

'Television,' Tom repeated. 'I thought you wanted to keep your face out of the spotlight, maintain a bit of anonymity.'

'Yeah, well.' Henry rubbed his temples, his voice mocking his own stupidity. 'At the time they made a few good arguments about how good it would be for sales and how I can't expect to stay out of the limelight forever.'

'And you're never one to let your career down.' Tom snorted. 'How long have you got before your privacy disappears?'

'The first television interview is in four months, just after book one comes out.' Henry sighed. 'That time is going to go like that.' He snapped his fingers.

'Ah,' Tom nodded, 'so this is where all this soul-searching is coming from. You're afraid more self-exposure is only going to worsen your gold-digger problem.'

'Well, what am I supposed to think?' Henry gazed out the window, pondering his failed relationships. 'It seems to be a fairly logical conclusion.'

'You know what it is?' Tom said with a sudden burst of inspiration. 'You're just hanging out at all the wrong places.'

'Huh?'

'You need to come out with me,' Tom explained, suddenly rising to his feet. 'Incognito!'

At first it had seemed like a pretty good idea, until they'd walked in the door of the Wet Elephant and Henry had cast his eyes across the enthusiastic crowd.

His brother had been right about one thing, there probably were no gold-diggers at this club. The women there were too young and too carefree to be thinking of marriage just yet.

He should have known that Tom would have difficulty realising he was talking about love and not lust. Tom didn't believe in love or marriage. Not after what their mother had pulled when they were kids. Tom was a confirmed bachelor, perfectly happy with his existence as the executive stud who loved them and left them. The 'no baggage' policy, he called it. He wanted to spend his life 'travelling light'.

But Henry wanted more.

Perhaps it was his in-built sense of optimism that prompted him to yearn for a deeper relationship or the close bond he had with his father that made him want children of his own.

However, instead of understanding that, Tom had dragged him off to a club that was filled with twenty-somethings high on hormones and alcohol. He really should have seen it coming.

Tom pulled Henry away from the dance floor toward some chest-high circular counters wrapped around a cluster of columns. He put his beer on this convenient platform and said, 'How do you expect to meet anyone if you don't give it a chance?'

'This is not exactly what I had in mind.' Henry scanned the room dubiously.

'What do you mean?' Tom demanded.

'Well, for a start,' Henry began, 'these girls are all too young for me. Most of them look like uni students.'

'For goodness' sake,' Tom scoffed, 'you're only thirty-two.'

'That's at least ten years on the girls in here.'

'Most of the girls in here,' Tom corrected. 'As for the rest of them, you're a famous writer; you've got dibs on anyone.'

'Keep your voice down,' Henry said through his teeth. 'We said I was going incognito. I don't really feel like talking release dates and Hollywood tonight.'

Over the last five years his novels had really taken off. It seemed the more successful he got, the less sincere people became. He'd met a startling number since then who had basically wanted to know him for one of three things.

Money.

Fame.

Status.

For this reason he didn't get out much, preferring the company of his brother to most others. It was a catch-22 because it meant that all the women he met were either in his industry or associated with it. They knew who he was before he was introduced as H. L. Carter, author of *The Carnegia Trilogy*, the biggest young adult story to hit shelves (and soon the screen) since the infamous *Twilight* series. That wasn't being conceited. That was just being honest.

'I must admit,' Tom grudgingly lowered his voice, 'I'm finding your whole attitude frustrating.'

You're finding my attitude frustrating!

'Tom, I'm not looking for a one-night stand,' he snapped, but his outburst did make his brother pause. Tom swirled the contents of his glass with a stubborn look on his face.

'Have four gold-diggers in a year taught you nothing? Commitment at this point is a waste of your time. You should enjoy your fame, for what that's worth. Be sensible later.'

Henry winced. He knew there was no point arguing with his brother. The man had made up his mind years ago. It was better if he just dealt with the problem himself. He felt his phone buzz in his back pocket and withdrew it.

Tom glanced over his shoulder to check out the caller ID.

It was their mother.

When his brother realised it, he grimaced and looked away. 'Still taking her calls, I see.'

'Not in a noisy nightclub I'm not.' Henry shook his head. 'I won't be able to hear a thing in here.' He turned the phone off and put it away.

'I seriously don't know why you bother.'

'She's our mother.'

Tom snorted. 'She wasn't our mother for twenty-five-odd years and then all of a sudden she turns up out of the blue begging forgiveness.'

'People change.'

'Yeah, *you* did.' Tom shook his head. 'As soon as you starting banking a million bucks a year she grows a conscience. A little too convenient, if you ask me. She makes your gold-digger girlfriends look like a bunch of nuns.'

Henry sighed. 'I thought we agreed you weren't going to use that phrase anymore.' He felt like his life was a revolving door. Just like the money they so prized, people came in and people went out. Nothing stuck. And every time he tried to ground himself he failed.

Was he wrong to believe that his mother really wanted to make amends for abandoning them as children?

Was he delusional to think that he could meet a girl who would love him and not his money?

Suddenly he just wanted to quit the club and go home. He wasn't going to meet anyone here.

'Listen, Tom,' he began, 'I really appreciate everything you're trying to do. But I don't want –' Henry lurched forward as somebody hurtled into the back of him. His first feeling was anger. Couldn't these crazy kids look where they were going? He turned around and managed to grab the girl just before she fell backwards. Her eyes were half-shut due to the bright strobe lights behind him.

But he'd seen enough.

She was an angel.

A blonde, blue-eyed, pink-lipped vision with skin like strawberries and cream. The delicate frame he was holding was small, slender and quietly sexy, dressed in sleek black slacks and a sleeveless red top with a scooped neckline. His hands dropped from her elbows as his jaw hit the ground somewhere between his feet. She was the kind of woman men died in battle for. Hell! If she asked him to take a bullet for her, he'd say, 'Where?'

Unfortunately for him, his star-gazing cost him big-time. One minute she was standing there looking at him, the next minute she had turned away. He heard her mumble something like 'sorry' under her breath and, before he had a chance to gather his wits, she'd escaped.

He slapped a palm to his head.

'Look, mate,' he felt Tom's hand on his arm, 'you're obviously not comfortable here, let's just go. Isn't the footy on tonight?'

'Tom,' Henry spoke without turning around, 'scratch everything I said before. I might just owe you big-time. I've just met her.'

'Who?'

'A girl who might be able to change my life!'

Loved the book?

Join thousands of other
readers online at

AUSTRALIAN READERS:

randomhouse.com.au/talk

NEW ZEALAND READERS:

randomhouse.co.nz/talk